The Road Back

The Road Back

Liz Harris

Copyright © 2012 Liz Harris

Published 2012 by Choc Lit Limited
Penrose House, Crawley Drive, Camberley, Surrey GU15 2AB, UK
www.choclitpublishing.com

The right of Liz Harris to be identified as the Author of this Work
has been asserted by her in accordance with the Copyright, Designs and
Patents Act 1988

A CIP catalogue record for this book is available
from the British Library

ISBN-978-1-906931-67-4

Printed and bound by CPI Group (UK) Ltd, Croydon, CR0 4YY

For my sister, Diana
My best friend since the day she was born
With love

Acknowledgements

The Road Back is entirely a work of fiction, but it would
never have been written had it not been for the album
compiled by my late uncle, Kenneth Behrens.

When stationed with the army in North India in the 1940s,
my uncle managed to get one of the few authorised passes
to visit Ladakh. Upon his return to England, he assembled
his photos and notes into an album, which he then passed
on to his daughters. That album is now in the Indian
Room of the British Library. When I read it, I fell in love
with Ladakh and its people, and I knew that I wanted to set
a story there.

My uncle's album gave me Ladakh for my location, and the
idea of having Patricia's father, Major George Carstairs,
compile a similar album. However, that is the extent
of my debt to my uncle. A charming, erudite, forward-
thinking man, my uncle was in no way the prototype
for Major Carstairs.

In order to gain a deeper knowledge of the Ladakhi
people and their traditions, I drew upon information that
I found in a number of books. In particular, I owe a huge
debt of gratitude to the superb book, *Ancient Futures:
Learning from Ladakh*, by Helena Norberg-Hodge, whose
intimate knowledge of the country and its traditions was
invaluable. For my knowledge of the nature of the terrain,

I'm indebted to the many people who travelled to Ladakh and later recorded their experiences on the internet, and to a variety of travel guides, especially the excellent *Trekking in Ladakh*, by Charlie Koram.

There are many people I could thank for their help, encouragement and support on my road to publication – but they are too many to name, alas. However, I must say a special thank you to my friend in the north, Stella, who reads everything I write and who is completely honest about it. Every author should have a friend like Stella. Thank you, too, to Sue, for helping me to ensure the psychological accuracy of my characters. Your advice was, as it always is, much appreciated.

The day that I discovered the Romantic Novelists' Association was a very happy day. Through the organisation, I've made some wonderful friends – they know who they are – learnt a great deal about writing and publishing, and had a lot of fun on the way to finding a publisher.

And what a publisher! A huge thank you to Choc Lit for their faith in me and for being such lovely people to work with. I feel extremely lucky to be with them, and I shall be eternally grateful to the Choc Lit Tasting Panel for taking the story of Patricia and Kalden to their heart.

Finally, I'd like to thank my husband, Richard, for being the great support that he is, and for putting up with me sitting in front of the computer, hour after hour, day after day. I couldn't have done this without you, Richard.

Prologue

Amy stood under a large black umbrella and stared at the tall, Victorian, semi-detached house on the opposite side of the road; the house where she'd begun her life, where she'd been cast off by the woman who'd given birth to her.

She put her hand into her pocket and pulled out a yellowing piece of paper. Holding the crumpled paper close to her chest to protect it from the rain, she read again the first of the words printed on it: her birth name, Nima Carstairs; the name of her birth mother, Patricia Carstairs.

She looked back at the tall house. She'd lived in that house for almost six weeks. Six weeks was no time at all compared with her years in Primrose Hill, where she'd lived before and after she'd married Andrew, but it was an important part of her life. She'd been someone else when she'd lived in that house: she'd been a Nima. And she hadn't been wanted.

Nima. What sort of name was that? Who would call their daughter Nima?

Her eyes were the eyes of a Nima; people were always remarking on her eyes. But apart from her eyes, would she have looked different, or liked different things, if she'd stayed a Nima? She'd not been able to stop asking herself those questions since the moment that morning when she'd first opened the letter that her father – her real father, the one who'd brought her up and loved her – had left for her to read after his death.

In his letter he'd written down the name of the home for unmarried mothers where she'd been handed over to him and his wife. Her eyes had filled with tears as she'd read that that day, thirty-two years ago, had been the happiest day of

1

their lives. He'd gone on to say that he felt she ought to have a way of tracing her birth parents in case she ever wanted to do so, and he'd tucked her Adoption Order into his letter. She'd felt very strange as she'd unfolded the order and seen the name that her birth mother had given her.

She'd always known she was adopted, but she'd had a happy childhood, loved and protected by her adoptive parents and loving them back in return, and she'd never felt any need, nor any desire, to find out about the people who'd given her away. Instinctively, she'd known that looking for her birth parents would hurt her mum and dad, and she wasn't going to do anything that would cause them unhappiness. Her birth parents had never been interested in her, and she wasn't interested in them.

The thrill she'd felt when she'd first read her name and that of her birth mother had taken her completely by surprise. She'd had to sit down.

For the first time ever, a powerful wave of curiosity had swept through her. Why had her birth parents given her away like that? Her mother had carried her for nine whole months – how could she have parted with her? She had carried her own baby for fewer than three months before her miscarriage earlier that year, but she'd been overwhelmed by grief, and so had Andrew, and they were still grieving. What kind of woman could ever give her baby away? What kind of man could let her?

She'd read her father's letter again, her vision blurred. He'd known her so much better than she'd known herself, and he'd wanted to help her do something he believed that one day she would want to do. And her mum must have agreed. The letter was dated two years earlier, just before her mother had died. Her father must have asked the solicitor to give it to her after they both had died. It had been their final act of kindness to her.

2

She'd read his words again, and had known instantly that she had to go at once to the house where she was born, no matter how bad the weather.

She folded the Adoption Order, put it back in her pocket and stared again at the house in front of her. The rain was bouncing off the grey tiles of the pitched roof, cascading in sheets over the edge of the eaves and falling on to the sloping roof of the bay window that flanked the heavy, dark blue door.

Her eyes on the house, she gripped her umbrella tightly, stepped into the road and walked across to the other side. Her boot hit the kerb and she looked down. The broken reflection of the house swirled in an oily puddle that had pooled in the gutter. A black sump reflecting another world. She stared back up at the house.

Day was fading fast, but there was no electric light in any of the rooms; the place looked deserted. She probably shouldn't have come on such a dismal day as this, but she had, and she wasn't going to stop now. She stepped on to the pavement and made her way between the moss-stained brick gateposts, past the squat stump of a tree that lay behind one of the gateposts, to the stone steps that led to the front door.

A shiver of nervous excitement ran through her as she went up the steps: her pregnant birth mother had walked up those same steps almost thirty-two years earlier. And she'd walked back down them again a few weeks later, leaving her baby behind, leaving Nima.

Why?

Reaching the narrow porch, she glanced at the tarnished bronze plaque next to the door. The house was clearly being used for offices. She put her ear against the door and listened hard, but she couldn't hear anyone moving around. Her heart sank. They must have left for the day.

She took a step back and looked along the front of the

house to the sash bay window surrounded by chipped white masonry, but she couldn't see into the room. Large droplets of rain hit her forehead and she moved back under the porch.

A button on an intercom next to the plaque told visitors to press for assistance, so she pressed the button and waited. The buzzer reverberated in the silent interior of the house. Reluctantly, she turned to leave. She'd have to come back another day, and make it earlier in the day.

A sound came from behind her. She spun round and saw that the front door was open and that a young woman in jeans and a cream polo-necked jumper was standing in the doorway.

'Can I help you?' the woman asked.

'Gosh, you made me jump!' Amy exclaimed. 'I thought that everyone had gone home.'

'There's only me at the moment, I'm afraid, and I'll be off shortly. But if I can help you at all, I'd be happy to do so.'

'I don't know that I need actual help. To be honest, I just wanted to see inside the house. I don't even really know why. My name's Amy Stevens and I've just found out that my birth mother stayed here when it was a home for unmarried mothers. I badly wanted to see where I started life. I don't suppose I could have a quick look round?'

Seeing the woman hesitate, Amy took the Adoption Order from her pocket and handed it to her. The woman ran her eyes over it and returned it.

'Come on in,' she said, opening the door wider.

Amy walked into the house.

A long, dimly lit hallway stretched out in front of her. Octagonal marble tiles, inset with small black squares, covered the length of the floor. At the far end of the hall, a greyish-white staircase led to a shadowy landing. The dark green walls of the hall were broken up by modern, semi-glazed doors, each with a plaque on the front. A large, gilt-edged mirror was fixed on the wall to the right of the front door.

Damp hung in the air. Amy shivered.

The woman laughed. 'I agree. It's not the most cheerful of buildings. But it's a job, and the people who work here are a great bunch, and that's all that matters. I expect you'd like to wander around on your own. You can go anywhere that's not locked. Let me know when you're ready to leave, will you? I'll be in the room over there.' She pointed to a door on the left.

'Of course, I will. Thank you.'

She looked around her. A sense of depression crept over her at the thought of having started life in such a cold, bleak place, and a lump came to her throat. She swallowed hard and took a step further into the hall. Her foot slid on the tiled floor. Glancing down, she saw that water was dripping on to the floor from her damp umbrella. There was a metal rack under the mirror, so she went and slotted her umbrella into it.

Straightening up, she caught sight of her pale reflection in the mirror. Turning back to the hall, her eyes wandered from one door to another. All were closed. Despite the woman's words, she had an uneasy sense of being an unwanted intruder. Her eyes strayed back to the mirror.

The person staring back at her was interesting, rather than pretty. To Andrew, she was beautiful, she knew, but really her face was a little too round, a little too wide. Her long, dark brown hair hung straight, and that narrowed her face a little, but she couldn't disguise her wide mouth. Andrew always said that when she was happy, her smile took over her whole face.

At the moment, though, she wasn't smiling; her eyes were glistening with unshed tears. Narrow, almond-shaped and heavy lidded, they were the eyes of a Nima, not of an Amy.

Did they come from her natural father, whose name she didn't know, or could they have come from her birth mother, the woman called Patricia Carstairs?

She walked slowly to the foot of the staircase and looked up at the dark landing. She had probably been born in one of the rooms up there and then handed over to someone else. Why, oh why, had her mother given her away, and why hadn't her father stopped her mother? What were they like, her birth parents?

PART ONE

Chapter One

The clock on the mantelpiece above the cast-iron fireplace ticked loudly in the silence that filled the back room of the small brick house in Belsize Park Gardens. The fire had been set, but the paper and coal were unlit.

Patricia sat very still on the wooden chair that had been placed in the centre of the room, her knees together, her fingers intertwined in her lap. His lips pursed in a line of displeasure, Major George Carstairs paced from one side of the sparsely furnished room to the other. Finally stopping squarely in front of his daughter, he stared down at her, his eyes cold.

'And how, exactly, do you account for your failure to prevent your brother from hurting himself?'

Patricia glanced up at the tall figure in front of her. Her fingers twisted nervously, and she looked back down at the floor.

'Well?'

'I did my best, Daddy,' she said in a whisper. 'I was reading my new book to James and he just fell over. He was sitting at the table, playing with his soldiers while I was reading to him, and then he fell on the floor and hit his head. I didn't know he was going to fall over. I'm sorry ...'

'Being sorry isn't good enough, Patricia.' Her father's chill tones cut across her words. 'It's nowhere near good enough. Your duty is to watch your brother's every movement, to see that he doesn't put himself in danger. Yet reading was more important than looking after your brother. Your instructions were quite clear. Was it asking too much to expect you to obey them?'

Patricia's eyes travelled over the patterned rug that covered the dark-stained boards on the floor of the front room and came to rest on her father's black shoes. They were polished to an ebony sheen. The last thing he did every night before he climbed the staircase to the bedroom that he shared with her mother was to polish his shoes.

'Look at me! Well, was it?'

'No, Daddy.' Her voice shook as she met her father's eyes. 'But I did do what you said I had to do if James fell over, like I always do. I wasn't afraid when he made that noise. I undid his shirt collar and looked for his tongue. And I put a penny in both of his hands. It's not my fault that his head hit the table. I didn't know he was going to fall down.'

'Not your fault, girl?' her father spat. 'You were alone with him! If you'd watched him more carefully, you'd have known what he was going to do. I cannot be here every minute of the day – I have to bring money into this house – and your mother has work to do in the kitchen. It's your job to watch your brother when you're not at school, but you didn't do that. You chose to read.'

'I promise I'll watch him much better in future.'

'I intend to make sure that you do just that. I'm going to teach you a lesson that will make you take your duty to your brother more seriously.' He took a step closer and leaned down towards her. 'I will not tolerate such laxity. Do I make myself quite clear?'

She nodded, staring up at him, her eyes wide open in anxiety. A movement of air brushed against her cheek and she sensed someone come and stand behind her. A hand rested lightly on her shoulder.

'I'm sure that Patricia did her best, George,' Enid Carstairs said, her voice shaking. 'It was obviously an accident, dear. You know how James often falls without any warning. You can see how upset Patricia is about the whole thing. She would never let James hurt himself if she could help it. She's a good girl, and she does her best to look after him.'

'Her best has been found wanting. Wars are not won where soldiers are found wanting. Patricia must learn that.'

He ran a slender finger slowly down the thin black line of his moustache.

Her mother's hand pressed more heavily on her shoulder.

'She's only seven, George. I've put a small dressing on James's head. It's only a little cut – nothing to cause alarm. He's vomited and he's now sleeping peacefully.'

'Every hurt that he suffers is a cause for alarm, Enid.' The Major's pale grey eyes didn't leave Patricia's face. 'Our focus at all times must be on helping him to get better. Patricia is old enough to understand that.'

He turned abruptly and walked towards the door. 'Follow me, Patricia,' he ordered without looking back. His footsteps echoed on the hard lino as he made his way along the corridor to the front room.

She burst into tears.

Her mother bent over and hugged her. 'Don't cry, darling. You know it only makes him worse. Just do as he says and go after him.'

'But it wasn't my fault, Mummy.' She clung tightly to her mother.

'I know that, sweetheart, and deep down so does Daddy. But you'd better go to him now, there's a good girl.'

'You go to him.' She clawed at her mother's arm, her face wet with tears. 'Tell him I'll be very good in future. I'll watch James all the time, I really will. I'll never read my books when I'm with him. Tell him, Mummy. Please.'

Enid pulled Patricia's hands away from her arms and stepped back. 'I have to get the tea ready, my dear. Go to your father or you'll make things worse for both of us. Go on now.' Tucking some stray strands of grey-flecked brown hair into the loose bun at the nape of her neck, she turned away and hurried out of the room.

Patricia gripped the sides of the seat with her hands, her knuckles white.

'Patricia!' she heard her father call. 'I'm counting.'

She gave a sharp intake of breath, slipped off the chair and ran towards the front room. The door was open and the Major stood waiting, a wooden ruler in his hand.

Enid perched on the edge of the bed, her eyes on her daughter's sobbing back.

'I wish I could have done something to help you, Patsy darling,' she said, pulling the blanket up over her daughter's shoulders. 'I did try, but you know what Daddy's like when he's angry. Please stop crying now. You'll make yourself ill.'

Patricia pulled the blanket over her head and cried more loudly.

Leaning forward, Enid gently uncovered her daughter's face. 'If you turn over, darling, you'll see I've brought you your tea, and I've given you our last piece of chocolate. You can have tea in bed as a treat, if you like. Then get some sleep.'

Her sobs slowing down, Patricia rolled over on to her back. She stared up at her mother with red-rimmed eyes.

'He hates me. Daddy hates me. He's always hated me.'

'Nonsense, darling. He loves you.'

'No, he doesn't. He loves James and he hates me. It's because he didn't see me when I was a baby. He saw James when he was a baby, but not me. That's why he doesn't like me.'

Enid stroked Patricia's long, blonde hair. 'You're wrong, Patsy – he does love you. He's just not good at showing it. It doesn't matter that he wasn't here when you were born. He's had the past five years to get to know you, and he knows what a lovely little girl you are.'

'Does he hate me because James is ill?'

Enid ran her finger down Patricia's cheek. 'He doesn't hate you, sweetheart.' She gave her a bright smile and took her hand. 'James being ill is very difficult for Daddy. It's hard for all of us, I know, but it's particularly hard for your father. He's used to being able to handle every situation, so he feels that he ought to be able to make James better. But he keeps on being told that there's nothing else that can be done for him. He won't let himself accept defeat, and he's taking his frustration out on you.'

She paused and looked anxiously at Patricia. 'That's a very grown-up thing to say to you, Patsy. Do you understand what I'm trying to say? Just because Daddy's very strict, perhaps a little too strict at times, it doesn't mean that he doesn't love you. He does.'

Patricia disentangled her hand from her mother's. 'No, he doesn't. He wishes I was ill and James was well.'

'You must never say that, darling. It isn't true. Daddy would be just as devastated if you were the one who was ill. You must believe that.' She leaned over and kissed Patricia on the forehead.

'No, he wouldn't.' She pushed her mother away, turned on her side and faced the wall. 'He hates me. And it's not fair.'

'I don't know what else I can say to convince you, darling,' Enid said helplessly, getting to her feet and looking down at Patricia. 'Eat your tea, then get some sleep. You'll feel better in the morning.' She hesitated a moment, then left the room.

Patricia heard the door click shut. She didn't move. If only Daddy had been at home when Mummy had gone into hospital for her to be born, but he hadn't been.

From the time that Patricia could talk, she regularly used to ask her mother to tell her the story about when she was born, and her mother would tell it to her again and again. Before long, she knew the story by heart.

She'd been born in Hampstead in June 1944. James was already two-and-a-half. Daddy had lived with them in London when James was little because he was recovering from a wound, but he'd been sent back to his regiment in North India two months before she was born. After the war had ended, he'd had to stay on in India as there were important things to do there, and he didn't come home until she was two.

Just after Daddy had gone to India, a bomb had hit their house. Mummy and James had been in the deep underground shelter at the time so they were safe, but it had been very frightening for Mummy, no longer having a house to live in and with another baby coming.

She had been very happy when a lady she knew, called Mary Shaw, had said that she and James could share her basement flat in Glenloch Road. Mummy had met Mary in the shelter. They used to lie on bunk beds next to each other, and try to pretend that the smell of wee wee in the air was really nice perfume.

Patricia had been in a great hurry to arrive, Mummy used to say with a smile. Three weeks before they'd thought she was going to arrive, Mummy had felt a pain and she knew that she would have to go into the hospital early. She'd been very worried about what to do with James, but Mary was kind and said she would look after him. James liked Mary and he could stay in a flat that he already knew. It had seemed perfect.

But things had gone wrong.

Mummy had had to stay in hospital for four weeks after she was born. During that time, doodlebug bombs started landing on London. They flew very low, Mummy explained, and they didn't have a pilot. They ran on fuel, and when the fuel ran out, the engine went very quiet, and a few seconds later the doodlebug fell out of the sky. Wherever they landed, they exploded with a big bang. Mummy said that the silence before they hit the ground was terrifying and people were very frightened of them.

The day that her mummy finally left the hospital was grey and unpleasant. The streets were empty, and all she could hear was the sound of the guns that were trying to stop the doodlebugs. She'd left the hospital and walked quickly down the hill, carrying baby Patricia in her arms, very excited at the thought of seeing James again.

It had been a whole month since she'd seen him. When she'd gone into the hospital, she'd told Mary not to come and see her because it would be too dangerous. And it would have been difficult to push the heavy pram up the steep hill to the hospital. But when she'd said that, she'd expected to be in the hospital for only a few days. As the days had turned into weeks, she'd begun to long to hear from her friend.

As she'd walked, her feet had crunched on bits of slate and broken glass that had been scattered across the pavement after a doodlebug attack. The air was thick with plaster and brick dust, and she'd tried not to breathe it in as she hurried past heaps of rubble that smelt of gas and burnt timber, praying that James was safe.

The closer she came to Mary's flat, the more excited she was. As soon as she'd seen the flat in the distance, she'd started to run and she hadn't stopped until she stood in front of the door. Her face a smile, she'd knocked on the door, but there'd been no answer: Mary and James were out. She'd taken her key from her pocket, unlocked the door and gone into the flat.

When she'd put baby Patricia into the large black pram in the corner of the room, she'd sat on the arm of a chair and started pushing the pram backwards and forwards, glancing around the room as she did so. That's funny, Mummy had thought, the picture of Mary's parents wasn't on the mantelshelf where it used to be, and Mary's collection of antique silver spoons had gone.

She'd stopped rocking the pram and stood up. Her heart thumping fast, she'd run into the bedroom and looked inside Mary's wardrobe. It was empty.

Mummy had hardly been able to breathe at that moment. She'd run back into the living room and stood there, her hand covering her mouth. Mary had disappeared and James had disappeared with her.

'What did you do next, Mummy?' she'd always ask at that point in the story.

'I picked you up and ran out of the flat. I'm not sure I even closed the door behind me. I asked everyone I saw if they knew anything about Mary and James. I asked the other people in the house – we shared a stove on the landing so we'd met each other – I asked the wardens and people in the air-raid shelter. Day after day, I stopped strangers in the street, went everywhere I could, asked everyone I met – but no one had seen them.'

'Poor Mummy.'

'I never saw Mary again. Eventually I heard that she'd been killed by a doodlebug. I imagine she'd been trying to take James out of London to safety. I assumed that he'd been killed, too. But a miracle happened, didn't it, darling?'

And Mummy would tell her how, six weeks after she'd left the hospital, James had been found by a nice air-raid warden. He'd been walking across the site of a bombed house a few streets away and had come across a little boy sitting on a pile of bricks. Even though he was filthy dirty and much thinner than the last time the warden had seen him, he recognised James and brought him back to Mummy.

'I was a very happy mummy when I had him back again, safe and not hurt,' Mummy used to say, sounding very sad. 'At least, I thought he wasn't hurt. But I was wrong, wasn't I, Patsy? He *had* been hurt. We just couldn't see it.'

Less than two weeks after James had been found, he'd fallen on to the floor, unconscious. His body had gone stiff, and he'd made a shape like an arch and had kept on jerking. At last, his body had relaxed and gone soft. He'd been sick and had then fallen asleep. Mummy said that she'd sat on the end of his bed all night, watching him while he slept.

She'd watched him closely the next day, and the day after that, and the following day, but carefully looking after Patricia at the same time, she'd assure her. The days passed and Mummy relaxed. Then, three weeks later, James fell down again. This time Mummy took him to the doctor. He said that it was too soon to know what to do and that Mummy should write down every detail about what happened when he fell, so that when the war was over, they would know how to help him.

When Mummy had returned home, she'd sat down to write a letter to Daddy to tell him about James being ill, but she'd changed her mind. James would probably get better, she'd thought, and she didn't want to worry Daddy if she didn't have to as he was very busy with the war.

But James hadn't got better; he'd got worse. Daddy had come home again when she was two. By then, James was four-and-a-half, and he was having a fit every week.

On the day that Daddy got home, James was so excited about seeing him that he had a very big fit and fell to the floor in front of Daddy. When Mummy had tucked him up in bed, she sat down with Daddy and told him how he'd got ill. Daddy didn't move or speak; he just sat there listening to her, staring at the spot where James had fallen.

The next week, he began to take James to see the best doctors in London.

All the doctors said that he must have been damaged by the bombs while he was lost, and they said that everyone in the family should be prepared for his fits to get worse and for it to be harder and harder to look after him by themselves.

Some of the doctors even suggested that they put James in a special home, but Daddy said no: James was going to get better and he was going to join Daddy's regiment.

By the time that she was seven, she knew exactly what to do when James had a fit.

She knew that her mummy and daddy relied on her to take care of him, and she was proud that she was a big girl and could help them. She didn't mind having to look after him – she loved him very much and she knew that he loved her – but she wanted her daddy to love her just like he loved James.

But he didn't. No matter how hard she tried to be a good girl, he only ever smiled at James. He never seemed to see her.

Her pillow damp beneath her cheek, she lay in her bed and stared at the wall.

Chapter Two

Kalden locked his hands behind his head and stared at the wall of white on the opposite side of the ravine. The sense of misery deep within him slowly drained away as he lost himself in the frozen slopes that faced him.

The longer he looked, the more his eyes became accustomed to the glare of the icy expanse and the more easily he could make out the myriad of shadowy indentations that broke up the snow-covered face of the rock. He moved his head from side to side, and fantastical shapes grew out of the snow and ice.

He took a step closer to the edge of the plateau. His father's features stared back at him, rough-hewn on the face of a distant crag. Smiling to himself, he traced the line of his father's brow in the rock, his heavy lids that hooded his eyes, the high cheekbones, his nose, his broad smile, and the curve of his chin and his throat, which went down, down into the strip of ice-green water that was cutting its way through the narrow valley.

Lowering his gaze, he followed the cluster of small ice-floes that clung to the tips of the white-crested water below, bobbing up and down on the backs of the waves. Mesmerised, he watched them until they'd rounded the bend in the river and were lost from sight. Then he raised his eyes to the shadowy peaks that towered above him, dusted with virgin snow. The hard light of the morning sun bounced off the sheer slopes and he squinted against its blinding reflection.

He sighed deeply. If only it were summer. How he loved the summer!

In the summer, he'd slide down the secret tracks buried in the steep slopes and he'd play at the water's edge. Sometimes he'd cross the river, stepping from one large stone to another, and then back again. Sometimes he'd run across the wooden bridge, making it sway precariously above the water that rushed beneath it. He was good at that and it was such fun.

And sometimes he'd get off the bridge on the other side of the river and clamber up the steep-sided, rocky paths to the high mountain pasture where he'd find his three brothers. He'd stay with his brothers, helping them round up the sheep and goats and putting them into the pens where the wolves couldn't get at them, or searching with them for the *dzo* and the yaks that had climbed the steep mountain slopes to graze at the edge of the glaciers.

When his mother and grandmother were at the high pasture, he was occasionally allowed to help them make the butter and cheese, although he was only eight.

When the day's work was done, he'd sit with Tenzin, Anil and Rinchen, watching the sun set over the mountain peaks, its golden glow lingering in the darkening sky and only fading away when the stars began to appear. Then they'd all go into the small, smoky room at the heart of the stone hut, and although they could hardly see each other in the flickering light of the wick lamp, they'd sing and tell stories. At night, he'd sleep alongside his brothers in the stone hut.

Summer was definitely the best time of all.

But it was a long way from summer now. It was going to be many months before the thaw would begin – months during which the mountain trails would be glazed over with layers of ice, and the wooden bridge would be buried beneath a solid bank of snow; months in which he would be unable to escape the village and lose himself in the vast emptiness surrounding it.

Once he'd tried to get across the river in the winter. The

bridge had been completely hidden beneath a thick white coat, so he'd slid down the track to the water's edge, taken off his yak-hair shoes and started to cross the ice-cold water at the narrowest part, clutching his shoes by their pointed tips.

But the earth and stones on the river bed had stuck to his feet. They'd hurt so much that he'd had to turn round almost at once and wade back. He'd had to sit on a lump of cold rock at the water's edge and struggle hard to pull the pebbles from his feet before he could begin to make his way back up the frozen track.

It had been much more difficult going back up the slope than it had been coming down. By the time he'd reached the top and had limped back to his house, his feet had been raw and he'd been in a lot of pain. His mother had been very upset at the thought of the hurt he could have done to himself, and she'd made him promise that he would never again try to cross the river in winter.

A shadow slid across the frozen rock and stayed there. He glanced at the sky. The sun was starting to fall behind the peaks – Tenzin's wedding was about to begin. It would begin the moment that the sun sank behind the high mountain.

He sighed again. He must get back to the village now, even though he didn't want to. Everyone at the wedding would be happy; he would be the only person who was sad, and he'd have to pretend that he wasn't. If only he could remain where he was, hidden in the white void, but he knew that he couldn't.

He loved Tenzin, and in his heart he knew that he should have stayed at the house and helped his other two brothers entertain the wedding guests who'd been arriving for the past two days. Instead, he'd disappeared and left Anil and Rinchen to fill the visitors' cups with *chang*, when he should have been standing alongside them and pouring the barley beer as the guests reached their house.

He felt a sharp stab of guilt, followed by a rush of anger at himself: he'd missed a valuable opportunity to make his family notice him.

He'd behaved like a baby, running off across the plateau like that. But he wasn't a baby – he was eight years old – and he should have been playing a full part in the life of the family. He was always saying that he wanted to stand shoulder to shoulder with his brothers for the rest of his life. It wasn't his brothers' fault that that was never going to happen, but it had been his fault that it hadn't happened that day.

A lump came to his throat and he swallowed hard. He should be happy for Tenzin that he was getting married – and he *was* happy for him – and he should have been doing everything he could to make it a lovely day for him, but he wasn't.

It wasn't that he hadn't done anything towards the wedding preparations: he had. He'd helped his mother to roast the barley from the fields, grind it into *ngamphe* and then mould the flour into the thick brown loaves that everyone would eat for breakfast during the three days of the wedding. After that he'd helped her to make the salty butter tea that they'd drink with the bread, and that they'd drink whenever they weren't drinking *chang*.

But it wasn't much in the way of help, and he felt ashamed.

Tearing his eyes away from the frosty peaks that pierced the sky, he pulled his thick, home-spun robe more tightly around him, tugged at the fur ear-flaps that hung from his sheepskin-lined hat and started to make his way back across the stony plateau to his village. When he got back home, he was going to make himself really useful, no matter how miserable he felt.

Glancing to his left when he was still some distance from his village, he saw that he wasn't far from the isolated, lime-washed house where the missionary teacher and his family lived. He stopped for a moment and stared at the house. It looked very lonely, standing by itself on the plain. There was no sign of the missionary, who'd moved into the house that summer, nor of his wife and son. Kalden knew that he had a wife and son because he'd seen them in Alchi when he'd gone there with his family soon after the missionaries had come to the area.

His family had been ambling along the steep, winding streets of Alchi that day. He'd been trailing behind them, sniffing the pungent odour of tea and spices that was drifting on the air, when he'd caught sight of the missionary family coming out of the dark interior of one of the wooden shops that lined the street. He'd immediately noticed them because of how funny they looked, and he'd stopped, open-mouthed, and stared at them.

They'd started to walk along the veranda in front of a group of shops further up the hill and then they'd paused. The boy stood a little to one side, leaning against one of the wooden posts that supported the roof of the veranda, hugging himself and rubbing his arms with his hands. He looked as if he was cold, Kalden had thought scornfully. He, himself, hardly ever felt the cold, and nor did his family or the other people in his village.

The missionary man had been wearing a short jacket and long trousers made of the same material as the jacket. He had a white shirt under his jacket. His father had never worn anything like that. His father always wore a long, straight robe and a tall, sheepskin-lined hat or a cap, like all the other men in the towns and villages. But the missionary didn't have anything on his head, and he had very short, fair hair. He looked very funny.

And the missionary's wife looked peculiar, too. She was wearing a dress the colour of the sky on a summer's day, with a short, brown, knitted jacket over it. She didn't have anything on her head, either, and there were no beads of turquoise or coral around her neck, no silver pendants, no conch-shell bracelets on her arms. They couldn't have much wealth, he thought.

If the mother and father had looked strange, the boy had looked really strange! He hadn't been able to stop himself from grinning at the sight of a boy with very white skin and fair hair, who was dressed in a woollen hat, a cream-coloured, loose, belted dress that went down to his knees, and knee-high socks of the same colour. He looked just like a Ladakhi boy, except that he looked funny and Ladakhi boys didn't.

A broad smile on his face, he had run a few steps to catch up with Tenzin. Pulling on Tenzin's robe, he'd glanced quickly at the boy again, then turned back to his brother. Laughing, he'd opened his mouth to say something about the way the missionary's son looked, but Tenzin had stopped him with a glance.

'Be kind in your thoughts, Kalden,' he'd said gently. 'We may not want them here, but they're living amongst us now and it's right that they want to look like us and do what we do. The boy will soon know how to wear our clothes and will then be comfortable in them.'

Kalden had let go of Tenzin's robe, feeling very ashamed of himself. His steps had slowed and he'd let his brother walk ahead and catch up with the rest of the family.

Turning towards the shop again, his eyes had met the eyes of the boy. The boy had smiled at him, and then swung his body around the veranda post. Kalden had stood in the middle of the narrow street, watching him. The boy had come to a stop, facing him. He looked about the same age as he was. They stared at each other.

He sensed that the boy wanted to talk to him – he looked lonely, and Kalden knew what it was like to feel lonely. He decided to go over and make friends with him. He took a step forward.

'No, Kalden.' His mother had put her hand on his shoulder. He'd been startled; he hadn't known she was there. 'These strangers have come to teach us to believe what they believe. But we don't want to be taught their beliefs. We know what is right, and we have our own monks and lamas to perform our ceremonies for us. We don't want these missionary people in our land. If we stay away from them, they'll go back to their home.'

And she'd taken Kalden by the hand and led him up the hill to where his father and brothers were waiting for them.

The only other time that Kalden had seen the strange boy was one afternoon when he'd been returning home after visiting his brothers on the high mountain pasture. He'd been passing quite close to the stream of melt-snow water that led to the missionary's house when he'd caught sight of movement by the low drystone wall surrounding the house.

Curious to see what was going on, he'd gone closer and seen that the boy and his father were trying to make mud bricks. Even from a distance, he could see that they were mixing too much straw with the soil that they were putting into the wooden moulds, and he'd laughed out loud at how silly they were. They'd heard him, and had turned and seen him standing there.

The missionary man had smiled at Kalden. '*Ju-le*. Come over and help us then,' he'd called out in halting Ladakhi.

Kalden's eyes had returned to the wooden moulds and to the pile of straw on the ground, and he'd laughed scornfully again. The boy had run off and hidden behind the wall, and he'd felt a moment's disappointment. The missionary had put down his scoop and walked over to where his son was crouching. Kalden had turned around and run all the way back to his village.

That night, as he'd lain beneath his yak-hair blanket, listening to the steady breathing of his brothers, he'd wondered why he felt so annoyed with himself, and so guilty. He shouldn't be feeling guilty – it wasn't up to him to help the missionary family make bricks that would keep the cold out of the house. They weren't Ladakhi so he didn't have to help them, and his mother had said that he should keep away from them.

He'd turned over on to his side and closed his eyes tightly against the guilt that refused to go away.

After that, every time that he'd crossed the plateau, he'd wondered whether he'd see the boy again, but he never had. And he'd never gone near their house again.

He turned away from the missionary house and continued his journey back to the village, his steps getting faster and faster. Soon he was in easy reach of the *chorten* that he had to pass on his way back home. Its pile of white-washed stone and mud, tapering to a peak topped by the crescent moon cradling the sun, told him that he didn't have far to go. He glanced up at the sky. Dark was falling. The most important part of the wedding would soon begin, and then they'd have all of the celebrations.

At the thought of the night ahead of him, misery welled up in him again.

He clenched his hands and pushed his fists hard into his eyes: he was going to drive back his sadness. He wasn't going to think about himself at all during Tenzin's wedding but was going to be a good brother to him. Dropping his arms, he ran past the *chorten* towards the cluster of white houses that nestled beneath the watchful gaze of the monastery that clung to the steep, rocky slope behind the village.

As he came close, he saw that the wedding guests were already on the frosty fields outside the wall, laughing and singing as they sat on the carpets that had been placed on either side of twelve huge pots filled with *chang*. Panting hard, he ran towards Anil and Rinchen, who were moving up and down the lines, filling everyone's cup with the barley beer taken from the large pots.

Just before he reached them, he stopped and anxiously scanned the crowd for his mother. She'd be upset that he'd disappeared for so long on such an important day. He wished he'd got back sooner.

Catching sight of Tenzin's bride, Deki, he stared at her. She was standing next to her mother, a little way away from the guests, fingering the turquoise-studded *perak* which was hanging down the back of her head to below her shoulders. One day Deki would have a daughter, he thought wistfully, and she'd pass the *perak* on to her, just like Deki's mother had given hers to Deki.

As he watched, Deki's mother gently pushed her daughter's hands away from the *perak*, then stood aside to let her move over to Tenzin, who was surrounded by guests. She went shyly to him and he stepped towards her, his face breaking out into a wide smile as he gazed down at her.

Kalden screwed up his hands and again pushed them hard into the sockets of his eyes.

'Here are your *kataks*, Kalden,' his mother said, coming up to him. 'You must throw them around the necks of Tenzin and Deki and wish them luck.'

He took the white scarves from his mother. 'Thank you, *ama*. I'm sorry I didn't get back earlier to help you.'

'It didn't matter.' His mother patted him on the shoulder, her eyes ranging over her guests. 'The members of the village *paspun* have done most of the work. They've been busy all morning, cooking and serving. And Anil and Rinchen were here to welcome the guests who arrived today, so you weren't needed. But it's sad that you weren't here to race the other children for the coins that Anil threw into the air when Deki arrived at our house.' She smiled down at him. 'But you're here now. Off you go to wish your brother and his wife good luck.'

Weaving a path between the guests, Kalden ran over to Tenzin and threw one of the scarves around his neck and the other around Deki's shoulders.

'Good luck, Tenzin. Good luck, Deki,' he said. But his words were lost in a gale of laughter as, at the same moment, Anil threw a *katak* around the neck of one of the village girls and drew her to him.

Rinchen put down his pot of *chang* and went over to join Anil and the girl, and the three of them began to move in a leisurely circle, swaying gently to the strains of the musicians and the sound of the drums. Gradually, more and more guests joined the circle, their laughter and merriment getting louder and louder.

Kalden stood for a few minutes and watched the dancing from a distance. It's not fair, he thought.

He spun round, ran to the opening in the wall surrounding the village and went quickly through the gap and made his way to his house. As he neared it, the brightly coloured prayer flags that fluttered from the carved upper balcony and roof top seemed to mock him. It's not fair, he repeated to himself, and he kicked the hard ground as he walked.

One of the women in the *paspun,* who was tending the huge cauldrons in front of his door, saw him approach and smiled. The smell of food made him realise that he was hungry, and he went over to her and was given a bowl of rice, goat meat, turnips and potatoes.

Carefully carrying his bowl, he went into his house, climbed the flight of wooden stairs and walked between the garlanded pillars on either side of the staircase into the large, smoky kitchen. Sitting down on the bench that ran along the far wall, he put his bowl on the low table in front of him and started to eat.

'Why have you come in here, away from our guests, Kalden?' a voice asked.

He jumped. Looking up sharply, he saw Anil come into the kitchen. Anil glanced across at him, then went over to the black, clay stove, threw some dried dung into it, blasted the dung alight with the goatskin bellows that hung from the wall, and came and sat next to him.

'I didn't know you were watching me,' Kalden said.

'That doesn't exactly answer my question.' Anil gave him an encouraging smile. 'Is there something worrying you, Kalden? You should be outside with everyone else, eating with them, joining in with the dancing, getting under our feet, making us laugh and feel happy that you are with us. Instead you are in here on your own. Why?'

Kalden ran his finger around the rim of his bowl.

'Tell me what's wrong. Let me help you. You're my brother, and I don't like to see your face so sad.'

'*Chi choen* – what's the point? And anyway, there's nothing wrong. I just wanted to be on my own. The visitors are getting silly. They're drinking too much *chang*.'

'A few of them maybe, but that's no different from every other celebration. They're enjoying themselves. This is your brother's wedding. You should be enjoying yourself, too, and helping him to celebrate.'

Kalden threw a glance at Anil, then quickly looked away.

'Is it that you don't like Deki?' Anil asked quietly. 'Are you sorry that she's coming to live in our home?'

'No, I do like her. She's very pretty and she likes laughing.'

'So?'

'Are you going to marry Deki one day, too?'

Anil laughed. 'I don't know. It's not something to think

29

about or talk about on Tenzin's wedding day. Maybe I will. I, too, like Deki. Would you mind?'

'No, not if it's what you wanted to do, and Deki did, too. And Tenzin was also happy. Will Rinchen marry her, too?'

'I'm not sure that Deki will want to marry the three of us,' Anil said with a grin. 'And Rinchen's only seventeen so I doubt if he's thinking about taking a wife yet. There's time for that in the future.'

Kalden looked at Anil. 'What about my future, Anil? I want to stay here, too.'

Anil put his arm around his shoulders. 'Is that why you've been avoiding the wedding celebrations today, because they remind you of the different life you'll have?'

Kalden nodded and looked down at his bowl.

'There's only land enough for three of us, and it can't be divided up. That's not the way we do things. You know that, Kalden. It's true that without land it isn't easy to marry, but it isn't impossible. You might be chosen by a girl who has land and who doesn't have any brothers.'

'But that's not very likely, is it? We know many people but we don't know any daughters who don't have brothers. My father's lucky that he didn't have brothers, only sisters. He knew he'd never have to leave the house. And you, Tenzin and Rinchen won't, either. But I will.'

'You'll go to the monastery, like the other younger sons,' Anil said gently. 'But you don't have to go this year, even though a lot of boys do at your age; you can wait until you're grown up. It'll be up to you to decide when to go. And when you've gone, you'll come back and stay with us – we will want to see you often, and we'll rely on you to help us at the times of sowing and harvesting. We'll also call on you for all of our family services. You'll always be a very important member of the family.'

'No, I won't. I'm not now and I never will be.' His eyes

filled with tears. 'Nobody listens to me now. You, Tenzin and Rinchen are the only important ones in the family because you're going to have the land. No one says it, but I know it. I want to be important like you are.'

'But you can't be, my brother,' Anil said quietly. 'You're the fourth son. You didn't choose to be the fourth son, but that is what you are. Although the life of a monk may not be what you would have chosen for yourself, you must learn to accept your place in the flow of life. If you can do that, you will find contentment.'

Breathing deeply, Kalden shrugged off Anil's arm and leaned forwards. His elbows on the table, he hid his face in the palms of his hands.

'You are much treasured, my brother, and you always will be. But you know that already, don't you?'

Kalden gave a slight nod.

'And is that not enough?'

He didn't move.

Chapter Three

Patricia stood on the corner of Belsize Grove and Belsize Park Gardens, clutching her leather satchel.

'I suppose I'd better get off home now, Ruth,' she told her friend. She kicked at a heap of cherry-blossom that had collected in the gutter and watched it float back to the ground. 'It'll soon be time for tea.'

'You're so funny, Pat. You look all miserable. If I had your news to tell my mum and dad, I'd be home by now. I'd have run all the way back from school to tell them.'

'If I had your mum and dad, so would I, but I haven't.'

'They're going to be ever so pleased with you.'

'No, they're not. They won't be interested. They've probably even forgotten what day it is.'

'Of course they won't have. I wish I'd got grammar so we could've gone to the same school.'

'I wish you had, too. I'm going to hate not being with you next year. But we can still be best friends, can't we?'

'Of course we can, if you don't think I'm too thick to be your friend. You'll probably make friends with the other brain boxes at your new school.'

Patricia aimed her satchel at Ruth. 'You're mad, Ruth, and you know it. I'll never like anyone else as much as I like you.'

Ruth beamed. 'You'd better not or I'll come after you with a big stick! Hey, do you suppose they cane people in a secondary school?'

'I suppose they must do. But probably only the boys, like in our school now. I hope so, anyway.'

'Me, too. But you're such a goody-goody that you'd never get caned, even if you were a boy.'

'Goody-goody yourself! You'd never have had the cane, either.' Patricia glanced along the road and sighed loudly. 'I'd better go and tell my parents now.' She dug the toe of her brown leather sandal into the pile of blossom.

'Are you going to see James at the weekend?'

'No, he got too excited last Sunday and just kept on fitting. It was awful. The Home said we shouldn't go again for a bit. He needs to settle into a routine. He's only been there a month.'

'Do you think they'll be able to make him better?'

'No, and he'll get even worse. Everyone says so. The fits have damaged his mind and he'll never get better.' She pulled her pale grey cardigan out of the satchel and put it on. 'I'm cold,' she said, buttoning it up. 'I wish I hadn't gone into summer uniform so soon.'

'So he won't be joining the army, then?'

'Not on your life. Remember never to mention the army in front of my father, won't you? It would just start him off.'

'Of course I won't. What do you think I am, thick? No, don't answer that.' She giggled. 'But I'm not likely to be talking to your dad, am I?' She paused. 'If you're not going to visit James this weekend, maybe we can go somewhere together?'

'You know I'd like to, but my father would never let me. He'd say it's one thing to go to your house for tea, with your parents being there, but it's quite another for us to go out on our own. If I suggest it, he'll blow a fuse and there'll be such a row.'

'You might be wrong about him. After all, we go to school on our own now, don't we? So what's so different about going out at the weekend?'

'Where were you thinking of going?'

'Anywhere really. We could get the bus to Chalk Farm, or maybe even Camden Town. Or we could go to the Saturday

33

morning film at the Gaumont State in Kilburn. Then you could come back to me and we could learn the words of 'Mambo Italiano'. I've got Alma Cogan singing it – Mum bought it for me this week. She wouldn't mind you coming round – she thinks you're a good influence on me. But I don't mind what we do.'

'I don't know why I even asked the question. I won't be allowed to go. I'll be told what to do, and that's that. Maybe I'll have to go shopping with my mother – big treat – or do my homework, read my books, be invisible. Better still, be James. You don't know how lucky you are.'

'But now that you're going to the grammar school, he might let you do more. It's only Thursday today so you've got time to get round him. Perhaps your mum can ask him for you. She could say that you've been working hard at school all week and you need a break on Saturday. I bet your father would say yes, especially when he hears you've got grammar.'

'My mother's much too scared of my father to say anything. And anyway, there'd be no point in it. He never listens to her, just like he never listens to me.'

'But like I said, you go to school by yourself every day, or with me. So why shouldn't we go out at the weekend?'

'Don't ask me why, but that's different. He might let you come over for tea, though. I could ask him that.'

Ruth shifted from one foot to the other. She flushed slightly. 'Thanks for the invitation, Pat, but I don't really want to go to your house, if you don't mind. Your dad's a bit scary. And you haven't got a gramophone, anyway.'

'OK, then, I'll ask him about Saturday, but I bet he says no. And he'll certainly say no if I'm late for tea, so I'd better get off now.'

'And I ought to go home and tell my parents the worst. No point putting it off any longer. You're lucky – your mum and dad'll be really proud of you.'

'That'll be the day. If by any miracle I *can* do something at the weekend, I'll tell you tomorrow. Meet you here at eight as usual. 'Bye, then.' With a backward wave of her hand, she started to run along Belsize Park Gardens in the direction of their narrow Victorian house, which stood half way along the road.

'Good luck with your dad,' Ruth called after her, and she turned and went in the opposite direction.

Patricia reached her front door, and stopped.

She stood and stared at the wooden door. Perhaps her father really would be proud of her, just like Ruth said. She tried to imagine his face looking pleased with her, and she wondered what he might say. Excitement rising within her, she stepped forward, knocked on the door and waited.

In the past, he'd never talked to her about school or anything, and he'd hardly ever read her reports so he might not know that she always got good marks. He might look really surprised, then smile and tell her that he had a clever daughter. And then, when she'd started at her new school, he'd talk to her at the end of each day about what she'd done in her lessons, and he'd be interested in everything she said to him. She'd matter to him. He'd no longer always sit by himself in the front room, thinking about James – he'd think about her.

Shivery expectation spread through her as she waited for the door to open. She tried to push the sensation back. She didn't want to hope too much.

Footsteps sounded behind the door. The door opened wide and her mother's anxious face looked down at her.

'Well?' she asked, stepping aside to let Patricia enter the hallway.

'Well what?' she called back to her mother as she went down the corridor to the kitchen. Enid quickly closed the

35

front door and hurried after her, her slippers sliding on the smooth lino.

'Well, what did you get, Patsy? Don't keep me in suspense any longer. I've been on tenterhooks all day.'

Patricia threw her satchel on to the kitchen table. 'I didn't think you'd remember what day it was.'

'You silly girl! How could Daddy and I forget something as important as this? I've been counting the minutes till you got home.'

'Where's Father? Is he in the front room?'

'Yes, he is, and you can go to him and tell him what you got yourself, but you must put me out of my misery first.' She stared eagerly at her. Patricia pursed her lips and gazed at the ceiling, watching her mother out of the corner of her eye. 'Well, did you get into the grammar school, darling?' Enid repeated. She clasped her hands together in front of her mouth.

Patricia nodded. Her face broke into a broad smile. 'Yes, I did, Mummy. Father will be pleased, won't he?'

'Oh, Patsy,' Enid cried, and she flung her arms around Patricia and hugged her tightly. 'I'm absolutely thrilled. And Daddy will be, too. Clever old you – it can't have been easy for you, what with James and everything. But I'm not in the least bit surprised. I knew you were a clever girl.' She kissed Patricia on the forehead. 'Now, go and tell Daddy your news. Working for the Assistance Board is really getting him down, and he's had a particularly bad day today. Good news like yours is just what he needs. He'll be so proud of you. While you're telling him, I'll go and set the table for tea.' She picked up Patricia's satchel and put it on the dresser. Then she took a tray from the side of the dresser and put it on the table.

Patricia remained standing next to the table, fingering the edge of the floral plastic table cloth.

'Off you go, darling,' Enid urged. She opened the door to the cupboard nearest her and took out three cups. 'Poor Daddy will be waiting.'

Still, Patricia didn't move. She stared at her mother. 'This'll make everything all right now, Mummy, won't it?'

Enid looked up from putting the cups on the tray, and met Patricia's eyes. She turned quickly back to the cupboard, and took out three saucers. 'Daddy loves you, darling,' she said, putting the saucers next to the cups. 'He always has.'

'No, he hasn't, but that's all right. I know he was worried about James. But with James in the Home now, he doesn't have to worry about him any more and he can think about me. He will, won't he?'

'You getting into the grammar school is going to please him very much,' Enid said, opening one of the drawers in the dresser. 'Things will sort themselves out, Patsy. You'll see.'

She took out three napkins and and placed them on the tray next to the china.

'Daddy,' Patricia called out as she knocked at the door.

'Come in, Patricia.'

She pushed the door open and went into the front room. The Major was sitting behind the large oak table that stood in the centre of the room, a pile of books on either side of him and an open map on the table in front of him.

He glanced up as she came into the room. She approached the table and hovered hesitantly on the other side from her father. Glancing down at the papers spread out before him, she saw a pile of sepia-coloured photographs lying on one of the corners of the open map. She leaned forward slightly and saw that the top photograph was of two men wearing unusual clothes.

'What are you doing, Daddy?'

The Major let out a short sigh. He leaned back in his chair, rested his elbows on the wooden arms of the chair and put his hands together, the fingertips of one hand resting lightly against those of the other hand. She noticed that the joints on the fingers of both his hands were thick and knobbly.

'Did you have some reason for interrupting me, Patricia?' he asked quietly

'Yes, Daddy,' she said, and her face broke into a wide smile. 'I've passed the eleven plus. I'm going to the grammar school in September.' Her eyes shining, she stared at him across the table.

He glanced to his right, to the small framed photograph of James that stood on the corner of the table.

'Ruth got secondary modern,' she said, playing with the bottom button of her cardigan. 'Most of the class did. Only six of us got grammar.'

The Major raised his eyes from the photograph. Patricia saw that they were moist. 'Are you crying because you're pleased with me?' she asked awkwardly. She pulled one of her pigtails over her shoulder and started to suck on the tips of her hair.

'I'm not crying, Patricia. You know I'm not one to make a scene. But this will be the one and only time that I hear such words from a child of mine. Of course, in an ideal world ...' He stopped himself, and gave her a smile that didn't quite reach his eyes. 'Well done, anyway.'

Her hands fell to her side. 'Aren't you pleased with me, Daddy? I thought you'd be happy.'

'Of course I'm pleased with you. Your success is a great achievement, and I don't mean to diminish it in any way. It is difficult, however, not to think that if James ... if James ...'

He coughed, leaned forward in his chair and looked down at the map in front of him. 'You will understand, I'm sure, a sensible girl like you, that it's hard to feel happy, as you put it, in such circumstances.'

'Yes, Daddy.' There was a lump in her throat, and she swallowed.

Staring at the top of her father's head as he peered at the map, she wondered whether she ought to leave the room. She glanced over her shoulder to the door, then turned back to look at her father. He'd picked up a ruler and pencil, and was underlining a place in the centre of the map. Then he put down the pencil, picked up the pile of photographs and started to look through them.

She watched him for a few minutes. 'What are you doing?'

The Major paused and looked up at her. 'It's my intention to make a written record of the trip I made to Ladakh in 1945. It's a most interesting country and a very beautiful one, and I think that my photographs and perceptions of the country may well be of interest to other people.'

She leaned over the table and tried to look at the map. 'Did you go there when you were stationed with your regiment in North India?'

'That is correct. A couple of colleagues and I were keen to visit Ladakh, as we'd heard that there was much of interest to see there. We had some leave due to us so we applied for visitors' permits and were given them, despite the fact that very few were issued at that time. I took photographs throughout our trip, and made extensive notes at the end of every day.'

'Is that what all those sheets of paper are?'

'Indeed it is.' He rested his hand lightly on the pile of documents nearest to him. 'It's going to give me a great deal of pleasure to compile this album. I had always hoped that I would visit Ladakh again one day, possibly with James. Regretfully, however, that will not now happen. Creating a record of the journey that I made will be something to show him. A compromise, one might say.'

'Where's Ladakh? We haven't done it yet at school.'

'In Asia, to the northeast of India and to the west of Tibet. May I suggest that you study the atlas that your mother and I gave you last Christmas? If you do so, you will be able to determine the co-ordinates of the country. Now, if there isn't anything else, you may tell your mother that I shall be ready for tea in precisely half an hour.'

'I was wondering about Saturday, Daddy.' Her voice shook. 'Ruth asked me if I could go out with her, perhaps for a walk somewhere or maybe to the cinema. Can I go, please?'

The Major put the photographs carefully back on the table, picked up a book from the pile of books next to him and opened it.

'Or can I go to Ruth's for tea? Her mother doesn't mind.'

Her father paused and looked up from the book. 'But I mind, Patricia. I mind very much. You are not yet eleven years old. It is for your mother and me to decide how you spend your time, not for your friend Ruth, and certainly not for Ruth's mother. I'm sure that you will have some school work to do at the weekend. I should be most disturbed to think that you were relaxing your standards now that you have achieved a measure of success.'

'I wouldn't do that. I promise.'

He put up his hand to silence her. 'Day after day, people come to the National Assistance Board and beg us to give them money, either because they are unable to earn their own income or, more frequently, because they are not prepared to do so. These people are a drain on the country's resources. I am determined that you will be able to provide for yourself. How you do so, of course, will be up to you. But this means that there must be no let-up in your endeavours.'

'I'll never be a drain like those other people, Daddy.'

'Indeed, you will not. This weekend, you will do your school work and then you will help your mother with some of her domestic activities, just as you always do. Now, perhaps you would tell her that I shall come for my tea in twenty-five minutes.'

'Yes, Daddy.' Her head down, she walked across the room to the door and started to turn the handle.

'One moment, Patricia.' Her father's voice reached her across the room.

'Yes, Daddy?' She looked back to where he was sitting.

He'd put his book down and was rubbing the joints on the fingers of his right hand. He looked very small behind the big table, she thought.

'When you write your weekly letter to your brother, it would be better if you didn't mention your examination success. We must strive to keep James from being aware of his limited capabilities. Emphasising the difference between his situation and yours would not be helpful.'

'I promise I won't mention it.'

'One further matter. I intend to make a start on my album this weekend and it occurs to me that there might be some ways in which you can assist me. After all, you are to be a grammar-school girl, are you not?' He gave her a slight smile. 'You might help me by sticking photographs to some of the pages, for example. I expect your mother would spare you from some of the household chores if we asked her nicely.'

Her face lit up. 'Oh, thank you, Daddy. I'd really like that.'

'You may go now, and again, well done.' He gave her a little nod, and she turned back to the door, pulled it open and ran through it.

In the split second before the door closed, she glimpsed her father reach out for the photograph of James and hold it to his chest.

Chapter Four

Ladakh, May 1955: Kalden, aged 11

'Kalden!' His mother's voice was carried to him on the back of the early morning air, but he was already out of his village, speeding past the tiny plots of cultivated land that lay beyond the village wall, past the tapering white stone *chorten,* and her voice died away in the wind.

As he ran across the patches of coarse grass breaking through the stony ground, and between lines of wild irises that stretched into the distance, the scent of wild currant and mint filled his nostrils. On he ran, not even stopping when in a streak of black and yellow, a golden oriole swooped low above him. His heart felt as if it would burst with happiness: summer was coming and he was going to do valuable work for people who needed him. A man's work.

By the time he reached the goats grazing outside the protective stone wall of the missionary's house, he was panting heavily, and he slowed down as he went through the gap in the wall to the area in front of the house. Coming to a stop just inside the wall, he looked around him for a moment or two, and then started to make his way slowly between the two small fields of turnips that led to the east-facing front door. Half way to the door, he knelt down to examine the progress of the vegetables.

A shadow of anxiety crossed his face, and he stepped off the path and walked carefully along the rows of planted furrows, his eyes on the ground. Reaching the edge of one of the narrow irrigation channels which was fed by the small stream near the house, he bent down and studied the flow of water.

The sound of loud voices erupted from inside the house,

breaking into the calm of the morning. He looked up sharply. Mr Henderson was shouting and he sounded very angry. He heard Peter say something to him, and then he heard Mr Henderson reply. He couldn't tell if Mr Henderson was still angry.

He stood up and stared at the house. The missionary's wife was speaking. Mr Henderson answered her. He didn't sound quite as angry as before, but nor did he sound happy.

Kalden bit his lip. Perhaps he ought to go away and come back another day. He needed to tell the missionary about the holes in the walls of some of the irrigation channels – if he didn't tell him soon, the vegetables would die – but the problem could wait a little longer. It would be better to talk to him when he was happy again.

He started to pick his way out of the furrows.

'Kalden!' he heard a voice shout out from behind him. 'Don't go!'

He turned towards the door as a fair-haired boy in a thick jumper and grey-flannel trousers burst out of the house and came running towards him. Kalden's face broke into a smile. 'Hello, Peter!' he called.

'Thank goodness you've come. Dad's in a rotten mood this morning,' Peter said, reaching Kalden and coming to a stop. 'I can't wait for him to get off to Alchi. He's going to ask if we want to go with him, but we don't, do we? Not when he's in such a bad temper.'

'You speak too fast, Peter. My English still not very good. I not understand when you talk fast.'

'Sorry. We don't want to go into Alchi, do we? We want to stay here, don't we?'

'*Ju-le*, Kalden.' Kalden turned and saw Mr Henderson coming up to them, a smile of welcome on his face. 'Or should I say "Hello"? We said that we'd only speak English to you, didn't we?'

'Hello, Mr Henderson.'

'I expect Peter's been telling you that I'm in a foul mood.' He glanced down at his son with an affectionate smile. 'I have to admit I've been a bit of a grouch this morning.'

'More than a bit,' Peter said. He grinned at his father. 'You've been horrible.'

'And he's probably also told you that I've got some purchases to make in Alchi today. I'll be back before evening. You boys are more than welcome to come along with me, if you want. But if you'd prefer to stay behind, Margaret's got *ngamphe* soup for lunch. She made it herself and very good it is, too. So, what's it to be: staying here or coming to Alchi?'

'I like stay here, Mr Henderson. *Ama-le* and *Aba-le* not pleased if I in Alchi with you. They not pleased I come here to house. Ask me stay in village.'

The missionary shook his head. 'I'd rather suspected that your parents were still unhappy about you coming to see us, even though they must know how much we need your help. This is a hard place to live for those who aren't born here. I don't know what we'd have done if you hadn't stepped in.'

'Stepped in, please?'

'It means, if you hadn't helped us. If you hadn't shown us what to do, I doubt we'd still be here.'

'I glad you here.'

'Well, thank you, Kalden. I'm pleased you feel that way. I just wish that others felt the same.'

'I sorry they not want you.'

'There's nothing for you to be sorry about, son. I can understand what they're worried about – they think we're only here to turn you all into Christians. Naturally we'd be delighted if that happened, but the main thing is to help all you children get a basic education.'

'Ladakhi children must look after land: do spinning, make dung cakes, look after little brothers and sisters, fetch water from stream, lots of things. No time for school.'

'The leader of Ladakh doesn't agree. He's said that every family has to send one of their children to school. Until we got here, your nearest school was in Leh, and that's miles away. If the children from the local villages came to us to be taught, it would be so much easier for them.' He shrugged his shoulders in a gesture of helplessness. 'But they don't want us here and won't come.'

'You good people. I like Peter. We friends. I like hear Mrs Henderson play music. And like pictures in books.'

Christopher Henderson put his hand on Kalden's shoulder and looked down at him. 'Bless you, son; you don't know how much pleasure it gives me to hear you say that.' He turned to Peter. 'To get back to the present. I take it that you and Kalden are going to stay here. Any ideas about what you're going to do?'

Peter looked at Kalden. 'What shall we do? We could slide down the slopes to the edge of the water.' He paused. 'Or we could go along to the next village and see what's going on there. Kalden's made friends with some of the children who live there.' He threw a sly glance at Kalden.

Kalden looked quickly down at the ground.

'Or Kalden could help you to get better at spinning, Peter. Now that's a thought. We'll need more blankets this winter and there's a pile of yak-hair just waiting to be spun.'

'Before spinning, must mend water channels,' Kalden said firmly.

Peter glanced along the furrows. 'What's wrong with them? They look all right to me. They've got water in them.'

'If Kalden says that they need repairing, then they obviously need to be repaired, and that's a priority. I'm sorry to disappoint you, Peter, but you may have to leave the village for another day, unless, of course, you finish the job fairly quickly.'

'We never finish anything quickly. Everything takes ages to do,' Peter muttered, a sulky expression on his face. He kicked the dust on the track and a cloud of sand swirled up.

Mr Henderson took a step back. 'Watch what you're doing, will you? Now, Kalden, what's this problem with the channels?'

'Water not stay in channels. Some of water go into ground before get to vegetables. Holes in side of channels.'

'How will you mend them? If you need my help, I can stay here. I could always go to Alchi another day.'

'You go Alchi. I show Peter. Peter show you tonight. Not hard. I mend with this.' He tugged at his homespun robe. 'Peter see what I do.' He pointed to the row of turnips at his feet. 'Turnips dry now, but soon have water.'

Christopher Henderson smiled down at him. 'What would we do without you, son? Thank you.' He looked at the heavy watch on his wrist. 'I really ought to get off if I'm going today. I'll leave you boys to it, then.'

A few minutes later, he set off on his bullock-drawn cart. Kalden and Peter waved goodbye to him, and stood and watched until he'd manoeuvred the cart through the gap in the wall and turned it in the direction of Alchi.

Peter turned to Kalden. 'How long do you think it'll take to mend the channels? It'd be fun to go to the village. We might see Dolma there. I think you like her. You do, don't you?'

Kalden shrugged his shoulders. 'She quite nice.'

'Quite nice! I'd say she's more than quite nice. She's very pretty.'

Kalden giggled. 'Then you marry her when you a man.'

'But it's you she likes. I can tell. And anyway, I don't know where I'll be when I'm a man. We may not even be here then.'

Kalden stared at Peter, his eyes opening wide in alarm.

'But I expect we will,' Peter added quickly. 'I wouldn't be able to marry her, though, because we wouldn't be able to talk to each other. She can't speak English and my Ladakhi's terrible. It *is* terrible, isn't it?'

'Yes,' Kalden said. They both laughed.

'Dad probably thinks I'm stupid,' Peter said, picking up two pebbles and banging them together, 'not being able to learn Ladakhi when you're so good at learning English.'

'Mr Henderson not think you stupid, Peter. He know you clever boy. You count and read. Ladakhi boys not clever; can't count and read. And you play music. You very clever.'

'I suppose so.' Peter's face brightened. 'He thinks you're clever, too. He's always saying how wonderful you are.'

A warm glow swept through Kalden. 'He really say I wonderful?'

'He's amazed at everything you know how to do. So, reading and writing isn't everything, is it?'

'But Mr Henderson in Ladakh to teach Ladakhi children reading and writing. Ladakh very hard country to live in. So reading and writing very important to Mr Henderson.'

'Maybe you're right.'

'Mr Henderson very upset this morning. Why?'

'I did a pretty dumb – pretty stupid – thing earlier on today. You know the stone wall he's been building to keep the goats away from those peas we planted? Well, I tried to walk along the top of it and it all broke. I forgot that the stones were only piled on top of each other.'

'You be hurt?'

'No, but I felt such an idiot. Dad was pretty angry, as you obviously heard. Now he's got to build the whole thing up again.' He looked across the rows of turnips, and sighed loudly. 'So what have we got to do to the irrigation channels? If we start now, we might have time for some fun afterwards. We can do the spinning another day. I hate boring old spinning. I wish we lived in England. No one spins their own clothes there – you just go to a shop and buy what you need.'

'Come on. I show how mend walls.' He beckoned to Peter to follow him, and walked towards the irrigation channels. As he did so, he unbelted his knee-length robe and started to pull it up over his head.

'Hey, what are you doing?' Peter squealed. He stood still and burst out laughing.

'You see very soon,' Kalden replied, his voice muffled beneath the folds of material. Giving a final tug on the robe, he yanked it off and waved it in the air, grinning at Peter.

'I know you've got another one underneath, but you'll be cold.'

'I not cold. Ladakhi boys not cold like English boys.' He held up the robe in his hand. 'This very old robe. Under old robe have new robe. New robe is good robe. *Ama-le* can't mend old robe again as lots and lots of mending in it, so we use old robe to mend channel. Me show.'

Peter stood and watched as Kalden tore the robe into large pieces, then crouched down and spread the pieces over the ground. He carefully scooped a handful of mud from the bottom of the irrigation channel, put the mud on one of the squares of material and wrapped the material around it. Then he pushed the mud-filled parcel into the place in the channel wall through which water was escaping.

'See,' he said, straightening up. 'Now wall good. It not take long. We mend walls, then we get dung from animals and make dung cakes. We put dung cakes on wall to dry in sun. If no dung cakes, not able cook food in winter and make fire, and you be very cold.'

'Don't mention winter. We haven't had summer yet! Right, let's see how quickly we can do everything. If we get a move on, we might have time to go and see Dolma when we've finished.' He knelt down beside Kalden, watched him make another mud parcel and then began to do the same.

'Do your parents shout at you a lot?' Peter asked as they each packed a mud parcel into the side of the wall. 'Like when they get angry with you because you keep on coming to see us?'

'Ladakhi people not get angry.'

'I know you've said that before, but surely they sometimes get really furious and yell at you, just like my dad gets angry with me when I do something I shouldn't.'

'*Chi choen*? What's the point?' Kalden smiled.

'How can you not argue? It's not natural.'

'Natural for Ladakhi people. All people in village must be friends with all other people in village. Need people to help with sowing and with harvest – with everything. So must all be friends.'

'I don't believe it. Everyone gets angry at some time or other – it's human nature. The people in Ladakh are the same as people everywhere else.'

Kalden shrugged. 'Maybe someone not very happy and get angry. But not often. Is not Ladakhi way to do things.'

'When you disobey your parents and come and see us, what happens?'

'We talk. They say they very unhappy. Me say missionary family need help to live here, and me give help. Me say parents not need me – brothers help parents with land. Brothers will have land, not me. Me help brothers and parents make ground ready for seeds; me go summer pasture with brothers – is good; me help cut barley and wheat when ready, and do whatever *aba-le* and brothers ask, but me not really needed at home. Me tell parents you be my neighbour and Ladakhi people must help neighbour.'

'Suppose there's a really, really big argument between

neighbours – I can't think what about at the moment, but suppose there is – what happens if the people can't settle it themselves?'

'Someone who know both villagers listen to one villager, then the other villager, and say what must be done.'

'Well, I think it's very strange. I can't see that system going down well in England.'

Kalden paused in the middle of rolling up the last mud package. 'You think you go back England soon?'

Peter sat back on his heels. 'I'd go tomorrow – I'm sorry, Kalden, but I would – but Dad wouldn't. That'd be accepting defeat. He's much too proud to give in and admit that he's failed. This is his mission in life. He's going to see it through, and the Church is going to support him all the way.'

'Is a good mission.'

'Oh, yes,' he said with sudden bitterness. 'It's very good. Life is hard here – there's no water and nothing will grow. The local people don't want us here and ignore us when they see us in the towns and refuse to send their children to our school. It's freezing cold for most of the year, and baking hot in the summer. And my mother – if we lived in England, she could go to concerts and things. We all could. She makes the most of it for my father's sake, but I know she'd rather be at home.'

'I sorry. I say wrong thing.'

Peter glanced at Kalden's face. 'I feel rotten saying that because I really like you, Kalden. You're my only friend, and when you go into the monastery, I won't have any friends at all.'

'I not go into monastery yet.' Kalden banged the final mud parcel firmly into position. 'I not think about monastery. You need me. I stay here.'

'But when your brothers take over the land, you'll have to move out of your house, and that might be quite soon.

With Deki married to all three of your brothers, and with them already having two babies, your parents will probably be moving into the little house next to your brothers' house soon. You'll have to go into the monastery then, won't you?'

'That not happen for long time. And anyway, maybe I marry and not go into monastery.'

Peter grinned and leaned forward, putting his face close to Kalden's. 'I know who you're thinking of,' he said, a sing-song lilt to his voice. 'And her name begins with D.' He sat back, stretched out his legs and stared excitedly at Kalden. 'I bet you *do* marry her. I heard Dad tell Mum he thought you were going to be really good-looking – much better looking than your brothers – and Dolma obviously thinks so, too – she giggles and goes all silly whenever she sees you.' He threw back his head and shouted, 'Kalden and Dolma are in love.'

'What a noise, boys!' Margaret Henderson called as she came out of the house. She came across to them. 'What are you up to?'

The boys scrambled to their feet, wiping the mud from their clothes.

'We've been mending the wall of the irrigation channels, Mum. The water was leaking out.'

Margaret smiled gratefully at Kalden. 'We seem to be saying thank you to you all the time, Kalden.'

'I pleased to help, Mrs Henderson.'

'Apart from the help you give us, I know how much Peter enjoys having your company.' She ruffled Peter's fair hair, and he pulled his head away in embarrassment. 'I expect both of you are ready for some refreshment now, aren't you? I still have some of the *gur-gur cha* that you brought us, Kalden. Would you like a cup?'

'What about me? I can't stand butter tea. It's much too salty.'

'Don't worry, there's apricot juice for you, Peter. I think I know by now what you like to drink.' She smiled at them both. 'So, do you want to come and have something to eat and drink? I heard Christopher telling you that I'd made some soup, so there's that, too.'

'Thank you, Mrs Henderson. You very kind.'

'Dear me, Kalden.' She laughed. 'You don't have to be quite so formal. Giving you a bite to eat is the least we can do after all your hard work. We want you to look upon our home as your second home. As it is, Christopher virtually looks upon you as a son. Now, shall we go in and eat?'

Kalden glanced towards the stone house in front of him, and then looked back at the missionary's wife. His face broke out into a broad smile. 'Yes, please,' he said.

Chapter Five

Patricia walked quickly across the crowded out-patient area of the Paddington Green Children's Hospital, tightening the strings of the green cotton hospital gown that she wore on Saturdays when helping out at the hospital, and went up the narrow back staircase to the small room at the top of the stairs where the nurses gathered in shifts for their afternoon tea.

She was late taking her tea break. While it hadn't been deliberate, she wasn't sorry to be the last to go. With any luck, all of the nurses would have returned to their wards by the time she got there and she'd have a quiet few moments in the middle of what had been an unusually busy afternoon. She liked the nurses a lot, but she was tired and not in the mood for conversation.

She pushed the door open and saw a nurse sitting at the table. Her heart sank: with only one nurse in the room, there'd be no way of avoiding talking to her.

'Hello, Sheila,' she said, forcing her face into a smile. 'I'm afraid I'm a bit late. Is there any tea left?'

'There is, indeed. More importantly, there are still some scones and strawberry jam. Help yourself.'

She went over to the table at the side of the room, poured herself a cup of tea from the large aluminium teapot and went and sat opposite Sheila.

'So, what did they give you to do today?' Sheila asked, spreading a thick layer of jam on her scone.

'Beds, beds and more beds! I'm sure I'll dream of making beds with hospital corners tonight. I've also done masses of sterilising today, and I've got to go to the sluice room after I've had my tea. That's something to look forward to.'

Sheila laughed. 'You poor thing. They're certainly working you hard, and you're not even getting paid for it. If you're doing this to see if you want to be a nurse when you leave school, I'm pretty sure I know what your decision will be.'

'Don't worry, I don't want to be a nurse. Not because of what they have to do – I like it here and I like the nurses – it's just that I want to go to secretarial school.'

'Not to university? You're at a grammar school, aren't you? Won't your parents want you to go to university?' Sheila pushed the plate of scones towards Patricia. 'Here, have a scone.'

'I don't want one, thank you. I'm not hungry.'

'No wonder you're so slim. With me, being hungry doesn't come into it.'

'My parents don't care what I do. My mother would probably like me to go to university, but my father doesn't mind what I do. I suppose I haven't really decided what to do yet. I could end up going to teachers' training college – I think I might like teaching. But whatever I do, I don't want to live away from home for three years. It wouldn't be fair on my father.'

'Why ever not?'

'Because I'm helping him with his book.'

'Is he a writer?'

'Not like you mean, but he's writing a book all the same. At first it was just going to be an album of notes and pictures about a trip he went on years ago to Ladakh – it's a country north of the Himalayas – but it's turned into a proper book now.'

'You're a bit young to be helping him write a book, aren't you? You can't be more than fourteen or fifteen.'

'I'm fifteen. I was fifteen in June. He's got arthritis in his hands, so he had to retire early. I mainly help him on

Sundays, doing all the typing for him, so it makes sense for me to go on a secretarial course.'

'Have you ever been to the place he's writing about – I've forgotten what it's called?'

'Ladakh. No, but I'd like to go. Father says he's going to go there again one day, as he wants to add a section about how the country's changed over the years. I don't know if it'll work out, though, with his hands being as they are.'

'He's lucky to have a daughter who's willing to help him in her free time. Most girls of your age would rather be out shopping with their friends, or going dancing.'

Patricia grinned at her. 'You must have met my friend, Ruth. She and her schoolfriends go on and on about Cliff Richard and Elvis Presley, and about boys. Rock and roll's OK, but not all of the time, and I don't really know any boys. You don't meet that many in an all-girls' school, at least not until the sixth form. The sixth formers have a dance every year with the boys from the boys' grammar school near us. I can't imagine what I'll talk to them about, though, when my time comes.' She pulled a terrified face.

'I'm sure you'll think of something. And if you can't think of what to say, there's always the other.' She gave Patricia a knowing look.

Patricia could feel herself going scarlet. 'And anyway,' she went on quickly, 'I don't mind helping my father. In fact, I quite like it. It'd be boring if everyone liked doing the same thing.'

'You said it. But why work as a nurse if you don't want to be a nurse? You could have got paid work in the zoo, for example. My cousin's your age, and she and her friends work there on Saturdays. They seem to have a lot of fun. Surely that'd be better than sluicing? Anything would.'

Patricia shrugged. 'I suppose it might be, but I find it quite interesting here as I already know a bit about nursing – I used to help with my brother who's been ill all his life. And my parents give me some money each week, so it works out fine.'

'Well, I'm sure we're all very glad that you came to us. I'm sorry about your brother, though. How old is he?'

'Seventeen. He lives in a Home now.'

'The poor thing.' Sheila got up and carried her cup and plate to the steel trolley in the corner. 'It must be very hard on your parents.'

Patricia picked up her cup and saucer and followed Sheila. 'He hasn't lived at home for about four years now. We visit him, though,' she added quickly, putting her crockery on the pile on top of Sheila's.

The door opened and a nurse put her head round the door. 'Oh, good, I've found you, Patricia,' she said, and came right into the room. 'I've been looking all over the place for you.'

'I was on my tea break. Have I done anything wrong?' she asked anxiously, a nervous flush spreading across her cheeks.

'No, not a thing. At least, if you have, I don't know about it,' the nurse said with a laugh. 'No, it's just that there's been a phone call from your mother. She'd like you to go straight home when you leave here.'

'I wonder what she wants.' She looked questioningly at the nurse.

'I can't help you, I'm afraid. I suggest that you go home now and find out for yourself.'

'But I'm meant to join Angela in the sluice room.'

'That can wait. I'm sure Angela can do whatever needs to be done by herself. You get off now and see what your mother wants.'

'If you're sure?'

'I *am* sure. I'll let Angela know that you've had to leave

early. Hopefully, there won't be any problems at home and we'll see you as usual next week. Now off you go,' she said, opening the door wider so that Patricia could go through it.

'Well, all right, then. Thank you.'

Undoing the ties at the back of her gown as she went, she hurried down the stairs to the sterilising room. She threw the gown into the linen bin, unhooked her brown woollen coat from the stand in the corner of the room and went as quickly as she could along the tiled corridor to the exit that led from the old part of the hospital.

The day was dying as she stepped out on to the pavement and made her way past the new red-brick hospital buildings. She crossed the street between two of the tall elm trees that flanked the road, went through an opening in the iron railings surrounding Paddington Green and immediately turned down the left-hand path that led towards Edgware Road.

As she hurried between the rows of plane trees that lined the path, dead leaves, golden-brown and crisp beneath her feet, crackled with every step that she took. Above her, the branches of the spreading plane trees had cut off the remaining light of day, and she shivered as she walked and drew her coat more tightly around her.

By the time she was half way across the green, the drone of thundering traffic filled the air and the conglomeration of buildings backing on to Edgware Road was clearly visible in front of her. Her steps slowed as she passed the marble statue of the actress, Sarah Siddons, and she stared beyond the statue to the distant tombstones that lined the north wall of the former burial ground.

She stopped short. It would take her ages to get back to Belsize Park by bus in all the traffic; the tube would have been quicker.

She hated the tube – she was always afraid that she

wouldn't be able to escape if anything went wrong and she used to worry that someone would fall on the line in front of her and be run over by a train. But the tube was quicker than the bus. Much quicker.

She turned and ran back up the path and across the road, back between the elm trees, back past the hospital. She didn't stop running until she'd reached the underground station.

Her mother opened the front door to her as she put up her hand to knock on the door. Patricia saw at once that she'd been crying.

Her hands flew to her mouth. 'What's wrong, Mummy? Has anything happened to Daddy?'

'Your father's all right, darling. No, it's James.' Her mother's eyes filled again with tears. 'The Home rang this morning. It was very sudden. No one expected it. James was fine one moment – well, as fine as James can ever be – and the next he'd had a massive fit. A really massive fit. And he died, Patsy. He died.' Her voice broke in pain-filled anguish, and she held out her arms to her daughter. Patricia burst into tears and ran to her mother. The door quietly clicked shut behind them.

'My darling James. But he didn't suffer at the end, and that's the main thing,' Enid wept, clasping Patricia to her. 'He won't have known what was happening. My poor, poor James. To die at seventeen. What life did he have?'

Patricia sobbed into her mother's shoulder. 'I should have written to him more often. I wasn't much of a sister to him.'

'Oh, yes, you were, darling.' Enid stroked the back of her daughter's fair head. 'You were a wonderful sister. Look how you used to help us with James, right from when you were a tiny little thing. You've always helped us look after him. No brother could have asked for a better sister.' Her arms tightened around her daughter.

Suddenly Patricia tensed and pulled back. She stared into her mother's grief-ravaged face. 'Where's Daddy?' she asked, her voice catching.

'He's in the front room, darling. I'd leave him for a bit. This has hit him very hard – it's hit us all very hard. I think Daddy's best left alone for a while. He'll come out when he's ready to talk to us. No, let's you and me go into the kitchen and have a cup of tea. That's what we'll do. It's time for tea, anyway.' She took a white cotton handkerchief from her apron pocket. Clutching it tightly, she led the way along the corridor.

Wiping her eyes with the back of her hand, Patricia followed her mother into the kitchen. She went straight over to the kettle and lifted it up, but Enid took it from her.

'I'll fill it up – just like I always do,' she told her. She tucked the handkerchief back into her pocket and gave her daughter a watery smile. 'Be a love and get the cake you made at school yesterday out of the pantry and put it on the table, and then perhaps you'd set the table.'

Her hands shaking, Enid filled the kettle with water and carried it over to the cooker. 'We'll have tea in here today,' she said, putting the kettle on to the stove and lighting the gas ring. 'We won't bother taking it into the back room. And we'll be really lazy and leave the plastic cloth on the table. That's what we'll do.' She stood in the centre of the kitchen and looked helplessly around her. 'Yes, that's what we'll do,' she repeated.

Patricia took the cake stand from the dresser, put it in the centre of the table, placed the cake on the stand and put the cake slice next to it. Then she went over to the dresser and opened the cutlery drawer. 'Shall I set a place for Daddy?'

'And why wouldn't you, may I ask? Am I not still a member of this family?'

Startled, she jumped at the sound of her father's voice behind her. She looked anxiously round at him.

'Of course you are, George,' Enid said. Twisting the corner of her apron, she stared across the room at her husband, who was standing in the doorway. 'You know you are.'

'I'm gratified to hear it,' he remarked, and walked stiffly into the room.

'I just wondered, Daddy. I thought you might be having your tea in the front room as you were still in there,' Patricia said. 'Because of James,' she added, her voice trailing off.

'Well, as you can see, I'm in here now. It's my intention to join you for tea, as I always do. Our custom is to have our tea together as a family and I see no reason to depart from that. We will do today what we have done every other day.' He sat down at the table.

Patricia hurried over to him, put a plate, cake fork and napkin in front of him, then she set the places for her mother and herself, put three cups on the table and sat down opposite her father.

'Would you like us to have tea in the back room, George?' Enid asked, hovering by the table. 'I can easily put everything on the trolley and take it in there, if you'd prefer it.'

'Not at all, Enid. We will do as you have suggested and take our afternoon tea in here today.' He unfolded his white napkin. 'It is perhaps appropriate that we allow ourselves some small departure from our habitual routine today, just this once. Just for today.'

There was a shrill whistle and a cloud of steam shot from the spout of the kettle. Enid rushed to the stove, took the kettle off the gas ring and poured the boiling water on to the leaves in the teapot, then she slipped a floral tea cosy over the pot and carried it over to the table.

'Patricia made the cake at school,' she said brightly,

putting the teapot next to the cups. She sat down and picked up the cake slice.

Patricia glanced across the table at her mother and saw that her face was white and her lips were quivering.

'It's a Victoria sponge sandwich, Daddy,' she said quickly. 'Some of the class put a sort of butter cream in the middle, but I put jam inside. Strawberry jam. I hope you like it.'

The Major sat still, staring down at his plate.

Enid cut three slices of the cake and put a slice on each of their plates. 'Would you pour the tea, Patricia, please? It should be ready by now.' Patricia leaned across and filled the cups in turn. Enid put a cup in front of each of them, then she picked up her fork, cut into her cake and took a bite. 'This is lovely, darling,' she said, with a little nod at Patricia.

'I hope it isn't too heavy.' Patricia picked up her cake with her fingers and bit into it.

'It isn't, Patsy. It's as light as a feather. Isn't it, George?'

There was no answer.

Patricia looked at her father. He sat motionless, his head slightly bowed, his face greyish-white in colour. His eyes were fixed on his plate, his cake untouched.

'Have a piece of Patricia's cake, George. It's very nice.' Enid's voice shook.

He didn't move. Silent tears started to roll unchecked down the furrows of his cheeks, and splashed on to his plate.

'Daddy.' Tears sprang to her eyes. She let her cake fall from her fingers. 'I'm so sorry, Daddy.'

'Later, Patricia,' he said. He pushed the plate away from him and stood up abruptly. 'I'll eat your cake later. And tomorrow …' His voice broke. 'Tomorrow we shall all go to see my son.' He turned and walked out of the kitchen, his back ramrod straight.

'I'm sorry, Mummy,' Patricia whispered through her tears.

Enid jumped up and ran to Patricia's side. 'I know, Patsy

darling,' she said softly, and she bent down and hugged her very hard. 'I know. And I'm sorry, too.'

Patricia switched on her bedroom light. Standing in the doorway, she looked around her.

Everything seemed the same as when she'd left her room that morning, but it also seemed different. Although James had never really been a presence in her life since he'd gone into the Home, a part of him had always been here in the house with them. It had inhabited every corner, shared the air that they breathed. But no more. For the first time ever, her room felt truly empty.

She heard her mother moving around in the kitchen downstairs, clearing up the remains of their silent evening meal, then she heard a door close. Her mother must have returned to the back room, expecting to find her there, not knowing that she'd come up to her bedroom. She'd been drained after a tiring day which had come to such an emotional end, and had felt the need to be alone, to lie quietly on her bed, read her book for a bit, and then close her eyes and put the day behind her.

She glanced across the room to her bedside clock and saw that it was still fairly early. She sighed heavily – exhausted though she was, she'd never get to sleep if she went to bed now.

She bit her thumb nail. Perhaps she should go back downstairs and sit with her mother for a little longer. She didn't really want to – she wanted to be by herself – but it would be a kindness to do so. Her mother would be alone, without anyone to share her sadness. Her father would never think of joining her. He'd stay where he'd gone after he'd left the kitchen – in the front room among his books.

She decided to do what she knew was the right thing, and she went back out of her room, pulled the door closed behind her and crossed the narrow landing to the staircase. Standing on the top stair, she glanced over the banister to the hallway. The kitchen door was closed, but the door to the back room was open. She went down a couple of stairs, bent slightly and stared across the hall into the back room.

The light outside was fading and the room was in semi-darkness, but she could see that her mother was sitting on one of the dark green chenille armchairs, staring across at the framed photograph of James that stood on the mantelpiece. As she watched, her mother suddenly jumped up, went over to the photo, picked it up and took it back with her to her chair.

She sank to the stairs and stared through the banisters as her mother ran her fingers slowly over the glass shroud that covered James's face, then raised the photograph to her lips and kissed it. Turning towards Patricia, she put the photograph on the table next to her and reached across to switch on the lamp. In the bright glare of the electric light, Patricia saw her mother smile at James.

Every nerve in her body screamed at her that she should go back to her bedroom and give her mother some privacy, but she couldn't move. Mesmerised, she watched her mother pick up her book, open it at the page where she'd put her leather bookmark and stare down at the lines of writing in front of her.

Patricia started to stand up. At the same moment, her mother looked up from her book and turned her eyes towards the open door. Patricia sank back down again. Across the emptiness between them, she could see that her mother's eyes were full of indecision. Then her mother took a deep breath, closed the book, put it on the table next to James's photograph, and stood up. She smoothed down her tweed skirt, and wa'ked out of the back room into the hallway.

Hidden in the darkness that had gathered on the landing, Patricia pressed herself against the banisters and sat very still. But her mother passed the foot of the stairs without glancing up. She went along the corridor to the front room, and out of Patricia's line of vision. Patricia heard her knock on the front room door. She sensed her mother waiting for her father to call her into the room, but there was silence. Then she heard her mother knock on the door again, slightly more loudly this time.

'Come in,' her father called, and she heard her mother open the door and go into the room. She didn't hear the door close.

Knowing that she ought not to do it, but unable to stop herself, she crept down to the bottom of the staircase, crouched on the lowest step and peered around the wall. She had a clear view along the corridor, through the open door and into the front room.

Her father was sitting in his usual chair behind the table, staring straight ahead of him, his glasses on the table in front of him. Patricia saw him nod slightly to her mother as she entered the room, then pick up his glasses and pull a pile of typewritten sheets towards him. Her mother hesitated a moment, then went and sat on the chair opposite him, with her back to Patricia.

There was a broken line of books along the middle of the table. A wall of words separating her parents, she thought.

'Yes, Enid?' Her father's voice was very quiet.

Patricia suddenly felt very nervous for her mother: when her father's voice was quiet like that, he should be left alone.

He leaned forward, pushed the books in the line closer to each other, and sat back against his chair. She wondered if her mother was able to see him above the books.

'Is there anything I can do for you?' he asked.

'Patricia's gone to bed,' she heard her mother say. 'I think she's already asleep.'

'Her ability to bring this day to an early end with sleep is, indeed, enviable. I fear that I shall find the welcome oblivion of sleep somewhat more elusive. This has been a sad day for me.'

'And for Patricia and me, too, George. For me, too,' her mother said. Patricia sat up in surprise. Her mother didn't normally talk to her father like that, sort of sharply, accusingly. 'He was my son as well as yours. I loved him, too.'

'I am well aware of that, Enid.'

Her father sounded very calm. Relief flooded through Patricia. She knew that her mother was wrong to speak to her father like that, but she'd had a terrible day and Patricia didn't want her father to get angry with her.

'I have no wish to disparage your grief, Enid, nor that of Patricia's. We are all mourning the loss of someone who was born with great potential. James lost the life he might have had and now we, in turn, have lost James.'

'That's right,' her mother said, her voice strange. 'I've lost my baby.' Her voice was getting louder; it sounded as if she was going to start crying again. 'So why are you sitting in here on your own? Why aren't you with me, helping me through this? We've lost a child, George.' Her mother hunched her shoulders, leaned forward, put her hands to her face and started to cry.

Patricia swallowed the lump in her throat, and watched her father get up, go round the table to her mother and stand beside her. He put his hand on her mother's shoulder. She stared in amazement: her father never touched her mother.

Her mother must have been as surprised as Patricia because she immediately stopped crying and looked up at him. 'You blame me, George, don't you? You've always blamed me for

James being ill, haven't you? You think it's my fault. You think I should never have left him with Mary. I know that's what you think. You've always held me responsible for what happened. You have, haven't you?'

Her mother put her face in her hands again, and her shoulders shook.

Her father slightly raised his hand, then he put it back again on her mother's shoulder.

Even though she couldn't see his face, she could tell from the way he was standing that he felt uncomfortable. 'I'm not aware that I have ever apportioned blame for James's affliction to anyone, Enid. It happened, and we've had to accept that and learn to live with it. I've done my best to do just that. That's all.'

'But that's not all, is it?' Her mother dropped her hands and looked up at her father as she spoke. Patricia caught sight of her face, and drew her breath in sharply. Her mother looked awful, not like her mother at all; her face was all swollen and desperate. 'Whether or not you admit that you blame me, it's there all the time. I know it is. It's been there every single day of our lives since you got back from the war. James would never have got ill if I hadn't left him. That's what you think, isn't it? But I had to go into the hospital, so maybe his illness is Patsy's fault, too. Is she also to blame, George?'

An icy hand gripped Patricia's heart. Her eyes went to her father's back, and she waited. He took his hand from her mother's shoulder and returned to his chair on the other side of the table.

'You are being ridiculous, Enid,' he said, sitting down and picking up one of the typewritten sheets next to him. His voice sounded very cold. 'You need to calm down and control yourself, my dear. I shall put your words down to your grief.'

Patricia felt herself relax.

Her mother stood up and wiped her eyes. 'You do blame me, George, and that's why, on all of the occasions over the past few years when we should have been together, comforting each other, you were doing exactly what you're doing now – hiding away in here. But you can rest assured that I won't embarrass you again by expecting more from you than you're able to give.'

She pushed back her chair, turned and started to walk towards the door. Patricia quickly scrambled to her feet.

'Just a thought, Enid,' she heard her father call after her. Her mother stopped where she was and turned round, her back to Patricia. 'Every person must deal with his grief according to his character. In my grief, my need has increasingly been for solitude. I accept that. It is evident to me, however, that your need is that I blame you for James's illness. But are you quite certain, my dear, when you look into your heart, that *I* am the person who's been blaming you for the past fifteen years? Is there not someone, weighed down with guilt, who is blaming you far more than ever I could, or would?'

Her mother didn't move. She stood still, staring in the direction of her father. The clock on the wall ticked loudly in the silence of the room. 'You do blame me, George,' her mother said at last, and she turned back to the door. 'Yes, you do.'

Patricia was half way up the stairs by the time that she heard the click of the door closing behind her mother.

Shaking, she ran into her bedroom and threw herself on to her bed. How dare her mother suggest that her father might blame her for James being ill! That was mean, mean, mean. Her mother was just jealous of the closeness between her and her father; that was it. She'd been really nasty that evening, trying to turn her father against her, and she'd never, ever forgive her for what she'd said.

Chapter Six

Ladakh, June 1960: Kalden, aged 16

Kalden stood in his favourite place at the top of a steep slope that fell sharply to the water's edge, and watched the thick morning mist inch its way up the crimson and green walls of the mountain, gradually uncovering the narrow ravine below and opening the beauty of the valley to his gaze. The dark stream at the foot of the craggy ridge, swollen with melt-snow water, snaked sinuously between clusters of fallen rocks and banks of crimson scree.

A spray of blue gentians nestled between two rocks at his feet. Peeping out from beneath them, he could see the tips of the wind-gnarled rose-bushes that clung to the sides of the slopes. In the burgeoning light of day, the flowers had started to unfurl their petals and were springing to life. Just like red butterflies, he thought.

A lonely bird swooped across the ravine.

He raised his eyes to the bird, and beyond the bird to the purple crests of the distant mountains, and he sighed with pleasure. It was going to be a beautiful day: summer was creeping over the plateau, melting the winter snow; Dolma had run her hand very slowly across his chest the night before and whispered that she liked him very much; and ahead of him was a day with Mr and Mrs Henderson and Peter. He couldn't have felt happier.

Mrs Henderson was going to start teaching him and Peter to play a tune she'd written for the three of them. Peter and he would play their recorders and Mrs Henderson would play the accordion. The recorder that the missionary family had given him the year before was the best present he'd ever had and he loved learning tunes to play on it.

He'd been very surprised when they'd given him the recorder and he'd tried to give it back, telling them that they'd already given him enough by teaching him lots of things, such as how to speak English and how to read. But they'd insisted that he take it. They all had their own instrument, Mrs Henderson had said, and they wanted him to have one, too; he was, after all, effectively a member of their family.

He'd learnt to play the recorder as quickly as he'd picked up the piano accordion. In fact, he'd soon caught up with Peter and overtaken him, which hadn't pleased Peter at all. But Mr and Mrs Henderson had been full of praise for the speed with which he'd learnt the instruments. He was a natural, Mrs Henderson used to say. A good all-rounder, Mr Henderson would add; a lucky boy to be so strong and powerful, as well as musical.

Since he'd been given the recorder, he'd hardly touched the accordion. He still liked it, but the recorder was easier and it belonged to him. What's more, he could carry it in the folds of his clothes and play it wherever he wanted.

From the moment that he'd learnt his first tune, he'd been waiting for the right time to play it to his family.

His chance had come during one of the long winter evenings when he and his parents and brothers had been sitting round the fire in the upstairs kitchen, listening to stories and singing and making music. Finally, there was a break in the conversation. This would be a good time to show them the recorder and what it sounded like, he'd thought. They knew he could play the drums, but so could other people in his village. No one in his village, however, could play the recorder. That made him special and they would be proud of him.

And he could see that they *were* proud of him as they listened to him play, but he could also see the sadness in their eyes.

'You play very well, my brother,' Anil had said when he'd finished. 'But this music comes from the missionaries. It reminds us that you still go to their house. And this is not good.'

'You are a Buddhist, Kalden, and you are going to be a monk,' Tenzin said, moving to sit next to him. He'd put his hand on Kalden's shoulder. 'You should now be spending more time with the monks, learning their ways, and less time with the Christians. Recorder music belongs to the world of the Christians.'

He'd thought of Dolma, and he'd opened his mouth to tell them that he might not be a monk after all, but Tenzin, his hand still on his shoulder, had started to sing a song about the approach of summer, and he'd closed his mouth again. There'd be time for that another day.

After that evening, he'd never played to them again.

He'd carried on helping his brothers and parents, doing everything he was asked to do: sowing seeds in the spring, tending the animals in the summer, harvesting the ripe crops in the autumn, making dung cakes and mud bricks, helping with the spinning, and joining his family and village in the celebrations that took place throughout the year. But when he'd done his chores and had spent enough time with Dolma for her to be happy, he'd go as fast as he could to his missionary friends.

That was where he was needed; that was where he belonged; and that was where he felt that he only ever really came alive.

It wasn't that he didn't feel strongly for Dolma. He did. It was just that the Hendersons had opened his eyes to the world that lay beyond his village, beyond his country, and he couldn't seem to stop himself from wanting to learn everything there was to know about that world.

But he knew that he couldn't carry on as he had been doing.

In between the hours that he spent with Peter and his parents, he and Dolma had been spending time with each other, and he sensed that his family was watching them anxiously, worrying about him and hoping very much that he'd find with her the future that they'd always known he longed for.

It was a future that he must now secure, or risk losing it. Tenzin had made that very clear when he'd taken him aside one afternoon not long ago.

'Dolma is a very pretty woman,' Tenzin had begun awkwardly. 'She is much admired by several young men, both from her village and from ours. You are not the only man to have feelings for her. But her eyes are for you only, my brother. And why not? You have grown into a fine man.' He'd given Kalden a wry smile. 'I think there will be many babies, and soon.'

Kalden had looked down at the ground.

'But you should not delay. You should go now to the *onpo* and ask if the stars are favourable for a match with Dolma. If they are, we will send presents and pots of *chang* to her family, and hope they will be accepted.' He paused. 'If this is what you want.'

Kalden had stood still. The white lime-washed house that stood alone on the plain had sprung into his mind. He pushed it aside.

'It is,' he'd said. 'You are right. I like Dolma and I want to be a married man, not a monk. I've not been thinking about the future, and I should have been. But I will now. Our parents will soon move next door. The babies are getting older and our house is already crowded.'

Tenzin nodded. 'Then speak to the *onpo* soon. If you do not, Dolma may give her affections elsewhere.'

'I shall do that,' he'd said, and he'd returned to his task.

Down in the valley, the winding stream was sparkling in

the shifting light of day, and warm air was creeping around him. He looked up at the clear blue sky and saw that the sun had edged above the mountains. It was time for him to go and see the Henderson family. Turning his back on the view, he began to pick his way over the rocky ground to the path that led to the missionary house.

As soon as the house came in sight, he began to run towards it across the flat ground, gathering speed as he passed a small wayside shrine, and not slowing down until he reached the drystone wall that encircled the house.

Peter was coming out of the house as he hurried along the path to the front door. His hands were thrust deep into the pockets of his lightweight trousers, and his face was troubled.

Kalden stopped sharply.

'*Ju-le, karu skyodat-le*, Kalden?'

'I am well, thank you, but hot,' Kalden replied. 'I been running.' He looked closely at Peter. 'And you, Peter? You are not smiling. Something is wrong?'

Peter glanced at him, and quickly looked away.

'It depends upon how you look at it,' Peter said. He looked down at his feet and kicked the ground. Dust flew in the air and he sneezed.

Kalden laughed. 'You always do that. You forget how dry ground is.'

'You're right. And to be honest, I'll be glad to see the back of it.'

The smile faded from Kalden's face. He stared at Peter, his brow wrinkling.

'What you mean, you be glad to see the back of it?' A frisson of fear ran through him.

Peter gave a strained laugh.

Kalden took a step back.

'Ignore me,' Peter said. 'My parents are having a row and

72

I'm in a mood, that's all. Let's go for a walk, shall we? I promise not to be bad-tempered for all of the time.'

'Yes, we can walk, if you like, unless there is something for me to do here. Mrs Henderson say she teach us music she written, but we can learn music another day.'

'That's decided then. If you don't want anything to drink, we can set off at once. To be honest, I can't wait to get away from the house for a bit. But if you're thirsty, just say so and I'll get you something.'

'No, we walk now. We pass a stream most likely and I drink there.' Kalden turned round, and walked back up the path alongside Peter. 'Why Mr and Mrs Henderson having a row and you in a mood?'

Peter's eyes didn't move from the ground in front of him.

'Why, Peter?'

'Kalden!' Mrs Henderson shouted in the distance behind them.

Peter gave an exclamation of annoyance. They both stopped walking and looked back at the house. Mrs Henderson was hurrying along the path towards them, closely followed by Mr Henderson, who was half hidden behind her. Kalden saw that her eyes were shining brightly and that she looked very happy.

'Where are you boys off to?' she asked, reaching them. 'You've only just got here, Kalden. Has Peter told you our exciting news?'

'I haven't said anything yet, Mother,' Peter cut in sharply. 'We're just about to go for a walk.'

'Maybe Kalden won't think it's such exciting news,' Mr Henderson said gruffly. 'Maybe like me he'll think it's depressing. Not exciting at all. Just depressing – too depressing to talk about.' He turned abruptly to his left and stalked off across the patch of turnips in the direction of the small orchard of apricot trees that they'd planted a few years earlier at the back of the house. 'Depressing and disappointing,' they heard him repeat as he disappeared from sight.

Kalden looked from Peter to Mrs Henderson. She looked anxious and not excited any longer. His heart beat faster. 'What is Mr Henderson talking about?' he asked. 'Why he sad? What is depressing and disappointing?'

Peter exchanged glances with his mother.

'Why don't you come in for a drink, Kalden?' she suggested. 'Then we can tell you what we've decided to do. You and Peter can go for your walk after that. How does that sound? What do you think, Peter?'

Peter gave a slight shrug of his shoulders. 'Why not? Come on, Kalden. We might as well go back.' Gesturing for Kalden to go with them, he went to his mother's side and started to walk with her to the house. Kalden hesitated a moment, then began to go after them, a step or two behind them all of the way.

They climbed the wooden stairs to the upstairs kitchen, and Mrs Henderson put out some dried apricots and poured them each a bowl of creamy yellow yak milk. Peter picked up his bowl and drained it. 'I can't wait to have a wider choice of things to drink,' he said, an expression of distaste on his face as he put the bowl back on the table.

His eyes moving warily from one to the other, Kalden picked up his bowl of milk, then put it down again, untouched. 'What are you saying, Peter? I not understand.' He turned to Mrs Henderson. 'What is Peter saying? Is he leaving Ladakh?'

'We're all leaving, Kalden, it's not just Peter,' Mrs Henderson said gently. She leaned forward and took his hand. 'We're going back to England as soon as we've arranged for our things to be shipped. We're going to contact our headquarters in England to find out where they need us to go next, but wherever it is, it'll be in England.'

'What about Ladakh? We need you here,' Kalden stammered. He felt the blood draining from his face.

'No, you don't, I'm afraid. The Ladakhi people have never needed us here, and they don't want us here.' She pulled her chair closer to Kalden. 'Deep down, you know that's true, Kalden. After almost ten years, the most we've achieved is to have an occasional small class for a week or two at a time. The few families prepared to let their children come to the school do so until they need the children to help on the land, and then we don't see them again. The majority of families still fear that we want to convert you all. That situation's not going to change. It's time for us to give up.'

'But must not give up. Mr Henderson say one child from every family must go school. It is rules. Child not go school if no school near village.'

She squeezed his hand. 'And then there's Peter to think about. He needs a wider education than I can give him. I've done my best, but even if I had sufficient knowledge, I wouldn't be able to teach him the science subjects that he ought to know – or at least have some grounding in – as we just don't have the equipment. There are things that he has to learn if he's going to get into university in two years' time. It's only fair that he has the same opportunities as everyone else of his age.'

'Into university?' Kalden echoed questioningly.

'Yes. It's where you go if you want to get what's called a degree. If he gets a degree, he'll be able to choose his career – the job that he'll do for the rest of his life.'

'So you leave Ladakh, Peter,' Kalden said, his voice flat.

'I'm really sorry, but yes. And if I'm honest, although I've got used to living here and I don't hate it like I did at first, that's only because we became friends and we've had lots of fun together. You're the only thing I'll miss about Ladakh. I want to go back to England and do all the things that

Mum used to do before she came here, and I want to go to university. Dad doesn't want us to go back, though. If he had his way, we'd all die here without me ever having had a life.'

'The Ladakhi people have a life, and they not go university,' Kalden said bluntly.

Peter shifted his position. 'That's different. They were born here. This is the only life they've known and their families are here. But I was born in England. I know I was only six when we left, but I still remember what it was like to fill a glass with water from a tap, to go to the toilet and pull a chain – you've no idea how much I hate going upstairs and sitting over a hole in the floor. And what it was like to switch on a light, and go to a shop to buy whatever I needed. Here we have to grow everything we eat and make everything we wear or use. I know I'll like living in England again. I'm not practical like you, Kalden. There's no future for me here.'

Kalden stood up. 'I go now.'

Peter jumped up and grabbed him by the arm. 'You're my best friend. I'll never have a better friend than you as long as I live. I know that. But it's not just me that'll soon be doing something different – you'll be moving on, too. You and Dolma, you'll get married and have children. You won't have to go into a monastery, so we'll both have a good life, and we'll always keep in touch.'

'Maybe I marry Dolma, I not know – we not talk. I have no land.'

'The land won't matter. She'll find a way round that, you'll see. Anyone can see how much she wants you to be her husband – all you have to do is look at her when you're near her to see that.'

'We'll be taking away with us the most wonderful memories of our time in Ladakh,' Mrs Henderson said, standing up. She put an arm around Kalden's shoulders. 'Peter's right, we'll never forget you, Kalden – you'll always be in our hearts and in our prayers. We've come to love you as part of our family. If we could, we'd leave you the house and the land, but it isn't ours to give away. We can leave you your favourite books and pictures, though, and anything else that you'd like. You'll have keepsakes from us, and we'll have our memories of you. That way, we'll always be close to each other.'

Kalden pulled away from her, spun round and ran to the top of the stairs. '*Ju-le*,' he shouted at them. 'Goodbye. I wish you never come here.' And he ran down the stairs and out of the house as fast as he could.

'Kalden!' he heard Mr Henderson call as he flung open the front door and ran out of the house. Glancing over his shoulder, he saw Mr Henderson coming round the side of the house.

He kept on running. They were leaving him. His family was leaving him. What kind of life would he have when they'd gone?

His feet hit the ground hard.

Peter was going away to have a real life, a life full of different people and interesting things to see and learn. Peter was going to be able to choose what he did in the future. He wouldn't have to marry a girl he liked a lot, but no more than that, to avoid having to do something that he'd really hate doing. Why hadn't he, Kalden, been born in England? It wasn't fair.

There'd be no more new books for him; no more accordion; no more new tunes for the recorder; no more climbing in the mountains with Peter; no more listening to Mrs Henderson talk about pictures; no more hearing Mr Henderson tell Bible stories; no more working outside with Mr Henderson, knowing that he needed him, relied on him.

When they went back to England, they'd take their world with them and he'd be left with nothing.

He reached the *chorten* on the outskirts of his village and collapsed in the dust at the foot of the stone pillar, his body shuddering violently. Raising his head from the ground, he stared ahead of him at the distant cluster of white houses and at the monastery that sat high on the rock behind them.

I hate them all, he whispered.

Exhausted, he fell back on the ground and let darkness creep around him.

Chapter Seven

'So what did your dad give you for your birthday – was it something really nice?' Ruth asked, glancing towards the window as she spoke. The fading light outside sent her reflection back to her. She shifted slightly to face the window and began to tease up the height of her bouffant hairstyle with her fingers. Then she turned back to Patricia. 'So what did you get, then?' she repeated.

'A sheepskin jacket,' Patricia told her, neatly folding the torn sheet of wrapping paper that had been pushed into the middle of the formica-topped table. She put the bottle of *eau de cologne* that Ruth had given her next to the paper. 'It's exactly what I wanted.'

Ruth laughed. 'Oh yes, it's just what you need for the summer. We're already in June, and winter's well and truly over. Your father has the maddest ideas.'

'Amazingly, summer will end and then it'll be autumn. And what comes after autumn? Oh, yes, winter again. Just because my birthday's in June, it doesn't mean that he's got to give me something I can only use in the summer. The jacket's perfect.'

'If you say so. But I prefer what my parents gave me. They paid for me to have my ears pierced and gave me some fantastic earrings. I can't wait to get out of these boring studs and start wearing them.'

Patricia shuddered. 'You'll never catch me having my ears pierced. I don't like needles. I didn't like watching the nurses give injections, and I certainly could never have given one myself. No, I'll stick to wearing clip-on earrings for the rest of my life, thank you very much.'

'It didn't hurt, and if it did, it was worth it. You can get much better earrings for pierced ears than you can get clip-ons.'

'Maybe you can, but I'm not bothered either way. Anyway, the jacket wasn't my only present. I'll get us another coffee – it's my turn – and then I'll tell you about the other present I got.'

Ruth glanced around the coffee bar. 'I wish you'd agreed to go into town instead of coming here. We could have found a much livelier place than this, and then you might have met someone dead good-looking and fallen madly in love with them, like I love my Johnny.'

'I'm not in any hurry to meet anyone. I'll meet lots of new people when I go to teachers' training college, and I'm quite happy to wait until then.'

'But that's not for more than a year. You'll need a boyfriend this summer if you want to have any fun.'

'I'm going to have fun alright, but not the sort you're thinking of. Dad and I are going hiking in Scotland for a couple of months. We're going to practise walking long distances.'

'Whatever for?'

'I'll answer that when I've got the coffees. Won't be a minute.' She got up, went over to the serving bar, and stood there idly fiddling with her pony tail while she waited to give the order.

'Here you are,' she told Ruth, returning a few minutes later with a couple of coffees. She sat down.

'You know, Patsy, you really ought to get some trendy things and find a new hairstyle, if you don't mind me saying so. You had the same hairstyle at primary school. If you had your hair done fashionably and wore a bit of make-up, you could be really pretty.'

Patricia laughed. 'Well, thank you very much indeed.'

Ruth smiled at her across the table. 'You know what I mean. You don't make the most of yourself. Max Factor does really good mascara and you could make your eyelashes look twice as long as they are. Come into the shop one day and I'll help you choose some things.'

'Funnily enough, I'm quite happy with my appearance, thank you.'

'Even if you don't want a boyfriend now, you will at college. You said so yourself. It's never too soon to start thinking about what you look like.'

'I give in. Before I go to college, you can tell me what make-up to get and how to put it on. That's a promise. But at the moment, there's too much happening that's really exciting for me to bother about lipstick and the rest.'

'Like what?'

'Like a trip.' Patricia leaned forward, her eyes shining. 'You know I told you my father's given me a second present? Well, he's going to Ladakh in May next year, and he's going to take me with him! We're leaving as soon as I finish my 'A' levels, and we'll be back just before college starts. I am so excited.' She sat back and beamed at Ruth.

Ruth wrinkled her nose in distaste. 'From what you've said about the place, I'm not sure that I'd want to go there. Now if it was two weeks on the Costa Brava, then you'd be talking.'

'Anyone can do that any time. I've typed up almost all of my father's book so I know masses about Ladakh. What could be better than going and seeing it for myself? And that's the reason for my new jacket – you have to have a thick jacket as it's high up in the mountains. So, there's method in Dad's madness, as you put it.'

'What about your mum? Is she going, too?'

'No, it would cost too much for the three of us to go. His pension isn't that large. Also, she's not been involved with the book so she doesn't know anything about the country. She's obviously not interested in it and wouldn't want to come.'

'There's no "obviously" about it. Your poor mother doesn't get a look in, does she? I feel really sorry for her. Your father should be taking her with him, not you. I bet he hasn't even asked her.'

'I helped him, not my mother.'

'That's only because he never gave her a chance. I know I don't see much of your folks, but whenever I do, he virtually ignores her. And you do, too. I bet neither of you ever include her in your conversation. I may not be clever like you, Patsy, but I can see that with you it's always been about you and your father. You run around after him like a skivvy. What he wants is what you want. I'm amazed you haven't decided to join the army to please him, or hasn't he suggested it yet?'

A stain of angry red spread across Patricia's face. She glared at Ruth. 'You haven't a clue what you're talking about. You've never lost a child. You don't know what my father went through and how devastated he was. I'm over the moon that we get on so well that he's going to take me with him, and you're not going to spoil it for me.'

'Your mother lost her son, too, but she gets left out of everything. How do you think she must feel, losing both you and James? As for your father taking you on the trip, I'd say that you've well and truly earned your place, typing that boring old book Sunday after Sunday.'

Patricia picked up a teaspoon and stirred her coffee furiously. Her lips tightened.

Ruth glanced at her across the table. 'Look, I shouldn't have said all that – it was none of my business. I'm really sorry, Patsy. Don't be mad at me – we're meant to be celebrating your birthday, not falling out.'

Patricia put her teaspoon down and picked up her cup.

She forced a smile to her lips. 'You're right, it's silly to quarrel. I hardly ever see you these days, now that your family's moved. We shouldn't be wasting valuable time, arguing about stupid things.' She sipped her coffee. 'Tell me about working in DH Evans and then, if you're really good, I'll let you tell me about Johnny all over again.'

Her mouth curved into a smile, and Ruth beamed back at her.

An hour later, they said goodbye outside the coffee bar.

Ruth turned to the right and started walking down Fitzjohn's Avenue to Swiss Cottage, and Patricia took the short cut through Perrin's Lane into Hampstead High Street. When she reached the high street, she turned right and made her way down the hill towards Belsize Park.

She thrust her hands deep into the pockets of her yellow lambswool cardigan. That last hour had seemed never-ending. Ruth had obviously been trying to re-capture the friendliness of the first part of the evening, just as she had, but neither of them had succeeded, and really they'd just been waiting until they'd been there long enough to be able to leave.

She speeded up her steps. It was Ruth's fault that the evening had turned out as badly as it had. She'd had no right to criticise her father in the way that she'd done. And as for calling her a skivvy! All she was doing was behaving like any normal daughter would – he'd got arthritis, after all.

And she was completely wrong about her mother. Her mother could have easily got involved with the Ladakh book if she'd wanted. Admittedly her father always made her mother a bit nervous – well, very nervous: he was the sort of person who knew exactly what he wanted and who didn't suffer fools gladly, as he put it – nevertheless, her mother could have volunteered to help him, but she never did. If she was left out, it was her own fault and no one else's. Trust Ruth to try and make it into something it wasn't.

She had altered over the years that she'd known her. She'd made new friends at her secondary school, who liked different things, and she wasn't the same Ruth any more. And then when she'd moved to Willesdon and it had become harder for them to meet, they'd drifted apart.

They'd recently begun seeing each other again a bit more frequently. That had been Ruth's doing. When she'd left school the summer before and had started working in DH Evans, she'd got in touch again and they'd gone out a few times. It was pretty obvious, though, that their lives were very different, and Ruth had been quite tetchy on occasions. Like that evening.

She wouldn't be at all surprised if she hadn't deliberately said those things about her family to upset her: not consciously – Ruth wasn't a mean person – but subconsciously. It could be that Ruth envied her, stuck as she was in a shop selling cosmetics, while she was going on a trip that summer and on an even more exciting trip in May. It was true that Ruth had Johnny, but Patricia had years ahead of her in which to find someone she felt strongly about, and then she'd have the man as well as many happy memories.

Her steps slowed. It must be wonderful, though, to love someone in the way that Ruth loved Johnny. She did hope that somewhere in the big wide world there was a man waiting for her to find him.

A chill breeze swept across her. She shivered, pulled her cardigan tighter around her and walked more quickly down the steep hill. As she hurried along, she glanced at the illuminated shops on either side of the road. Her mother had walked past those very shops just a month after she'd been born, carrying her in her arms, still unaware of what she'd find when they got back to Mary's flat. Of course, not all of them were the same shops – some of the original shops had been bombed out of existence – but some were.

Her mother used to tell her that it was almost impossible for people to imagine what the High Street had been like at the time of the bombing. But Patricia could imagine it, down to the smallest detail.

Whenever they had walked back from her primary school or from a morning playing at Whitestone Pond, her mother would tell her how shop after shop had been reduced to rubble. She'd brought the scene so vividly alive that Patricia had almost been able to taste the brick dust in the air and smell the burning wood and sulphur fumes.

Now, years later, the shops had been rebuilt and were better than the old shops, and most people had almost forgotten what it had been like before and during the war. But for Patricia, the bright new shops would always remind her of the June in which she'd been born: the June in which James had begun to die.

She shook herself. She must stop thinking like that or she was only going to get upset. What happened to James was one of many awful things that had happened during the war. It wasn't her mother's fault; it wasn't anyone's fault, and she shouldn't dwell on it. It was only getting to her that evening because of the row she'd had with Ruth.

She passed the Town Hall and started down the stretch of wide pavement that led to Belsize Grove. On the other side of the road, a little further down the hill, the underground station was clearly visible. The entrance to the deep-level air-raid shelter where her mother had met Mary Shaw was just past the main entrance to the station.

She glanced towards it, then turned away and stared fixedly at the pavement in front of her. She must force herself to think only about the future, not the past.

When she reached her house, she went in and quietly

closed the door behind her. She slipped out of her cardigan, slung it over the coat stand in the corner of the hall and started along the corridor past the front room. The door was closed. The light shining through the crack at the bottom of the door told her that her father was in there, but she was sure that he wouldn't want to be disturbed.

A little further along the corridor, she heard a sound coming from the back room. Her mother must have waited up to hear about her birthday evening. She went quickly to the foot of the staircase and started up the stairs, making as little noise as possible – she just wasn't in the mood for any more conversation that evening; she'd had more than enough as it was.

'Is that you, Patsy?' her mother called from the back room. 'You're earlier than I expected.' She heard her mother open the door. 'Come and tell me what Ruth had to say for herself, darling.'

She reached the landing, ran into her bedroom and closed the door behind her.

Through the wall, she heard her mother's footsteps on the hall lino as she went along to the kitchen, looking for her. 'Where are you, Patsy?' her mother called.

She opened her bedroom door, hurried on to the landing and leaned over the banister. 'I'm sorry, Mother,' she called. 'I've come up to bed – I'm very tired and I've got an early morning ahead of me. We had a really nice time. I'll tell you all about it tomorrow, I promise. Goodnight.' She went back into her room and shut the door.

She leaned back against her door, her heart thumping loudly. She could tell that her mother was standing in the kitchen doorway, and in her mind's eye, she could see her looking vaguely around the empty room, wondering what to do next. She could almost feel the weight of her mother's disappointment and loneliness.

Well, it wasn't her fault, she thought, swallowing a rising sense of guilt. She moved away from the door. It wasn't anybody's fault. Things were as they were and they all had to cope with them as best they could. She went across to her bedside table and switched on the lamp. Her mother being unhappy had nothing to do with Ladakh or her father or her. Ruth didn't know what she was talking about.

She took the box of cologne out of her handbag and threw it on to the bed.

Chapter Eight

Ladakh, September 1961: Kalden, aged 17

Carried in the arms of the autumn wind, the strains of the harvesters' songs soared across the ochre and grey wilderness, over the crumbling stones of the wall and the house where the missionary family once had lived, over wayside shrines, rippling many a mantle of multi-coloured prayer flags as they drifted to the far reaches of the plateau where they met the mountains and gradually faded away.

Kalden stood still and listened.

In past years, his heart would fill with happiness when he heard the reapers' songs as he went out to the fields to help with bringing in the fruits of the year's toil. But not this year. This year, his heart was heavy, and he would not be singing with them.

In the early weeks after Peter and his family had abandoned their house, the vegetable patches, the orchard, the place that had been their home for so many years, taking their world with them, Kalden had gone to the house most days, waiting, hoping.

Unable to accept that they'd truly left for good, he'd repaired the surrounding stone wall, made dung cakes, tended the vegetables, plugged leaks in the irrigation channels, picked the ripe apricots from the trees and spread them out to dry on blankets that he'd laid out on top of the flat roof, and he'd piled armfuls of alfalfa and hay next to the apricots, ready for the missionaries' animals during the long, hard winter ahead.

On occasions, when night had fallen before he'd finished what he needed to do, he'd stay there overnight, using the blankets and few pieces of equipment that they'd left behind them, and he'd feel close to them again. For weeks on end, he'd done everything he could to keep the place alive, all the while scanning the distant horizon, waiting to see the family return.

In vain, he'd waited. The Hendersons didn't return, and no other missionary family had taken their place. Finally, he'd had to accept that they'd gone for good.

He'd thought about living in their house himself, since nobody else was going to live there. His family, however, had tried to make him recognise that he'd be too far from the village to be given help when he needed it. However hard he worked, it would be difficult enough to grow and harvest sufficient crops by himself to feed himself throughout the year; if he had to feed a family, too, he'd face an impossible task.

What's more, Tenzin had added later, when they were on their own in the kitchen, if Kalden was living so far from their community, it would not encourage anyone to want to be his wife.

If he'd had any doubt about Tenzin being right, Dolma had made the situation very clear not long after that.

A few days after Tenzin had spoken to him, he and Dolma had been walking around a field of ripening wheat on the outskirts of her village. The missionary house still in his mind, he'd decided to bring up the subject of their future together.

'I am sorry that in the last few weeks I have not seen you as often as I would have liked, Dolma,' he'd begun. 'But when the missionary family left, there were many things to be done at their house. They are now finished, and I am thinking about making a home there for myself, and for a wife.' Suddenly very nervous, he'd tried to smile at her. 'I would like you to be that wife.'

She'd put her hand on his arm, and left it there. He'd looked down at her hand, and then back up at her face. She'd been gently shaking her head.

'I feel very close to you,' she'd told him. 'But I would not be happy living where the missionaries lived. It is too far from my family and my friends.'

'It is away from our villages, yes. But it is not so far that we could not come back to see our families, and not so far that our families could not come to see us. And we would make a new family, too. You and I ...'

She'd put a finger to his lips. 'There is something I must tell you.'

He'd moved her hand away and stared at her, waiting.

'For much time now, you have not been coming to see me. At first I am upset, but then I begin to accept it. Namgyal, who lives in my village, sees that you are no longer visiting me, and he has come to me. In recent weeks, we have often been walking together and have become friends. We are happy together and Namgyal is now going to see the *onpa*. If the signs are favourable, my family will accept the gifts he sends, and we will marry and live in the family house that he shares with his brother.'

A tightness had closed around his heart. He'd taken a step back.

'It does not make me happy to hurt you, Kalden. You are a good man and you make me feel something inside me that no one else can make me feel. But I think it will not be a very deep hurt for you. I have not wanted to face it, but I have known for some time that your heart has only once been truly captured, and that was by your missionary friends. That is so, is it not?'

He'd looked at her, then slowly nodded.

Her smile had held a trace of regret as she'd turned away and gone back to her village.

After that time, he'd stopped going to the missionary house for anything other than the occasional visit, during which time he'd trail disconsolately through the deserted building and among the overgrown vegetable patches, trying not to think about things as they used to be.

Instead, whenever his help wasn't needed by his brothers, parents or neighbours, he'd filled his days by walking across the plateau and among the mountains, exploring further afield than he'd ever been before. At the height of summer, he'd gone as usual to the high mountain pasture with his brothers, but when they'd got there, he'd wandered off on his own.

When the long, cold winter had come, he'd sat on his bench in the shadowy corner of the kitchen, his recorder in his pocket, watching his family and neighbours laugh, dance and tell stories to each other. Whenever they turned to him, he'd nodded, smiled or laughed with them.

But whatever he did, wherever he went, no matter how much he struggled to suppress his memory of the days when music, books and new ideas had given a purpose to his life, the Hendersons were always with him in his mind. Not Dolma – he never really thought about her – only his second family.

Although he'd never written to Peter after the Hendersons had returned to England – he didn't write well enough, and anyway there was nothing interesting to say – he'd received some letters from Peter. In his letters, Peter told Kalden that his parents were busy helping in a poor part of London, and that they were really enjoying the feeling of being wanted and needed. He mentioned his new school, the orchestra he'd joined and the friends he'd made, but he didn't say much about them. Kalden could tell, though, that Peter loved every minute of his life in England and that the family would never return to Ladakh.

At first, there were only a few weeks between the letters from Peter, but the gaps became wider, and as he went out of the village to join the harvesters in the barley fields, it suddenly hit him that he hadn't heard from his friend since the barley seeds had been sown.

He didn't blame Peter for not writing to him any more: there was no point in writing as they'd never meet again. And what's more, Peter would know that the delivery time for letters sent to Ladakh was completely unpredictable, and that whatever he wrote would be out of date long before his letter reached Kalden.

This wasn't the fault of the runners who carried the letters between the peasants' stone huts along the road from Leh; it was the fault of the weather. The runner could only do his stretch and pass the post bag to the next runner when the weather allowed it. In bad weather, it could be weeks before a letter reached its destination, which in Kalden's village was a small post hut that stood just outside the village wall.

And in a way, he was glad that he didn't hear from Peter any more. He didn't want to learn any more about something he could never have, and he knew that Peter wouldn't be interested in being reminded about things that he'd been delighted to leave behind. For both of them, that part of their life had ended.

But just occasionally in the evenings, he would sit in the corner of the kitchen, his eyes on his brothers and Deki as they played with their children, and although he didn't want to, he'd find himself wondering what Peter and his parents were doing at that very moment, and he was filled with envy.

Envy. It was a word that he'd never heard before he met the Hendersons. He'd first come across it in one of the books he'd read with Mrs Henderson, and she'd explained that it was an unpleasant emotion that one person felt for another, when that person wanted something, or someone, that the other person had.

When Mrs Henderson had finished explaining the word, Kalden had looked at her in amazement. It was very strange that one person could feel that way about another, he'd said. Ladakhi people didn't envy each other; they needed each other, so they had to be friends. Everyone helped everyone else, and they all shared what they had.

Mrs Henderson had smiled at him and said that he was very lucky to live with people who didn't know what it was to be guilty of the sin of envy. Envy, she'd told him, could destroy a person's peace of mind. She'd looked at Kalden to see if he'd understood.

He'd nodded, although he still hadn't really grasped what it was to feel envious of someone else. It was only later that same evening as he'd lain beneath his blanket that he'd cast his mind back to the way he'd felt when each of his brothers had married Deki, and he'd wondered if that feeling had been envy.

When the Hendersons had left Ladakh, and he'd received his first letter from Peter about his life in England, he'd known that it had been. Envy had become much more than a word and an explanation: it had become a pain that ached deep within the core of his being. He missed the life that he'd had, and he was eaten up with envy of his friend.

When he reached the harvesters in the golden fields that ran down to the small stream, he switched his sickle to his right hand and joined the first line of reapers who were swinging their sickles through the ripe barley. His heart was heavy as he worked, as he knew that this would be the last harvest during which he'd be living with his family.

His parents had said that the following spring, when the fields had been ploughed and the new seeds sown, they would be moving into the tiny house next door. At that time, he would have to pack up the few things he treasured and go into the monastery to begin the life of a monk. He had no choice.

Of course he'd come back every year to help his family and the other villagers with the sowing and reaping, but things would never be the same again once he'd left his home. He knew that, and so did they. In despair, he looked at the fields around him, then he lifted his sickle high and swung it hard through the barley stalks.

By the time that he stood upright again, the sun was hot and almost everywhere around him there was stubble where once there'd been barley: the harvesting would soon be done. The reapers alongside him were singing and laughing as they wielded their sickles, cutting the last of the barley stalks low to the ground, but he didn't feel like singing and laughing. Next year, when he stood with them, he would have the shaven head of a monk. Raising his arm, he ran his fingers through his dark hair.

'*Skyot*, Kalden! Come! We need your help,' he heard Tenzin call to him from the side of the field.

Handing his sickle to a nearby child, he went over to join Tenzin and Deki, who were with a group of the villagers. They were binding the stalks into sheaves and loading them on to each other's backs, ready to be carried to the threshing area. He stood still and let them balance several bundles on to his back, and then he followed a laden Deki towards the large circle of packed earth where the newly cut crop was being threshed.

Reaching the threshing area, he stood patiently until it was his turn for Anil to pull the sheaves from his back and throw them on to the threshing circle, then he started to turn away to return to the field for another back-load. As he did so, he caught sight of his seven-year-old nephew, Tashi, and he remembered that Tashi was acting as the thresher for the first time. His face broke into a smile, and he paused to watch Tashi at work.

Tashi was beaming broadly as he ran around the threshing circle, following the animals which were trampling the crop with their every step as they went round and round, attached to a pole in the centre of the threshing circle, the *dzo* in the middle and the horses and donkeys on the outside.

'*Ha-lo baldur, ha-lo baldur,*' Tashi kept on shouting at them, encouraging them to keep on moving.

In his hand, he clutched a wicker basket, and every so often, he lunged forward behind an animal and caught the animal's dung before it could land on the ground and spoil the grain. Each time that he did this, he giggled excitedly and looked around him to make sure that everyone had noticed how skilful he was.

Kalden stood and watched Tashi for a few minutes; Tashi, a second son, who was learning to work the land that would one day belong to him and his brothers. With a sigh of resignation, he turned away.

Seeing Anil at the side of the threshing area, he went over to him rather than go straight back to the fields, and stood in silence while Anil ceremoniously placed a small religious figure on top of first one pile of threshed grain then another, each time saying a small prayer of blessing for the harvest. The grain blessed, Anil stepped back to let it be put into sacks.

'Tashi is having fun, and doing a good job; a man's job,' Kalden told his older brother.

'Yes, he is,' Anil said. He glanced at all the piles of grain waiting to be blessed, and turned to Kalden. 'And this is a job for you, my brother, I think,' he added with a wry smile, and he handed the figurine to Kalden.

His eyes on Kalden's face, he let his hand rest gently on

his brother's shoulder for a moment. Then he dropped his hand and moved off in the direction of the harvested fields to find Rinchen and Tenzin and help them with the animals that had been brought down from the summer pastures to graze on the stubble left behind in the fields.

Kalden stared after Anil until he was out of sight, then he looked down at the small figure in his hand. It was shaped a little like his recorder, he realised. His mind raced back to the first time that he'd held his recorder in his hand. What a moment that had been. If only ... He blanked his thoughts. *Chi choen*? What's in the past is in the past.

He swallowed hard, placed the figurine on the heap of grain closest to him and said a prayer to the spirits, asking them to bless the harvest.

With the harvesting finished for that year, the festival celebrating the success of the harvest could now begin. The harvest thanksgiving was one of the occasions that they looked forward to every year, and there was a buzz of excitement among Kalden's family and friends, who this year were crowding into the large kitchen on the first floor of Kalden's house for the festivities.

All around them, the kitchen was a blaze of colour. Garlands of wheat and barley encircled the wooden pillars at the top of the staircase. Caught in the light from the butter lamps that glowed on the low table in the centre of the room, their hues vied with the brilliance of the villagers' clothes. A number of the men from the village had dyed their long, straight robes from their natural beige to the deep crimson red of the mountain scree, and every woman wore a richly coloured brocade waistcoat over her full, flowing robes.

On their heads, Deki and the other wives wore their jewelled *perak*, the turquoise and coral stones catching the gleam of the fire and shining like brightly coloured stars. The necks of all the women were encircled with necklaces, their arms with bracelets and their fingers with rings. Their jewels danced in the golden light of the lamps.

The music and laughter in the kitchen almost drowned out the sound of the monks who were in the family's altar room above the kitchen. Chanting to the rhythmic beat of the drums, they offered prayers for the happiness and prosperity of Kalden's family and for all the families in the world, and placed before the altar pyramids of barley dough that they'd made and decorated with butter and flower petals.

Below them in the kitchen, Kalden tried not to hear them as he and his brothers moved among the guests, pouring butter tea and *chang*, offering further refreshment and waiting patiently while their guests went through their refusals before finally accepting it. When at last everyone had something to drink and eat, and the singing and dancing had begun, Kalden took himself over to his bench in the corner of the kitchen and sat there nursing a cup of *chang*, a solitary figure at the edge of the crowd.

'*Ju-le*, Kalden. *Khamzang*?' Kalden looked up and saw that Wangyal, who lived with his wife in the post house just outside the village, was standing in front of him.

'I am well, thank you, Wangyal,' Kalden said. 'Please, sit and drink your *chang* with me.'

'*Ju-le*,' Wangyal said, and he sat down on the opposite side of the low table. He glanced across at Kalden, and pulled nervously at his wispy white moustache.

Kalden looked at him curiously. 'What is it, Wangyal? You seem to be worried.'

'I have something to ask of you,' Wangyal said. He took a sip of *chang*.

'What is it you wish to ask me?'

'Two people are coming to us from the country England.

They will be staying in my house, the post house. They will arrive at the start of the next sowing season and will leave after the harvesting.'

Kalden's heart missed a beat. 'Do we know these people?' His hands tightened around his pot of *chang*.

Wangyal shook his head. It was a father and daughter, he told him, who had asked to be found a house in their area. A mail runner had brought a message about them from someone important in Leh. The person had asked if they could stay in the post house, and he had agreed. He and his wife would move into their sons' house as soon as the visitors arrived. Their sons' house was close by, and they would be able to cook for the visitors each day, and look after them and the post house during their stay.

The important person in Leh had also said that the visitors would need a pony-man to be their guide for the whole of their stay. Kalden knew well the mountains and plateau, and he was greatly hoping that Kalden would agree to be the visitors' pony-man for the summer and would take them everywhere that might be of interest to them.

'I do not want to,' Kalden said bluntly.

'No one in our village speaks English.' There was a note of urgency in Wangyal's voice. 'Only you. Please, will you help me with these English people?'

He looked down at the pot in his hand. Inside his head, an accordion and a recorder started to play. Pages of books flashed before his eyes. His heart began to race, and he looked across the table at Wangyal.

'I must go into the monastery next year after the sowing is completed, Wangyal,' he said quietly, struggling to stifle the strains of the music that threatened to fill every corner of his mind. 'You know that.'

Wangyal leaned forward eagerly. 'You can choose when you want to go into the monastery. Your brothers will be happy for you to stay longer with them, and their children, too. *Ladak ma-ldemo duk*. We know that Ladakh is very beautiful. We will all want them to see that beauty and to have a joyful time in our village. Please, will you be their guide, Kalden, and stay with us until they leave?'

Kalden raised his eyes and stared beyond Wangyal to the wall behind him, and through the wall to the stone house that stood alone on the vast plateau, through the front door of that house where he'd been needed, through into the fullness of the life enclosed within its walls, and his face broke into a slow smile.

'*Kasa*. I will,' he said. The music in his head swelled to a crescendo and broke around him into a mighty euphony of glorious sound. 'Yes, I will.'

Chapter Nine

To Ladakh, May to June 1962:
Patricia, aged almost 18; Kalden, aged 18

Major George Carstairs surveyed the four people standing in a small group near him and turned to Patricia.

'They'll do,' he said. 'Two bearers, a cook and a leader should be sufficient for our needs. We are, after all, only two people, and our stay in Ladakh is merely for the summer months. I suspect that the bearer leader – Sonam, I believe he's called – may prove to be *ganda,* which means lazy, Patricia. That wouldn't surprise me in the least.'

'Well, they all look very pleasant to me, especially the one who's also going to be doing the washing-up. He's obviously shy, but he seems quite charming.' She smiled at the bearers and they beamed back at her.

'What you mean is, they all smile a lot,' her father said tersely, following her eyes. 'Not quite the same thing, I regret to say. I saw any number of smiling people at the Assistance Board. They would smile week after week as they turned up for their handouts, perfectly able-bodied people, living off the workers of the country. Don't allow yourself to be influenced by appearances, Patricia. You need to remain on your guard at all times.'

'I will, Father.'

They waited until the bearers had finished loading the donkeys with the food for the journey, their luggage and camping equipment, then they stepped forward and let themselves be helped on to the back of their ponies by the bearers.

She looked around her from her elevated position. 'It's

hard to believe that we're almost in Ladakh at last. I'm so glad you brought me with you, Father!'

A smile crossed the Major's lips. 'I, too, am looking forward to our trip, Patricia. I have nothing but the happiest of memories of my time here in '45, and I'm very much looking forward to retracing my steps. This is the realisation of a long-cherished dream.'

'I know that, and I'm ever so pleased that I'm going to be sharing it with you. I still can't get over how lucky we are that your friend was able to find us somewhere to stay in the area that you stayed before. That's the icing on the cake.'

'Indeed, that was a stroke of luck,' the Major nodded. 'But I wouldn't go as far as to say that Gordon is a friend. He lives in Northumberland and I only ever see him at the annual regimental dinner. But you're right. We are, indeed, fortunate that Gordon was able to put me in touch with a contact of his in Ladakh, who has managed to find us suitable accommodation. And we're somewhat privileged, too, in that we're going to be allowed to fly back to England from Leh Airport, even though we aren't diplomats or official personnel. The fact that we may have to wait a few days for a flight home is a small price to pay for the convenience it'll afford us.'

'I hope the village house is nice.'

'I am sure it'll be satisfactory. Of course, we mustn't expect home comforts, and our food may well prove rudimentary, but that will all be part of our experience.'

'I wonder if Mother wishes she was with us.'

'Your mother will be far happier going to her little bookkeeping job each day than she would be here,' the Major said stiffly. 'She's never shown any interest in Ladakh, and she wouldn't have had the stamina for the travelling involved. That said, we shall write to her regularly. Our first letter will be when we reach our destination. We can relate the high points of our trip. I imagine that staying in a post house will facilitate our contact with England, although any postal service relying on runners is bound to be haphazard.'

Patricia turned to watch the last of the bearers get on to his pony. 'Thank goodness the head bearer speaks some English. I wish he was going to be our pony-man for the summer. It would have made everything so much easier.'

'His English is very basic. We'll be better off with someone who knows the region thoroughly, even if they don't speak English. The Ladakhi words we've learnt should serve us well, and we have books with us. I pride myself on having a degree of common sense, and I'm sure we'll manage very well when Sonam has left us.'

'Leave now. Short ride on pony. Long rest,' Sonam called out, signalling to the other bearers to follow him as he moved his pony forward.

'I fear that Sonam's choice of adjectives rather supports my initial impression of our head bearer,' the Major murmured dryly as his pony started moving.

Patricia laughed. 'Long ride or short, this is going to be the best leg of our trip so far. I felt sick for the whole of the bumpy bus journey from the airport to Lahore. The train to Rawalpindi was so noisy that I couldn't sleep a wink, and then that awful taxi drive to Kashmir, with all those hairpin bends. The only easy bit so far was the lovely avenue on the way into Srinagar, the one with poplar trees on both sides. But I'm not complaining. I couldn't be enjoying myself more.'

'I'm glad to hear it. As you say, the pony will be the most pleasant mode of transport thus far. Quite how comfortably you'll be able to sit down in a day or two is, of course, another matter,' he said with a slight smile.

'I know that the next stop is Gagangir. How far away is it, do you think?'

'According to my calculations, about forty-five miles. If I recall correctly, it's a very lovely forty-five miles that takes us through the valley of the River Sindh. But it's a testing track for a novice rider and you should prepare yourself for some awkwardness of movement at the end of the day, Patricia, whether the day has been spent in walking or riding on the pony. We shall ride for most of the way, but I'm hoping that we'll be able to cover some of the ground on foot, just as I did in 1945. When we stop, I'll get the camera out of the bags – we must take a few photos of the journey for the book.'

One behind the other, they followed Sonam along a narrow trail that led them past groups of small wooden houses, their long upper verandas overhung by eaves and a sloping roof, deep into the heart of the Sindh valley. Surrounded by the beauty of the mountains, they rode in silence.

When they reached Gagangir, they had a short rest and then set off on foot for the eight-mile trek to the Sonamarg, their destination for the first night. One steep track led to another, and they soon needed their long hiking sticks. By the time they reached Sonamarg, Patricia was exhausted.

'I can't believe how unfit I am,' she said, panting. 'That hiking in Scotland doesn't seem to have helped at all. And you were right about getting stiff after several hours' riding. I hurt where I didn't know that I had anything *to* hurt.' She leaned heavily on her stick and stared across the fields of gold to the snow-covered mountains that rose up against the clear cerulean sky. 'It's easy to see why this is called the golden meadow. Seeing it was worth every single difficult step to get here.'

Her father smiled warmly at her. 'I suspected that you'd feel the same appreciation of the landscape as I. But now may I suggest that we see what that rascal of a cook has been up to since he went on ahead,' he said, and he started to stride across the meadow towards the cluster of tents that had been erected at the foot of the pine-clad slopes of the mountains.

She stared at his back, a glow of happiness spreading through her. Then she hurried after him, her energy renewed. As they drew near to the tents, they saw that the cook had set up their camp at the edge of a crystal stream that was running swiftly along the base of the mountain.

'Excellent,' the Major said, eyeing the blazing camp fire and the tea of buns and cakes that had been laid out for them. 'Excellent,' he repeated. 'And I do believe that I can detect the smell of our supper cooking.'

The next morning, they set off early on the nine-mile journey to Baltal.

'Baltal lies at the foot of the Zoji-la Pass,' the Major told her. 'The entrance to Ladakh is on the other side of the Pass. We are nearly there, Patricia.'

The terrain was easier for the ponies, and they had time to enjoy the sight of the wild spring flowers that stretched back from the snow-bordered path along which they rode. All around them, the scented air was filled with the music of cuckoos and larks.

When they reached Baltal, they ate their sandwiches while the ponies and donkeys had a rest. After lunch, Patricia decided to walk a few steps along the trail they'd be taking when they set off again. 'It's a very steep track,' she called back to her father a few minutes later. 'And very foresty, too, by the look of it. It's not going to be as easy as it was this morning.'

'It *is* a difficult path,' the Major said, coming up behind her. 'We're about to enter the Pass itself, and we'll be traversing pine forests for the next few miles. But this is not altogether surprising since we're in the rain shadow of the Himalayas. Enjoy the richness of the vegetation here,

Patricia – Ladakh is much more barren. There's very little rain at Ladakh's altitude.' He glanced at his watch. 'Time to set off, I believe, if we're to get to the Rest Hut at Machoi before nightfall. Tomorrow, we'll be in Ladakh.'

The ploughing and sowing was about to begin. Spades would be breaking the ground, and ploughs turning the soil. But before the villagers shattered the peace of the worms, the spirits of earth and water had to be shown that they were honoured. A day had been devoted to pacifying them, a day without meat or *chang*, a day of prayers, but that day was now drawing to a close.

Kalden sat in the corner of the kitchen and listened to the sound of the monks in the altar room above him. Next year he would be up there, chanting the ritual prayers with them. By agreeing to help Wangyal with the English people, he was delaying the start of his life as a monk, but it was no more than a short delay. He glanced at the ceiling, stood up and ran down the stairs and out of the house.

As he went over to join his family and the villagers who were standing around the small heap of clay bricks that had been built for the spirits, he heard footsteps behind him and he realised that the monks, too, were leaving his house. Looking around, he saw monks coming out of the other houses as well. The light of day was fading fast and they needed to make the rest of the offerings before the sun fell behind the mountains.

The monks all gathered around the brick altar, offering yak milk to the spirits. Then they and the villagers moved to the nearby stream to throw more offerings into water which was swollen with melted snow. Standing at the rear of the crowd, Kalden watched them for a few minutes, then he turned and walked slowly back to his house.

The next day he rose early and made his way through

the gap in the village wall to the edge of the fields beyond. Standing there, lost in thought, he stared with unseeing eyes in the direction of the women spreading manure into the furrows.

A sound from behind him jogged him from his reverie, and he turned and saw Anil and Rinchen approaching, carrying a wooden plough between them. Tashi and his brothers were just behind them, leading a huge *dzo* and holding bags full of seeds. Members of the *paspun* and some of the other villagers were following with large pots of *chang* and a number of silver-lined cups.

He watched as the children fastened the *dzo* to the plough and the villagers organised themselves into working groups. Then he glanced at the side of the field to where a monk in scarlet robes was chanting the sacred texts, unconcerned that his voice was lost in the laughter from the villagers, who were joking and singing as they threw handfuls of seeds into the newly ploughed furrows.

Surveying the scene around him, Kalden's heart was heavy.

Higher and higher into the Zoji-la Pass they rode, the moss-green pine trees of the lower slopes gradually giving way to barren stretches of ground where their every step sent up a cloud of dust that reached their shoes and hid the small wayside shrubs that bordered the track.

Once or twice, Patricia glanced down into the valley. Each time she recoiled in fear at the sight of the sheer walls of crimson scree which dropped from her feet into a dark void, and she swiftly looked away again.

'It's really scary when you look down,' she told her father on one of their short breaks.

'Not for those who have seen the whites of the enemy's eyes on the field of battle, it isn't,' the Major replied, taking the can of water that the bearer held out to him and putting it to his lips.

'Well, it's pretty frightening to me. I think I'm finding out that I don't like heights.'

Higher still they climbed. Just as she was beginning to wonder if they'd ever get to the top, they passed through a patch of yellow poppies and came out on a large crag of purple rock that overhung the valley. They got down from their ponies and gazed in awe at the panorama spread out before them.

A movement in the valley caught Patricia's eye, and she knelt down to peer over the ridge. A solitary wild horse was running the length of the mountain stream that wound its way through the heart of the valley. 'It's all so beautiful,' she sighed, and stood up again.

'You can see now why I haven't been able to get this journey out of my mind in all these years,' her father told her. 'And why I resolved to make the journey a second time, this next time with James. I'm confident that he, too, would have enjoyed it. But sadly that wasn't to be.'

A lump came to Patricia's throat.

'You're right, Father,' she said quietly, her voice sounding strange to her ears. 'James would have loved it, just as I do. Even though I've helped you with your book over the years and seen the photos and notes you made, nothing, absolutely nothing, has prepared me for the real thing. And James would have felt the same.'

The Major turned to look at her. 'You are a good daughter to me, Patricia. I may not have said this often enough over the years. Grief does strange things to a person. But I want you to know that I am very happy to be sharing this experience with you.' He gave her a small nod, and turned back to survey the view.

'Thank you, Father.' Her vision blurred, and she blinked several times.

'Move now, *acho-le*,' Sonam said, coming up to them with a wide smile. 'Snow. Ice. Must get Rest Hut soon.'

Their short break over, they struggled on foot up a tortuous track that took them into dense snow and ice. When they reached the first of the rivers that they had to cross, they found that thick snow had formed a bridge beneath which the water rushed. Sonam led the way across the snow-bridge, cautiously followed by the Major and Patricia. The bearers and cook brought up the animals, food and baggage in the rear.

Once over the bridge, they trudged through snow and waded through icy streams for what felt like an eternity, until at last they crawled up the hill that led to the Rest Hut at Machoi. Their cook quickly put together a meal, and as soon as they'd finished eating it, they fell into their beds and slept.

Kalden closed his eyes tightly, shutting out the light. The sun was already up, but as the seeds had been sown and there was nothing left to do but water the crops, he didn't feel the need to get up for a while, especially as he'd had a restless night. He sank lower into his bed and pulled the blanket over his head to block out the sound of the voices outside.

But the muffled tones of the *churpon* and his brothers reached him through the blanket. They were standing right under the carved balcony that hung from the front of his bedroom, discussing the irrigation canals.

The *churpon* had only just been appointed by the village to be their *churpon* for that year, and he was keen to make a start on controlling the flow of the water that ran from the stream into the canals, and from there to the crops in the fields. His brothers were offering advice about the order in which he should block and open the canals to make sure that all of the village households had an equal share of the water.

Kalden's mind went back to Mr Henderson's irrigation channels and to how hard he'd had to work to plug the leaks and keep the water flowing.

He threw back his blanket and sat up. All that belonged to the past, and he refused to think about it. And when the two visitors came, he'd have to work extra hard to ensure that they didn't make him remember what he was trying so desperately to forget.

They must now be only days away from his village, those English people. His heart beat faster: he was dreading meeting them. He swung his legs over the side of the bed and stood up. Yes, he was dreading meeting them, but he couldn't wait for them to arrive.

Patricia's aching muscles were beginning to ease when they left the Rest Hut early in the morning and headed for the Dras Valley, which lay on the far side of the Zoji-la Pass.

To their great relief, they soon left the snow and ice behind them and found themselves crossing one area after another of treeless, rocky ground, interspersed with patches of coarse grass. The journey being easier, they reached the top of the slope that led down to the River Dras in unexpectedly good time.

The Major got down from his pony, walked to the edge of the ridge and stared in front of him. 'We are now looking at Ladakh,' he said. He coughed and patted his handkerchief pocket. Patricia saw that his eyes were glistening.

Sonam came up behind them, his face anxious. 'We go now.' He pointed to the sky. 'Many times blizzard here. Is good now. But better must go now.'

They climbed back on to their ponies and continued along the trail. The scree-like surface of the slopes gradually gave way to gently undulating lush green pastures that were carpeted with wild flowers, and they were able to relax and ride side by side.

'Look, there's a *dzo*!' Patricia exclaimed as they passed a field in which a wooden plough was being pulled by a large animal that looked like a bull.

'That is correct,' the Major said. 'And we'll see many more of them before our trip comes to an end, I'm sure.'

When they reached Dras, they left their bags at the white Rest House, and wandered among the scattered village houses until it was time to return for their evening meal.

'This is a pretty little house, isn't it?' Patricia remarked as they waited for their food to be brought to them.

'Indeed, it is,' the Major replied. He gave her a slight smile and pointed to the wall beside their table. 'Do you see any names that you recognise?'

She looked at him questioningly, then leaned forward and peered closely at the wall. 'Only one,' she said, and she sat back and smiled broadly at her father. 'And, funnily enough, the surname is the same as mine.'

'It's a tradition that all Europeans who stay here sign the wall. As you can see, when I was last here, there were approximately forty names ahead of mine. Not surprisingly, the list is somewhat longer now.'

'Yes, but not that much longer, considering the number of years since you were last here.'

'This is not a journey that everyone could, or would, make.' He glanced again at the names. 'We must both sign the wall before we set off for Kargil tomorrow.'

'I bet you're the first person to sign twice.' She laughed.

'That would, of course, be a distinction of some sort,' the Major said in quiet satisfaction.

The following morning, they left early to cover the fifteen-mile journey to Kargil, riding first on pony-back through willow-fringed glades and hamlets, and then walking with the aid of their sticks along undulating, stony tracks. The afternoon trail took them deep into the narrow, rocky gorges through which the River Dras roared, and then past cultivated strips of land, separated only by lines of wild irises and the occasional willow or poplar.

As soon as they reached the outskirts of Kargil, their cook went on ahead. By the time that they reached the polo ground where they were to spend the night, their camp had already been set up and their food prepared.

'We've now travelled one hundred and twenty miles from Srinagar,' the Major remarked as they sat outside the tent in the dying light, each wrapped in a blanket against the cold night air.

'I can't believe how far we've come,' she said, pulling the blanket more tightly around her. 'I expect I will tomorrow, though, when we explore the Bazaar. All the books said it was quite amazing.'

'Then to ensure that we're in a condition to do justice to the sights we're going to experience, I suggest that we turn in now.'

As they walked along the narrow winding streets of the Bazaar the following morning, Patricia's eyes darted from one stall to another as she struggled to take in everything around them. Occasionally they paused to peer into the open-fronted shops or at the stalls displaying cheap cloths, trinkets, knives and assorted knick-knacks, or the Major stopped to photograph something unusual.

While she stood waiting for her father, her eyes followed the young girls of her age with interest. They all wore a woollen hood over their heads and a long-sleeved, full-length dress, belted at the waist, and they all had several strands of brightly coloured beads hanging around their necks. Suddenly realising it was her eighteenth birthday, she turned to her father. 'I know we don't normally make a fuss of birthdays,' she said, 'but I'm glad I was in Kargil for this one. It's been unforgettable. Now I can't wait to see what our village is like.'

'We still have a few days of travel ahead of us, I'm afraid,' the Major said as they resumed walking. 'They'll be difficult days, with a number of streams to cross. You'll need to be alert for stones hidden beneath the water. A couple of bearers tripped over concealed stones in '45 – one of them was hurt quite badly, as I recall. And you must also approach the bridges that span the gorges with caution. It's not uncommon for Ladakhi people to lose their lives by falling off such a bridge.'

'I will be careful, don't you worry, Father. And now I want you to choose something I can get you as a souvenir – not that you'll need it. We're going to remember this summer forever.'

'Kalden!' Tashi shrieked, running after Kalden as he was walking through the village on his way back to his house, pulling a *dzo* behind him.

'You are in a great hurry, young Tashi,' Kalden said. He stopped and smiled down at his nephew. 'Is anything troubling you?'

'*Skyot*! Kalden. You must come with me,' Tashi said, and he pulled at Kalden's robe.

'What is it?'

'Wangyal has an important message from Leh. It's about the visitors from England.'

A wave of fear swept through Kalden.

What if they didn't come after all, those English people who would be able to tell him about England! He'd been planning to talk to them about the books he'd read and to have the sort of conversation that he'd had with his missionary friends. They had to come; he'd prepared for their visit; he longed for their visit. They had to come.

'I'll go to Wangyal as soon as I've tethered our *dzo*. You can tell him that, Tashi.'

Tashi spun round to run to the post house, but stopped sharply. 'Oh, he's here!'

'*Ju-le*,' Wangyal said, hurrying up to them.

'*Ju-le*, Wangyal. Is there any problem with the English visitors?' Kalden put his arm around Tashi's shoulders.

'Not at all,' Wangyal answered with a broad smile. Kalden relaxed his hold on Tashi. 'I have just heard that they left Kargil a few sunrises ago. They will soon be in Alchi, and then with us. We are moving out of the post house today and into our sons' house. You must now get the ponies and everything you will need for when you take the visitors into the mountains. That's what I've come to tell you.'

'I have done that, Wangyal. Relax, my friend. We are ready, aren't we, Tashi, for the visitors?'

Tashi nodded his head vigorously.

'Yes, I am ready, Wangyal,' Kalden repeated, and he turned and stared in the direction of Alchi.

Their final overnight stop was in Alchi, an hour or so from their destination.

Eager to bring their journey to an end, they left Alchi as soon as they'd finished their breakfast and in the middle of the morning they reached the outskirts of the village that was to be their home for the summer.

As they approached the village they saw that some of the villagers were working in the fields outside the wall, laughing and talking as they bent over the furrows. When they saw the visitors arriving, they stopped what they were doing, stared at them, and then waved at them before turning back to talk excitedly among themselves. The Major inclined his head towards them and Patricia waved back.

The moment they reached the post house, she slid down from her pony and started to walk back along the track. Her father followed a little way behind her.

'They obviously knew we were coming,' she called to him, stopping and waiting for him to catch her up. 'They don't seem at all surprised to see us.'

'It's a small village. Come, Patricia. We should go back and look at our house. We can meet our neighbours on another occasion. For the present, let's see what the bearers are up to.'

'We're going to have a wonderful time here,' she said as they walked past the bearers, who had started to unload the ponies. 'I can just feel it.'

When they reached the top of the short path that led from the stony track to the post house, they stopped and stared at the single-storey, whitewashed building that stood half way between the drystone wall encircling the village and the track that stretched across the plateau. Tiny wayside flowers grew along the edge of the road, breaking up the hard ground with sporadic patches of colour. On one side of the house there was a vegetable patch, and on the other, a well-trodden path led to a narrow gap in the wall.

Patrica turned round and stared across the track to the ploughed fields. At the far side of the fields there was a small stream, and further away still, a second stream seemed to meander into the distance.

'They will be glacial streams,' the Major said, following her gaze. He turned back to the house. 'This will be very suitable for our needs, I think. Now, let's see if there's anyone in the house.'

He started down the path towards Sonam, who had taken some of their canvas bags to the front door and was standing by the door, the bags at his feet.

'*Ju-le*,' Sonam called out, and he pushed open the door. He hesitated a moment on the threshold, then took a few steps into the dark interior of the house. The Major and

Patricia stopped half way down the path and waited for him to reappear. A minute later he came out, shrugged his shoulders in their direction and started to walk to the side of the house. He stopped and looked back at the Major.

'Me go village, *acho-le*,' he said, and he pointed to the narrow gap in the wall.

The Major nodded his approval, and he and Patricia strolled back to the ponies and donkeys, and watched as the other men unloaded the rest of the bags and carried them down to the house.

Just as the last of the bags was being lifted down, they heard Sonam's voice. He was talking to someone on the other side of the village wall. They hurried back down the path and reached the door just as he rounded the corner of the house, accompanied by a short, elderly man with a sparse white moustache, who was wearing a maroon robe, belted at the waist, and a cream woollen hat.

'This Wangyal,' Sonam told the Major and Patricia. 'Wangyal house.'

'*Ju-le*,' Wangyal said shyly.

'*Ju-le*,' they replied.

Beaming at them, Wangyal left Sonam's side and started to go through the doorway into the house. '*Skyot*,' he said, beckoning them to follow him.

Patricia began to go after him, then stopped abruptly. 'Do you think we ought to tell Sonam and the others that they can leave now, Father? They've still got a way to go before they reach Sumdo, and they want to be there before dark. We don't need them for anything else here, do we? I don't think there'll be anything from now on that we can't deal with ourselves.'

'You're right, Patricia. Everything seems to be in order and there's no reason for them to tarry here. We have to start conveying our wishes by ourselves at some point, and that point might just as well be now. I shall pay them and then we can dismiss them.'

He turned to Sonam and gestured to him that he wished to pay him, and that he and the other bearers could then go on their way. Sonam nodded his understanding and gratitude. After the Major had paid the agreed sum and he and Patricia had managed to convey their satisfaction with everything that the men had done throughout the journey, the bearers took the ponies and donkeys and rode off down the track to pick up the path for Sumdo.

Patricia watched them leave, and then followed her father into the house.

The light was dim in the sparsely furnished room, but she was able to make out a pile of brass pots and pans in one of the corners, and a large wooden barrel on the ground next to them.

'I expect the barrel is for their barley drink – the *chang* that the bearers had each evening when they thought we weren't looking,' she said with a laugh.

'I think you're probably right.'

'And those clay pots over there might be for milk and yoghurt.'

'Yes, that must be so.'

As she became more used to the light, she saw that there was a row of smaller clay pots on a wooden shelf that ran around the room, and that there were two large bins at the side of the kitchen stove. She went over to one of the bins and lifted the lid. 'And this must be barley flour. I'm glad I'm not going to be doing the cooking. I wouldn't know where to begin.' Suddenly remembering that Wangyal was there, she smiled at him.

A wooden bench ran along the side of the wall to the left of the entrance, and there was a long, low table in front of it. On the other side of the table, a large chair stood facing the stove, with a smaller chair at its side. Several stools were backed against the far wall.

Sensing that Wangyal was looking anxiously at her, she smiled again at him and nodded her approval of the house. He smiled broadly back at her.

'It's fine down here, don't you think, Father? Shall I go and look upstairs?'

'No, I'll do that,' the Major said, and he picked up one of the canvas bags and began to climb the wooden stairs. 'Maybe you'd like to make a start on sorting out the bags and seeing what stays down here and what goes upstairs. And perhaps you can make our friend here understand that I should like some refreshment as soon as possible.'

'I'll do my best,' she said. She turned to Wangyal. 'Food and drink?' she asked, pointing to herself and then pointing up the stairs after her father.

His brow furrowed. '*Hamago*,' he replied, shaking his head and looking bewildered.

'*Chu skol*?' she asked hesitantly. 'And *cha*?' She couldn't remember the word for food, but if she'd pronounced the words for boiled water and tea correctly, he might think of bringing some food with the drinks.

'*Hago*.' He chuckled, his brow clearing, and he ran out of the hut. In the distance, she heard him shouting, 'Kalden! Kalden!'

The Major's footsteps sounded on the stairs as he came back down, an air of satisfaction about him. 'In addition to our rooms, we've got a Spirit Room upstairs,' he told her with a smile. 'The room next to it is the latrine.'

'I must go and have a look in a minute. I asked Wangyal for something to drink, and I'm sure he understood me. I think I said the words right – at least, I ought to have done, we've heard Sonam and the cook say them often enough. I

117

hope he doesn't bring any of that salty butter tea, though. It'd make me thirstier than I already am.'

'I'm sure you were correct in what you said, Patricia. We have, after all, been learning Ladakhi for several months now, and furthermore, we've had a modicum of practice in the last few days.'

'It's a bit easier remembering the words in Belsize Park than it is in the heat of the moment here.' She laughed. 'I totally forgot the word for food.'

'*Sal* is food, I believe, and *zo* is eat.'

'Wangyal went out of here shouting for something called a kalden. Have you got any idea what a kalden is?'

'Kalden is who, not what,' a voice said from the entrance to the house. 'Me Kalden.'

She spun round and saw a dark shape outlined in the doorway.

'You speak English!' she exclaimed.

'Not speak very well. Forget much.'

'That's fantastic, isn't it, Father?' she cried, clapping her hands together in glee. 'Fancy there being someone here who can speak English!'

'Me Kalden, pony-man. Wangyal ask me help you when you in Ladakh. Me help.'

He stepped into the room.

She looked up at his face, and she caught her breath.

Her hands fell to her sides and she took a step towards him. Their eyes met. At exactly the same moment, each smiled at the other.

Chapter Ten

They would be wise to rest for the first week, the Major told Patricia as they relaxed on their first evening after they'd eaten the meal that Wangyal had brought them. Although they'd adjusted to the high altitude during their journey to Ladakh, they were obviously both tired and needed to regain their strength. He would tell Kalden that they would not be going anywhere for several days, although they might need him to interpret for them if they found it too difficult to make themselves understood.

'How lucky to find someone here who speaks English,' she said, swallowing her disappointment at having to wait for a week before they'd see Kalden again and start exploring the area.

'We are indeed fortunate,' the Major said. He stood up. 'And now I think we should turn in, Patricia.'

The following morning, any lingering sense of disappointment faded away as they strolled past the village, staring across the fields to the shimmering plateau and to the majestic, snow-capped peaks that towered above it. When they reached the *chorten*, they turned round and walked slowly back.

'What a setting!' she exclaimed, gazing from the mountains to the monastery that was crouching on the rocky slope behind the white lime-washed village houses.

'Yes, it is,' the Major said, smiling at her. 'It's typical of the villages in this area. Now, let us begin our exploration of the village itself.'

They went into the village through the wide gap in the wall, and started to amble along the path that looked as if it ran through its centre. As they walked, they became aware of a growing buzz of excitement in the air. Some of the villagers came out of their houses, holding out pots and bowls as a way of offering them refreshment. Each time, the Major and Patricia shook their heads and smiled their refusal. The people they passed on the path stopped and stared at them, running their eyes over their clothes, peering curiously at their faces, all the time smiling warmly in welcome.

'We must seem very strange to them,' the Major remarked as a group of young children ran up, giggled and ran away. 'I imagine that apart from the occasional missionary, we're the first Westerners that most of them have ever seen.'

'Judging by the way in which they're all staring at my legs, it's also the first time they've seen a woman in jeans. But they don't seem to mind us being here. In fact, they seem really pleased to see us.'

Their slow progress through the village was made even slower by the Major stopping at regular intervals to instruct Patricia about the aspects of Ladakhi life that they encountered on their way, and by the end of the morning, when it was time to return to the post house for their lunch, there was still much of the village that they hadn't yet seen.

When they got back to the post house, they found Wangyal hovering uncertainly there, waiting to serve them a thin, pancake-shaped bread, along with a bowl of soup that had been thickened, they later decided, with unroasted barley flour.

'I think we'll leave the rest of the village for tomorrow, Patricia,' the Major said when they'd finished their meal. He got up from the table. 'I must admit, I'm somewhat tired now, and I think I'll retire for my afternoon rest. What will you do?'

'I'll sit outside and read for a while. It'll be lovely and warm in the sun.'

Once the Major had settled himself upstairs, Patricia picked up her book, tucked it under her arm, carried a wooden chair out of the house and sat down in front of the vegetable patch. Her book in her lap, she stared for a while at the distant fields and glistening streams, then she opened the novel at her bookmark and started to read. As she turned the page, the sensation of being watched swept over her.

She looked up sharply, put her book down, got up and went up the path to the track. Standing at the top of the path, she looked in both directions, but there was no one to be seen, nor was there anyone in the fields opposite. Could it have been Kalden, she wondered? But surely he'd have come over and spoken to her?

Biting her lip, she walked a little way along the track, her steps crunching on the stony ground, loud in the silence of the tranquil afternoon, but the track and the fields were definitely empty. After a few minutes, she turned back, returned to her book and carried on reading without further interruption until her father appeared and suggested that they take a short, late-afternoon walk.

'It'll be good to have the chance at last to practise the Ladakhi words that we've learnt,' Patricia said as they made their way along the edge of the fields towards the streams. 'I know we said a bit to the bearers, but not really much more than *Ju-le*. Obviously *Ju-le* is a godsend as it means just about everything under the sun – hello, goodbye, good morning, goodnight, please, thank you – but it'll be nice to use some other words, as well.'

'Indeed,' her father agreed, and they walked along in silence, drinking in the quiet beauty of an afternoon that was turning to gold in the light of the slowly dying day.

'What are you looking for, Patricia?' the Major asked suddenly.

Startled, she glanced at him. 'Nothing,' she said quickly. 'I'm not looking for anything. Why?'

'It's only that you keep looking back towards the village and you seem to be searching the fields for something.'

She coloured slightly. 'I'm just looking at the different views – it's all so beautiful. And I'm watching the birds.'

'Indeed, I didn't know that you were interested in ornithology.' The Major raised an eyebrow.

'I'm not usually. It's just that everything here is so ... so heightened, if that makes any sense.'

'Yes, it does,' he said warmly. 'I know exactly what you mean. We are at one in that. There is something about this country that quite captivates a person.'

'Yes, there is,' she murmured, and she fixed her eyes firmly on the ground ahead for the rest of their walk, altering her focus only when the Major pointed out an item of interest.

Much later, curled up under her blanket for the night, she wondered what Kalden had been doing all day.

The following morning, the Major decided that they would attempt to complete their tour of the village before lunch. They could then go for an afternoon stroll in the area around the village after he'd had his rest.

Accordingly, they set off immediately after breakfast, walking quickly to the spot where they'd broken off their exploration the day before, and then slowing down. When they turned to go down one of the winding lanes that separated the village houses, a large two-storey house, towering above the buildings on either side, immediately confronted them. The Major stopped and stared up at the frontage of the house.

'Look at that, Patricia! Look at those carvings on the balconies and windows, and all around the doors – they're unusually ornate, even for Ladakh.'

Leaving her standing at the top of the lane on her own, he went closer to the house to inspect the designs. While she waited for him to finish, she glanced idly around at the other lanes.

'See, Patricia, the design is constructed mainly around the lotus,' the Major called over his shoulder, peering at the pattern around the window closest to him. 'Not that it's surprising to find the lotus featured, given that it's the symbol of purity and lies at the heart of Buddhism.' He took a step back from the house. 'I really must take a photograph of this window – the craftsmanship that went into it is quite astounding. Come and see for yourself.'

As he slid his camera from his shoulder, she started to go and join him, when a movement to the side of her caught her eye. She glanced towards it. Kalden was just coming out of one of the lanes, walking in their direction.

Her face broke into a smile.

She swept her hair back behind her ears, and turned to face him as he emerged from the shadows cast by an overhanging balcony and stepped into the dazzling rays of the morning sun. He saw her. His steps faltered, and a smile spread slowly across his face. A beautiful man with a golden smile, she thought, flushing slightly, and she found herself walking towards him.

'That such attention is paid to something purely decorative is indicative of Ladakhi values,' her father's voice came from behind her.

'Kalden's here,' she called, pausing fleetingly and turning to her father, who was trying to capture the whole house in the camera lens. 'Shall we go and say hello – or, rather, *Ju-le*?' She laughed. Without waiting for an answer, she continued walking towards Kalden.

The Major clicked the camera, put it back in its case and went quickly after her.

'*Ju-le*, Patricia-*le*,' Kalden said as Patricia reached him. 'You and Major-*le* see village? Village very good. Yes?'

Patricia opened her mouth to reply, but the Major had reached her and placed himself at her side. 'We like your village very much, Kalden,' he said. 'It's everything we could have hoped for. And we've been made to feel most welcome by everyone we've met.'

'Me very pleased, *acho-le*. And you, Patricia-*le*, you like village?' His dark brown eyes rested on her face.

'Very much, thank you,' she said self-consciously. She smiled up at him, and he smiled back. Her heart missed a beat. 'As my father said, everyone's very kind,' she added quickly. 'It's such a shame that we can't have a proper conversation with the people we meet, but we can only say a few words in Ladakhi.'

'Patricia is excessively modest on our behalf,' the Major said stiffly. 'I'm confident that we'll prove able to manage more than just a few words.'

'Me help you learning Ladakhi, you help me learning better English. Me forget much English. Is good idea?' Kalden asked, slightly moving his head to include the Major in his question.

'Yes, it is. It's a very good idea, isn't it, Father?' Her eyes shone.

'Indeed, it is.' The Major paused. He ran his fingers down the line of his thin moustache. 'I know I told you that Patricia and I would keep to the village and the area surrounding the village during our first week, Kalden, but I think that perhaps we might feel up to taking a short trip or two in the next few days. Would you agree, Patricia?'

'Yes, I would, Father. I feel very rested now and I'm dying to visit some of the places you've written about in your book.'

The Major looked gratified. 'In that case, Kalden, may we plan a short expedition – a short trip – for tomorrow, shall we say?'

Kalden's smile broadened. 'That good plan. Ponies ready. Where you like go, *acho-le*?'

'Somewhere that isn't too far. We should not be over ambitious at this early stage of our visit. Perhaps we could go along the edge of the River Indus, and get in some walking as well as riding. Would that be suitable for a day's outing?'

'Is very good plan. We go pretty village near river and we come back. Little temple in village. We leave when sun come up and we back in village before sun fall behind mountains. Me speak Wangyal about food. Is good?'

'That sounds perfect; just the ticket, Kalden, thank you. Now, Patricia, I suggest that we continue with our tour of the village. We'll see you tomorrow morning, Kalden, at sun up, as you say. Good-day to you.' And the Major began to walk briskly in the direction of the lane from which Kalden had appeared.

With a quick smile at Kalden, Patricia started to run after her father. 'Isn't it funny hearing them say *-le* after our names every time that they speak to us? I don't think I'll ever get used it. Major-*le*; Patricia-*le*.' She laughed.

'That's the Ladakhi way of showing respect,' the Major said, turning into a lane. 'But we, too, show our respect for the other person by using the appropriate mode of address and by our demeanour.' He gave a sigh of satisfaction and smiled at her. 'I would say that, all in all, we've made a good start to our stay here, wouldn't you?'

'It couldn't have been better, Father.'

Behind them, Kalden stood in the middle of the path, staring towards the lane down which Patricia had gone, with her hair flying behind her, a stream of gold. Long after she'd disappeared from sight, his eyes were still fixed on the lane.

The following morning, Kalden came early to the post house and they set off on pony-back across the plateau in the direction of the River Indus, reaching the river at a point where the stream was narrow and sluggish.

After a short break, they started along the path that followed the river upstream, keeping to the inner edge of the track as it took them higher and higher above the muddy waters of the Indus. At one point, Patricia inadvertently glanced over the side of the path, and felt quite dizzy when she saw the height to which they'd climbed.

Moments after that, the path curved sharply to the left. They rounded the bend and saw ahead of them a long suspension bridge which was swaying above the deep gorge of the Indus. She stopped her pony and stared in horror at it. Her eyes travelled down to the ravine far below, and she shivered. It was the deepest they'd seen, and the bridge looked more precarious than any other they'd crossed so far. The blood drained from her face.

Kalden glanced at her. 'Can take different bridge over river. Better bridge,' he said hastily.

'Nonsense,' said the Major brusquely. 'If this is the best way to our destination, this is the way we shall go. Isn't that so, Patricia? We'll show Kalden what the British are made of, will we not?'

Kalden looked anxiously at her.

'Of course, Father. I'll be fine, Kalden, really I will.' She forced a smile. 'After all, how could I not be? The bridge is covered in prayer flags of every colour, and all those prayers are being carried on the back of the river to the spirits. They'll see that we're safe.'

'*I* see you are safe, Patricia-*le*,' he said quietly. 'You not fear when you with me.'

Edging his pony over the rocky outcrop that led to the bridge, he dismounted, and indicated that Patricia and the Major should also get down but remain where they were, then he began to walk slowly across the bridge, pulling his pony behind him. When he reached the far side, he tethered the pony, and returned. One at a time, he led the other two ponies over the bridge, and then, standing on the far bank and holding the bridge steady with his hand, he beckoned to the Major to cross to him.

'Do be careful, Father,' Patricia said, putting her hand on his arm.

He shrugged off her hand, stepped on to the bridge and walked slowly and evenly to the other side, his eyes fixed straight in front of him.

'It's much easier than it looks,' he called back to her, 'even with my arthritis.'

Her heart in her mouth, she put a hand on the rope handrail on either side and began to edge her way across the bridge, her eyes on Kalden. When she reached what she thought must be about half way across, she heaved a sigh of relief and glanced over the side of the bridge. She saw the drop beneath her, and froze. Paralysed with fear, she gripped the rope handrails in a panic and shut her eyes, trying to blot from memory the sight of the gorge below.

Before the Major had registered her terror, Kalden was on the bridge, walking steadily towards her.

'Patricia-*le*,' he said quietly when he reached her side. 'I here.' He stepped closer to her and carefully manoeuvred round her. Then he slipped one hand around her waist and put the other next to hers on the rope handrail. 'You be safe with me. We walk together.'

She felt the hard muscle of his chest against her back and the strength in the arm around her. Her body relaxed and she let him guide her across the bridge, one step after another, until they reached the path on the other side.

'We there,' he said as they stepped on to firm land. He looked down at her, and he let his hand fall from her waist.

'Thank you, Kalden,' she said, her voice shaking with

relief, her eyes glistening. 'Thank you.' She turned to the Major. 'I'm sorry, Father,' she stammered. 'I'm sorry for being such an idiot and letting you down. I don't know what came over me. Like you said, it wasn't that bad.'

'I'm coming to realise that you don't have the best head for heights, Patricia. That is not your fault and it's something we couldn't have known in advance. I sincerely hope, however, that you'll try to conquer your fear while we're here. We're surrounded by mountains and rivers, and we'll be somewhat restricted if we can't use the traditional means of getting from one side to the other. Every ravine is threaded by streams, and they have to be crossed and re-crossed.'

'I'll try, Father. I'm sure I'll be all right in future.' She tried to look reassuringly at them both. 'I'm sure I will.'

'We go now,' Kalden said. 'We sit soon, Patricia-*le*. Is good?'

'Thank you,' she said, looking up into eyes that were warm with sympathy and understanding.

Before long, the ground opened out into a fertile tract that ran down to the Indus and reached the water in an abundance of pink roses. As soon as she was close to the river, she slid off her pony and ran down to the water's edge. Crouching on the ground, she inhaled the scent of the roses.

'They smell glorious,' she sighed, standing up as the Major and Kalden reached her. 'It was worth any number of frightening bridges to get to such a wonderful spot. I can't think of a nicer place to have come on our first day out. This was an inspired idea, Kalden – a very good idea, I mean.'

'Indeed, it was,' the Major echoed. 'And now I think we'll eat.'

They found a spot on the river bank, and ate the *ngamphe* that Wangyal's wife had prepared for them. *Ngamphe* was barley flour mixed with tea, Kalden explained. It was something that they'd have a lot for lunch as it was easy to carry and it would give them energy.

When she'd finished eating, Patricia lay back on the grass and stared up at the clear blue sky and at the mountains and crags that towered above her. A bird began to sing in the poplars that fringed the bank on the opposite side of the river.

'Just listen to that bird. What sort of bird is it, Kalden?' she asked, rolling on to her side to look at him.

'Sorry. Me not know English name.'

'It's a golden oriole,' the Major cut in. 'They're quite common here.'

'And what's that sound?' she asked, sitting up as strains of a different music burst into the air, mingling with the song of the oriole.

'Music come from temple. Lama sing prayers.'

'Is a lama the same as a monk, Kalden?' Patricia asked.

'Lama is Buddhist teacher. Monk not teacher. Monk lives in monastery, but can come into village and do services. Follows teachings of Buddha and cuts hair from head. Lama not have to cut hair. Lama only have to cut hair if also a monk.'

'I see. Thank you.'

'You want visit temple in village, Patricia-le?'

'Yes, we'd like that, Kalden,' the Major said, and he stood up. 'Is it close enough to walk from here? I could do with stretching my legs a little.'

'Yes, Major-le. Can leave ponies here.'

They set off for the short walk to the village, Kalden leading the way, followed by the Major and then Patricia. Just inside the entrance to the village, they saw the lama squatting in front of a small, white, square building. That building was the temple, Kalden told them.

Standing alongside chattering villagers wearing multi-coloured velvet caps fringed with black fur earlaps, and long grey woollen robes, edged with sheepskin and tied at the waist with blue girdles, they watched as the lama slowly turned over the leaves of a wood-bound book whilst chanting the sacred texts. Every so often, he paused to strike his drum and cymbals. An old man in priestly red clothing, hovering at his side, regularly refilled the lama's bowl with a liquid that Patricia thought was probably *chang*.

'Many Ladakhi temples like temple here. Now me show where lamas live,' Kalden said after they'd watched the lama for several minutes and the Major had taken some photographs, and he led them round the back of the temple to another small building.

Two rows of lamas were sitting just inside the building, surrounded by idols, lighted tapers and masks as they ate their midday meal from bowls. In front of the building sat an old lama with a patch over each eye. In one hand he held a small metal prayer-wheel inscribed with the mantra '*Om mani padme hum*', which he was chanting over and over again, and with his other hand, he twisted the wheel continually.

'Each turn of wheel is prayer,' Kalden told them. 'Many prayers mean good future life.'

'He means their reincarnated life, Patricia. The prayers will help them to be born into a higher quality form. Is that not so, Kalden?'

Kalden nodded cheerfully.

Patricia threw Kalden an amused glance, aware that he hadn't understood a word of what her father had said. He caught her eye and quickly looked away. Under the golden hue of his skin, she was sure that she saw him blush. Smiling to herself, she hurried after the two men, who'd started to wander through the village.

It was a small village and despite the Major's enthusiasm

for examining every inch of the place, they'd soon seen everything there was to be seen and Kalden suggested that they start on their journey back. The Major agreed and promptly set off in the direction of the ponies, leading the way.

'Your English is really very good, Kalden,' Patricia told him as they followed her father. 'Where did you learn to speak English?'

'Long story,' he said. 'Not story for today. Soon be back to pony.'

'Then you've got to tell me another day, when we've got more time. Do you promise you will?' Her eyes met his.

'Me promise,' he said. They smiled at each other. They were both still smiling when they reached the ponies.

While Patricia and the Major unhooked the ponies from the rocks at the base of the slope, Kalden quickly went over the tract of ground where they'd eaten their lunch, collected their bowls and put them into the goatskin bag which he hung on his pony.

'Go back different bridge,' Kalden told the Major when they were ready to leave. 'Long walk, but small bridge. Small bridge good for Patricia-*le*.'

Patricia threw him a look of gratitude.

'I'm not sure that that's a good idea, Kalden,' the Major said. 'I think that Patricia should face the first bridge again. When one falls off a horse, it's a mistake not to climb back into the saddle at once. However, the choice is yours, Patricia.' He stared questioningly at her, an eyebrow raised.

'I prefer to go back the way we came, Father,' she said quietly. 'My father's right, Kalden. I have to prove to myself that I can get to the other side of any bridge that we come across.'

'That's the spirit, girl,' the Major said, and he swung his leg over his pony.

Kalden threw a sidelong glance at the Major's back, tightened his lips and pulled hard on the strap of the goatskin bag.

'As we become more used to our environment, we can go further afield, Kalden,' the Major said while Patricia was climbing on to her pony. 'In a couple of weeks, I might ask you to arrange for the three of us to go to the village of Sumdo Chinmu via the Stakspi La. It was a memorable trip that I'm keen to repeat. It would mean an overnight stay, of course, but I believe that the shepherd's hut I stayed in all those years ago is still in use as a Rest House.'

'Can do that,' Kalden said, getting on to his pony. 'If you ready, Patricia-*le*, we go bridge again.'

She nodded, and the Major started to lead the way towards the narrow track.

'I be with you, Patricia-*le*,' Kalden said, and he gently urged his pony forwards.

The following morning, ignoring her father's instructions to leave their washing for Wangyal's wife to do, Patricia collected their dirty clothes and made her way past the fields to the stream that was furthest from the post house. She dropped the clothes in a heap on the ground, knelt down, put a shirt into the water and started to scrub it.

'Not do, Patricia-*le*!' she heard Kalden call, and she turned round to see him running towards her. 'I go to see Major-*le*, but see Patricia-*le* at water. Not wash clothes here. Drink water in stream. And village there drink water.' He pointed downstream, where Patricia knew there was another village. 'Come,' he said, and he gathered the clothes in his arms and led her to the stream that ran along the edge of the fields. 'Not drink water here. Water go to fields. Wash here.'

'I'm sorry. I didn't realise … ' Patricia began. He stopped her with a slight shake of his head.

'Me know,' he said, and he smiled deep into her blue eyes. She smiled back at him, and they stood there, motionless, each staring into the other's face. Their smiles faded. The clothes slipped from his hands and his arms fell to his sides.

She felt a sudden longing to move closer to him, to put her hands against his chest and slide her fingers beneath his shirt. A hot glow spread through her body, and she felt herself go red. She looked quickly down at the clothes at her feet. 'I'd better get these done, then,' she said in a rush, and she crouched down and picked up the shirt closest to her.

'Me help?' he asked, kneeling next to her, inches from her.

'Thank you for offering, but I don't mind doing them. I'm sure you've got more important things to do than helping me.' She attempted a laugh, her eyes on the clothes.

'Not more important than be here with you, Patricia-*le*,' he said quietly.

Her laugh died away. She raised her eyes and looked at him.

'Kalden!' they heard the Major call from the direction of the post house.

Their heads spun round and they saw the Major fast approaching them, his eyes riveted to the spot where they knelt. Patricia scrambled to her feet, closely followed by Kalden.

'Hello, Father,' she said, colouring. 'Apparently, I was using the wrong stream for washing the clothes, but I'll know in future. And Kalden's offered to help me do the washing. That's nice of him, isn't it?' She pushed her hair back from her face.

'Indeed, it is. I had intended to ask Kalden to join me in a cup of tea while he and I planned a walk for tomorrow – I think we'll consider today a rest day – but if you feel in need of help with the washing ...'

'Of course I don't,' she cut in hastily. She turned to

Kalden. 'I'm fine, thank you. You and Father start planning the walk, and I'll join you as soon as I've finished here.'

'Come, then, Kalden,' the Major said. He turned and started to walk stiffly back across the coarse grass. Kalden followed a step or two behind him.

She stared after them for a moment. Butterflies fluttered deep inside her in a way that she'd never felt before. Taking a deep breath to steady herself, she bent down, picked up the shirt again and submerged it in the water.

'Many walks here. Not need pony,' Kalden said as they headed in the direction of the *chorten* the following day, a rucksack on each of their backs. From across the stone-strewn plain, they could hear the sound of the prayer flags flapping noisily in the wind long before they reached them.

'Must stay on left of *chorten*,' Kalden told them gravely as they approached the tapering stone structure. 'And on left of *mani*, too,' he added a little further on as they passed a low stone wall inscribed with prayers.

'It's nice not to have to take the ponies. We've done masses of riding in the past month, and even when we were walking, we still had to pull our pony,' Patricia remarked a few minutes later. 'Don't you think, Father?'

'I agree. A long walk is just what our muscles need, and at a brisk pace.'

Pausing for a moment, she turned to look back at the village, her eyes slowly climbing from the upper storeys of the white houses to the rock that rose up behind the houses. Higher still her gaze went, until it reached the monastery.

It looks like a person watching them all the time, she thought, and she turned back to the track and walked quickly to catch up with the two men. As she came up behind them, she saw Kalden glance over his shoulder at her.

'The monastery's quite frightening,' she said as she

reached him. 'I wouldn't like to live on the side of the rock like that.'

He stared ahead.

Before long, they'd left the village and *chorten* far behind them and had struck out across barren ground, a seemingly never-ending stretch of light brown rock beneath the canopy of the bright blue sky.

'House over there missionary house. Missionary family from England,' Kalden said suddenly. He stood still and pointed to an isolated house at the far side of the plateau, only the top part of which could be seen above the stone wall that surrounded it.

'A missionary family, you say,' the Major remarked. 'I can't imagine that they'd be very popular in such a Buddhist region.'

'Not popular. Gone now.' He turned away and continued walking.

'Did you ever speak to the family?' Patricia asked.

'Yes, Patricia-*le*. Me meet family. Me friends with family.'

'What were they like?'

'In the spirit of helping each other with our languages, Kalden,' the Major interposed, 'I trust that you won't object to my pointing out that when you refer to yourself, and when you are the person doing the action, it is usual to say *I* and not *me*. For example, to use your last statements, you would say *I* met the family, not *me* met the family; and *I* was friends with, not *me* was friends with. I trust that that helps.'

'Thank you, Major-*le*. I remember now.'

'Did the missionary family teach you to speak English?' Patricia asked.

'Yes. But they gone long time now. When family go, not speak English. Forget English.'

'And is that where you got your trousers from?' she

135

asked, glancing down at his legs with a smile. 'You're the first Ladakhi man I've seen in a pair of trousers.'

'Missionary man give trousers. Ladahki robes more hot, but I like wear trousers. And when go, missionary man leave me many trousers.'

'I don't think you should question Kalden so, Patricia. It's not appropriate.'

'I'm sorry, Kalden,' she said, and she fell silent.

The route that Kalden had chosen took them up a broad band of sloping sand and stones. They paused several times on the way up to the cluster of crags that they could see at the top, and sat on a rock for a rest. Sometimes they gazed back at the view across the wide plateau as they sat there; other times they stared ahead at the snow-covered peaks of the mountains.

'The silence here is quite amazing,' Patricia said at one point, perched on a rock between Kalden and her father. 'I never before understood what people meant when they said that silence was deafening, but now I know.' She turned to Kalden. 'What I'm saying, Kalden, is that it's very quiet here and very beautiful.'

The smile he gave her lit up his whole face.

'We see river soon, down in valley,' he said. 'Very pretty. Me like valley. No,' he stopped himself, laughing. '*I* like valley. No, I like *the* valley. Summer, I cross river – the river – with brothers. Go to mountain pasture. Is good.'

'How many brothers have you got?' Patricia asked.

'Three,' he replied. He got up and started to walk up the path to the top of the slope.

'That's quite a drop!' the Major exclaimed, joining him at the top and peering cautiously over the rim of the crag into the ravine below. 'How on earth do people get to the bridge at the bottom?'

'Paths go down side of mountain,' Kalden said. 'Go down

path, over bridge and up track on other side of mountain. Family go to mountain pasture over bridge. When take animals, take wide path down mountain. Not go on this path.'

'I suggest that we have our lunch now,' the Major said, stepping back from the edge of the rock. 'And after lunch, you can take us to the bottom of the slope.'

'Path here very difficult if not Ladahki. Have lunch and go to wide path. Is good?'

'I think you underestimate our strength and stamina, Kalden,' the Major said, tersely. 'As an ex-army man, I have experienced difficult terrain. I'm sure you'll find that we're well up to the challenge. Isn't that so, Patricia?'

She walked gingerly to the edge and peered over. 'I'm not so sure, Father. It looks quite difficult. Perhaps we ought to do as Kalden suggests and find an easier path. Maybe when we're more used to the mountain tracks, we can attempt this one.'

'Nonsense! By the time that we've had our lunch we'll be fighting fit and ready for anything Kalden can throw at us. Come on, what do you say?'

His face anxious, Kalden turned to Patricia. She met his eye, then looked away. 'We'll do whatever my father says,' she said quietly.

They finished their lunch, packed everything into their rucksacks and slipped their rucksacks on to their backs.

'Right, Kalden,' the Major said briskly. 'Lead the way.'

Worry written all over his face, Kalden led them over the granite crags to a point slightly further along the ridge. Patricia kept as close to him as she could; the Major followed behind her. They came to a slender gap between two of the crags, and Kalden stopped.

'We go here. Is place to put foot under rock. Then take

path to river. I watch you, Patricia-*le*,' he said, and he gave her a reassuring smile. 'I here. You be safe. Me go first, next Patricia-*le*, next Major-*le*.'

'We'll be fine. Don't you worry about us, Kalden,' the Major said.

Sliding between the crags, Kalden put his foot into a hollow just under the ridge and took a step down. He turned and held his hand up to Patricia to help her. She took a deep breath, squeezed through the gap and grabbed his hand. Putting her foot out, she felt around in the air for secure ground. For an instant, all sense of space dissolved and she seemed to be floating in a void.

'Kalden!' she cried in alarm.

'I here. You good.' His hand tightened around hers.

She inched her foot further to the right, and found the indentation in the rock.

'I've done it,' she cried in relief as she felt the firm ground beneath her, and she gave a little laugh of triumph. Then she took her other foot off the edge of the ridge and found herself standing next to him at the top of a single track path. Still gripping his hand, she peered round him and saw that the path wound diagonally down the steep slope of the mountain.

'That's amazing,' she said. 'You can't see any of this from the top.'

'You good, Major-*le*?' Kalden called up to the Major, who was stepping on to the track after Patricia. 'Me help?'

'I'm fine, Kalden. Indeed, I've faced more demanding tests of courage than this in the past,' he said. 'If you just help me put my foot in the correct place … Ah, there we are. Thank you.' And he joined them.

'Now we go down to river.' Kalden glanced down at Patricia's hand for a moment, then released it. Turning, he led the way along the narrow path.

At about three quarters of the way down the mountain, the path widened into a small ledge.

'Have rest?' Kalden suggested, and he stopped. 'Much loose stone near end of path. Need be careful.'

'A rest's a brilliant idea,' Patricia said, and she promptly sat down and leaned back against the wall of the mountain. 'I could do with stopping for a moment, although it isn't as bad as I thought it was going to be. The hardest part was getting on to the track in the first place.'

'Next bit very hard,' Kalden told her, sitting down next to her. 'We go very slow.'

'I don't think we need to stop until we reach the bottom, do we? There can't be much further to go,' the Major said, looking restlessly around. 'You heard my daughter, Kalden; she's finding it all quite easy. I think we can continue.' He stepped over Patricia and Kalden's legs, and started down the last part of the scree-covered track.

'Major-*le*!' Kalden cried out. He jumped up and rushed after the Major, who'd increased his speed and was disappearing round a bend. Patricia scrambled to her feet and hurried after them. Hearing her footsteps behind him, Kalden stopped and turned round.

'You go slow, Patricia-*le*,' he told her. 'Many stones on track. If go slow, not get hurt. Me go Major-*le*.' And he went on ahead, glancing anxiously back at her with every step that he took, and twice going back to help her over a rough spot.

As they rounded the bend, they saw that the Major had paused just before the bottom of the path, which stopped slightly short of the water's edge, and was taking stock of his surroundings. The river was swollen and flowing at a great speed through the ravine. To the right of him, the hanging bridge was swaying a few feet above the white-tipped crests of the water. Running parallel with the bridge, linking one side of the river to the other, was a row of large boulders which protruded from the water like a broken chain of stepping stones.

'The water's quite high – presumably because of the melted snow coming down from the mountains,' the Major called up to them. He shaded his eyes with his hand and stared across the water to the far bank. 'I see no reason, however, why we shouldn't bypass the bridge and cross to the other side by stepping from one rock to another. More of an adventure. The rocks are large enough and are clear of the water.'

'Not cross river on stones!' Kalden cried. He started to run down the path. 'Bridge good. Stones not good.'

'Nonsense,' the Major called, walking forward. 'It certainly wouldn't be the first time that I've used such a means to cross a river.'

'Bridge good, Major-*le*. But stones not good.'

The Major gave a short final jump and landed on the stony ground at the foot of the path. Kalden's voice was lost in the loud rattle of the scree that began to slide noisily down the track after the Major.

Patricia started to run. The pebbles beneath her feet began to move and she cried out in alarm. Clattering loudly, the pebbles picked up speed as they slithered down the slope. Her arms flailing, she struggled to stop herself from falling backwards. Kalden spun round, ran the short distance back up the slope and grabbed her by the wrists to steady her. Holding her firmly, he pulled her to the side of the mountain and hugged her to his chest as the ground moved beneath their feet.

The pebbles came to a stop, and they pulled apart, their self-consciousness instantly lost in their concern for the Major. Kalden tightly gripped Patricia's hand and led her carefully down the track. The eyes of both of them were on the Major, who'd gone over to a pile of boulders clustered at the water's edge and was climbing on to the rock closest to him. He stood on the rock and faced the line of boulders stretching across the river.

'We come, Major-*le*. Not move.'

'You're wrong if you think we'd fall off the rocks, Kalden,' the Major shouted above the roar of the water. 'If they're all like the one I'm standing on, we'll certainly be able to give the bridge a miss. Don't you agree, Patricia?'

He turned to look at his daughter with a confident smile, stepped on a patch of wet weed, and slipped. Giving a startled cry as he lost his balance, he fell from the rock and crashed heavily on to the hard ground at the water's edge.

'Father!' Patricia screamed.

Kalden dropped her hand and sped down the rest of the track and across the stones to the Major. Patricia went after him as quickly as she could, her heart thumping and her eyes smarting in the cold wind.

'Are you alright, Father?' she cried, reaching him and kneeling down beside Kalden.

'Don't fuss so, Patricia,' he said irritably, struggling to sit up. 'Damned silly thing to do. Help me up, Kalden, there's a good chap.' He put his arm up and Kalden took it. Patricia leaned forward and took his other arm.

'We take Major bottom of path,' Kalden said, and they helped the Major into a position from which he could stand.

With their support, he put his left foot squarely on the ground and eased himself up. Then he put some weight on to his right foot. Crying out in sudden pain, he lifted his right foot off the ground and clung tightly to Kalden and Patricia, staring down at the ground in front of him, breathing heavily, his face creased in agony.

'We help, Major-*le*,' Kalden said gently. 'You hurt.' He eased the Major's arm around his shoulder and Patricia did the same to his other arm. Together they half carried him to a large rock at the foot of the slope, and helped him to sit down.

'Well, that was unexpected,' the Major said when he'd recovered his breath. 'I'm sorry, Kalden. My fault. I should have listened to you. You were in command.'

'Think you not able to walk, Major-*le*,' Kalden said flatly.

'I'm sure I will be. I'll try again. Move back and let me stand.' He raised himself from the rock, gave an involuntary cry of pain and immediately fell back. 'I fear you're right,' he gasped. 'Damned foot seems to have taken a bit of a knock. Bloody nuisance.' Breathing heavily, he leaned forward and manipulated his foot. 'Well, it's not broken,' he said straightening up, his face ashen. 'It's just a sprain. But I regret I'm going to require assistance to get back to the top.'

'Me help. Me strong,' Kalden said.

'And I'll help, too,' Patricia added. 'What's it best for me to do, Kalden?'

'Best behind Major-*le*.'

'If you give me your arm, Kalden, that'd be a start. Good man.' The Major took Kalden's arm and pulled himself up, leaning against Kalden. Patricia took her father's rucksack from him and placed herself behind him, ready to steady him if he looked like falling. Very slowly, they made their way up the track, with Kalden half carrying the Major, who was in visible agony.

'Much time before sun go behind mountains,' Kalden said, wiping his forehead with his arm as they reached the ledge half way up the path. He leaned back against the rocky wall, the Major next to him. 'We not worry, Major-*le*.'

Finally, after a number of short breaks to help the Major, who was clearly in distress, they reached the top of the slope. Kalden went first through the gap between the crags, then he leaned down to help pull the Major up after him. His face contorted with pain, the Major had to put his injured foot on to the rock more than once before he was safely on level ground.

'I'll be all right, Kalden,' Patricia called up to him. 'You help Father.' And she grasped the roots of a bush that was overhanging the path and pulled herself up on to the ridge.

Although their trek back across the plateau was easier than the climb up the steep slope, they made slow progress and the sun had already begun its descent behind the distant summits by the time they were close enough to the village for Kalden to leave them. Assuring them that he'd be back as quickly as possible, he ran off to get a pony on which the Major could complete the rest of the journey.

'I'm sorry about being such a fool, Patricia,' the Major said gruffly as they sat next to each other on a small boulder, waiting for Kalden to return.

'You just concentrate on getting that foot better, Father,' she said. 'Don't think about anything else.'

The face that he turned to her was weary with pain and exertion. 'I was pig-headed and stubborn, and you must know that I realise that I am entirely at fault. The pain I am in is a just punishment.' He paused for a moment, and she opened her mouth to speak. 'No, Patricia,' he said quietly. 'Let me say what I want to say. I know that I am not always ... easy, for want of a better word. You're a good girl, and I appreciate that. If I haven't always made that clear ... well, that is to my discredit.'

'Thank you, Father,' she said. 'That means a lot to me.'

The sound of hooves broke into the still of the late afternoon, and they saw Kalden returning on a pony. Together with Patricia, he helped the Major into a sitting position on the back of the pony with his right foot hanging down alongside the stirrup, and they started to make their way back to the village, one on either side of the Major.

The sun was disappearing behind the dark peaks, bathing the ground in a deep orange light, by the time they reached the short path that led to the post house. Kalden raised his arm to help the Major get down from the pony without putting his injured foot on the ground.

'I'm sorry about this, Patricia,' the Major said, leaning back against the flank of the pony, sweating with exertion, 'but Kalden will have to show you around until I'm fit enough to come out with you both again. I shall need to rest my foot for at least a couple of days.'

With one hand on the pony's rein and the other under the Major's elbow, Kalden glanced at Patricia across the back of the pony. She met his gaze and she saw the fatigue in his dark brown eyes disappear in the sudden fire that flared up in their depths. Her heart pounded.

The sun faded from sight and darkness fell.

Chapter Eleven

Patricia stared in concern as Wangyal led the village *amchi* across the room to the Major, whose face was pale and drawn as he sat in the large chair in the downstairs room of the post house, his right foot resting on a blanket that had been folded into a small square and placed on the low table under his foot. The candle that burnt on the table threw dark shadows into the corners of the room.

Chanting under his breath, the *amchi* bent over the Major's foot.

'I think we should take Father to Leh – obviously not this evening, but tomorrow morning,' Patricia told Kalden, who was standing next to Wangyal. 'There's bound to be a hospital there. After all, it's the capital.'

'*Amchi* good man; he know what to do.' Kalden gave her a reassuring smile. 'He good *amchi*. His father good *amchi*. His grandfather good *amchi*. He make Major foot well. You see, Patricia-*le*.'

'I do hope you're right,' she said, biting her lip. 'We're only here for a short time. It'd be awful if Father had to remain in the post house for most of our stay – there were so many places we wanted to go to.'

'Foot be good soon,' Kalden said firmly.

The *amchi* picked up her father's wrist, held it for a moment, then put it down and did the same with the other wrist. The light was dim and Patricia moved closer to the Major to get a better view of what the *amchi* was doing. He gestured for the Major to open his mouth, then he studied his tongue, and looked into each of the Major's eyes, one after the other.

'My father's only sprained his ankle,' she said. 'Why's he looking at his tongue and eyes?'

'*Amchi* know what to do,' Kalden repeated. 'Not worry, Patricia-*le*. You see.'

The *amchi* picked up his goatskin bag and took out a bunch of herbs, a bowl, a short piece of wood and some small pots. Then he crouched down and started to grind the herbs with a little water and some black powder from one of the small pots, all the time chanting what Patricia supposed was a mantra.

Then he stood up, leaned over the Major's leg and spread the greenish-brown paste over his bare foot. Finally, he covered the Major's foot with a cloth, stepped back and said something to Kalden in Ladahki. Kalden nodded.

'*Ju-le*,' Kalden said. He turned to Patricia and beamed at her. 'Major foot better soon. But he not walk for many days.'

The *amchi* said a few more words to Kalden, who looked at the Major in sudden amusement. Patricia stared questioningly at him.

'*Amchi* give mantra for you to chant, Major-*le*.' Kalden laughed. 'I tell you mantra. You chant it. You get better very quick.' The Major and Patricia both smiled.

The Major turned to the *amchi* and cleared his throat. '*Zumo kangp-e nanga gyal rak*,' he began. '*T'uk-je-che*.' He leaned forward slightly to bring Kalden into his line of vision. 'I've tried to tell the *amchi* that the pain in my foot already feels better, Kalden, and to thank him for his help. If I have made a mistake in the words that I've used, perhaps you would make sure that the *amchi* knows how grateful I am to him. It was very kind of him to come so quickly. Do thank Wangyal, too, for his help, there's a good man.'

Kalden conveyed the Major's message to the *amchi*, who smiled broadly at the Major, then gathered his belongings and went out of the house accompanied by Wangyal.

'What a relief to know that you'll be up and about in a day or two, Father.'

A spasm of pain crossed the Major's face as he tried to move his injured foot. 'I fear it may be a little longer than that. But you're not to sit around the house, waiting for my foot to be better. No, you must go out and explore the area. Take photographs of everywhere you go. We'll have them developed back in England, and then you can show me what you've seen.'

Patricia opened her mouth to protest, but the Major held up his hand to stop her. 'I insist upon it. Kalden can start showing you the cultural highlights in the immediate vicinity. I saw them the last time I was here. I don't need to see them again. By the time that you've seen everything there is to see locally, I shall be fighting fit and ready to join you in some trips that will take us further afield.'

'But I can't leave you by yourself all day long. Suppose you need something.'

'Those are my wishes, Patricia. And I won't be completely by myself – Wangyal won't be far away. Now, have I been understood?'

'Yes, Father. Thank you very much. It's very kind of you.'

'Nonsense, girl! This lamentable situation is entirely my own fault. It's not a matter of kindness at all. Why should you suffer because I acted in a foolhardy manner?'

'Nevertheless, I think it's very generous of you to be willing to stay alone for most of the day, Wangyal or not. But I'm still worried about how you'll manage when I'm out. You mustn't put any weight on your foot until it's absolutely ready.'

'I'm well aware of that, thank you, Patricia. Kalden, perhaps you would ask Wangyal if his wife would like to help me out over the next few days. Of course, she and Wangyal will be recompensed for any extra work they undertake.'

'Recompensed? Me not … I not understand word, Major-*le*.'

'Recompensed means rewarded, given some money.'

'Money not needed. Wangyal and wife be happy to help.'

'Then all is satisfactorily settled. Now you may both help me upstairs. It's late and I feel in need of rest. I shall partake of my meal upstairs.'

The Major held out his arm to Kalden. Patricia hurried to the other side of her father and together they manoeuvred him to the foot of the narrow wooden stairs. Then she stood back and let Kalden take the Major slowly up the stairs and help him to get ready for bed.

'Thank you for all of your help today and for bringing the *amchi* to Father so quickly,' she said when Kalden had come back down again and she was walking with him to the front door. 'I couldn't have managed without you.'

'I sorry Major-*le* hurt. I pleased to help.'

'Well, thank you, anyway,' she repeated, and she opened the front door. 'Oh, look at the sky!' she exclaimed, and she flung the door wide open and stepped out of the house. 'It's so black that every single star stands out like a diamond. In London, there are always lights on somewhere or other so there's a yellowish glow in the sky every night. But here, you're aware that you're on a planet hurtling through space. It's quite frightening, feeling so little under such a big black emptiness.'

'I not understand.'

She laughed and looked across at him. 'I'm sorry, Kalden. I haven't a clue how to explain what I mean. You're used to this,' she said, pointing to the sky. 'I'm not. All I'm trying to say is that the night sky in Ladakh is beautiful.'

'I glad you like,' he smiled. 'Me, too. I like.' He looked up at the sky.

She followed the line of his upturned throat, the cut of his jaw, the curve of his mouth, and she was shaken by a sudden violent urge to lean forward and touch his face, to feel his golden skin beneath her fingertips. Her knees felt weak.

He looked down at her and she quickly turned away.

'Very beautiful,' he said quietly.

She wondered whether he meant the sky. Desperately, she hoped he didn't. Her face felt hot in the cold night air.

'About tomorrow,' she began, suddenly self-conscious. 'I think I ought to stay around the house to help Father get into a routine. We could go out the following day, though, if that was all right with you.'

'It very all right, Patricia-*le*. First time we go out, I take you my favourite place. We see mountains, valley, river. Is beautiful place.'

'That would be lovely. Thank you. For now, then, *Ju-le*.'

'I see Wangyal *tho-re* – I see Wangyal tomorrow. I come here with Wangyal and Wangyal's wife to make plan for Major-*le*. You, me, go out next day.'

'That sounds perfect. Well, then,' she said awkwardly, and she stepped back into the doorway. 'I'll see you tomorrow.'

'Goodnight, Patricia-*le*,' he said softly.

His heavy-lidded eyes slid slowly across her face. She could almost feel their caress on her skin.

'Goodnight, Kalden,' she whispered.

For a long moment each stared into the other's face, unsmiling, then he stepped back, raised his hand in a slight wave and turned away. Standing in the open doorway, she watched as he went up the path, turned along the track towards the village, and was gradually swallowed up by the black of night.

She went back into the house, closed the front door behind her, and leaned back against the door, breathing heavily. She stared around the dimly lit room, her gaze coming to rest on the low table where the candle still flickered, where Kalden had been standing. In fewer than two days she'd be going on a trip with him, just her and Kalden, just the two of them alone.

Her heart beat fast.

Every time she looked at him, her stomach turned over and she felt the strangest sensation deep inside her. And when he wasn't with her, she couldn't stop wondering what he was thinking, what he was doing. This must be what Ruth had meant when she'd talked about the way she felt about Johnny.

Whenever she'd listened to Ruth on the subject of Johnny, she'd laughed inwardly at what she'd thought of as silliness. But as Ruth's words sprang again into her head, she heard them with different ears, and she could have wept with shared emotion. Oh, if only Ruth were at her side at that very moment!

She stepped away from the door, went over to the candle and blew it out.

The following afternoon, having made herself comfortable outside the house on a wooden chair that she'd taken from indoors, she opened her book.

The sun was at its height, and after a few minutes of intense heat beating down upon her, she got up and moved the chair into the shade at the side of the house. Sitting back down, she let her eyes travel over the fields of green shoots to the glittering streams beyond them; to the plateau that stretched out behind them, its barrenness broken up by sparse patches of green and smatterings of wild flowers; to the white-tipped peaks of the mauve and grey mountains that rose above the plateau, piercing the azure sky.

The air was fragrant with the perfume from the flowers. Her book lying unread in her lap, she sat back, closed her eyes, inhaled the scented aroma and listened to the marmots whistling to each other in the distant mountains. It was the perfect afternoon, and the next day promised to be even more perfect. She couldn't wait for it to begin.

'What your book, Patricia-*le*?'

She opened her eyes, startled. 'Gosh, you made me jump, Kalden.' She laughed, sitting upright. 'I didn't hear you come up.' She pushed her hair behind her ears and glanced down at her legs. She wished she'd changed into something prettier after lunch and wasn't still wearing her jeans and an old, white, cotton shirt.

'I come see if you want go walk.'

Her heart leapt. 'I'd love to,' she said at once, and closed her book. Then her heart sank. 'But what about Father? I don't see how I can. I ought to stay here. He could wake up at any time and Wangyal won't be back till later. It would have been nice, though.' She sighed wistfully. 'But it's probably better to wait till tomorrow – Wangyal's going to be here all day tomorrow.'

'Only short walk not far from house.'

She glanced again at the snowy peaks, their caps turning to gold in the rays of the sun. Then she looked back up at Kalden, a dark silhouette against the bright sun.

'Well, just a short walk, then,' she said. 'After all, Father *is* asleep.' She stood up and dropped her book on to the seat of the chair. 'We'd better not be too long, though,' she added. Pulling a pale blue ribbon out of her pocket, she tied her hair back from her face and they started walking along the dusty track.

'This is really lovely,' she said, staring around her at the desolate beauty of the landscape. 'And do you know what – I feel free.' She threw back her head, raised her arms and spun around. 'I – feel – free!' she shouted. She came to a halt, laughing. Kalden grinned at her in amusement, and they resumed their walk. 'I do love my father,' she told him, 'but it's just so great to be on my own for a bit. Obviously I'm really sorry that he's hurt himself, but at the same time, it's going to be fun, having a few days without him. I hope that doesn't sound too awful.'

'It not sound awful,' he said. He smiled at her, then looked away and they walked along in silence for a while.

'Not that way, Patricia-*le*,' Kalden cried suddenly as they reached the *chorten*. He grabbed her hand and pulled her towards him. 'Must walk left of *chorten* and *mani*.'

'I'm sorry, I forgot.'

'You not be Buddhist, but is good to keep left,' he assured her.

His hand still firmly grasping hers, they went past the *chorten*, past the *mani*, and struck out across the sun-baked plateau. Whenever their eyes happened to meet, he imperceptibly tightened his hold on her hand, and they smiled at each other before turning back to the path ahead.

'Book you read, what book called?' Kalden suddenly asked, breaking into the silence. 'When a boy, I read books. I read with missionary people, Mr and Mrs Henderson.'

'*Pride and Prejudice*. It's by someone called Jane Austen. She lived a long time ago. I think it would be a very difficult book for someone who isn't English. Do you know it?'

'No, not know book. You tell story.'

'I can't really. There's not a lot of story to tell. It's not that sort of book. But it's my favourite book – it's beautifully written and I love what story there is. Does that make any sense?' She laughed.

'No,' he replied with a grin. 'You try tell story.'

'Well, it's about a family. There are five daughters, and their mother wants them all to marry men with lots of money.'

'Husbands must have much money? Much money is very good thing?' He stopped walking and turned to her.

'No, it isn't,' she said quickly. 'Being a good person is more important than having lots of money. But the mother in the book thinks money is important.'

He started walking again, his face throughtful. 'In book, girls want husbands?' he asked after a few minutes.

'Some of them do, but I'm not sure about Mary, the third daughter. Like me, she loves reading. She just wants her family to notice her and to think she's clever. I always feel sorry for Mary. She's not as pretty as her older sisters and not as clever.' She looked at his bewildered face and burst out laughing. 'I don't think you'd like the book, Kalden.'

'If you like book, I like book,' he said gravely.

'Maybe, but I'm not convinced.'

'What is name of fourth daughter?'

'Kitty. Why?'

'Kitty is happy?'

'I suppose so. Why wouldn't she be?'

'Not good to be born number four.'

'Why not? What's so different about being the fourth child?'

'Not important,' he said, and fell silent.

His grip on her hand loosened and she glanced across at him. His smile had disappeared and his face was sad. She stood still. 'What's the matter, Kalden?' She grasped his hand more tightly. 'Why are you upset? Is it something I said?'

He looked down at the ground. 'Not upset. I good.'

'But you're not. What's wrong? Please tell me.'

'Nothing to tell. We walk now. Yes?'

'All right, then.' Worried, she turned back to the track and they started walking again, their hands still loosely clasped.

'Patricia-*le* is beautiful,' he said after a few minutes, his eyes on the dusty track. 'Patricia-*le* have husband in England?'

Her heart jumped. 'No, there's no one in England, Kalden.' She felt herself going red. His fingers tightened again around hers and their arms brushed against each other.

He stopped walking and turned to her. His dark gaze stared into her face. 'Patricia-*le* has beautiful eyes.'

She turned her head away, and pressed her free hand to her hot cheek, trying to cool herself down.

'Very beautiful blue eyes,' she heard him softly repeat behind her.

'No, they aren't,' she said with a nervous laugh. She fixed her eyes on a cluster of rose-bushes that seemed to be growing out of the smooth rocks at her feet, their deep red flowers stark against the stony backdrop. Two small speckled lizards darted across the surface of the rocks and slithered between the cracks. 'They're just ordinary.'

'Not ordinary.' His eyes burnt into the back of her head and she turned to him.

'We must talk about something else,' she said with an awkward laugh. 'You keep making me go red.'

He stared down at her flushed cheeks, and his face broke into a slow smile. He had a dimple in one of his cheeks when he smiled, she noticed. 'We walk then,' he said, and he glanced up at the sky. 'Sun soon go behind mountains. We go back house now.'

A wave of disappointment shot through her. 'I suppose you're right. It's been a lovely afternoon, though, and I don't want it to end.'

'I glad you like afternoon, Patricia-*le*. I want you be very happy here.'

'I already am,' she said.

'I very glad.'

Their eyes met.

Abruptly, Kalden dropped her hand, took a step away from her and began to walk quickly in the direction of the village, his head down.

For a moment or two, she stared after his retreating back, puzzled; then she started to go after him, slowly at first, then faster and faster, increasing her speed until she caught up with him. Sneaking a look at him from time to time as they walked along, she saw that his eyes were blank, and she felt her anxiety grow. Gradually, he slowed down.

She noticed that he occasionally glanced at her hand, which was hanging by her side, but he didn't make any move to take it.

'Where is mother, Patricia-*le*?' he asked after a while.

'Back in England. She wasn't interested in coming to Ladakh with us. To be honest, I don't think Father ever suggested that she come along. She wouldn't have liked all this walking and climbing. What about your family? You haven't told me anything about you or your family.'

'I not interesting,' he said bluntly.

'I don't believe you.' She laughed. 'Just the fact that you speak English is interesting. More than that. It's amazing. Apart from Sonam, who was our chief bearer on the journey from Kashmir, we haven't met anyone else here at all who knows English. That alone makes you very interesting.'

'I pleased I interesting,' he said with a wry smile.

'You said the missionaries taught you English. Did you go to their school?'

'Ladakhi children not go to missionary school. Ladakhi people not want missionary family here. But I friends with family.'

'When did they leave?'

'We do one harvest after family leave. Missionary boy, Peter, want go university in England. And Mrs Henderson want Peter go university. Mr Henderson very sad – he want stay in Ladakh. But family go back to England.'

'Was Peter the same age as you?'

'Yes. Peter my friend. All family my friend. I help family live in Ladakh. Ladakhi life hard if not Ladakhi person. Missionary family speak bad Ladakhi and I help family speak good Ladakhi. Family help me speak English.'

'You must miss them.'

'Yes.' He started walking more quickly again. 'Miss family, miss pictures, miss books, miss music. Mrs Henderson teach me play accordion. Give me recorder for present. Me like play recorder.' His voice was wistful.

She bit her lip. 'I'm sorry, Kalden. I shouldn't have brought the subject up. You obviously miss them a lot.'

He glanced at her anxious face, reached out and took hold of her hand. 'You not be sorry, Patricia-*le*. I not sad now. Before you come Ladakh, I very sad. But you come, and I be happy now. You nice, Patricia-*le*. And Major-*le*,' he added quickly.

'I'm glad you're feeling better about things now,' she said. 'It's not much fun being sad.'

Their hands tightly clasped, they continued along the stony track. When the mass of colourful flags that fluttered around the *chorten* was clearly in sight and they could see the roofs of the village houses in the distance beyond the *chorten,* Patricia suddenly stopped walking.

She cleared her throat. 'Kalden.'

'Yes, Patricia-*le*?'

'We're going to be spending a lot of time together in the next week or ten days, so we're going to become friends, if we're not already, aren't we?'

'I feel you are already my friend, Patricia-*le*.'

'Then I think you should show it.' She gave a self-conscious laugh. 'Before we go any further, I want you to say the following words after me. Say, "You are my friend, Patricia."'

'You are my friend, Patricia-*le*,' he repeated.

'No, that's not exactly what I said. Let's try it again. Say, "You are my friend, Patricia." Repeat exactly what I said.'

A smile of understanding spread across his face. 'You are my friend, Patricia,' he said softly. 'Patricia. Patricia.'

'That's better. I hope it wasn't too painful. I just thought it was time we stopped being so formal when we are together. Now we can continue walking.'

Both of them were smiling into the open space in front of them as they reached the *chorten* and walked past it.

'See,' Kalden said, holding up their entwined fingers. 'See. I am like Englishman. I hold woman's hand. Ladakhi man and woman not hold hands outside house. English man and woman do. I see Mr and Mrs Henderson hold hands. Is good.'

'Yes, is very good.' She laughed. He moved closer to her. She felt the taut muscle in his arm rub against her soft skin, and a thrill shot through her.

As they neared the village wall, a loud burst of music rang out in the air above the houses. Startled, she looked up at the monastery. Kalden's gaze followed hers.

'Is monks,' he muttered, and he dropped her hand.

Moving slightly ahead of Patricia, he went past the main entrance and along to the post house. Wangyal had just come out of the house and was disappearing round the side when they reached the top of the path to the post house.

'Father must be awake!' Patricia exclaimed. She put her hands up to her hair and pulled her ribbon tighter. Kalden thrust his fingers into his belt.

'So, Patricia-*le* … Patricia,' he said, stopping. 'I see you tomorrow. I come in morning and we go for day in mountains. Me show – I show – favourite place. We take food. I go now see Wangyal about *ngamphe* for tomorrow. Is good?'

'Is very good, Kalden. I can't wait for tomorrow!' she exclaimed. She felt herself go scarlet, and she quickly looked away.

'And I not wait, Patricia. All night I think of tomorrow,' he said quietly.

'Is that you, Patricia?' they heard the Major call from inside the house.

'I'm just coming, Father,' she shouted. ''Bye then, Kalden.

Come early, won't you?' And she turned and half ran down the path. Pushing the door open, she paused and looked back at Kalden. He was standing motionless, staring at her. She smiled at him again, then disappeared into the dark interior of the house.

As he walked slowly along the winding lanes to his family's house, he found himself whispering her name over and over again. He reached his front door, heard the sounds of family life within, and stood still. Looking up, he stared at the darkening sky.

It was Patricia's face that he saw.

He inhaled deeply, squeezed his eyes shut, and welcomed the all-consuming red-blackness that blotted out her image. She was never going to be a part of his life – she couldn't be – and he must stop himself from thinking about her, stop himself from dreaming. Such dreams could only end in pain. He must remind himself of that at the start of every day that Patricia lived in his village.

Releasing his breath, he opened his eyes, walked into the house and closed the door firmly behind him.

Chapter Twelve

July

Side by side they sat at the edge of the plateau, high above the narrow ravine.

Lowering her gaze from the mountain peaks whose summits were veiled in shadow, Patricia's eyes slid down the slope on the opposite side of the gorge. For a few moments, she watched shifting bands of light move slowly across the face of the rock, leaving a swathe of deep purple in their wake, and then she looked down into the heart of the valley, and followed the curve of the winding river until it disappeared from sight.

She leaned back on her elbows and glanced sideways at Kalden. 'Do you realise that it's been more than a week since my father's accident? Time's flying by.'

'For me, too, Patricia.'

'And do you realise that although we've spent most of that time alone with each other, I still don't know you at all?'

'Not much to know. I'm only pony-man.'

'No, you're not. You're my friend, a friend who often looks sad, even when his mouth is smiling,' she said quietly. 'A friend who seems to be moving further away from me, not closer.'

He stared ahead of him, his face impassive.

She shifted her position to face his profile. 'I feel really awkward asking this, but there's something I want to know. I'm a bit embarrassed about asking you, though.'

'Something is wrong?' He turned to her, alarm in his eyes.

'Oh, no, there's nothing's wrong,' she said quickly. 'At least, I hope there isn't. No, I just wanted to know why we

159

don't hold hands any more when we're out. Apart from that first afternoon, you've only taken my hand when you've thought I might need help, and then you couldn't let go of it fast enough. Why, Kalden? I rather liked it when we held hands.'

'Me, too. I like it very much.' He studied the ground. 'But is not a good idea. When we hold hands, I feel close to you. The more we hold hands, the more close I feel to you. Then, when you go back England, I be hurt. Is better not holding hands.'

'You must do what's best for you,' she said after a short pause. 'No one likes getting hurt, and if you think you'll be hurt …'

She turned to look back at the opposite slopes. A sudden breeze caught her hair and blew it around her face. The breeze died down, and her hair fell lightly across her eyes, a veil of gold.

'I should have tied my hair back today,' she said, pushing strands of hair away from her face in irritation. 'I thought I'd leave it loose for once, but I'm not sure it was such a good idea now.'

He glanced at her. 'Your hair is very beautiful; like field of ripe barley in sun.'

'You make my hair sound like a bowl of cereal,' she said with a laugh.

'Ripe barley is very beautiful. But your hair is not like porridge,' he added, a note of amusement in his voice.

'Porridge!' she exclaimed, and burst out laughing. 'How on earth do you know about porridge?'

'Peter talk and talk about porridge. He miss having porridge for breakfast. One Christian feast day, Mrs Henderson got porridge for Peter from England. Peter and I eat porridge. Is good, but not beautiful like hair of Patricia.' He paused. 'I should not speak like this.'

'You mean, in case you get hurt?' Their eyes met. Kalden was the first to look away.

He picked up a large stone from next to his foot and threw it hard down the slope. They sat still, listening to the stone ricochet against the hard rock wall until it landed with a dull thud on the boulders and shale at the edge of the water.

'Did your family mind you being friends with the missionaries?'

'Yes,' he said shortly. '*Ama* and *aba* – my mother and father – not like me going to the Henderson family and are pleased they are gone. But I miss the family. I hurt very much when they go and I still very sad they are gone.'

'You said they left a year ago. That's a long time to be feeling so sad.'

He picked up another stone and threw it down the slope. 'In England, many things happen in one year, and every year is different. In Ladakh, life is same this year as last year. We plough fields, we sow seeds, we look after crops, we harvest. Then it gets very cold and we have long rest, with parties, festivals and stories. We eat food we grown in year before and we wear clothes we made. Then comes good weather and we plough fields again and sow seeds. Nothing is different. Nothing makes me stop remembering my friends,' he said flatly.

'But people make their own changes in life, don't they?' She paused imperceptibly. 'They get married, for instance, and have a family of their own.'

He shrugged his shoulders, his face expressionless.

'I'm sorry, I never thought to ask before. You're not married, are you, Kalden?' She held her breath.

He gave a short, mirthless laugh and turned his eyes to the sky. 'No. I'm a fourth son.'

She felt herself start breathing again. 'It's not the first time you've said that you're the fourth son. What does it mean, apart from the fact that you've got three older brothers?'

He jumped up and vigorously wiped the seat of his trousers. 'We go back now. We take a different path and go along *kongka* – along the ridge. Path go around top of plateau and we see river as we walk. Then we go between big rocks back to track, and track takes us back to village. Is very beautiful walk. Come.'

Trying to shake off a growing sense of despair, she watched as he busied himself, picking up their lunch bowls and putting them into his rucksack, then she got to her feet. 'I suppose you're right, we ought to be moving,' she said, and she adjusted the collar of her white, cotton shirt and tucked her jeans more tightly into her boots. 'We said we'd be home earlier today, what with the *amchi* coming again this evening.'

They put their rucksack on their back and set off along the single-track path which skirted the rim of the high plateau, the river below them on their right and a mass of jagged crags on their left. Kalden led the way and Patricia followed him closely until the path widened sufficiently for her to walk at his side. Lost in their thoughts, neither spoke, but each glanced at the other from time to time.

When they'd gone some distance, the track narrowed again and veered sharply away from the line of the river in order to avoid a pile of huge boulders perched on the edge of the ridge. Before skirting the boulders, Patricia stood still and stared ahead of her at the blue-green river which stretched out to the hazy horizon, meandering sinuously between the sheer walls of scree that rose from the depth of the ravine, their colours and shadows changing minute by minute in the fickleness of the afternoon sun.

'It really is lovely.' She took a step closer to the edge of the plateau, and felt Kalden move to her side and place his hand lightly under her elbow. 'You can see for miles from up here, and every single inch is beautiful: the river, the mountains, the flowers.'

She turned to him, and he dropped his hand. 'Come, we go, Patricia,' he said quietly, and he went back to the path.

'Even the swinging bridges look pretty from up here,' she remarked when they'd passed the boulders and were walking parallel with the river again. 'Not that I'm keen to go over any of them again. I haven't forgotten how precarious they feel.'

'Precarious? What does this mean?'

'It means dangerous. As if the bottom of the bridge could break at any minute, or as if the whole thing might suddenly move and you'd fall over the side.'

'Some people fall over side. Many bridges are only thin planks of wood. Planks are tied together. End of bridge stands on heavy log, and log stands on a pile of stones. Bridges *are* precarious. See, I learn new word. But we leave river path here,' he said, coming to a halt in front of a thin fissure between two tall crags. 'We get to track through here.' He stepped into the thin shaft of light that slanted to the ground between the two rocks. 'Is difficult. Very small space and many rose-bushes on rocks. Sharp thorns on bushes.'

'I'll be fine,' she assured him, and she followed him closely, her eyes fixed on the back in front of her as she edged her way forward.

'Thorns, Patricia! You watch,' Kalden suddenly shouted just before they reached the light at the end of the passage, and he stopped. She peered around him and looked at the ground. Wild rose-bushes were growing from the base of the stony outcrops on either side of them and stretching in a tangled mass across their path.

He held up his hand. 'You wait.'

Using his legs, he carefully pushed some of the thorny

branches to one side, then he flattened himself against the rock, trapping the higher-growing branches between his back and the rock. 'You walk now,' he said. 'Path be wider after bushes.'

Holding her hand, he helped her to pass in front of him. Once she was clear of the prickly tendrils, he followed her, cautiously releasing the branches as he went, and they walked along the widening path, side by side, her hand still in his.

As they emerged into the glare of the afternoon sun, he let her hand fall. She looked pointedly down at her hand and then questioningly up at him.

'No more roses,' he said, avoiding her eyes, and he led the way across the parched ground to the track.

'I know what you said about being hurt, but I still don't really understand what you mean,' she said, keeping pace with him. She put her hand on his arm, and he stopped where he was and turned to her.

'I close to Henderson family. When they go, I very sad. You go back to England when harvest done. You and me, if we get close, I be very sad when you go – but a different sad, a worse sad. You and me, we not friends like missionary friends. They call me son. Peter like brother to me.'

'And me?'

'You not see me as son or brother,' he said with a wry smile. 'I feel that. And I not see you as sister. Not at all like sister.' He took hold of both her hands and stared hard into her face. 'You are woman and I am man. When I hold your hand, I hold the hand of a woman, a woman who is very special. And I feel like a man. That is not good, not with a woman who is special. I must not hold hands with you, Patricia,' he said, and he released her hands. 'I not want to hurt very much when you go back England.'

She looked up into his face. His lids lowered, but not

164

before she'd seen the longing and desire that burned in the depths of his eyes.

'You know, Kalden, sometimes it's worth getting hurt,' she said, her voice shaking, and she leaned forward and tentatively kissed him on his lips.

Brushing against him, she felt the lean muscle of his chest against her body, and she shivered. Goosepimples ran along her arms, and she quickly stepped back, colouring. 'I know I shouldn't have done that after what you said, but I did it anyway because I wanted to.'

She turned away, shaking, and started to walk along the track, leaving him standing there, staring after her.

Minutes later, he caught up with her and walked in silence at her side, his hands deep in his trouser pockets, his eyes on the ground.

'I wish you'd say something,' she ventured after a while. 'I never normally behave like that – I've never done such a thing before. I wouldn't. I don't know what came over me. Yes, I do,' she added with a slight smile in his direction. 'But if it's not something that you want … '

He stopped walking and turned to her, his face ragged with despair. 'I do want, Patricia. I must not, but I do want,' he burst out, his voice thick with emotion.

The blood drained from her face. 'What is it, Kalden? Please tell me what it is. Is it something to do with my father?'

He shook his head, his eyes bleak, and looked away.

'Please tell me,' she begged. 'The *amchi*'s coming tonight. Father will be coming out with us again very soon, maybe even tomorrow. This might be our last chance to talk properly. Please, *is* it to do with my father?'

'Not your father. My brothers.'

'I don't understand.'

'It very complicated.'

'But I want to understand. Start by telling me the names of your brothers,' she said, desperately.

'Tenzin, Anil and Rinchen.'

'And have you any sisters?' she prompted.

'No sisters. Just three older brothers.'

'Are they all married?'

'Yes. They married to Deki.'

'Which one's married to Deki?'

'All are married to Deki.'

She stared at him. 'Are you saying that all of your brothers are married to Deki, or that there are three women called Deki?'

'One woman called Deki. All brothers married to same Deki. They have children and are very happy. Deki is very nice.'

'I know that Ladakhi women used to have more than one husband, but I thought that wasn't allowed any longer.'

He shrugged. 'Woman having more than one husband is good for Ladakh. In Ladakh, land is always kept in one piece for whole family. Whole family looks after land. Not much water in Ladakh. If every brother has wife, many wives in one family and many babies. But still only same piece of land and same little water. That makes big problem.'

'So sharing a wife is a sort of population control?'

He gestured helplessly with his hands. 'I not understand population control.'

She stared at him, and a thought struck her.

A sense of dread crept through her. She moved away from him and turned to stare with unseeing eyes at the jagged peaks of the mountains. She could feel his gaze on the side of her face, but she couldn't bring herself to look at him.

'Are you, too, going to marry Deki? Is that what you're trying to tell me? As you're the youngest brother, you've got to marry the person chosen by your older brothers. Is that it?'

He laughed mirthlessly. 'No, I not marry Deki.'

Weak with relief, she looked back at him. 'Why not? Why not marry her if she's already part of your family and that's the way things are done here?'

He took a deep breath. 'Wife not marry four brothers. And I not want to marry Deki, anyway.' He started walking again.

She ran after him. 'Then I still don't understand.'

'I not want to talk about me. I not interesting. I want to talk about you, Patricia. Have you brothers and sisters in England?'

'But … '

'You have brothers and sisters?'

'No sisters, but I did have one brother. His name was James.'

'James go to university?'

'No, he died when he was seventeen. He was very ill for most of his life.'

'Oh, Patricia, that is sad.' He stopped walking. His eyes full of sympathy, he took hold of her hand and gently squeezed it.

'Yes, it was. My parents still haven't got over what happened to him, and they probably never will. But really, dying was the best thing for him. He'd suffered for so many years and he was getting worse all the time.'

'Losing brother very sad. Must miss brother.'

'Yes, I do,' she said slowly. 'But if I'm truly honest, although I was obviously really upset when he died, he'd been living somewhere else for so long – since he was eleven years old – that he hadn't been part of my life for years, so I don't miss him as much as I might have done. And things at home became easier after he died. A weight seemed to have been lifted from everyone. So yes, it was sad that James died, but in a way it was also a relief. You're the first person

I've ever told that to.' She smiled. 'It must be because you're special to me, just like you say I am to you.'

He raised her hand to his lips, kissed it, then enclosed it in both of his hands. 'If I not think about you as I do, it be easy to laugh, to hold your hand, to think only about today, to do what we want. But you are more to me, and this would not be right.'

He squeezed her hand, then dropped it, and they continued making their way past tiny strips of pastureland where yaks and *dzo* were grazing, past the *manis* and *chortens* dotted across the plain, past the fields outside the village where the stalks of ripening barley were growing tall in the heat of the summer days, their minds empty of everything except their awareness of the other.

The rays of the dying sun were casting long shadows across the dusty ground by the time that they reached the post house. As they went down the path, they saw that the front door was open and Wangyal was in the doorway, beaming in welcome. He stood aside to let them enter, closed the door behind them and hovered just inside the room.

The *amchi* was already in the house, and they saw that he was putting his herbs and small pots back into his bag. Patricia went quickly over to her father and looked at his foot.

'What did the *amchi* say, Father? I can see that he's put some more of that mixture on your foot, but not as much as before.'

'I think we'll have to wait for Kalden to tell us what the *amchi* thinks,' the Major replied. 'I gathered that he's satisfied with my progress, but there were one or two things that I didn't quite pick up.'

After a short conversation with the *amchi*, Kalden smiled at the Major and Patricia.

'*Amchi* say foot much better, Major-*le*. The … ' He held out both his hands to indicate size, gradually narrowing the space between his palms, and glanced at Patricia for help.

'The swelling,' she said. 'The swelling's gone down?'

'Yes, that is so, Patricia-*le*. The swelling's gone down. Must now move foot every day, Major-*le*, and soon you be able stand on foot. If foot hurt when you stand, then is not ready to be standing on, and must wait a day before you try to stand on foot again.'

'Thank you, Kalden. I must say, I'm greatly impressed by your *amchi*. He's achieved much in a very short amount of time. I shall take his advice and give myself a programme of exercises. Then in a couple of days, I shall try to stand on my foot. I'm sure that I'll soon be able to walk short distances. I'm very much looking forward to resuming my exploration of the area, which I suspect will happen within the week.'

'That's wonderful, Father,' Patricia said, and she forced a smile to her lips. 'We can't wait for you to be fit enough to join us again.'

Her eyes strayed to Kalden's face and she saw the disappointment she felt mirrored in his eyes. A lump came to her throat and she swiftly bent over the table and made a fuss of straightening the blanket that was folded beneath her father's foot. Kalden turned away to speak to Wangyal.

Wangyal would shortly be bringing them their meal, he told them when he'd finished talking to Wangyal, and he asked if there was anything the Major wanted to discuss with Wangyal while they were all together. If not, both he and Wangyal would go back to their houses. Since the Major hadn't any instructions to give and couldn't think of anything he wanted to know, Kalden said goodnight to them both and started to follow Wangyal out of the house.

'What time I come tomorrow, Patricia-*le*?' he asked, pausing in the doorway.

'You and I will be occupied in the morning, Patricia,' the Major called after her as she went towards Kalden. 'I'd like you to help me establish an exercise routine for my foot, if it's no trouble. I'd be grateful if you confined tomorrow's walk to the afternoon.'

'Of course I will.' She looked up at Kalden, who nodded his understanding. 'Where shall we go then?' she asked him. 'We won't have very long.'

'I think of somewhere,' he said, and he gave her a quick smile, turned and walked away.

Her eyes followed him until he was lost from sight. Her only thought was that she couldn't wait for the following afternoon to arrive.

Chapter Thirteen

There was only about one area left to explore near the village, Kalden said when he arrived at the post house early the following afternoon, and he suggested that they go there as it would be perfect for their limited amount of time that day.

He told her that it was the small village that lay downstream, where the villagers drank the water from one of the streams that flowed past the fields outside Kalden's village. The children from both villages played together. Sometimes they married each other, he added.

They'd go to the village, have a look round and then pick up a trail which would lead them in a wide arc around the back of his village. That way, they'd return home from a different direction. The walk wasn't difficult and it wouldn't take too long.

Not minding where they went, so long as they went there together, Patricia fell in with his suggestion, and they set off as soon as Wangyal had arrived to settle her father down for his afternoon rest.

She wasn't surprised to see that the neighbouring village was very similar to Kalden's village and that the people were equally warm and friendly. But unlike Kalden's village, they weren't used to her appearance, and everywhere they went children screamed with delight and chased around her, and the older villagers stopped what they were doing, beamed and shouted '*Ju-le*', their eyes widening with astonishment as they looked at her jeans and unadorned neck and wrists.

Kalden repeatedly explained to them that Patricia-*le* and her father were staying in his village, getting to know the Ladakhi way of life and exploring the area, and she would then say a few words of greeting in Ladakhi, which clearly pleased them. But finally, he threw her a look of desperation and suggested that they give up any idea of seeing the rest of the village and get out as quickly as possible.

Laughing, she agreed, and they went as fast as they could to a small opening in the wall at the back of the village. As they slipped through the gap, a brightly coloured tree just outside the wall caught her eye, and she stopped in front of it. Clusters of dried apricots had been hung from the branches and loaves had been spread out on the ground in front of it. She looked questioningly at Kalden.

It wasn't unusual to find such a tree outside a village, he said, coming over to her. It was a tree for the good demon which lived near the village. The villagers put offerings by the tree to keep the demon happy: a happy demon was good for the village.

He took one look at her face, laughed, dropped his rucksack on the ground and took out a small canvas bag. Scooping a handful of dried apricots from the bag, he gave a few to her, and went over and placed the rest at the foot of the tree.

'And now we, too, be looked after by good demon,' he said with a grin as he put the empty bag back into his rucksack. Straightening up, he pointed towards a small mountain in the distance, some way beyond the apricot trees that were growing in the fields outside the village. 'We go there now. But we turn before we get to mountain and go across plateau to our village.'

'It doesn't look very far away,' she said, putting a dried apricot into her mouth. 'It shouldn't take us long to get there.'

An hour after they'd left the neighbouring village it seemed to Patricia that they were still some way from the mountain.

'I can't believe how far away the mountain's turned out to be,' she said, stopping to draw a breath. 'It's a lovely walk with all the birds singing and the sun, but we don't seem to be getting any closer to the mountain.' She shaded her eyes with her hand and gazed at the dark shape rising up against the clear blue sky. 'I'm glad we're not going that far.'

'Air in Ladakh is very clear. Mountains seem very near, but are not. If you tired, we can make shorter walk. Not go closer to mountain, but go back to village now.'

'Oh, no,' she said quickly. 'I'm fine, really I am. I don't want to go back a minute sooner than we have to. No, let's do what we were going to do.'

'We hold hands, then,' he said, and he held out his hand to her. 'I help you.'

'If you're sure?' she asked, hesitantly.

'I very sure,' he replied, taking her hand firmly in his. 'I very sure,' he repeated, and they started to walk forward, their hands entwined.

When they reached the point where the stony track turned away from the mountain, they struck out across the shimmering plateau and made their way past fields full of wild irises and a profusion of herbs, the scent of which enveloped them. Far away to their right, against a backdrop of hazy pink and mauve mountains, there was a faint outline of what Patricia thought must be a wall, the only sign of human life in the world of nature.

'I do love it here, Kalden.' She sighed. She felt him tighten his fingers around her hand, and a wave of happiness spread through her as they walked along.

Suddenly she realised with a jolt that Kalden's body had tensed and that he'd started to stare up at the sky every few minutes. She turned to him, but before she could ask what was wrong, he stopped walking, dropped her hand and looked up. Turning around on the spot, he studied the sky in every direction. Then he took her hand again, and began to walk more quickly, his face anxious.

'What's the matter, Kalden? You look worried. What is it?'

'Birds no longer singing,' he said shortly.

'It's getting colder; perhaps that's why.'

'That not why,' he said, and he looked up at the sky again. She followed his gaze and saw that the sky was changing at a frightening speed: the blue had almost vanished, and the sky, now sombre and overcast, was fast breaking up into small low clouds that were streaked with a steely grey.

'Sometimes get very strong winds in Ladakh,' Kalden said, a note of urgency in his voice. 'Winds come suddenly. I think strong wind come. Must find shelter. Missionary house near here. We go there. We go there fast.' As he spoke, a powerful gust of wind swept around them, throwing a column of swirling dust into the air. Patricia coughed.

He put his arm around her shoulders and together they ran towards the distant wall, racing against a wind that was becoming stronger and stronger with every passing moment, fighting hard to make headway across the moving ground, not daring to stop and catch their breath until they reached the wall which encircled the abandoned house.

They sank to the ground behind the crumbling wall, crouching low. Kalden leaned across Patricia, trying to shelter her with his body. Covering their heads with one of their hands as clouds of sand and stones spun in the air above them, with the other hand they clung tightly to the top of the wall, desperately trying to stop themselves from being blown away.

The fierce winds were gathering force, roaring from every direction, prising apart the loose stones of the wall and hurling them into the air. The lump of stone that Patricia was clinging to came away in her hand and she gasped with fright.

Kalden leaned close to her to make himself heard above the booming of the wind. 'Not stay here. We go to house,' he shouted. 'We be safe in house.'

With both his arms tightly holding her, he helped her struggle to her feet. Their heads down, they tried to run along the path between the overgrown turnip fields, battling with their every step against the ferocity of the wind. They reached the front door, and he threw himself against it with his shoulder. It swung open. He pulled Patricia into the house and slammed the door behind them.

Panting heavily, they stood in the small downstairs room and looked around them, their eyes stinging from the grit and the wind.

'I sorry, Patricia,' he said, when he'd caught his breath. 'I should see wind coming sooner.'

'It wasn't your fault, Kalden. You weren't to know how quickly everything would change. But it was certainly scary. That good demon must have been fast asleep.'

'Sadly, can't blame good demon. Was my fault. I should have known – I live here all my life. Was not looking at sky, was looking at Patricia.'

'Well, don't look at me now,' she said with a laugh, suddenly self-conscious. 'My hair's a real mess and I've probably got sand and dust all over my face. I must look a fright.' She raised her hand to smooth down her hair.

'You look beautiful,' he said quietly. He caught her arm mid-air and placed it gently by her side. 'Very beautiful.' Raising his hand, he ran his fingers slowly through her hair, then he let his arm fall to his side.

She shivered.

'You are cold,' he said quickly. 'Strong wind go soon and air be warm again. Is more warm upstairs and we have blankets. We go upstairs till wind stops. Is good?'

She nodded, and followed him up the wooden stairs to

the first floor. He went into the first room he came to. She lingered in the doorway, and watched as he took two folded blankets from a shelf.

'This be Peter's room,' he told her, unfolding one of the blankets while he held the other tucked under his arm. 'Many harvests go since we make these, Peter and me. Peter is in bad mood when we make blankets – he not like doing this. Come, Patricia, you soon be warm.' He spread the blanket over the floor, and indicated that she should sit on it.

She hesitated, still in the doorway. 'You come, Patricia,' he said gently. 'If we be close together under blanket, you be warm.' He gestured to the blanket again, and she went over to it. Her every sense heightened by nervousness, she sat down.

He dropped the second blanket on to the corner of the first, and disappeared down the stairs. A few minutes later he returned with a short, lighted candle, its flame flickering ominously with his every movement. He put the candle on the shelf, picked up the second blanket and came and sat next to her. Unfolding the blanket, he tucked it around them both, cocooning them in a sudden rush of heat. She felt his leg touch hers, and she shivered again.

'You cold, Patricia?' he asked in surprise.

'No, I'm not,' she said quickly, glancing at him. Their eyes met. Both immediately turned away. He edged slightly away from her.

'When wind stops, we go,' he said. '*Nima* will make us warm again when we go out of house.'

'*Nima*?'

'The sun. *Nima* means the sun. Without *nima*, there is no warmth, no life. There be more sun today. Wind not stay long.'

'I hope you're right,' she said, hugging her knees to her chest under the blanket, acutely aware of him next to her.

Afraid to look at him lest her eyes revealed how much she longed to be sitting still closer to him, to feel his body against hers, she looked around at the bare walls and the almost empty shelves, and she forced herself to try to imagine what it must have been like for Peter to live in a totally different culture for most of his life and then go back to England.

Her knee drifted sideways and touched Kalden's leg.

'Do you know what Peter's doing now?' she asked, quickly pulling her knee back up and tightening her arms around her legs.

'I not know. Have not had letter for much time. Peter very busy and letters take long time to come in Ladakh. But Peter will be happy. He go to school that help him with his lessons, and then he go to university. Peter be able to choose what he do.' His voice was filled with yearning.

'But we can all choose what we do, within limits, can't we?'

'Not in Ladakh, not if you fourth son.'

She twisted round to face him. 'This time, you've got to tell me what you mean, Kalden. Why can't you choose what you do? Please tell me.' She put her hand lightly against his cheek and turned his face to look into hers. 'I can't bear to see you unhappy like this. Why does it matter that you're the fourth son?'

'Because I not able to marry, Patricia,' he said, and he gently moved her hand away from his face.

'Why can't you get married? Maybe not to Deki, but to someone else?'

'Land go to first three sons. Not enough land for fourth son. Without land, man cannot marry. So I not marry.'

'What will you do then, stay in the house with your brothers and Deki?'

'I go into monastery. I be monk.'

'A monk!' Her hand flew to her mouth. 'When?'

'After the harvest, when you go England. If you and Major-*le* not come to Ladakh, I be in monastery now. But I not want to think of that today.' He paused. 'Listen!'

She looked up at the ceiling. 'What is it? I can't hear anything.'

'And I not hear anything. I not hear wind. I go and look.' He slipped from beneath the blanket, tucked it back tightly around her, and went swiftly down the stairs.

A dull pain ached deep within her, and she brought her knees back close to her chest.

Almost immediately, he reappeared at the top of the stairs. 'Wind is gone and sun is come. We go home now,' he said briskly. He leaned over and offered her his hand.

'But suppose you fell in love with someone?' she asked, her heart beating fast. She ignored the outstretched hand, and pulled the blanket right up to her chin.

'I once had friend. She marry man with land.'

'I'm so sorry, Kalden.'

'Not be sorry. I try feel deeply for her, but I not feel enough deeply.'

As he leaned forward and started to prise the blanket from her fingers, he glanced at her face and saw that her eyes were full of unshed tears. He straightened up and looked down at her. 'You not be sad for me, Patricia. From time I born, I know I be monk one day. I accept this.'

'I'm not just sad for you,' she said, and she pushed the blanket away from her and stood up. 'I'm also sad for the person you could have loved and who could have loved you.'

He stared at her, his forehead slowly creasing. 'I not want to understand what you say,' he said flatly. 'Must not understand.' He turned away.

'But you do understand, don't you?' She caught hold of his arm. 'I've been waiting for you for all my life, Kalden, and I didn't even know it till the moment I met you. And I know it was the same for you. You feel the same as I feel. You do, don't you?'

He pulled his arm away from her, his eyes ablaze. 'You know I do. But I must not. We must not talk like this. Is not good. I not free man. I never be free man.'

'Even if you've got to be a monk one day, you're not a monk now. Surely you're entitled to some happiness, if you want it.'

'You think I don't want, Patricia? I do.' He grasped her hands. 'From the day you come to Ladakh, I see only you. I look at the sky and I see you. I look at the fields and the flowers and I see you. I look at the mountains and valleys and you are there. I look at the water that brings us life and I see you. You are that life. You are everywhere for me. From moment I see you, you fill my heart. And I am scared at what I feel for you.' He buried his face in her hands

'And I feel the same way about you, Kalden,' she said quietly.

He dropped her hands and stepped back. 'But we can never be, not you and me. You are not a woman for a game, for fun. You are a woman for a man to have forever. I cannot be the man. I cannot ... but I want. I do want.'

She took a step closer to him. 'If *you* want and *I* want, then nothing else matters.' Her voice shook. 'There are worse things in life than getting hurt.'

'I not afraid of getting hurt. I hurt every day when I think of you leaving. But I not want to hurt you, so we must go now.'

Their eyes met, and locked. Standing in the centre of the room, neither moved.

The beat of their hearts loud in the silence of the afternoon, he took a step forward and cupped her face in his hands. Bending his head, he brushed his lips against hers. Then his hands slowly slid down the column of her neck, across her shoulders, down her arms, down to the tips of her fingers.

'Beautiful Patricia,' he said so softly that she could hardly hear him, and he pulled her close to him.

'Oh, Kalden,' she breathed, and she wound her arms around his back, and pressed against the lean muscle of his chest. His male scent of salt and sweat enveloped her, and she leaned up to kiss the hollow of his throat. She felt his body hard against hers. The dull ache became a heavy throb.

Her heart pounding, her hands flew to his shirt, her fingers fumbling with the buttons.

He put a hand on hers and stilled them.

Staring deep into her eyes, he finished unbuttoning his shirt and pulled it off, his muscles rippling beneath his smooth golden skin. She caught her breath. Raising her hand, she very slowly ran her fingers across his bare skin. Her lips parted, and she looked up into eyes that were staring down at her, dark with longing,

'Oh, Patricia, I do want,' he said, and he brought his face down to hers and kissed her full on the mouth.

They lay quietly for several minutes, their arms around each other, Kalden's face buried in her hair, Patricia's face lost in the hollow of his neck.

'We must get back to village,' he said at last. 'It soon be dark and Major-*le* be awake.'

'I suppose you're right.' She sighed and curled up closer to him.

He raised himself on his elbow, and kissed her lightly on the top of her head, on her forehead, on the tip of her nose, on her mouth.

'You're my golden man, Kalden,' she whispered, and she slid her hand to the back of his neck. 'I do love you.'

'Love.' He smiled into her face. 'Ladakhi people not have this word love, but I hear Henderson family talk of love and

I know what this means to you. And I know that I love you, too, Patricia.'

'You don't have to say that.'

'But it is the truth. Until the harvest ends, we can love, and I take that love with me for rest of my life. But we must go now.' He gave her a rueful smile and started to get up. Reluctantly, she followed him.

Standing together on the blanket, they faced each other, their bare skin gleaming in the amber light of the candle, the tips of their fingers touching.

'I love you, Patricia,' he said. 'I will always love you.'

They hurriedly threw on their clothes, ran out of the missionary house and made their way along the track towards the village, their feet crunching on the pebbles thrown across the path by the wind. Hand in hand, half walking, half running, they went as quickly as they could, their eyes drawn frequently to each other.

The light was fading by the time they got to the *chorten*. Seeing a group of boys coming towards them, laughing and chasing each other, their hands fell to their sides. Every so often one of the boys stopped where he was, bent over to the ground, picked something up and put it into a bag. When they got closer, she saw that they were collecting animal dung.

They'd make the dung into pats, Kalden told her, and they'd put the pats on the village wall the next morning to dry in the sun. When dry, they'd be added to the store of dried dung to be used for cooking and heating during the winter.

'But I not want to think of winter,' he said, and he took her hand again and didn't release it until they reached the outskirts of the village.

'We go for walk tomorrow?' he asked as he followed her down the path to the post house.

'I do hope so,' she said quickly. 'For the whole day, if possible. I just hope Father isn't furious about how late we are.' She took a deep breath and opened the door.

The Major was sitting in the centre of the room, his chair facing the front door, and his foot resting on the low table. A strong stick was propped up against his chair.

'You've moved your chair round, Father!' she exclaimed, coming into the room. 'And you're wearing a sandal on your foot!' Her heart sank. 'You had cloths wrapped around it when we left.'

'Which was a long time ago, a very long time ago. After you'd left, I sat outside for some time, but the wind got too much for me and I had to come in. I hadn't realised that I was going to be left alone for quite so long. I'd rather assumed that you would be back for tea, or that Wangyal would look in on me, but it seems that I was wrong on both counts.'

'I'm really sorry, Father. But as you said, the weather suddenly changed. One minute there was sun, the next there was a horrendous hurricane. It was terrifying. We were out on the exposed plateau, completely unprotected. We had to find shelter as quickly as possible and stay there until the wind had died down – no one could have walked in it, it just wasn't safe.'

'Yes, yes,' he said irritably.

Kalden stepped forward. 'Wind also in Alchi. I go and see if Wangyal back from Alchi, Major-*le*. If he back, he bring you tea now. If he not here, I bring tea.'

'Thank you, Kalden. You may then go back to your house. Tomorrow you and Patricia will be taking your last walk alone. The sprain was less serious than it first seemed, and the *amchi*'s medicine was excellent. I'm happy to tell you that my foot is now much better.'

'That's excellent news, Father!' She forced herself to look happier than she felt.

'Indeed, it is. Tomorrow I shall walk a little in the village, building upon the exercise that I've taken today, and after that I shall be fit for action once again. Perhaps you would plan a short walk for us all for the day after tomorrow, Kalden, bearing in mind that I should not attempt too much too quickly.'

'That very good news, Major-*le*. I go now to Wangyal.' He glanced at Patricia. 'Patricia-*le*, I come to you tomorrow after breakfast. We go to the *gompa* at Rizong that you want to see. I ask Wangyal to give us food for lunch.'

'Thank you, Kalden. That sounds ideal,' she said.

With a massive effort, she turned back to her father, forcing herself not to watch Kalden until he'd disappeared from sight. She put a bright smile on her face. 'That's excellent news about your foot. I'm very much looking forward to us all being together again.'

'I, too, Patricia,' he said, looking gratified. 'And I'm pleased to note that Kalden has been showing you some of Ladakh's culture. You'll enjoy seeing the painted blocks at the monastery tomorrow which depict the main events in the life of Buddha.' He sighed deeply. 'I still recall the effect they had on me when I saw them in 1945.'

'I know. I remember you writing about them in your book – that's why I told Kalden that I'd like to see them.'

'Now, I suggest that while we wait for our tea, we look at the map and make a list of the places of interest that we want to see before our visit ends. Obviously, you've already visited some of the places on our original list, but there will still be plenty left for us to see together.' He leaned forward and picked up the folded map from the table in front of him. 'Pull up a chair and help me to open the map.'

As she dragged a chair over to her father, she surreptitiously glanced at her watch and tried to work out how many hours it would be before she saw Kalden again.

Chapter Fourteen

August

Patricia sat on the wooden chair in the downstairs room, her rucksack at her feet. She could hear the sound of her father moving around in the room above her as he packed for the overnight trip to the high pasture. She sighed inwardly. He'd soon be down, probably at about the same time as Kalden arrived, and then they'd set off. And as with every other day since her father had started coming out with them again, she and Kalden wouldn't have any time by themselves.

Several times in the first few days after her father had starting joining them on their trips again, she'd come very close to telling him how she and Kalden felt about each other, but she'd always stopped short at the last minute. Her every instinct, born out of years of living with her father and getting to know the way in which he thought, made her suspect that he might be horrified at the idea of a relationship between his daughter and someone who came from a world so different from theirs.

However, she'd finally decided that she needed to take the first step towards introducing him to the idea of her being in love with Kalden, and one evening she'd hesitantly suggested that they ask Kalden to share their meal the following evening.

'He's a pony-man,' he'd told Patricia sharply. 'He's a pleasant man and a useful companion on our trips in that he's well-versed in the flora and fauna of the area, but he's essentially an uneducated man. One doesn't invite people like that to the dinner table.'

She'd swiftly turned away to stop her eyes from revealing the anger she felt, and the sudden fear.

Any lingering thoughts she'd entertained about telling her father that she and Kalden were in love had disappeared in that moment, and she'd settled for making the most of the few moments together that she and Kalden could snatch. Being able to walk along next to him, to think about him and to know that he was thinking about her, was better than nothing – it made her feel alive, made her feel loved. It wasn't nearly enough, but it was all that they could safely have.

The thud of something falling on the upstairs floor cut into her thoughts. It was followed by an exclamation of annoyance. Her father must be making heavy weather of packing his things, even though this was the second overnight trip that they'd undertaken since his foot had been better, and their first one had been much more ambitious than this.

Their first overnight trip had lasted for three days.

'My foot is clearly back to normal,' the Major had announced one evening at the end of a visit to Alchi. He'd held out his leg and flexed his foot. 'We've been limiting ourselves to day trips for long enough now, and I feel that I'm ready for the challenge of going further afield.'

'This is good, Major-*le*. You want me plan a trip that takes two days?'

'I think we can be more ambitious than that, don't you? There are three places that I'd like to visit: the derelict fort at Basgo, the large monastery at Likir – I'm particularly interested in seeing the collection of arms and armour there – and the painted caves at Saspol. Bad weather prevented me from visiting the caves in '45, and I'd like to redress this. I rather suspect that we're looking at something a little longer than a two-day trip.'

Kalden had nodded. 'That is so, Major-*le*.'

Two days later, they'd set out on a three-day trek. First they'd skirted the edge of the high ground to the east of

Alchi, then they'd crossed the plateau and headed down into the valley of the Indus.

'I'll always hate these bridges,' Patricia said, eyeing the high suspension bridge that hung above the Indus. 'I wish there was another way round, but I know there isn't.'

'You'll be fine, Patricia,' the Major said, and he rode up to the bridge, and dismounted, waiting for Kalden.

Kalden smiled reassuringly at her. 'I be near you, Patricia. You be safe. You always be safe when I with you.'

Once he'd reached the other bank with the ponies, Kalden steadied the rope handrails for the Major to cross, and then indicated that Patricia should start to walk over the bridge. She put a hand on each of the ropes, stepped on to the wooden base and made her way steadily to the opposite bank, her eyes straight ahead of her.

The Major nodded with satisfaction when she reached him. 'Well done, Patricia.'

They'd got back on their ponies and picked up the trail to Basgo.

Their journey had taken them along a path that was roughly parallel with the Indus. At one point, they'd passed a group of monks in red robes coming towards them and Patricia's eyes had met Kalden's. Both had swiftly turned back to the sandy landscape around them.

They'd camped overnight on gound at the foot of the village of Basgo, which towered on a cliff above them, the ruins of its ancient citadel dominating the skyline, and the following morning they'd spent a couple of hours wandering among the temples and the broken walls of the fort and towers. They'd then set off for Likir.

'Is the monastery actually in the village itself?' Patricia had asked Kalden as they rode a little way behind her father over the rocky ground that was taking them away from Basgo.

'No, monastery is outside village. We go through village and take path to monastery. Is not very far. There is much to see in monastery. Many weapons and big clay statues of Buddha. I think everything be very interesting for Major-*le*.' Patricia glanced at him, and they grinned at each other. Their spirits lifting, they'd urged their ponies forward and caught up with the Major.

An hour after they'd passed through Likir, they reached the monastery, a cluster of white buildings dominated by a large statue of Buddha. They got down from their ponies, and the Major took a few steps forward and stood staring up at the statue. Patricia threw a hopeful glance at Kalden.

Giving her a quick smile, he went up to the Major. 'Patricia-*le* looks very tired Major-*le*. Perhaps should have short rest. I can stay with her.'

'That's not a bad idea, Father,' Patricia said, going over to them. 'I do feel quite tired and I wouldn't want to hold you up – there's a lot for you to see here.'

'By all means, have a rest if you wish,' the Major said. 'But I shall take Kalden with me. I may need help with some translation.'

She hadn't needed to look at Kalden's face to know that he felt as disappointed as she did.

'I'll come with you, and try to keep up,' she'd said.

Their final overnight stop had been at Saspol. The Major had seemed quite tired on the journey to Saspol, and they'd frequently stopped to rest. Several times he'd appeared to be asleep, and Patricia had moved to Kalden's side, or he had moved to hers, but on each occasion the Major had suddenly sprung into life and asked for an explanation of something that had caught his eye or remarked upon something that had just occurred to him.

As soon as they'd reached the painted caves, their final destination, the Major had placed himself between Patricia and Kalden. All they'd been able to do was look helplessly at each other as they'd slowly progressed through the thirteenth century rock-cut temples, listening to the Major talk at length about the brightly coloured miniatures of the Buddhist deities depicted on the walls.

When they'd finished looking at the paintings, and had spent several minutes staring at the beautiful view of the Indus Valley that opened out from the caves, they'd trekked back to the post house, where the Major had declared himself completely satisfied with every aspect of the journey.

The following day, still excited by the success of the trip, he'd asked Kalden if it would be possible for them to visit the high pasture used by his family. Kalden had said that it would, and they'd decided to give themselves a few days' rest, and then to go up into the mountains, and stay the night there.

Later that same morning, when Patricia was talking to Kalden in front of the post house while they were waiting for the Major to join them on a short stroll through the village, Kalden had quietly told her that he thought that the Major suspected there might be something between them. He'd started to notice that whenever he and Patricia began a conversation, the Major would interrupt them and draw him to one side. It was happening so often that he was beginning to think that it couldn't be a coincidence.

'You're mistaken,' Patricia had assured him. 'Father would never be able to keep silent about such a thing. If he thought there was anything going on, he would say so. And he wouldn't have suggested another overnight trip.'

'I hope you right, Patricia.'

'I am. If he's behaving as you say he is, it'll be because he's the sort of man who expects to be the centre of attention at all times. This means that he's the one who's always got to be talking or be the person spoken to. I bet that even when he's asleep, his antennae quiver if anyone else is given attention,' she'd added with a laugh.

With the aid of her hands and arms, she'd managed to explain the meaning of antennae, and Kalden had laughed with her, but his eyes had been anxious as he'd glanced towards the post house.

Since that day, she'd watched her father and seen for herself that he did, indeed, draw Kalden aside if she was talking to him, and she'd begun to wonder if Kalden could have been right after all.

If her father did suspect something, but hadn't warned her about it, it could be a sign that he was prepared to look kindly upon her relationship with Kalden, and she'd been wondering again whether to tell him that she loved Kalden. In the end, she'd decided to wait until she was more certain about how he'd react. In the meantime, they must avoid doing anything to make him suspicious, if he were not already so.

The sounds coming from upstairs told her that her father had finished putting the things he'd need into his rucksack. He'd now be pulling on the shoes that he'd cleaned before going to bed, and then he'd come on down and tell them all what to do. She leaned forward, folded the flap over her rucksack, pulled the cord tightly and sat back in her chair.

Domineering, that's what her father was. She'd never before seen it quite as clearly as she could see it now.

From as far back as she could remember, she'd blamed his strictness and distance from her on his misery about James. She'd understood his grief. He was her father, and she loved him and felt for him. But deep down she'd always hoped that one day he'd see her for the good daughter she strove to be.

First as a child, and then in her teenage years, she'd been the best daughter she could, and she was certain that he'd finally come to appreciate her and that theirs was a strong relationship. But was it strong enough to survive the knowledge that she had fallen in love with a man he wouldn't invite to the dinner table? Of that she wasn't sure.

In the clear light of day, and with a clarity of vision given her by her love for Kalden, she could see now that the passage of years filled with sadness and frustration – sadness about James and a situation he was powerless to change, and frustration that he was trapped in a peacetime job that he hated – had turned her father into a rather selfish, self-centred man, a man who was rigid and unbending to those around him, a man who thought he always knew best.

But he was still her father and she loved him, and she didn't like doing something behind his back that might one day add to the grief that the past had already heaped upon him. And upon her mother.

She glanced around the room, and her eyes came to rest on a piece of blank paper lying on the table in front of her. She'd write to her mother as soon as they returned from the trip to the high pasture. It was quite a long time since she'd written; much too long, in fact. They'd be back early the following afternoon. She'd go first to visit Deki's sister and her baby, and then she'd come back and write to her mother.

Deki's sister, who lived on the other side of the village in the shadow of the monastery, had just had a baby. Patricia had met her once or twice when she and Kalden had stopped at his house for a drink at a time when Deki's sister had been visiting the family, and although they'd never done anything more than smile at each other, she thought she seemed very pleasant; and she liked what she'd seen of Deki, too.

The previous afternoon, when Kalden had finished telling them about the arrangements for the trip, he'd mentioned that the *onpo* – the astrologer, he'd translated – had said that people could now start visiting Deki's sister as her first seven days of being alone with the baby since its birth had passed, and all the signs were favourable. He was going to go and see the baby as soon as they'd returned from the *phu* – the mountain pasture – and he wondered if Major-*le* and Patricia-*le* would like to go with him. His family would be there, too, he'd added.

The Major had politely declined, saying that he was likely to be quite exhausted by the time that they returned, but he'd told Patricia that she might accompany Kalden, if she wished. He would be interested in learning about the Ladakhi customs at the time of a birth. When she came back, she would be able to relate everything she'd seen in case there was something he could use in his book.

Soon after that, Kalden had left, telling them that he was going to arrange for gifts of butter and flour, and for the dough figurines that he and Patricia would take with them when they went to visit Deki's sister. The Major had promptly picked up his pad and jotted that down.

Patricia had hardly been able to sleep that night, she was so excited about the forthcoming trip. It would be the first time she'd gone with Kalden to one of his family celebrations, and even though they weren't going there as a couple, it meant something special that they'd be going there side by side as friends.

'I'm sorry to have kept you waiting, Patricia,' the Major said, coming down the stairs. 'My organisational skills seem to have deserted me this morning.'

'Don't worry, Father, Kalden's not here yet.' There was a knock on the door. 'I take that back,' she said with a laugh, and she jumped up. 'That'll be him.'

'It's very good of your brothers to allow us to stay with them, Kalden,' the Major said as they headed across the plateau to the ravine. 'Before we left England, I told Patricia how much I hoped to go to the *phu*. We're keen to see the sorts of things that the Ladakhi do in the summer, and also to have the time to enjoy the view from such an altitude.'

'Brothers happy you come, Major-*le*. Mother also happy. She there with brothers.'

'I didn't realise that we were to have the pleasure of meeting your mother, too. Delightful.'

Kalden turned to Patricia. 'Rucksack not too heavy, Patricia-*le*?'

'It's heavy, but not too heavy, thank you. And that's because you're carrying almost all of the supplies for the three of us, as well as everything else you're carrying.'

'Is necessary bring more barley flour, salt, tea and dried apricots for brothers.'

'It would be better not to talk, Patricia. We need to conserve our energy for the climb ahead of us. As I'm sure Kalden does, too.'

They took the wide path that led down to the narrow wooden bridge at the foot of the valley and crossed to the other side of the river without difficulty, then they began to climb up the mountain track. At the entrance to the first mountain pass they reached, they paused to look at a cairn festooned with prayer flags. Kalden suggested that they take a short rest, and they did. Then they continued their journey and didn't stop again until they reached their destination.

The top of the track opened out on to a wide expanse of undulating pastureland. Panting from their exertion, the Major and Patricia took a few steps across the grass, dropped their bags and stared around them, spellbound, at the sprawling vista of crags and towering peaks that stood proud against the blue sky, their snow-covered tips glittering in the bright light of the afternoon sun.

Patricia turned to look back down the path they'd walked

up. 'Look at the view of the ravine from up here. Mother would have loved it.'

'Indeed, it *is* very lovely, Patricia,' the Major said, following the direction of her gaze. He paused a moment. 'I sometimes feel that I should have considered bringing your mother with us. However, as I've said before … the difficulty … the rigours of the journey being as they are … We'll make sure that we include a detailed description of these two days when next we write. Better still, we shall take a photograph that we can frame for the wall and give to your mother on our return. I think she would like that.'

'I'm sure she would, Father. It's a lovely idea. And I shall write to her tomorrow, as soon as I've been to see Deki's sister.'

The Major nodded. 'We will both do so.'

'You come, please,' they heard Kalden call.

Turning, they saw that he was standing in front of a stone hut set back on the pastureland, handing the extra bags that he'd brought with him to one of his brothers. They picked up their rucksacks and went over to join him.

'The chairs are a most welcome sight, Patricia,' the Major remarked as they reached the hut and saw the four wooden chairs that had been set out in front of the hut. They hovered by the chairs. Kalden indicated that they should sit, and they sat down next to each other. He then went and sat opposite them, put his bag on his lap, took out the lunch that Wangyal had made for them and handed them each a bowl.

'Anil and Rinchen are with animals. Tenzin go in house to bring us salty butter tea,' he told them. 'Tomorrow Tenzin come back to village with us. Has things must do in village.'

Just as they were finishing their lunch, Tenzin came out of the hut carrying three small pots.

'*Ju-le*,' he said with a smile, and handed them each a pot of tea. He returned to the hut, and reappeared a few minutes later with another pot of tea. He went over to the fourth chair, moved it slightly away from the other three, and sat down.

Patricia took a sip of her drink. 'That feels amazingly good!' she exclaimed as the buttery liquid slid across her parched lips, coating them with grease. 'My lips were about to crack, they were so dry, but this has really made them feel better.' The Major nodded, trying to stifle a yawn. 'You must be tired, Father,' she said quickly. 'It's been one hill after another, which is exhausting. Why don't you have a short sleep so that you can enjoy the rest of the day?'

'I must confess, I do feel a trifle weary.'

'You could rest in hut, Major-*le*,' Kalden suggested.

'Thank you, Kalden. You know, I think I might just do that, if you're sure that I won't be inconveniencing anyone. If I'm going to help with herding the animals later, which I hope your brothers will permit me to do, I'd like to feel somewhat fresher than I do at the moment.'

Kalden rose to his feet. 'I take you into house, Major-*le*.' The Major stood up, and together they went to the hut. As they disappeared through the doorway, Patricia heard Kalden promise to ensure that her father was awake well before it was time to put the sheep and goats into the pens, away from the reach of the wolves.

When the Major was settled, Kalden came back out and went over towards the empty chair next to Patricia. He started to sit down, glanced at Tenzin, stopped where he was and straightened up. For a moment, the two brothers stared at each other, neither saying a word.

Then Tenzin said something in Ladahki and Kalden replied. After a short exchange of words with Tenzin, Kalden went and sat opposite Patricia. A few minutes later, Tenzin got up, made a brief comment to Kalden, and went off to join Anil and Rinchen, who could be glimpsed in the distance among the *dzo*.

'What did Tenzin say to you?' Patricia asked Kalden.

He shrugged. 'He say is better I not sit next to you. And he ask why I always wear trousers when I with you, not Ladakhi robes. I tell him it is easy in trousers and I like them. Next he ask what we are going to do now, and if we want to go with him and Anil.'

'What did you tell him?'

'That we are going to watch *ama* – my mother – make cheese. But I not say how long we watch *ama*,' he added, and they smiled slowly at each other. 'So come, Patricia. We go see cheese.'

They went round to the back of the stone hut, and Patricia saw that there were a couple of smaller stone huts across a stretch of pasture. This was where his mother made cheese, Kalden told her, leading the way over the grass to the first of the huts. They went inside just as his mother was taking a cheese out of its mould. She looked up, smiled at them, then put the cheese on a block and started to press down on it, pushing the liquid out.

From time to time, she paused and glanced up at Patricia. Nodding slightly, she'd turn her gaze to Kalden, look at him long and hard, and then return to the cheese, pressing it more forcibly each time.

'Although *ama-le* and *aba-le* are now in small house,' Kalden said while they watched his mother working, 'they still part of family. They help in fields, they come to mountains in summer, making cheese and butter and helping with animals, and they help with grandchildren, too. They still very busy, very important people in the family.'

'They're really lucky, always being at the heart of their family. It doesn't work like that in England. Mind you,' she added with a smile, 'I don't know quite how keen I'd be to have my father involved in everything I did for the rest of my life.' They both laughed. His mother looked up sharply and spoke to Kalden. He replied, then nudged Patricia to start moving.

'*Ju-le*,' she said to Kalden's mother, who nodded at her again, unsmiling, and she went out of the small building, followed by Kalden, who immediately moved to her side.

As they walked away, Patricia could feel his mother's eyes on her back. She glanced over her shoulder and saw that his mother was standing in the doorway, watching them, her expression inscrutable.

'I don't think your mother likes me,' she said, turning back.

'Is not that. *Ama-le* worry about my heart.' He gave her a wry smile, and led them on to a narrow path that tapered down a steep slope. 'We not far from hut for herders,' he said, taking her hand. 'If you like, we go to hut.'

'I do like,' she said, and her steps quickened.

By the time that they reached the hut, both of them were running.

Later, with Patricia enclosed in Kalden's arms, their clothes in disarray on the floor, they lay with the front door wide open and watched the sun paint the sky a vivid red and gold as it sank behind a black silhouette of jagged peaks.

Slanting through the doorway, the rays of the dying sun found their bodies and dressed their naked skin in a mantle of gold. Kalden looked down at Patricia's face, his eyes darkening.

'Sun is beautiful,' he said, 'but you more beautiful.'

He leaned over and kissed first her upper lip, then her lower lip. Then he raised his hand, and lightly traced the arch of her brow with his thumb, the line of her cheekbones, the curve of her mouth, the slope of her shoulders. Bending his head, he buried his face in the shadowy hollow between her breasts.

'I wish I be with you forever,' he whispered into her soft skin.

'And I do, too,' she said. 'I really do.' She trailed her fingers down the length of his spine, wrapped her legs around his back, and pulled him to her.

'Kalden!' Tenzin's voice from afar broke into the calm of the late afternoon.

They flew apart. Then they heard Tenzin shout something else out. He was still some distance from them, but closer.

She scrambled up from the bed. 'What's he saying?' she asked, snatching up her jeans and T-shirt.

'He asking where we are.' Kalden stood up, picked up the clothes he'd thrown over a stone bench and started pulling his trousers on. 'But he know where we are.'

Patricia stood still and stared at him, panic in her eyes. 'If he knows, do you think he'll tell my father? I don't know what he'd do if he found out.'

He dropped the shirt he was holding, put a hand on each of her shoulders and stared deep into her eyes. 'I be with you, Patricia. You not worry. You be safe when I be with you,' he said quietly.

'And we've forgotten to wake him up! It's getting dark; they'll have rounded up the animals by now. He'll have to know some time, but not now, not like this.'

He gave her a wry smile. 'Tenzin able say Good Morning in English, but that be all. And he is my brother – he not try to tell Major-*le*. You not worry.' He bent down and kissed her.

She tried to smile, and they finished dressing, left the hut and went quickly to the narrow path.

When they reached the foot of the path, they saw Tenzin standing at the top, a dark figure, stark against the crimson sky. They glanced at each other. Kalden gave her a reassuring smile, then they turned back to the path and started to walk up. As they got close to Tenzin, they saw lines of worry etched into his face. His expression relaxed as they came nearer, but his relief was mingled with anxiety.

Just before they reached Tenzin, Kalden motioned to Patricia to stop walking, and he went up to his brother by himself. He stood still and waited for him to speak. Tenzin said something, and Patricia heard the concern in his voice. Kalden answered him evenly. She strained harder to make out what they were saying. Tenzin definitely repeated *ma-cho* several times, which she knew meant don't do, and also *lama*, monk. And she was pretty sure that she heard him say *gyalla mi-rak*, it's not good, on more than one occasion. But the rest she couldn't follow as they were speaking too quickly.

At one point, Tenzin put his hands on Kalden's shoulders and looked into his face with undisguised anxiety. And with love, Patricia saw. A lump came into her throat.

Kalden gently removed Tenzin's hands, and stepped back. After a further short exchange during which she heard Tenzin say *dzo* a couple of times, Tenzin threw her a look of displeasure, spun round on his heels and walked briskly in the direction of the hut.

She went quickly up to Kalden. 'What did he say?'

'Nothing important,' he said, and they started walking again.

'You can tell me honestly what he said. I know he doesn't like me.'

'He doesn't know you. If he know you, he like you. He is worried for me, worried I get hurt. He sees in our faces that we feel much for each other, and he reminds me I am to be a monk.'

'But you're not a monk yet so you're not doing anything wrong. Did you tell him that?'

'Tenzin is worried only that I get hurt. He is good man. He says we tell Major-*le* that we been looking for *dzo* that have gone away, and that we have to go far to find them. This afternoon, Major-*le* look for missing *dzo* with Anil and Rinchen, so he believe what we say.'

'I hope you're right, but we'll soon find out – there's Father now and he doesn't look happy.' She went a few steps ahead of Kalden. 'Father,' she called, hurrying up to the Major, who was standing rigidly in front of the main stone hut, watching them come towards him, his lips set in a thin line of anger.

'I'm sorry that we've been gone for so long,' she said as soon as she reached him, her words tumbling out on top of each other. 'It was the *dzo*. They'd wandered off and gone miles away. It took us ages to find them.'

The Major's face relaxed a little. 'I see we were on the same mission,' he said tersely. 'It would, however, have been preferable to have been on that mission together. There were one or two things that I would have liked to have known and I could have done with Kalden's help.'

'I'm sorry it took us so long,' she repeated. She saw his face relax a little more.

'Well at least you're back in time for dinner. If I understood everything correctly, we're going to eat in their small kitchen. It'll be somewhat cramped, I daresay, not to mention smoky because of the fire, but I'm sure we'll manage.'

'They're bound to make you as comfortable as possible, Father.'

'I think I can endure discomfort for one night, Patricia. What is a degree of discomfort when compared with the chance to live like the natives for an evening? No, whatever the inconvenience, tonight is going to be an invaluable part of our Ladakhi experience.' He patted his stomach. 'I must confess that I'm ready to eat. Healthy labour brings with it a good appetite. And it'll be interesting to have food prepared by someone other than Wangyal, or rather his wife.'

'Me, too. I'm looking forward to that. I'm so hungry, I could eat a *dzo*,' she said, with a laugh.

'You might be about to do just that,' the Major remarked dryly, and together they turned to go into the house, Patricia acutely aware that a few steps behind them, Kalden followed, his eyes on her back.

The next day, having stopped at the post house for only as long as it took to leave their rucksacks and see the Major comfortably settled for a late afternoon rest, Patricia and Kalden went directly to the far side of the village to visit Deki's sister and her new baby.

'He is so sweet!' she exclaimed, leaning over the bed to look at the baby, Chospel, who was half hidden in his mother's arms. '*Bumbarik*!' she said. She glanced back at Kalden, who was staring at the baby over her shoulder. 'I hope that was the right word for congratulations for when someone has had a baby. If I'm wrong, will you say the correct thing, and also tell her that Chospel's lovely?'

In a few sentences, Kalden conveyed Patricia's words to Deki's sister, who beamed up at her and changed her position slightly so that Patricia had a better view of Chospel's face. As Patricia gazed down at the tiny face, at the shiny dark hair that stood up in silken tufts, at the soft golden skin, at the eyes tightly closed against the flickering light of the wick lamp, at the minuscule fingers curling in the air, her eyes misted.

'He is lovely,' she whispered, 'really lovely.'

Deki's sister said something to Kalden. 'We are two of her first visitors,' he translated. 'She thinks we bring good luck as you are special visitor.' Then he pointed to the willow-plaited ceiling. 'That arrow we put up there also bring her good luck. It keeps bad demon away. She is very happy to have much chance for good luck.'

'Well, I hope the arrow's more successful at keeping the bad demon away than the dried apricots were at keeping the good demon happy,' she said, laughing.

'You don't think good demon was helping us that day in the strong wind?' he asked in amusement. 'I do, Patricia, and I feel that he still with us,' he added, staring into her face, his eyes full of love.

There was a sudden noise behind them. They jumped and turned round. Tenzin stood in the doorway, holding plates of flour, butter and tiny models of an ibex. His eyes were on Patricia.

'*Ju-le*,' she said hesitantly.

'*Ju-le*,' he muttered, and came into the room.

She stepped back to let him go over to the table beside the bed. He placed his gifts next to the presents that Kalden had brought, leaned over and stroked the baby's cheek. Then he spoke softly to Deki's sister, and she smiled gratefully up at him.

Straightening up, he looked from Kalden to Patricia and back again to Kalden. He said something to Kalden, who shook his head and gestured indecision with his hands. Throwing a quick smile to Deki's sister, Tenzin started towards the door. As he passed in front of Kalden, he stopped, put his hand on his brother's shoulder, looked long into his face, then he removed his hand and left the room.

'He want to know if I go with you to party,' Kalden said.

Patricia looked questioningly at him. A baby is born to the whole village, he explained, and when the baby is a month old, the whole village celebrates with a big party and presents.

'It is only possible if Major-*le* comes, too. If I go with you to party and Major-*le* not come, whole village will know what I feel for you. Major-*le* will know, too. But perhaps Major-*le* will want to come. Is part of Ladakhi way of life,' he added with a wry grin. 'But we go for short walk now. Major-*le* wake up soon.'

They said goodbye to Deki's sister, promising her that they'd try to come and see her and Chospel again before long, and then they went downstairs. As they left the house, a little boy ran past them into the house, his arms full of dough animals.

'*Ju-le*,' he shouted over his shoulders as he ran up the stairs.

'That be Tashi,' Kalden said, laughing as he looked back at the stairs. 'My brothers are his fathers. He very good boy.' He turned back to the path and they strolled towards the main entrance to the village. 'After village party,' he continued, '*onpo* will say when Chospel can go out of house for first time. It must be a day when all omens are favourable.'

'So he'll be at least a month old before he gets any fresh air,' she said in amazement.

'This is to help baby. Before she take Chospel out of house, she will rub butter on his head and put soot and oil between his eyes. This keep evil spirits away. Chospel will wear long robe that she make for him, and a woollen hat with a silver *om* on it.'

'Aren't babies born in the summer very hot in those clothes?'

'Most babies are born in the summer,' he said. She looked at him in surprise. 'Is very good way to spend long, dark nights,' he added dryly.

She laughed, and they walked along in silence for a little while.

'Where's her husband?' she asked suddenly. 'The only man there was Tenzin. They're not both married to your brothers, are they?'

'She not married. We all look after Chospel – my parents, my brothers, people in village.'

'You mean she's an unmarried mother, and no one minds?'

'I not sure what you mean, Patricia,' he said, as they went out of the village and walked slowly towards the golden fields where the ripening barley was rippling gently and swaying in the hot afternoon breeze. 'We walk along stream to go back to post house. It take longer, so I keep you longer with me. But what you mean when you say, and no one minds?'

'Doesn't anyone think it's wrong for her to have a baby without being married?'

He shrugged his shoulders, and took her hand as they stepped off the track and walked alongside the tall barley. 'Is better to have husband, yes, but sometimes man and woman feel strongly for each other. They not married but they have sex. There may be a baby. Is better for woman to have husband when there is a baby, but we care for baby anyway, like we do every other baby.'

'That's the perfect way of looking at it. Unfortunately, people in England don't feel the same way about such a situation.'

'What do people feel in England?'

'That it's a disgrace to have a baby if you're not married. Do you understand what the word disgrace means?' He shook his head. 'In England, you're not meant to go to bed with – to have sex with – a man unless you're married to him.'

'So in England, woman not ever have sex with man unless he is husband?'

'They shouldn't, but they do, of course. And if they get pregnant, everyone knows that they've had sex when they shouldn't. It's seen as a disgrace, something terrible. Things are starting to change now, but most families would still think it a huge disgrace if an unmarried daughter had a baby. They would feel ashamed.'

'This is not good. And people like you and me, who cannot get married? They must not ever have sex?'

'Being unable to marry doesn't alter a thing. So you see, just as you say that you're not a very good Ladakhi man because you wear trousers, not robes, and because we hold hands, I'm not a very good English girl.'

'I very happy about that, Patricia,' he murmured, smiling into her eyes.

She stopped walking and turned to him. 'I love you, Kalden. I love you so much.' She lifted his hand and put it to her lips.

'And I love you, too, Patricia. I not know before that I could ever feel like this – so happy, so close to someone, so always wanting to be with her, every minute of day, every minute of night.' He put his arms around her, pulled her close to him and hugged her tightly. 'Every day, I look at the barley and I see it rising higher, growing more golden, and I know that I am one day nearer to the day you leave me. The harvest soon begins, and when the harvest is finished, you go to England and I go to the monastery. And I am hurting now.'

She took a step back and looked at him. 'And I am hurting, too,' she said. 'So why are we going to do what is going to hurt us both?'

He raised his hand to her face and ran his fingers slowly down her cheek.

'Take your hands off my daughter!'

They spun round.

Crushing the delicate barley stalks beneath his feet, the Major stood in the golden field, his hands on his hips, legs astride, his eyes white with anger.

The blood drained from Patricia's face.

Chapter Fifteen

'Follow me, Patricia,' the Major said curtly.

His face grim, he strode down the path, flung open the front door and walked into the post house.

'Say something, won't you, Father?' Patricia pleaded, half running down the path after him.

Hesitating on the threshold of the house, she hovered a moment in the doorway, caught among the shining particles of dust that swirled in the lengthening rays of the afternoon sun. Then she stepped into the dark interior of the house and closed the door behind her, shutting out the warmth of the day.

'You didn't say a word all the way back here, Father,' she said, moving closer to him. 'I'm really sorry. I wanted to tell you about Kalden and me, but … '

'There is no Kalden and you, madam,' he cut in sharply, his voice bitter-cold with anger. 'You have disappointed me more than I can say. You are an educated girl from a family of some standing. Kalden is a peasant. There is no common ground between the likes of us and peasants. In behaving as you have done, you've cheapened yourself, and by association, you have demeaned your family.'

'Father …'

'My sole comfort is that your mother knows nothing of your reprehensible conduct. But that is cold comfort. When Wangyal brings us our food this evening, I shall make it clear to him that I wish to speak with Kalden after breakfast tomorrow. At that time, I shall inform you both of my plans. You may go to your room now. I have nothing more to say to you.' He walked over to his chair and sat down heavily, his back to her.

'I'm not a child any longer, Father,' she said very quietly.

'That is a moot point, Patricia. You've just turned eighteen years of age, which is three years short of the age of majority. You have yet to embark upon your course of higher education, and whilst this will equip you to support yourself in the future, for the present you are entirely dependent upon me. No, I would not define your state as one of adulthood. Nor would I describe your underhand behaviour as adult behaviour. You will now go to your room, please.'

For a moment or two, she stared at her father's rigid back, then she slowly turned away in despair, crossed the room to the stairs and climbed to the upper floor.

Throughout the long night, she lay on her bed, her eyes wide open, unable to push back the panic that crawled through her body and tightened its fingers around her heart.

'Kalden,' she whispered into the bleak emptiness that surrounded her.

'And that is what is going to happen,' the Major announced with clipped precision, his eyes narrow as he surveyed them both with distaste. 'My decision is irreversible. I trust that I have made myself clear.'

Standing side by side, neither Patricia nor Kalden said a word.

'Is that quite clear?' he repeated icily. 'Kalden?'

'Is clear, Major-*le*, but is not possible. I understand you want me go to Leh with you while you arrange for you and Patricia go back to England. Journey to Leh takes two days, maybe three days if weather not good. It take two days in Leh to make your arrangements, perhaps more days if no one is at airport. Then journey back take two more days.'

'We shall be gone for as long as it takes. And you'll kindly refer to my daughter as Patricia-*le*.'

'In next few days, everyone in my village is needed because

206

we get ready for harvest – we help other families and other families help us – and for me this is also very important time as I start preparations to go into monastery. It is not possible for me be out of village for many days.'

The Major opened his mouth to speak, but Kalden continued.

'I find you pony-man in Alchi, Major-*le*, and I take you to pony-man. I ask pony-man bring you back here after Leh. But I do not go to Leh with you. I stay with my family and I do what I must do in my village.' His face resolute, he met the Major's eyes.

'What do you mean, preparations to go into the monastery?' the Major snapped. Kalden glanced sideways at Patricia, resignation etched in his face. Then he pulled his gaze away and looked back at the Major. 'I become a monk, Major-*le*. I not marry like my brothers. I go into monastery near this village. This year I must go with monks into our Spirit Room for two-day festival of Skangsol. This is festival we have when harvest ends. After Skangsol, I leave my family and go live with monks.'

'I see.' The Major stroked his moustache with cold deliberation. 'I see,' he repeated. 'I must confess, I had wondered what your position would be, knowing the traditional status of the fourth son in a Ladakhi family. It had occurred to me that you might choose to be a coolie since you obviously enjoy walking in the mountains.'

'I not want to be coolie. I choose to be a monk.'

'A somewhat surprising choice, given the manner in which you were holding my daughter yesterday,' the Major retorted icily. He paused, pursing his lips thoughtfully. 'Very well, Kalden,' he said finally. 'I accept that, given the circumstances, it would be difficult for you to accompany me to Leh. Indeed, I am now wondering whether a better plan would not be for Patricia and me to move out of the post house in the next day or two and go together to Leh. We could stay there until the day of our flight. I trust you would be able to arrange suitable accommodation for us?'

'I try, but is not easy at harvest time. There not be many houses to stay in Leh, and people from these houses go back to villages for harvest and Skangsol. There be no one to get food for you and look after you. But if you wish, I try to find house that is not too much worse than post house. I ask pony-men in Alchi if they know something not too bad.'

An idea sprang into Patricia's mind. She felt a sudden surge of hope and stood very still, her mind working fast.

The Major turned to her. 'I think we can allow Kalden a couple of days in which to arrange for a pony-man and for the provisions that we'll need on the journey to Leh, also to find us some accommodation there, can we not? That would allow us almost two days in which to pack our possessions. Have you any objections to such a plan, Patricia?'

'No, Father,' she said, injecting a note of despair into her voice and letting her shoulders visibly slump. 'I can be ready to leave in two days.' She paused, and looked at her father, concern on her face. 'I'm a bit worried, though, that we might not be able to get a flight out of Leh for at least a couple of weeks. I think you said the airport's only used by diplomats and soldiers, didn't you? I don't know how you go about these things. I assume you'll have to get in touch with Gordon's contact, won't you? But that could take some time, especially if he isn't here at the moment. I suppose it doesn't matter, though, if we have to be in Leh for three or four weeks – there's bound to be some accommodation there that isn't too uncomfortable, and I'm sure we can manage to look after ourselves. Anyone can get used to anything.'

The Major frowned. He looked around the room, his expression thoughtful. His stance relaxed a little.

'Shall I start packing now, Father?'

'Just wait a minute, will you?' he muttered irritably. 'I'm beginning to wonder if I'm hurrying us out of here with unnecessary haste. If Kalden is to be engaged with the harvest and the monks, there might not be any need for you to accompany me to Leh at this point. We could revert to my original plan, which is that I leave you here, go to Leh to arrange for the earliest flight possible, and then return here until it's time to leave for the airport. I should not wish to find myself living in discomfort for what might be, as you quite rightly point out, as long as a month.'

Neither Kalden nor Patricia moved.

'If there were anyone here at all who spoke English – apart from Kalden, that is,' the Major said stiffly, 'I would consign you to his charge during my absence, Patricia. But since I am unable to communicate my wishes to anyone in the village other than through Kalden, I must adopt an alternative strategy.'

She held her breath.

The Major turned to face her. 'I have conscientiously brought you up to know the difference between truth and falsehood. I pride myself that I have set an example of rectitude before you, and that you – my daughter – are incapable of speaking anything other than the truth. If I leave you here tomorrow and go alone to Leh, do I have your word, your solemn word, that you will remain inside the post house until I return and that you will not communicate in any way at all with Kalden during my absence?'

Relief flooded through her. She lowered her head. 'I promise, Father,' she said quietly.

The Major glanced at her. A curl of satisfaction twisted the edge of his lips, and he turned to Kalden.

'You have overstepped the mark in that your behaviour towards my daughter, whether or not she was a willing party, has been inappropriate, to say the least. Apart from our journey together to meet the pony-man in Alchi, I do not wish to see you again. You will not come near this house, unless instructed to do so by me, and you will not contact my daughter in any way. I want your word – the word of a man who is about to take up the life of a holy man – that you agree to this.'

Patricia glanced surreptitiously at Kalden. His head bowed, his body conceded defeat. She looked back at her father, and then down at the floor.

'I not want to bring trouble to you and Patricia-*le*,' she heard Kalden say, the tone of his voice bleak. 'And I not want to bring disgrace on *ama-le*, *aba-le* and my brothers. It does not make me happy to agree, but I will agree to this.' He walked over to the door, paused and looked back at the Major. 'I be here after breakfast tomorrow. I take you to Alchi.' And he left the room.

Patricia's eyes stayed fixed on the stone slab beneath her feet.

It had been a long day.

From the moment that her father had set off for Alchi on the first leg of his journey to Leh that morning, she hadn't been able to stop thinking about him being with Kalden, and wondering if they'd spoken to each other on the journey and what would happen when Kalden got back. No matter how hard she'd tried to occupy herself, she'd been unable to think about anything else all day. And she still couldn't. She'd never felt so helpless and so restless in all of her life.

And an equally long evening stretched out ahead of her.

She stood up – she'd have to find something to take her mind off Kalden. It wasn't worth writing to her mother as she'd probably see her before the letter reached her. She'd get her notebook from upstairs, and read it through.

She ran up the stairs, picked up her notebook from the

shelf in her room and took it back downstairs with her. She lit a couple of candles, and then sat down and started to read through everything she'd ever written in the book.

When she came to the end, she let it slip through her fingers to her lap and stared ahead of her, lost in thought. The girl who had filled the pages of that book had been a very different person from the girl who was sitting alone in the post house, weighed down by the knowledge that her father had gone away to arrange the journey that would take her from the man she loved, and would always love.

That girl had spent so much time trying to please her father and get his attention, that she'd neglected her mother and had failed to show her that she loved and valued her.

That girl had been so certain that after years of being in the shadow of her father's love for her brother, she had stepped out from that shadow and been seen for herself, and that her father had finally appreciated having her as his daughter.

As she'd sat in England, wide-eyed and eager, writing down the Ladakhi words that her father had chosen for them to learn that week or adding to the schedule of places that they were going to visit or jotting down her thoughts about their forthcoming trip, she'd been so confident that they'd genuinely bonded at last, and that their relationship had been growing stronger with each passing day, fed as it was by their mutual interest in a country that only he had visited, but that she increasingly longed to explore.

But now, little more than three months after they'd arrived in Ladakh, that relationship was in tatters and she was the object of her father's contempt.

Perhaps if he had known that she truly loved Kalden and that he loved her, he might not have dismissed their relationship as merely a casual tryst. Hope had stirred as she'd lain in bed throughout the long night, thinking about her father's anger that afternoon when he'd found her in Kalden's arms, and she'd agonised about whether to tell him in the morning, before he left for Alchi, what Kalden meant to her, wondering if he'd feel differently if he knew that theirs was a real love and that they wanted to stay together forever.

Assuming that Kalden *did* want her to stay with him forever.

Once, only once in the night, had she allowed herself to wonder if he felt as passionately about her as she felt about him, but that moment had swiftly passed as she'd seen in her mind the love in his eyes whenever he looked at her. No, he cared about her as deeply as she cared about him, and if her father realised that, there was a chance that he might accept them as a couple.

But the word 'peasant' had swum into her mind, followed by the expression on her father's face as he'd said the word, and her hope had died before it had been properly born – he would never let her marry a man whom he thought inferior in every way.

Knowing in her heart that to be true, her eyes wide open, she'd lain on her bed, dreading the coming of the day.

When the morning had finally come, she'd had one glimpse of Kalden – just one fleeting glimpse to last her all day, and for a lifetime.

She and her father had just finished a silent breakfast when there'd been a knock on the front door. It would be Kalden, she realised, come to take her father to the pony-man in Alchi. She'd immediately got up to open the door, as she always did, but her father had ordered her to go up to her room: the door would not be opened for as long as she was downstairs.

She'd opened her mouth to object to the way in which he was treating her, but she'd bitten back the words lest she antagonise him and make him re-think going to Leh by himself. Instead, her head bowed in visible submission, she'd gone slowly up the stairs, her eyes surreptitiously on the door behind which Kalden stood. When she'd been three-quarters of the way to the top, the Major had opened the door and gone out to join Kalden. He'd closed the door behind him as quickly as he could, but it had been open long enough for her to see that Kalden's face was drawn and strained.

She'd heard their footsteps going up the path, and she'd desperately longed to run down the stairs, open the door and hurry after them, just to see Kalden again, no matter how brief the moment. But she knew that she mustn't. If her father saw her staring after them, Kalden would be lost to her forever.

If he wasn't already lost to her.

Her heart heavy, she'd come back down the stairs, and had sat in the chair, her eyes on the door, waiting as the day had crawled by.

'Patricia!'

She started in surprise, and jumped up. Her notebook fell to the floor.

'Patricia!' Kalden whispered again from outside the post house, his voice urgent. 'I back from Alchi.'

Her heart thumping fast, she ran to the door and flung it open. He slipped into the house, pushed the door shut behind him, threw his arms around her, pulled her to him and buried his face in her hair.

'My Patricia,' she heard him murmur, his voice muffled by her hair.

For several minutes, they clung wordlessly to each other. Then he pulled away, put his arm around her shoulders and led her to the long bench at the side of the room.

'Come, Patricia, there is much to say,' he said. 'I know I promise Major-*le* that I not talk to you, but I not speak the truth. I not a monk yet,' he added with a wry smile. Then, his face suddenly serious, he took her hand. 'I not know what you are feeling all this day, but I know what I feel. I feel deep, deep love for you. I cannot think of life without you.'

'And I love you so much that it hurts, Kalden.' She clutched his hand tightly. 'I can't bear the thought of leaving you. I've never been as unhappy as I've been since yesterday.'

'Then we live together,' he said.

'Live together?'

'We have said we stay together, so we have only to choose where we stay. I think first that we can live in Ladakh. We can make our home together here.'

'In Ladakh? I don't understand. I thought you were going into the monastery because there wasn't anything else you could do. Or are you thinking of being a coolie? You'd hate being a coolie, though.'

'Yes, I not want to be a coolie, and to be a coolie will not put food in our bowls. But a place we can live is missionary house. It belong to missionary church, but church not use it since Mr and Mrs Henderson leave. Missionary house already special to us. House is empty, but I can make house good again. Is little far from village, but I can grow food and we can live there. That is one thing we can do.'

'I'd rather be here with you than back in England without you,' she said without hesitation. 'We'll do that.'

He tightened his hand around hers. 'At first I think this is good idea. But then I think of missionary wife. Mr Henderson is happy here, and Mrs Henderson want to do what makes him happy, but she miss life in England – she miss music, books, people, food – and she feels sad that Peter cannot live like other English boys. Harvests pass, and she becomes more and more sad. Deep in my heart, I know that one day you be unhappy in Ladakh. You have mother in England. You can do many things in England you cannot do in Ladakh. Life in Ladakh is difficult if you not born in Ladakh. It be too hard for you here.'

'You're wrong, Kalden. Being with you is all I need to be happy. It doesn't matter where we are.' She leaned against his shoulder, put her arm across his chest and snuggled up to him.

He smiled sadly. 'I wish it is so, but it is not. Ladakhi people not know what it is to live in place like England. They not miss what they never have. But you know and you will miss it, even if today you think you will not. When we have children, you will feel about our children like Mrs Henderson feel about Peter. I not want that to happen. I want you to be always happy.'

She glanced up at him. 'So what are you saying, Kalden?'

'That I come to England with you,' he said very quietly.

She straightened up and stared at him. 'But you'd have to leave your family and the life you've always known. England's so different from here. It would be very strange and very frightening for you.'

'One of us must leave a family if we wish to live together. You are the life I want, Patricia. You will be my family, and the children we will have.'

She leaned back against his arm, biting her lower lip thoughtfully.

'You know, I think it could work, you coming to England,' she said slowly. 'You speak excellent English and you can read English, too. You'd certainly find work. It might not be as good as you deserve, but the more you learnt, the better the job you'd be able to get. I can work and bring in money, too, and we can rent a flat.' She looked up at his face, her eyes shining with excitement. 'Our first home together.'

He hugged her tightly. 'I very happy, Patricia. I feel I want to stay with you now and not leave you again, but I must not – I must get ready for journey. We will go before Major-*le* gets back. He is back in six or seven days, maybe more – I ask pony-man to go very slowly to Leh and back to village – but that is not long and we must leave post house very soon.'

'All we have to do is get to an airport in India. I've got some money of my own. It's not a lot, but it'll be enough for our tickets to England. We'll go back the way we came, through the Zoji-la Pass to Srinagar.'

'I have different idea. When Major-*le* comes back, he will think we go to Srinagar, but we will not. We will go south to Chiling and then we follow the Markha river to Lato. At Lato, we travel south on road that goes from Leh to Manali. So if he start to follow us, he go on wrong road.'

'Is the road to Manali a good road?'

'The road is high in the mountains. We go down the side of the mountains, round and round, until we come to grazing land. But it is a good road. Any road that takes us to place where we can be together is good road.'

She nestled up to him again. 'My mother's going to love you. And I'm sure Father will accept us when he sees how happy we are.'

'I hope that very much. I know that is what you want.'

'And we can come back and visit your family. You won't have to lose all contact with them. We'll come back as often as we can.'

He kissed the top of her head and straightened up. 'I go back to house now. I not want anyone to know we are together. Is better that way.'

'You're right, of course,' she said. She sighed. 'I can't wait to be able to do whatever we want.'

'And I feel that, too. Tomorrow I go and find bearer in

Alchi. We take one bearer and three pack-ponies. We change ponies for *dzo* when we get to very high ground. *Dzo* better for mountain tracks. When I in Alchi, I get food for trip as we not have any cook. I come back late from Alchi as I not want anyone to see ponies and food. While I in Alchi, you pack clothes and things you need, and we can leave early in next morning. I ask bearer to be with us when the sun rises. We will start our life together with *nima*, the sun.'

'I'm so happy,' she breathed.

He put his finger under her chin, tilted her face to his and kissed her full on the lips. 'I love you, Patricia,' he said, his voice thick with emotion. 'I not know the words to tell you, but for rest of my life I show you every day. You and me, we are one person.' He stood up and looked down at her, his eyes ablaze with love. 'I not want to go now, but I must. I see you tomorrow night when I back from Alchi.'

She caught his hands in hers. Bending over them, she kissed the palm of his right hand, then the palm of his left hand, then she pressed his hands to the sides of her face. 'I love you,' she said. 'I always will.'

Chapter Sixteen

The air was cold and the ground hard when they set off from the post house an hour before the sun had fully risen. Determined to put as much distance as possible between them and the post house in the first couple of days, they went as quickly as they could in a south-easterly direction.

'What's the name of our bearer?' Patricia asked towards the middle of the morning when they'd slowed to a more comfortable pace, feeling able to relax a little now that the village was far behind them.

'Lobsang. It means that he has very kind heart.'

'That's nice.' She smiled at Lobsang's back, then glanced over her shoulder at the long expanse of track behind them. 'Do you think we'll be able to keep this speed up all the way to Manali?'

'We must. Lobsang see we do. Road to Manali is high up and sometimes it snows before end of September. Road always closes in October, maybe even by end of September. Lobsang must leave us and be back on lower ground before snow comes, so must be in Manali before end of September.'

Lobsang turned round and beamed at them. Kalden said a few words to him and he replied, looking up at the sky, and then turned back to the track.

'Lobsang worry about snow coming early. He say we go quickly,' Kalden told her, and they speeded up their pace again.

Having travelled all morning with only one short break, they reached the Dungdung Chan La early in the afternoon. Deciding to go through the mountain pass and then stop for their lunch, they started to ride into the pass. A moment later, Kalden pulled his pony to an abrupt halt and stared from one side to the other, at the Stok Range soaring majestically in the east, and at the rocky pinnacles of the Zanskar Range stretching away to the south.

'What is it?' she asked, anxiously.

'Might be I never again see family and people I know since day I am born. I do what I want, Patricia – I want to be with you – but I feel for my family.' He turned round in his saddle and gazed back at the shadowy peaks of the mountains where he'd grown up.

She nudged her pony closer to his and leaned across to him. 'We'll come back, Kalden,' she said softly, resting her hand on his. 'I promise we will.'

'I hope this, but I not know. I have locked picture of mountains in my mind, and I keep it with me forever.'

He took a deep breath, turned away from the past and fixed his eyes firmly on the way ahead.

Urging their ponies forward, they followed Lobsang along the ridge towards the valley, riding side by side. Every so often, her eyes strayed to Kalden's pale face, and she leaned across and rubbed his arm, sending him waves of sympathy and understanding. Each time, he smiled back at her, but she saw that his eyes were full of sorrow.

The track narrowed as they got closer to Chiling and they were forced to ride one behind the other. With Lobsang in front of her and Kalden behind, she had no choice but to keep her eyes on the path ahead and on Lobsang's back.

Just before they reached Chiling, Lobsang pointed to a small stretch of pasture land to their right on which grey-brown sheep were grazing, and he indicated that they should stop there and have some food. Both they and the ponies needed a short rest before they went any further, he told Patricia through Kalden.

'You *will* see your parents again, Kalden. We'll make sure of that,' Patricia said as they sat on the grass together, a little way back from Lobsang. She picked up a lump of dried cheese and a piece of thick brown bread, broke each in half and gave him a piece of each. 'You must eat something. You haven't eaten anything all day. You've got to keep your strength up.'

He smiled across at her. 'I all right now. You not worry.' He put his arm around her and bit into the bread.

'Are you sure we've got enough food for the journey? We've only got enough bread for one more day, and we didn't bring many bags of *ngampe*. I know we've still got several bricks of tea, butter and salt, but there are only a few blocks of cheese left. It doesn't seem much for three people for such a long journey.'

'It be enough. If we carry much, we go slowly. We make many meals with food we have, and it easy to carry. Tomorrow we make porridge with *ngampe*, cheese and salt butter tea – Peter always say it look like porridge, but not taste like it. We roll mixture into little balls and we boil little balls in pan with water. If it rains, or if we not find wood to make fire, we not cook them – we eat them with water. *Ngampe* porridge is very good for long trips.'

She made a face of disgust, and he laughed.

'Yet another reason to get to the end of our journey as quickly as possible,' she said. 'I wish I could say that it sounds delicious, but I can't.' She yawned, lay back on the grass and stared up at the clear blue sky. 'Just look at that sky! There's not a cloud to be seen.'

Kalden gave her a smile, got up and went to help Lobsang put everything they'd used back into the canvas bags that hung from the ponies. When they'd finished, he came over to her. 'We go now, Patricia, or you want we rest longer?'

'Definitely go now,' she said. Yawning again, she stood up, wiping the dust from the seat of her jeans. A worried expression on his face, Lobsang watched her as he stood holding the ponies. He said something to Kalden. Kalden glanced at Patricia, nodded to Lobsang and went over to her.

'Lobsang thinks we go only a little further today. We stop on other side of Chiling. After Chiling, must cross very deep ravine before we get to the big river. Ravine is dry, but we use high bridge to get to other side. Before we get to bridge, there is a pasture just like pasture here. Lobsang thinks we tired and suggests we camp on pasture and cross ravine tomorrow.'

'Can't we cross over first and then stop for the night? I'm terrified that Father will return from Leh sooner than we thought and come after us. I know it's silly – he doesn't even know which way we've gone – but I can't help worrying. It doesn't feel as if we've come very far yet, and I'm not that tired. And what about the snow? Shouldn't we go as far as we can each day before stopping?'

Kalden went back to Lobsang, followed by Patricia, and they had a short conversation.

'Lobsang says there is hut on other side of ravine, not far from bridge,' he told her. 'Perhaps there be other pony-men in hut, and they give us information about road to Lato. I have told Lobsang that we cross river today and stay in hut tonight.'

'That sounds the best thing to do; thank you. That way, we can set off tomorrow before daybreak if we want. If we spent the night on this side of the ravine, we wouldn't be able to cross the bridge in semi-darkness so we wouldn't be able to leave as early in the morning.' She smiled gratefully at Lobsang, and the three of them mounted their ponies and picked up the trail again.

Riding behind Lobsang for the next leg of the journey, they stared in silence at the view on either side of them. When they reached Chiling, they skirted the village and made their way along a winding track that was bordered by a profusion of willow, rose and sea buckthorn.

'I feel the size of an ant, sandwiched between such massive rock formations,' she said at one point. 'And look at those huge mounds of earth – they look just like spires.'

Gradually, the path became steeper and more uneven, and they were forced to keep their eyes firmly on the rocky ground ahead of them.

'How will your parents know where you are?' Patricia asked as they sat on the grass in the small clearing where they'd stopped for a rest before crossing the bridge. 'Won't they panic when they can't find you?'

'Tenzin will tell them.'

'Did you tell him where you were going?'

'Yes. I could not go without telling him, and I ask him to tell *ama* and *aba,* but not until they ask about me. I trust Tenzin; he not let them worry.'

'What did he say when you told him you were coming to England with me?'

'That he not surprised. He say he know for long time that I feel much for you, and he see in your eyes that you feel same for me. He say he always think I never be very good monk. He think I be better husband. I think so, too.' He gave her a lazy smile and squeezed her hand. Then he turned his attention to Lobsang, who was speaking to him at the same time as staring up at the sky.

'We very near bridge,' Kalden translated. 'Lobsang ask if you sure you want to cross bridge today. It is late now and sun be soon behind mountains. He thinks we stay here for night. He sees we tired.'

'He's right that I'm tired, but I'm not too tired to continue. I'd rather cross the bridge now. But it's been a really difficult day for you, Kalden, leaving your family and all that, and if you've had enough and you'd prefer to stop now, then that's what we'll do.'

'We go over bridge now,' Kalden said, and he told

222

Lobsang that they'd cross the ravine and then stop for the night in the hut.

A little further along the track, the path gave a sudden sharp twist and they found themselves riding up a short stretch of rocky ground between heaps of stones that had been piled together at irregular intervals. Astride the top of the path stood two large crags. Passing between the crags, they saw a narrow bridge hanging high above a dark ravine that fell away at their feet.

Patricia stopped sharply. Her eyes flew to the bridge – to the overlapping wooden slats that formed its base; to the wide mesh of the rope handrail; to the gently swaying movement – and she shuddered.

Jagged crags jutted out from the ridge that overhung the valley and blocked her view of the ravine. Cautiously she inched her pony forward and peered down the slopes of the crimson scree to the dry river bed below. Her line of vision was broken by the clusters of rose-bushes that had managed to take root on the barren slopes of rock, their tangled branches reaching out into the emptiness above the gorge, but she was able to make out a jumble of large boulders at the foot of the cliffs, which marked out the line of the river bed.

She followed the path where the river had been, watching it narrow, widen again, and then disappear behind a grey wall of rock. Then she turned her head to the right and stared up at the tall cliffs that dominated the valley, cutting out the rays of the dying sun. Shivering, she looked back at the bridge in front of her.

'I'm glad that the bridge goes across the narrowest part,' she said. 'I don't like the look of it at all. I'll be very pleased when we're on the other side. And I'm glad we don't have to go any higher in the mountains today. They look quite scary in this light.'

'When we go in high mountains, we get *dzo*,' Kalden said. 'Is already high up for ponies, but ponies are good. Lobsang choose well. And bridge will be easy crossed. Is good.'

'Poor Kalden. You sound very tired. It's not surprising as you've had such a hard few days.'

'I a little tired. I not sleep last night. I think about today. But I good.'

She held her hand out to him and he took it. Their eyes met, and they tightened their hold on each other.

The sound of Lobsang calling to them brought them back to the moment. He was standing at the edge of the bridge, holding his pony and indicating that they should get down from their ponies and join him. They swiftly dismounted, and Kalden reached across to take Patricia's reins from her. Lobsang saw what he was doing and motioned to him to stay there, speaking to him in Ladakhi.

Translating, Kalden told Patricia that Lobsang was going to take the ponies across the bridge one at a time. He would tie the ponies a little way along the track on the other side. When all three ponies had been safely tethered, Patricia would cross the bridge to Lobsang, who'd be waiting on the other bank.

Although it wasn't necessary, Kalden added, he would hold the rope handrail at his end of the bridge, keeping it steady while she walked across, and Lobsang would hold the handrail at the other end, so she would know that she was safe. When she reached the other side, he would cross the bridge.

'You be all right, Patricia,' he said. 'Soon we be in hut together.'

His arm around her shoulders, they watched Lobsang slowly make his way across the bridge, pulling the first pony behind him.

'You see,' he said as Lobsang stepped off the last wooden slat, the pony close behind him. 'Bridge is good.'

The light was fading fast by the time that the last pony had been tethered on the opposite side of the river. Lobsang glanced anxiously up at the darkening sky as he took his position at the far end of the bridge, a hand on each of the handrails. He shouted a few words to Patricia.

'He want you go now,' Kalden said, and he gave her an encouraging smile.

Nervously biting her lower lip, she squarely faced the bridge and put her foot on the first of the wooden strips. Determined not to look down, she began to edge her way to the other side, her eyes firmly on Lobsang, her body trembling. Half way across, her steps faltered. A sudden tremor ran along the length of the rope, and she realised that Kalden had tightened his hold on the handrails.

'I'm all right, Kalden,' she called over her shoulder, her eyes still on Lobsang. 'I'm not looking down. I'm fine.'

Her heart racing, she took another step, and then another, each step bringing her closer to Lobsang, closer to the other side of the river. Desperate to bring to an end the sensation of swaying above nothingness, she took another step, more quickly this time. And Lobsang was there, just in front of her, an arm's length away, only one more step away.

Relief flooded through her. As she put her foot on the slat in front of her, she took her hand off the handrail and held it out to Lobsang. Her toe slid under the wooden slat and she stumbled. Losing her balance, she fell forward, and cried out in sudden fear.

At the very moment that Lobsang caught hold of Patricia's hand and pulled her to safety, the bridge lurched violently. A cry of terror pierced the air and fell to the ravine, where it died away.

Neither Patricia nor Lobsang moved. Behind them, way, way below them, they heard three muffled thuds. Then silence.

She screamed and spun round.

Where Kalden had stood, there was nothing: only the bridge, swaying from side to side in ever-decreasing arcs as it settled slowly back into position, a gaping hole in its wooden base marking the place where Kalden would have put his feet.

'Kalden!' she screamed, and she jumped forward on to the bridge.

Lobsang pulled her back. Frantically gesturing for her to stay where she was, he showed with rapid hand movements that he, not she, would go back. She nodded quickly, her eyes wide with fear as she stared transfixed at the gap in the wooden slats, feeling her face go chalk white.

Pressing her clenched fists to her mouth, she stood with her back against the cold rock, and watched Lobsang wait for the bridge to steady itself and then walk quickly and evenly into the gathering gloom. When he reached the middle of the bridge, he paused and stared over the handrail into the ravine below. Then he looked back at Patricia and slowly shook his head.

A low moan escaped her. 'Kalden.'

Despair rising within her, threatening to choke her, she stared at Lobsang's back as he continued across the bridge to the hole in the wooden base. He turned to her and pointed to the large hole at his feet, miming the way in which some of the slats had fallen into the valley. By his arm movements, he showed her that the hole was too wide for him to get past it to the other side.

His hands firmly gripping the rope on either side of the bridge, he again leaned over the handrail and stared into the valley below. 'Kalden-*le*!' he shouted. 'Kalden-*le*!'

'Where are you, Kalden?' Patricia screamed from the side of the ravine.

She stepped forward, grasped the rope handrails, one in

each hand, and started to walk across the bridge to Lobsang, all fear for herself forgotten. Ignoring his shouts and frantic hand movements as he begged her to slow down, she kept on walking until she reached his side. Stopping, she stared down in horror at the gaping hole where the slats had been, and through the hole to the black void that lay below.

'Oh, no,' she moaned.

She raised her eyes to the shadowy crags. 'I want Kalden,' she whispered. 'I want Kalden,' she repeated, more loudly. Tightly gripping the handrails, she leaned over the side. 'Kalden!' she screamed into the ravine, tears streaming down her face. 'Kalden! Answer me! Please, answer me!'

Her voice came back to her as the sun dropped behind the high mountain peaks, and a shroud of darkness covered the valley.

'Kalden!' she shouted again. But her voice was lost in the depths of the gorge, and silence was her answer.

Lobsang took her gently by the arm and spoke to her, his face anxious, his eyes creased with sympathy. Sentence after sentence fell from his lips, words she couldn't understand, but a meaning that was clear. It was already dark and they must leave the bridge at once. They must go to the ponies and get themselves to the hut as quickly as they could.

Unable to move, she stared fixedly into the blackness beneath her.

Balancing carefully, Lobsang wrapped his arms around himself and pointed to the sky. He mimed the cold. It would get colder and colder and they would freeze in the Ladakhi night if they didn't get to warmth and shelter, he made her understand. There was no hope for Kalden, his expression said, and he shook his head again as he looked down at the black ravine: no one could survive a fall like that. They could do nothing for Kalden; they must leave.

He took her arm and made a move to guide her back across the bridge.

She pulled away from him. 'I can't. He might be alive.' Her voice rose. 'You don't know that he's not. We've got to look for him, find him. He might be alive, and it's cold. We've got to get to him.' She tried to push past him, but he grabbed her and held her fast.

Words poured out of his mouth, his face worried, frightened. He pointed up to the sky and the mountains; he pointed down into the ravine. He put his hands together in a plea to her, then he pointed again to the sky and mimed snow and cold. '*Ju-le*,' he begged her. '*Ju-le*.'

His hand firmly on her arm, he started to walk, making her walk with him. Numb, she let him half carry her across the bridge to the track on the other side. She took a couple of steps along the track, stopped and pulled free of Lobsang. Turning round, she stared back across the ravine. The crags had dissolved into the black of night and she could no longer see the rose-bushes.

'Kalden,' she whispered into the silent emptiness. 'I will love you till the day I die.'

Lobsang put his hand under her elbow, gently led her to the ponies, helped her on to her pony and then mounted his. Her arms fell helplessly to her sides, and he took her reins in his hands and guided her pony and Kalden's to the shepherd's hut. Then he helped her down, and tethered the ponies alongside the four others that were already there.

Wrapped in a blanket, her face deathly pale, she sat in the corner of the smoky room while he talked with the pony-men there. From his expression and gestures, she knew that he was describing what had happened and telling them about the hole in the bridge. From time to time, the eyes of the pony-men strayed to her, openly curious, but warm with sympathy. Gradually, their conversation petered out and each of the men took a blanket from the large pile at the side of the small room and settled down for the night.

Lobsang came across to Patricia and tried to explain to her what he'd been saying, pointing first to the other men, then in the direction of Chiling. Then he pointed to Patricia and himself and to the sky, and she knew that he was telling her that they must continue their journey as soon as morning came, reminding her that snow was imminent. She nodded, her eyes bleak with despair.

He hesitated a moment, then took a step closer. Looking intently at her, he started to make round circles in the air with his hand. She turned her head away, desperate for him to go away and leave her to her grief, but he wouldn't. He tapped her on the shoulder, and again made circles in the air, this time with greater urgency, and repeating the word '*Om*' several times.

Suddenly she realised what he was doing. He was trying to comfort her by telling her that death wasn't final; there would be a new life. Life and death were part of the same circle, he was showing her with his round movements. She forced herself to nod. He looked pleased and moved away. Taking a blanket from the pile, he made himself a bed in the far corner of the room and closed his eyes.

Throughout the long night, she clutched the edge of her blanket to her chin, her eyes wide open as she stared back into the past and tried not to look into the future, a future without Kalden. Silent tears trickled relentlessly down her cheeks and fell on to the cold stone floor.

Chapter Seventeen

Her canvas bag still covered with the dust of Ladakh and India, Patricia knocked on the front room door, opened the door and went in. She paused for a moment, took a deep breath and then walked over to the large table behind which her father sat. Standing in front of the table, she waited for him to look up.

The Major kept his eyes on his book.

She glanced quickly around the room while she waited for him to acknowledge her presence. There was something different about the room, but she couldn't identify what it was, and she returned her gaze to the top of her father's head. His hair was rapidly thinning, she noticed.

The clock on the mantelpiece ticked loudly. She stood there for another minute or two, stepping nervously from one foot to the other, then she heard the sound of movement behind her. Looking back over her shoulder, she saw her mother hovering in the doorway. Enid gave her an encouraging nod and she turned back to the table.

'Father,' she said awkwardly. 'I'm back.'

He looked up at her, his grey eyes cold. 'That is somewhat self-evident, Patricia, given the fact that you are standing here, in my room.' His eyes returned to his book.

'Did you get the letter I sent to you and Mother from Dehli, telling you what happened to Kalden? I posted it before I got on the train. It's just as well that I sent it when I did – I had to keep on changing trains as I went from one country to another and I wouldn't have been able to send it to you after that for ages,' she said. 'My letter telling you how Kalden died,' she added after several minutes of silence.

'We did,' the Major said tersely. He pushed his book to one side, took off his glasses and looked up at her. 'I am sorry for Kalden's parents, losing their son in such a pointless way – no one knows better than I how the death of a son can destroy a father's life. They are fortunate, however, in having other sons, who will no doubt bring them comfort in the years to come, even more so since those sons have remained true to their cultural identity and their family. Now, if there's nothing else.' He put his glasses back on, pulled his book in front of him and started to read again.

'I should like to come back home to live with you and Mother, if I may.' Her voice shook with nerves. She sensed her mother leave the doorway and come over to stand behind her.

The Major looked up from his book and directed a raised eyebrow at his daughter. 'I am most surprised to hear that, Patricia. I understood from your letter that prior to leaving Ladakh you had felt ready to dispense with any further education, seek employment and set up home on your own. Am I to infer from your request that you have since changed your mind?' Very deliberately, he removed his glasses and placed them on the table.

'Everything's different now, Father, now that Kalden's not here. I'd like to live with you and Mother, and go to college as I'd planned to do. With Kalden ...' Her father leaned back against his chair and raised his hand to stop her mid-sentence. Her voice trailed off.

Staring at her in studied concentration, he ran his thumb and index finger down his moustache and pinched his lower lip between the two fingers.

'I am prepared to let you return to my house,' he said at last. She heard a slight sigh from behind her as her mother let her breath escape. Warm air brushed against the nape of her neck. 'But only upon the following conditions. You will never again say Kalden's name, nor will you mention him in any way, neither explicitly nor implicitly. You will never talk about our visit to Ladakh – it is to be as if we were never there together. There will be no mementos of him, nor of any aspect of the trip, in any part of the house, and that includes your room. To this end, you will destroy the film in your camera. Now, do I have your word that you accept these conditions?'

'But, Father …'

'I wish to forget your willingness to enter into a relationship that would have brought nothing but shame to your family, and in future I shall focus solely upon the happy time that I spent in Ladakh in 1945. Do I make myself quite clear?'

'Yes, Father,' she said quietly, her face ashen.

'When you've emptied your bags, you will throw away everything that originated in Ladakh, for example, the bag you are holding. You may keep only the bags that we took with us when we left for the ill-fated expedition.'

A lump in her throat, her fingers tightened around the strap of the bag.

Moving his head slightly, the Major included his wife in his line of vision. 'And I want your word, too, Enid, that you will do your utmost to ensure that Patricia observes my wishes. Have I your word on that?'

'Of course you have, George.' Patricia felt a sympathetic squeeze on her arm.

'Very well, then. We can move on. You've expressed a wish to take up your place at college, Patricia, which is a wise decision. A person needs a worthwhile goal, and the discipline of academic routine will help you to put this summer behind you. And talking of routine, Enid, I shall be ready for tea in half an hour.'

'Certainly, George.'

'Since we are again three in number, I suggest that we

cease eating in the kitchen and revert once more to eating in the back room as befits a respectable family. And now perhaps you will both leave me as I wish to finish reading this chapter before I have my tea.' Picking up his glasses, his eyes returned to his book.

Patricia turned round and started to follow her mother out of the room.

'Just one further thing, Patricia,' the Major called as she reached the door. She paused. Her mother continued hurrying along the corridor towards the kitchen. 'No doubt you won't be surprised to learn that I've decided against extending the Ladakh book. There will not now be a section describing the Ladakh of today.'

'I understand, Father,' she said quietly.

As she closed the door behind her and started to go slowly upstairs to her room, she suddenly realised what it was that was strange about the front room: every single book about Ladakh, every map, photograph and document, had been cleared from her father's table – they'd either been destroyed or stowed away in a place where they couldn't be seen.

She went into her bedroom, closed the door and looked around at her future, her eyes empty.

The following morning, she unpacked her bags and then, at the Major's request, went round to Belsize Park to collect his copy of the *Hampstead and Highgate Express* from the newsagent's opposite the tube station. She came out of the shop, tucked the newspaper under her arm and strolled into the centre of the wide pavement.

Standing there, she stared around her. When she'd last stood there, May blossom had been drifting from the trees to the wooden benches that faced the road, but the blossom was now long gone and the leaves on the trees were a golden-brown. There was now also a hint of a chill in the air, which hadn't been there four months earlier. Apart from that, though, everything was the same as it had been in the days before she'd gone to Ladakh.

Parades of shops with flats above them still lined both sides of the road, the newspaper kiosk still stood on the right of the entrance to the tube station, the posters in front of the Odeon cinema on her left were just as garish as they'd been in May. To her right, in the residential area down the hill, large houses still topped sweeping flights of wide stone steps. Yes, everything was exactly the same as it had been in May. Everything, except one thing. She had changed. The change didn't show, but it was there.

She had gone to Ladakh a quiet, shy girl, whose only goal had been to win love and approval from her father, who'd believed that her father had finally come to love and value her. But she'd got it wrong. In Ladakh, she'd learnt what it was like to be truly loved, and that had shown her the shallowness of her father's feelings for her and the selfishness that underpinned his life.

That naïve girl had remained in Ladakh.

In her place, the woman who had loved Kalden with the same passion as he had loved her had come back to England. Theirs was a love that many people never knew in the whole of their life. It was a love that had changed her forever, and it would never die. She didn't need mementos and she didn't need to talk about him in order to remember him – he lived in her mind every minute of the day; he lay at her side every minute of the night.

It was the only way that she'd been able to go on without him.

At the first light of day on the morning after Kalden's fall, she'd run from the shepherd's hut to the ravine, desperate to find him, desperate to be with him, not caring what happened to her. But Lobsang had reached her as she'd been about to step on the bridge. He'd gripped her arms and forced her to look into his face. She could do nothing for Kalden, he'd made her understand, his face frantic. They had to set off at once for Manali: snow was coming. They weren't prepared for snow and would be at risk.

'*Nyerang-a ha go-a?*' he'd asked her, repeating the question over and over again.

She'd slowly nodded that she'd understood.

Without releasing his hold, he'd taken her back to the hut and helped her on to her pony. Leaning across from his pony, he had taken hold of her reins and pulled her pony along the track alongside his. Her head bowed, she'd sat in a daze, misery gnawing at her heart, eating into her with agony as she was taken further and further away from Kalden.

As the days had passed, she'd found that she could close her eyes, day or night, and see Kalden's face in front of her, and from that time on, she'd never been alone.

She glanced around her once more, and then started to walk slowly down the hill, glancing idly in the shops as she passed them by. When she drew level with the chemist's shop, she stopped sharply and thrust her hand into her pocket. Her fingers curled around a small spool of film, and her heart thumped fast – there were some photos of Kalden on the film, taken in the early days of their visit. No matter what she'd promised her father, she'd have the film developed. She didn't need photos to remember him by, but just to have them, to have something to touch … She half ran into the chemist's shop.

'That'll be a week from today, Miss. Is there anything else I can do for you?' the chemist asked, handing her a ticket.

There wasn't, she told him, and she put the ticket in her jacket pocket, picked up her newspaper and left the shop.

She'd get a Saturday job, she decided as she walked briskly down the hill, a new lightness in her step. She needed some money of her own and it'd be good to do something totally different on Saturdays. When her father had finished with the paper, she'd look in the Situations Vacant column and see what there was. If she found that having a job interfered with her college work, she could always stop.

Her spirits lifting, she turned into Belsize Grove and made her way down the road to Belsize Park Gardens.

'What about the library?' Enid asked.

'Well, what about the library?' Patricia looked up from the newspaper.

'When I changed my book last week, I noticed that they were advertising for Saturday staff. That'd be the ideal job for you. You love reading.'

'Which library, Arkwright Road or the branch in Antrim Grove?'

'Antrim Grove. I usually go there now as it's much closer.'

'That would be perfect. I can easily walk to Antrim Grove. I'd love that. Kalden and I used to go out walking for hours.' She stopped abruptly, and her hand flew to her mouth.

Enid leaned across the kitchen table and squeezed the hand that held the newspaper. 'I know you miss him, Patsy darling, and I wish I could help you. I hate seeing you suffering like this. But you know what your father's like.' Her voice trailed off and she glanced at the clock. 'Why don't we go to the library now and pick up an application form? You can tell me all about Kalden as we walk.'

Patricia nodded. She pulled out a handkerchief and blew her nose.

Her mother got up from the table, put her cup on the draining board and went down the corridor to the front room. Patricia heard her knock on the door, open it and tell the Major that she and Patricia were going to the local library to see about a Saturday job they were advertising.

She couldn't hear her father's response, but she returned to the kitchen a few minutes later, a wide smile on her face.

'I've said we'll be back well before it's time for tea. If you're ready, we can go now, darling,' she said, and she untied her pinafore.

Scraping her chair back from the table, Patricia followed her mother to the door.

Less than a week after she'd returned her completed application form to the library, she was given an interview with the Librarian there. A day later, she received a letter offering her the job. Her mother hugged her, and her father nodded his satisfaction.

'I'm not surprised that they've offered you the position,' the Major remarked. 'I imagine that your experience with the children at the hospital will prove advantageous to the library. They have quite a large children's section there. Indeed, too large, I sometimes think. Children today have no conception of the meaning of silence.'

'I'd better sort out what to wear,' she told them. 'And I really ought to put my summer clothes away and get out the rest of my winter things. In fact, I think I'll make a start on that before lunch.'

She went up to her room, opened her wardrobe doors and started taking out her summer things. As she threw her jacket on to the bed, the ticket for her camera film fell from one of the pockets. She picked it up and looked at it. It was one day short of a week since she'd left the film to be developed. The chemist had said that the photos wouldn't be ready for a week, but they just might be back early. She glanced at her watch. It was almost one o'clock – if she moved quickly, she could get to the shop before it closed for lunch.

She sped downstairs and told her mother that she had to get something from the shops, but wouldn't be long.

Running all the way, she reached the chemist's at exactly one minute to one o'clock.

The chemist looked up as she approached the counter, out of breath. He stared pointedly at his watch, then took the ticket from her, flicked through the photographs awaiting collection, pulled out a packet and gave it to her. She glanced round for something to buy as she had to have a parcel to carry into the house, saw the sanitary towels in the aisle behind her and grabbed a box of Kotex. The chemist put it into a paper bag, and she paid him and left the shop.

Slipping the photographs into the paper bag, she hurried back down the hill. Much as she would have loved to have sat on one of the benches and looked through the photographs, it would make her late for lunch, and in her mind's eye, she could see her father sitting rigidly at the table, his eyes on the clock on the wall. Her mother would bear the brunt of his ill humour and she didn't want to put her through that if she didn't have to. Also, looking at the photos in a rush wasn't really the way in which she wanted to look again on her Kalden's face.

Her mother opened the door as she reached the house. 'Lunch is ready, darling.'

'Just let me pop upstairs and wash my hands first. I won't be a moment.'

'I'll start dishing up, then.'

As she hurried up the stairs to her bedroom, she heard the sound of plates being put on the table.

She hastily looked around her room, trying to think of a place for the photos where no one would look. Her eyes lit on the bottom drawer of her chest of drawers, where she kept her sanitary towels, and she went over to the drawer and pulled it open. As she slid the new packet of Kotex into the drawer, she saw with surprise that she already had two boxes. Slipping the photos beneath the boxes, she wondered idly when she'd had her last period. She couldn't quite remember.

Her system must still be unsettled after all the travelling she'd done, she thought, standing up, not to mention the shock she'd suffered over Kalden's death. Now that she was settling into a routine again, she'd soon get back to normal.

She closed the drawer, went into the bathroom, washed her hands and ran lightly down the stairs to the kitchen. Travelling could have that effect on women, she told herself as she took her place at the table.

Chapter Eighteen

Late October

Several times when they met up in the evening, Patricia had come near to telling Ruth what she suspected, but the moment had never seemed quite right, and each time she'd held off.

They'd first seen each other again shortly after Patricia's return from Ladakh.

At the start of the evening, each had been ultra polite to the other, and Patricia had realised that neither had truly recovered from the things that had been said at the time of her seventeenth birthday. She'd also sensed that Ruth was still upset that she'd been so tied up with her plans for the trip to Ladakh that she hadn't gone to Ruth's engagement party.

Hoping to get things back to normal between them, she'd asked Ruth to tell her all about the party and about Johnny. Ruth had beamed at her, produced photographs of the party and had held out her hand for Patricia to admire her engagement ring, a tiny sapphire with a diamond chip on either side of it.

Unwilling to introduce a note of sadness into the evening, Patricia had decided not to tell her about Kalden on that occasion, but to continue trying to get their friendship back to where it had been a few years earlier. With that end in view, she'd plied Ruth with questions about her plans for the wedding and honeymoon, about where she and Johnny were going to live, about her job at DH Evans, and about whether she wanted a boy or a girl when the time came.

Gradually they'd relaxed into a genuine warmth, and by the end of the evening, it was clear Ruth had thoroughly enjoyed herself and she was the first to suggest that they meet up again as soon as possible. It was on the second occasion that they'd met that Patricia had told Ruth all about Kalden. Her face full of sympathy, Ruth had hugged her friend.

'You'll meet someone else, someone from round here, honest you will, Patsy,' she'd told her. 'When you go to college, maybe. And I'll tell Johnny to be on the lookout for a bloke for my best friend. It's a crying shame that he hasn't got a brother. There might be someone in the garage where he works.' She'd hugged Patricia again. 'You'll be all right. I just know it.'

Patricia decided that she'd probably said enough about Kalden for that evening, and that she definitely wasn't going to bring up the subject that was increasingly dominating her thoughts. That could wait for another evening.

A week later, she and Ruth had gone to the cinema together to see *Flower Drum Song*. As they'd got up from their seats at the end of the film, Patricia suggested that they go for a drink somewhere nearby. She'd waited long enough to tell Ruth what she suspected and she desperately needed to talk to someone; she was going to tell Ruth that evening.

'Some of those Chinese men are good-looking in a sort of way,' Ruth had laughed, tucking her arm into Patricia's as they left the cinema. 'But I could never fall for anyone like that, good looks or not. They're much too different from us.'

Patricia had glanced at Ruth's face, and she'd changed her mind.

Sitting on her bed, she stared at the photograph of Kalden. His eyes were half closed as he squinted against the sun to look straight into the lens of the camera. Her heart raced – he looked so good-looking, so strong and so alive. A powerful surge of longing for him swept through her body, shaking her to the core.

She raised the photo to her lips, and kissed it. 'I think you're going to be a father, Kalden,' she whispered to him. 'I'm telling you this because I'm sure you can hear me. I'm really scared, but I'm also very, very happy. I do hope that our baby looks exactly like you.' She smiled at the face that stared up at her from the celluloid. Lightly she ran her fingers over his features, then she hugged the photo to her chest.

'Patricia!' she heard her mother call from downstairs. 'Do you want to come round the corner with me? I've got to get some things from the shops, and you said earlier on that you wanted a walk.'

'I'll be down in a minute. I'm just putting my jeans on,' she shouted. With a last glance at Kalden's face, she got up, went over to the chest of drawers and put the photo back in the bottom drawer.

Then she hurried to the wardrobe, took out her jeans, stepped into them and started to pull up the zip. Half way to the top, she stopped – the two sides of the zip no longer met. She stared down at her stomach, and her heart beat faster – not only must she definitely be pregnant, but it was starting to show.

She pushed the wardrobe door wider open and studied her reflection in the full-length mirror. Yes, her stomach was certainly a little rounder. Not enough to be obvious to anyone else but her at the moment, but it soon would be.

Panic rising within her, she took off her jeans and put on a gathered skirt; she'd have to tell her parents very soon.

She'd tell her mother first, she decided as she went down the stairs. Her mother would hate the idea of her daughter being an unmarried mother, that was for sure, but on the other hand, she very much wanted to be a grandmother, and this would be her only chance – she could never love anyone else but Kalden. Hopefully, her mother's desire for a grandchild would outweigh the fact that she wasn't married.

As for her father, she dreaded telling him. She knew him well enough to know that he'd see this as a shameful situation. Her only hope was to try to counteract that by pointing out that if the baby were a boy, he could join the Major's regiment. The thought of having a grandson might just help him to see her pregnancy in a positive light. She was far from convinced that it would, but tell him she'd have to, and she couldn't leave it too long after telling her mother.

She stepped off the bottom stair on to the hard lino and glanced towards the kitchen. She'd tell her mother that morning while they were out – she would know what to do next.

'You're very quiet, Patsy,' Enid said a little later as they walked up Belsize Grove towards the shops. 'Is anything wrong?'

'No, there's nothing wrong as such,' she said, suddenly very nervous. She bit her thumbnail. 'Actually, I wouldn't mind getting a cake. We could stop at Grodzinski's and treat ourselves, and then we could sit on a bench and eat it. There's something I want to tell you.'

'It all sounds very mysterious. All right, then, we'll get that cake, but we mustn't let it ruin our appetite. You know what your father's like.'

Enid stared at her, her face ashen.

'Say something, Mother,' Patricia urged. 'You're going to be a grandmother. It's what you wanted, isn't it?'

She saw the alarm in her mother's eyes, and felt a stab of fear. She'd been so happy at the thought of having Kalden's baby that deep down she'd felt sure she'd be able to persuade her parents to feel the same. But maybe she'd been naïve. Her mother looked anything but pleased, and if she couldn't convince her *mother* …

'Please say something, Mother.'

Her mother turned a chalk-white face towards her, her eyes watering. 'Have you thought how your father will take this, Patricia? Have you thought what he'll say, what he'll do?'

'Well, yes, I have a bit. I thought he might like the idea of a boy who could join his regiment ... if it *is* a boy. Obviously, not to replace James ...' Her voice trailed off. 'Aren't you pleased for me?' she whispered. 'I'll always have a part of Kalden. You know how much I love him.'

Her mother took her hand and squeezed it. 'I can understand how you feel, darling, really I can. You must believe that. But there are other things to think about, too. Like your father.'

'Father loves me in his own way and he'll want me to be happy. I know he was furious when he found out about Kalden and me, but that was instinctive. If he'd had longer to get used to the idea, he'd have come round in the end, I'm sure.'

'That's neither here nor there, Patricia. There is no Kalden any more,' her mother said gently. 'There are only the neighbours,' she gestured around her, 'and the people we know, such as your father's regimental colleagues. Heaven knows, you would have found it hard enough with a child of mixed race if you and Kalden had been married, but to have such a child without a husband ... It would be far more difficult than you can possibly imagine. For a start, I'm quite certain that the child would never be accepted into your father's regiment.'

'Kalden and I would have managed whatever happened,' Patricia cut in quickly. 'And our child would have been loved – and will be loved – and that's the most important thing.'

'Maybe you would have managed, but we won't ever know. The thing is, you're not married. You would be an unmarried mother, which brings shame in itself, and worse than that, your child would be a half-caste. How do you think your father would cope with that?'

Patricia pulled her hand away from her mother and slid back against the bench, her half-eaten cake forgotten. 'So you're saying that Father's bound to be against me having a baby and that you don't like the idea, either. Even though the child will be the only thing I have left of Kalden. What the neighbours might think is more important than what I feel. Is that it?'

'If we lived on a desert island, I'd be so happy for you. I know how much you miss Kalden and how you'd love to have such a permanent reminder of him. But we don't live on a desert island.' She gazed at Patricia with sympathy. 'I'm sorry, darling, but that's the truth.'

'What do you think Father will say, apart from the fact that he's not pleased?' Patricia asked after a short pause. 'If I'm pregnant, there's not really a lot he can do about it, is there? Except kick me out of the house. But that would also bring disgrace upon the family and I can't really see him wanting to go down that path. Can you?'

'The most important word at the moment is "if". You said, *if* you are pregnant. You don't yet know for certain that you are. There are lots of reasons why a woman misses a few periods. I suggest that we don't say anything to anyone until we're absolutely sure of what we're facing.'

'Fair enough.'

'The first thing is to make a doctor's appointment for as soon as possible – we'll ring up from the public phone in front of the cinema. I'll come to the doctor's with you and your father will think we've gone shopping. And talking about shopping, I suggest we finish our cakes, buy what we need and go home.'

The doctor's examination was brief, but thorough. From the expression on his face as he went back outside the screen, leaving her to get dressed, Patricia knew that her suspicion had been confirmed.

She finished dressing and went and sat next to her mother on the other side of the doctor's desk. Her mother gave her an encouraging smile, then they turned back to the doctor, who was rapidly scanning her file. When he'd finished, he picked up his pen and asked about her periods. Glancing occasionally at her mother's drawn face, she gave her dates to the best of her recollection.

She was definitely pregnant, the doctor said at last, putting his pen down on the blotting pad. He'd done a blood test and would send it away, but there was no doubt in his mind about the result: the physical evidence was unmistakable. She could expect to give birth around the middle of May. His eyes slipped to her left hand. Instinctively, she slid her right hand on top of her left. Her mother's arm brushed hers as she leaned across and put a hand on top of hers.

His face impassive, the doctor looked from Patricia to Enid and back again to Patricia, then he suggested a date for a further appointment. They agreed the date and walked out of the surgery into the overcast morning.

'I've never liked Dr Saunders,' Enid said as they started walking up the tree-lined hill towards Belsize Park Gardens, the dead leaves crackling under their feet. 'He's not what you'd call a friendly man. Your father likes him, though, and I have to admit that the advice he's given George over the years about his arthritis has been quite helpful. What do you think of him?'

Patricia didn't answer.

Enid glanced at her. She was walking along, her eyes fixed on the ground and her hand resting on her stomach. Enid fell silent and turned away.

Beneath the wool of her skirt, Patricia could feel the slight swell of her baby, her gift from Kalden, a gift she already loved.

With every step that she took, memories of Ladakh

flooded into her mind. She saw before her the stone-covered plateau, the steep slopes of red and crimson scree, the diverse shades of grey in the rocks, the snow-capped peaks that towered above the plateau, the *chortens* and the *manis*, their colourful prayer flags fluttering in the breeze, and she saw Kalden.

They reached the top of the hill and turned to the left. A tap on her arm pulled her out of her reverie, and she realised that Enid was telling her to step off the pavement. Looking up, she saw a young woman pushing her pram towards them along the narrow pavement. She stepped into the gutter and stood still. Enid walked a little further on, then paused to wait for her daughter.

'How old is your baby?' Patricia asked the woman as the pram drew alongside her. The woman stopped where she was. Patricia peered into the pram and gazed at the tiny face that was almost hidden by a pile of blankets.

'She's two months,' the mother replied. 'I'm taking her for her check-up.'

'She's lovely,' she said, and she smiled into the pram. 'She's really sweet.'

'She's not that sweet when she's yelling at two in the morning, I can tell you! Have you got any kids?'

'I'm having a baby in May.'

'Good luck to you, then. I hope it's a better sleeper than Claire.'

And the mother moved off.

Enid resumed walking and Patricia hurried to catch her up. 'Shall we tell Father when we get back home?'

'I think we might as well. There's no point in putting it off any longer, is there? The blood test will only confirm what we already know. But if your father appears to be in a bad mood, we'll leave it for another day. We'll play it by ear, as they say.'

The Major sat behind his desk in the front room and heard Patricia in silence, his back ramrod straight, his lips set in a grim line. Enid stood nervously behind her daughter. Patricia finished telling him about the baby and waited for him to speak, but he sat motionless, unspeaking, his eyes looking beyond her. She cleared her throat, willing him to say something.

'Am I expected to congratulate you upon the conception of a bastard?' he asked at last, his voice hard. Patricia heard her mother catch her breath. 'Animals fornicate and as a consequence, produce young. Is the fact that you have achieved what the lowliest beast can achieve a matter for praise? Well, is it?' he asked sharply, his eyes ice-cold.

'Of course not, Father,' she said, her voice shaking. 'But it was a bit more than that. I love Kalden. My baby is the result of love.'

'Love, you call it! I think lust might be a more accurate word – lust for a man you hardly knew, for a man who could never have offered you a future. Kindly don't dress it up, madam.'

'I loved him and I'm not ashamed of it.'

'And I suppose that you're not ashamed of ignoring the teachings of the Christian Church and letting him have what he wanted out of wedlock? Where is your self-respect, girl? We expected you to value yourself more highly. You may not be ashamed for yourself, but I am ashamed for you, as no doubt is your mother. We deserved better from you than public disgrace.'

'There's no disgrace in loving someone like Kalden. You never really got to know him, but I did. He was a wonderful person, kind and loving.'

'I think we are all now well aware of the nature of his love. That is only too evident from your present predicament. When both of you were so late in returning that day at the mountain pasture, I did wonder fleetingly if there could be anything untoward between you, but I believed in you, Patricia, and I refused to entertain thoughts that placed you in a bad light. I took your words at face value. It would appear, however, that you lied to me then, just as you lied to me before I left for Leh, and no doubt on many other occasions, too. What kind of love gives rise to lies?'

'You can twist it any way you want, Father. But if Kalden hadn't died, we would have got married and we would have been very happy. I will never feel ashamed of having his baby.'

'You may feel what you wish, Patricia, just as your mother and I are entitled to feel as we do. And in the same way, it is up to you to choose what you do. After all, you will have to live with the consequences of your decision.'

She looked at her father, confused. 'What choice have I got? I'm already pregnant.'

'As you have made very clear. Let me assure you, Patricia, that I do not expect you to attempt to procure for yourself a miscarriage, nor to go to any of the so-called backstreet abortionists, about whom one hears such horror stories. No, your choice is a very simple one: you either give up the child for adoption as soon as it is born or you keep the baby.'

'I'm going to keep the baby, of course.'

'Whichever course you decide upon, you will have to defer taking up your place at the teaching college until next year, but that should prove possible. Should you choose the option of adoption, you may remain at home until your condition becomes unmistakable. I shall then find somewhere for you to stay for the final months of your pregnancy. It will be at some distance from here – I should prefer the neighbours not to be over familiar with every detail of our private life. When the time for the birth approaches, you will be admitted into a home for unmarried mothers. I believe that there are several such places around. As soon as the child has been handed over to its new parents, you may return home.'

'I will never agree to that.'

'You will naturally need time to think about it. However, I am sure that you will agree, upon reflection, that it is a generous offer. I am, of course, prepared to meet every expense that is incurred.' He paused a moment, and cleared his throat. 'You may not feel it at the moment, Patricia, but I do love you and I want only what is the best for you in the long run.'

She stared at her father, frightened. 'I couldn't give up my baby. I couldn't give him up. I love him. It's all I've got of Kalden. Please don't make me do that.'

'I am not making you do anything, Patricia. The choice is yours.'

'Then I'm going to keep my baby. That's my choice.'

'Then you may remain here until your condition becomes clearly visible. At that point you must leave this house and find your own lodgings. You will make your own arrangements about the birth and you will find yourself somewhere to live after the child is born, somewhere that will accommodate a baby.'

'But how will I pay for everything? I won't be able to work when I'm really large. And once the baby's born, I'll have to look after him, so I won't be able to work then, or not very easily. What would I do with the baby while I was working?'

'That is for you to determine. My time in the National Assistance Board suggests that you may well be eligible for some sort of benefit – most people seem to be. I imagine that there is some form of assistance for unmarried mothers. You might wish to research available benefits while you await the birth, if keeping the child is the course of action that you decide upon.'

She turned to her mother in panic, but Enid gestured her helplessness and shook her head. She turned back to her father, and stared at him in a silent plea.

'I have set out the options as I see them,' he said, standing up. 'Of course, you may come up with a plan that I have not thought of, in which case you will pursue that plan, if that is your wish. Whatever you choose to do is entirely up to you, Patricia. I suggest that you now go to your room and give the matter some thought.'

'Please, Father …'

'I think I have said all that there is to be said.' He looked beyond her to his wife. 'Regarding tea this afternoon, Enid, you and I will take our tea together in the kitchen. You may take Patricia's tea to her room. She will wish, I am sure, to remain in her room to consider the options I've put before her.'

He walked out from behind the desk and crossed the room to the door. Opening the door, he motioned to Enid to go through it, and then he opened it wider for Patricia. She stared at him, unable to move.

'You may leave now, Patricia,' he said from the doorway.

Numb within, she walked slowly across the room. When she was almost out of the room, he laid his hand gently on her shoulder.

'I am not entirely without sympathy for the position you find yourself in,' he said awkwardly, 'although I am aware that it may sound as if I am. You are my daughter and you have been a good daughter to me. Furthermore, I do recognise that in the period prior to learning of your relationship with Kalden, I found him to be a pleasant young man.'

'Thank you, Father,' she said quietly. 'You don't know what it means to me to hear you say that. Thank you.'

He held up his hand to stop her. 'But I cannot lie and say that I am not pleased that your relationship with him has

251

ended. I *am* pleased – it was an unsuitable liaison – but I do regret very much the way in which it ended. And despite the fact that I abhor the way in which you have behaved, I can see that this must be hard for you.'

She audibly caught her breath, her eyes widening in hope.

'But I cannot, and I will not, allow our name to be dragged through the mud,' he went on, and her hope faded. 'Not just for my sake and your mother's, but also for your sake. You are still very young and you have a good future ahead of you, provided that that future remains unsullied. As your father, it is my duty to do my utmost to ensure that it does.' He paused.

'I understand, Father.'

'Good. I have laid before you the two options as I see them. It's up to you which one you choose. In all conscience, I can do no more.' He opened the door a little wider. She took a step forward out of the room, then turned back to look at him. They stared at each other for a moment, neither saying a word, then the Major firmly closed the door.

Chapter Nineteen

April to May, 1963

Patricia walked slowly up Highbury Fields, her mother at her side. Past the open-air swimming pool she went and past the expanse of grass that lay beyond it, her eyes firmly on the gravel path in front of her. She was not going to look to the left to see the children playing on the fields; she was not going to let herself hear them laughing and talking to each other. Her eyes down, her feet moving one in front of the other, she reached the tennis courts, passed them, and came out on to Highbury Hill, leaving the fields and the children behind her.

'Let me get my breath,' Enid said. She stopped in front of the clock tower in the middle of the crossroads at the top of the hill, perched on the edge of its stone surround and put Patricia's suitcase on the ground next to her. 'Even though you haven't brought a lot, your case is beginning to feel quite heavy. That was more of a hill than I realised. And if *I'm* tired, you must be even more so, darling.' She nodded towards Patricia's swollen stomach.

'I'm fine. Do you want to go back and sit on one of the benches for a bit – you'd be more comfortable there than here? If you're tired, that is.'

'No, let's do this now.' Enid forced a smile, stood up and picked up the suitcase again. 'We don't want to shilly-shally, do we? We're nearly there now. Might as well get it over with.' She squeezed her daughter's arm.

'But it's not going to be got over with, as you put it, for another month, is it? In fact, it'll be even longer than that. They're not going to take the baby away the minute it's born.' She started to move away, glancing up at the clock tower as she did so. She stopped abruptly. 'I'd call that colour ox-blood, wouldn't you? Ox-blood and gilt. How very appropriate since it marks the place where I'm going to betray Kalden by giving his baby away. And what's more, there's even a sun dial on top of the tower. The sun was going to be the symbol of our life together. How wrong can you be?'

'Let's go, Patricia,' Enid said quietly. She took her arm and they started to walk.

A little way down the hill, Enid stopped and stared across the road at one of the terraced Victorian houses that lined the pavement. Patricia glanced at her, then followed her gaze to the other side of the road and stared at the house opposite her. Neither of them said a word.

A tangled mass of holly grew over the outer railings and overhung the pavement. Between the house and the railings, half hidden by one of the brick gateposts that stood on either side of the iron gate, the branches of a dying tree reached up to the April sky. Like hands, she thought. The branches were just like hands, long bony hands with lots of veins – every vein, every artery visible beneath a transparent skin: dying hands. She looked away from the decaying tree and stared down at her stomach. Her baby was kicking.

'I think it's going to be a boy,' she said. 'It kicks all the time. I bet he'll be good at football.'

'Don't be too sure of that.' Enid smiled with her mouth. 'James hardly moved at all, but as for you – you couldn't keep still for a minute. That baby could just as easily be a girl.'

Patricia's eyes returned to the tall house and climbed to the grey slate roof where two chimneys stood: tall, narrow chimneys, which made the house seem loftier, more fearful.

'I'm going in now,' she told her mother abruptly. 'As you

said, we might as well get it over with. We'll say goodbye here.'

'Won't you let me come in with you? I want to see your room, see that you've got everything you need.' Enid's eyes pleaded with her.

'I'd rather be on my own. It'd be easier.'

'I feel as if I've let you down, Patsy.' Her eyes filled with tears and she put out her arms to hug her daughter. 'I didn't know what to do. I know you want to keep your baby – of course, you do – and I wanted to help you do that. But I didn't know how. You do know that, don't you?'

'I do know that, Mother.'

'If only I had a bit more money of my own, but I don't. I make very little, and what I bring home, we need. But if I had anything at all to spare, I'd give it to you so that you could keep the baby. Whatever the neighbours thought. But I haven't.'

'I understand, Mother.'

'I tried to talk to your father – I asked him to let you come home with the baby. I told him that you being happy was the most important thing of all. But you know your father, dear. He loves you, and he's so sure that he's right about this being the best thing for you that he won't even listen to me. You know what he's like, don't you, and you don't blame me. You don't, do you?'

'I do know what he's like. Yes.'

'And Daddy found you a nice place to stay for the last few weeks, didn't he? Mr and Mrs Taylor were kind to you and looked after you well, didn't they? We did the best we could.'

'They were fine, really they were.' Patricia pushed her mother's arms away. 'I'm sure you did everything you could, Mother,' she said. She took her suitcase from Enid's hands and started to cross the road.

'I did, didn't I? There was nothing else I could do.'

She reached the other side, and stepped out of the gutter and on to the pavement.

'Don't blame me for this, Patsy. I love you, darling,' she heard her mother call.

Without looking back, she walked between the gateposts and climbed the stone steps that led to the porch. Across the road behind her, she could hear Enid crying. Her back to her mother, she raised her hand to the iron doorknocker and rapped it twice. Then she stepped back from the porch and waited.

A movement to the left of her caught her eye. She turned towards the sash window just in time to glimpse a girl with long brown hair disappearing from sight.

She turned back to the door. At least she wouldn't be on her own in the Home, she thought as she waited for the door to open. That was a relief: she hadn't relished the idea of it being just her and the people in charge. There was a sound of steps approaching the door. A bolt of fear shot through her, and she gripped her suitcase more tightly as the door opened.

'You must be Patricia Carstairs,' a thin, angular woman said. 'My name is Miss Waterson. Come in.'

Trembling, she stepped out of the sun into the dark house. Miss Waterson closed the front door behind her. 'Follow me,' she said, and led the way along the narrow hallway, her footsteps reverberating loudly on the black-and-white marble tiles.

Trying not to make too much noise with her feet, Patricia followed her to a room at the far end of the hall. As she passed the foot of the staircase, she heard the sound of a baby crying on one of the upper floors, and she paused and looked up at the landing at the top of the flight of stairs.

'Try not to dawdle, there's a good girl,' Miss Waterson

said, her hand on the door to her office. 'I've got some papers for you to sign, and I'd like to get you sorted out before lunch.'

'Well, that's your part of the administration out of the way, Patricia. Your father has already dealt with the financial side of things,' Miss Waterson said, making a neat pile of the documents that Patricia had signed. She gave her a brief smile. 'You're a fortunate girl to have such supportive parents. Not all of our girls are in the same happy position. But to move on because time is short, for the time that you're with us, we would like you to look upon this as your home, not as a prison.' She paused and smiled again.

'Thank you,' Patricia murmured, feeling that she was expected to say something.

'But that doesn't mean that there aren't any rules, I'm afraid. Just as an efficient house is run according to rules, so, too, is this Home.' She held out a sheet of paper. 'I would ask you to study our rules and to abide by them. I feel that I should warn you that any infringement of the rules will result in the withdrawal of your television and radio privileges, and possibly in restrictions on your right to use the telephone. I think you'll agree that that is not unreasonable.' She paused again.

'No, Miss Waterson.'

'If you have any money with you, I'd like you to leave it with me. If you wish to use the telephone or buy anything from the Home, you can ask me for the necessary sum.'

Patricia shifted awkwardly in her chair.

'As far as visits are concerned, I expect your father will have told you that your parents are not allowed to visit you while you are here. We find that visits from the outside are too upsetting for the girls. You won't see your family again until you leave the Home, which will be approximately six weeks after the birth of the child. Now, do you have any questions that you wish to ask?'

'Nothing, thank you,' Patricia said quietly.

'Good. We'll leave it at that then. Perhaps you'd leave your purse with me now.' She paused and waited for Patricia to put her purse on the desk. 'As I said before, we want you to feel at home during what will obviously be a difficult time for you. You mustn't hesitate to come to me if you have any problems, and if there's anything I can do to help, I will.'

'That's very kind of you. Thank you.'

'One of the other girls, Valerie Merton, has been assigned to you, and she will give you a timetable. We follow the same routine every day, with the exception of Sunday, when you will be taken to church in the morning and you will not have to do any cleaning that day. However, if you break any rules, you might find yourself losing your free time on Sundays.'

She got up, walked past Patricia to the door and opened it. 'Ah, good, you're here, Valerie,' Patricia heard her say. 'Be sure to explain the system for cleaning the Home to Patricia, and show her the duty rota. Her name is already on it.' She turned back to Patricia, and smiled again. 'You may go to your dormitory now,' she said. 'Valerie will take you there.'

'Hang on to those smiles – you won't get any more,' Valerie murmured under her breath as she led Patricia up the stairs to the room in which she was to sleep. 'And I'm Val, not Valerie. The old cow knows that. Are you Pat or Patricia or something else?'

Patricia found that she couldn't answer her for the lump in her throat.

There were about twenty girls in the house, Val told her. Their dormitory was full and like the two of them, all of the girls in it were in the last weeks of their pregnancy. The girls who'd already had their babies slept in a different dormitory and weren't allowed to mix with the girls waiting to give birth.

'Why not?'

'So they can't tell us what's it like in the hospital and how awful the nursery is, I 'spect. Last week, when none of the Gestapo were around, I got talking to a girl who had her baby a couple of weeks ago – she lives on my street – and she said that it's bloody cold in the nursery, not to mention dirty. Typical of this lousy dump.'

'I thought Miss Waterson seemed all right. Can't she do anything about it?'

'Ha! You'll see how all right she is soon enough,' Val said. 'Now, let's go and eat.'

Later that night, as she lay on her back beneath a thin blanket, Patricia closed her eyes and waited to see Kalden's face, just as she'd done every night since the night when he'd fallen to his death. But for the first time since she'd lost him, she couldn't see him. Stiff with grief and fear, she lay on the hard bed and waited all night for Kalden to come to her. In vain.

The following morning, Val showed her the rota and pointed out that she and Patricia were down to clean the hall floor after breakfast.

'It's like we've got to be punished. We have to work every day like you wouldn't believe,' Val told her as they each took a metal bucket full of water and a scrubbing brush from the scullery and went out into the hall. 'And we're meant to be grateful to them 'cos they let us live in this shithole and take us to hospital to have the baby.' She clumsily got down on her hands and knees at the entrance to the hall. 'Right, I'll show you what to do.'

'Are your parents making you give up your baby?' Patricia asked a few days later when she and Val were scrubbing the marble tiles of the hall floor for the second time that week.

'In a way, but not really. I mean, I'm only seventeen, aren't I? I don't really want to be saddled with a kid at my age when I've never even looked after myself. I suppose I might have thought about keeping the baby if my mum and dad would have helped, but they don't want to know, do they? I can bring it home, they said, but I'd have to look after it myself. And I can't do that on my own. It's not just the money – you can get a bit from the government, though it's hardly a fortune – it's all the things you've got to do for a baby.'

'But whatever your parents said, they might feel differently when the baby was born.'

'Too dodgy. Suppose they don't? And I want to go out and have some fun, and get married. Who's going to want to take on someone else's kid? No, it's probably just as well that I can't keep it.'

'What about your baby's father?'

'That was just a one-night stand, nothing serious. I got unlucky. But I can tell you one thing – I'm not going to do it no more with no one, not till I've got a ring on my finger. That's for sure.'

Behind them, they heard the office door open and footsteps come towards them. They bent their heads over the floor and scrubbed harder.

'Don't forget the staircase, you girls, when you've done the floor. You're down to polish it today.' Miss Waterson stepped on to the patch of floor that they'd just washed.

They sat back on their heels, their scrubbing brush in their hands. 'No, Miss Waterson,' they said in unison.

'I want to see my face in the banisters when you've finished. If I can't, I'll ask you to do it again. Now I suggest that you stop talking and concentrate on what you're meant to be doing. And I, too, need to concentrate, which I can't do whilst you're making such a noise.' She turned and went back to her room.

'The cow,' Val muttered angrily. 'She's just in this for the money. Maureen and Brenda did the staircase yesterday. It doesn't need doing again today, and she knows it. And what's she want to see her face in the banisters for, anyway? She's a right ugly bitch.'

When they'd finished the hall floor, they collected some rags and paraffin from the scullery and lumbered slowly to the top of the wooden staircase. They were panting hard by the time that they reached the upper landing, and having checked that no one was around, they sat down heavily on the top stair.

'What about you?' Val asked when they'd recovered their breath.

'What do you mean, what about me?'

'You know. The same as you asked me. Are your parents forcing you to have your baby adopted?'

'They said that I could choose what to do, but if I wanted to keep the baby, I'd have to leave home and manage on my own without their help. That's what I was going to do at first, so I went to the National Assistance people and they said that I'd get some money, even though it wouldn't be a lot.'

'You can say that again! They're so stingy, you don't even get three pounds.'

'I liked the woman who interviewed me – she didn't preach or look down her nose at me. She did say, though, that I should think seriously about what was best for my baby. A married couple wanting a baby would be able to offer it much more than I could, she said. They'd give him a good home and love him. But she said it nicely. When she could see that I'd no intention of giving my baby up, she told me about the benefits and suggested that I ask the Council about social housing. She did warn me, though, not to get too hopeful.'

'And did you go to them?'

'You bet. I applied the next day. And what do you know, I'm unmarried and I'm having a baby, so I'm obviously no better than a prostitute, and the Council certainly wasn't going to help people like me.'

'Smug hypocrites.'

'So much for that, I thought, and I decided to see what I could rent on benefits. Honestly, Val, you've never seen anything like some of the bedsits I went to, and they weren't that cheap, either. There are lots of people looking for places to rent, and landlords can charge what they want for dingy little rooms, with everyone in the house sharing the same dirty bathroom. Some of the houses were even full of rats. I couldn't take my baby into places like that.'

'Of course you couldn't. And your parents really wouldn't help you when it came down to it?'

'They were only prepared to help if I gave my baby up for adoption.'

'That's really mean of them.'

'I don't know that it's mean, as such. My father's convinced that he's making me do what's best for me. The trouble is, he doesn't really understand what I feel; how much I want my baby. That's not being mean. It's being wrong.' Her voice caught.

'We'd better stop talking about our babies or we'll both start blubbing,' Val said, with a forced laugh. 'Come on, Pat, you rub the paraffin into the wood, and I'll dry it off with the cloth. Then we'll take turns rubbing the polish in. We'll pretend we're grinding old Waterson into the wood, and that'll make us feel better.'

Slowly they worked their way down the staircase, sitting on the stairs whenever possible to take the weight from their knees. When they finally reached the bottom, Patricia stood back and surveyed the sheen that ran up the flight of stairs.

Stretching herself, she leaned back and tried to rub the small of her back with her hand.

'Thank God, that's done,' she said wearily. 'Fancy them making us work as hard as this in our condition.'

'What would your dad say if he knew? Would he tell you that you could go back home at once? Mine wouldn't – he'd say that it'll teach me a lesson.'

Patricia thought for a moment. 'I don't really know,' she said slowly. 'I'm certain that he wants me to be treated well, and he thinks that that's happening. In fact, I think he'd be very angry if he found out that I wasn't being properly looked after. On the other hand, though, he doesn't want anyone to know that I'm pregnant, and if I went back home looking like this, they would. I don't really know what he'd say, but as I'm not going to tell him, I'll never find out.'

'You might be wrong about what he'd say. Why don't you tell him? It's awful here and you might be able to escape.'

'But I don't want to leave. I want it to be awful. Maybe not quite as awful as it is, but I want to be punished – not punished for being pregnant, like they're doing here – but punished for agreeing to give my baby away.'

'But you didn't have much choice, from what you said.'

'Maybe I did, maybe I didn't. I don't know anything any more. Anyway, let's go and have our tea now.'

That night, as Patricia lay in her bed, her eyes closed, she wondered if that would be the night that Kalden would creep into her mind again. But as with every night since she'd moved into the Home, he failed to come. She opened her eyes and turned her head towards the cupboard where she kept her handbag. Her photo of Kalden was in the bag.

She knew that she could get up, open the cupboard door, take the bag out and look upon his face again. But she hadn't done it on any of the other nights and she wasn't going to do it that night. She wasn't going to do it while she was in the

263

Home, nor when she was in the hospital. Maybe she wasn't going to be able to look at his face ever again.

She lay back on her pillow and gazed up at the ceiling. This was no place for Kalden. She was glad that he wouldn't come to her while she was there: she didn't want him to see what she was about to do.

Eight weeks later Patricia walked down the stone steps that led from the Home, went through the gate and on to the pavement, her suitcase in her hand.

Her father stood next to her mother on the opposite side of the road, facing her, waiting for her. She crossed the road and walked up to them.

'I called her Nima,' she said. 'My baby's name is Nima. It means the sun.'

PART TWO

Chapter Twenty

Patricia sat in the chair by the window in her small upstairs room. Her heart beating fast, she read the letter again.

Dear Patricia Carstairs,

My name is Amy Stevens. I have reason to believe that we are connected.

I am 32 years old. I was born in Highbury, London, in May 1963, and my birth name was Nima Carstairs.

If you believe as I do that there is a connection between us, and you feel that you would like further contact, you can get hold of me at 62 Ainger Crescent, Primrose Hill, N.W.1. My telephone number is 0171 9768.

Yours sincerely,
Amy Stevens

Nima. She said the name aloud when she finished the letter, and she turned and stared through the window. The sun was shining brightly. Her Nima. She might soon be meeting her. Meeting her child. Her stomach churning, she looked back at the letter and read Amy's words for the third time. Her hands fell to her lap.

Had Nima – No, Amy; she must think of her as Amy now. Had Amy been adopted by people who loved her and treated her well? Had she been happy? What would she think of her?

Her heart missed a beat. Would Amy blame her for not keeping her? Would she be angry that she'd been given away and hate her for what she'd done? She'd have to make her understand that she'd had to do what she did. She couldn't have done anything else.

Or could she?

She felt nauseous. As the years had passed, that question had come into her mind more and more frequently. She'd always managed to push it away – what had happened, had happened, and that was that; she'd done the only thing she could do in the circumstances. But would her daughter agree? Would she understand that she'd had no choice?

She looked down at Amy's address. It was a Primrose Hill address. Camden Town was no distance at all from Primrose Hill. If Amy had always lived there, she would probably have shopped in Camden Town on occasions – they could even have been in the same shop at the same time, and not known.

She glanced out of the window again. Over the years, people had kept on telling her to get out more, to make a life for herself, but she'd ignored them all – the past was where she'd wanted to be, and that was where she'd stayed. But if she'd listened to them she might have met Amy. If she hadn't always kept her eyes on the pavement when she'd been out of the house, she might have seen her in the street, in a shop. She'd have known her at once – her baby had Kalden's eyes.

Clutching the letter tightly, she got up and started to pace the small room. She'd reply to Amy. Of course, she would – Amy was her child and she wanted to meet her, was desperate to meet her. But what should she say? How much should she put in her first letter?

She went over to a shelf, picked up a pen and pad, went back to her chair, opened the pad and stared at the blank piece of paper. Then she started to write.

Dear Amy,

Thank you very much for your letter. I can't deny that it came as a huge shock, but a very welcome shock. I'm really thrilled that you've contacted me.

There is nothing in the world I want more than I want to meet you and get to know you. I can't tell you how much I hope that you feel the same.

With best wishes,
Patricia (Carstairs)

She read through what she'd written, then she carefully folded the letter, put it into an envelope, stamped and addressed the envelope and hurried down the stairs and out of the house. As she made her way along the street to the post box, her eyes scanned the face of every person she passed.

Four days later, the postman brought Amy's reply.

Dear Patricia,

I'm quite willing to meet you – I wouldn't have got in touch with you had that not been the case.

What about meeting at Marine Ices, opposite the Round House in Chalk Farm – say next Saturday, at 11 a.m.? It's central to both of us. If that doesn't suit you, perhaps you would suggest a different arrangement.

Yours sincerely,
Amy

It did suit her, Patricia immediately wrote back, and she was very much looking forward to meeting Amy. She addressed the envelope and got up to go and post it. As she did so, she caught sight of herself in the mirror that stood on the shelf. She went closer to the mirror, and stared at her reflection.

She hadn't realised it before, but she looked every bit her fifty-one years of age, and maybe even older than that. Her hand went to her greying shoulder-length hair. Perhaps she should give her hair a colour rinse before she met Nima – before she met Amy. She seemed to have gone grey overnight. And her hair could also do with a trim. She must look her best on Saturday. She wanted Amy to like her.

They stared at each other across the table.

'Well, I don't look much like you,' Amy said, leaning back in her chair.

'You look like your father.'

'I guess that figures if I don't look like you, and I don't.' Amy picked up a menu and opened it.

Fingering the edge of the table cloth, Patricia smiled tentatively across the table. 'It's strange, isn't it, meeting like this?'

Amy glanced up at her. 'You can say that again. To be honest, I know this was my idea, but I don't really know why I suggested meeting you. I had the best mum and dad in the world – they were amazing parents – and I don't need any more.'

'Do they know you're here?'

'I wouldn't go behind their backs, if that's what you mean.' She paused. 'Mum died two years ago, and Dad died a few months ago.'

'I'm very sorry.'

'What about – you abandoning me or my parents dying? Look, you don't have to answer that. Let's get some coffee, shall we?'

'I'll get them. How do you like your coffee?'

'Black, please. No sugar.'

'Would you like a scone or something with it?'

'No, thanks. Just the coffee.'

A few minutes later, Patricia returned to the table with two coffees and sat down. She took a sip of her drink. 'You've got a ring on your finger, I see. What's your husband's name?'

'Andrew. He's an architect.'

'An architect, is he? That's nice.'

'I look after his books for him.' Amy stared pointedly at Patricia's left hand. 'I take it you didn't get married, or if you did, you're not married any more.'

'I never married.'

'Have you any children?'

'Just you.'

'I don't really count, do I?'

Patricia took another sip of her coffee. 'What about you – have you got any children?'

'I had a miscarriage four months ago. We still haven't got over losing our baby.'

Patricia put her cup back on the saucer and looked across at Amy. 'I'm so sorry. Losing a baby is the hardest thing that can happen to anyone.'

'Especially if you don't choose to lose it.'

She picked up her drink again. 'How did you find me?'

'Dad left a letter for me to read after his death. It had the address of the house in Highbury where you gave me away, and also the Adoption Order. He thought I might want to know more about my background one day. It wasn't difficult to find you – you've got the same name and you live in the same sort of area as you used to. Andrew did the leg work.'

'That was kind of him.'

'He's a kind man. He'd have been a great dad. Rather, he will be a great dad when the time comes.'

'You haven't asked about your father, Amy – your birth

father, that is,' Patricia ventured after a few minutes' silence. 'Do you want me to tell you about him?'

'I suppose I must want to know something about you both or I wouldn't have contacted you like I did. I wasn't going to, you know – I don't need you – but losing my baby like that … and Dad dying … well, I suppose I suddenly wondered how anyone could give their child away.'

'I understand,' Patricia said quietly. 'And I wouldn't blame you if you hated me.'

'I don't hate you. You have to know someone to hate them. I don't know you at all. You're not part of my life and never have been.' She paused. 'So where is he, then, my birth father? Presumably, he's Asian or something like that. There's no way I got these eyes from a full-blooded Englishman. And I obviously didn't get them from you.'

'He was born in Ladakh.'

'Where's that? I've never heard of it.'

Patricia smiled. 'Not many people have. It's a shame as it's a beautiful country. It's north east of India – north of the Himalayas – and west of Tibet.'

'That explains Nima, then. I wondered where the name came from.'

'*Nima* means the sun. You were going to be the sun in our lives. When I was eighteen, my father and I went on a trip to Ladakh, and that's where we met Kalden, your father.'

'My father's name is Brian Galloway, and my mother's name is Maisie Galloway. My birth father's name was Kalden. I think that was what you meant to say, wasn't it?'

'You're right, of course. I'm sorry. I'll try to be more careful with my words in future.'

'So I'm the result of a holiday romance, am I? That's too corny for words.'

'Not in the way that you mean, you're not. Kalden and

I genuinely loved each other. He was so good-looking, he took my breath away the moment I met him. And he was such a wonderful person. How I loved him!'

'And that's why you gave your child away to someone else, is it? Yes, that makes good sense.'

'You don't understand. How could you? Long before we knew I was expecting you, we decided to stay together forever. Kalden was killed as we were leaving Ladakh to come back to England – he fell off a high bridge.' She stared at Amy, who was looking down at the table. 'I'm afraid that he died,' she repeated. 'If I hadn't insisted on crossing the bridge before we stopped for the night ... if I hadn't been in such a hurry to get off the bridge at the other side ... it might never have happened. But it did. And he died.'

Amy raised her eyes to Patricia's face. 'I'm glad you loved each other and that I wasn't the result of a meaningless one-night stand. That would have hurt.'

'I can't tell you how often I've re-lived that moment just before we started to cross the bridge. Whenever I re-live it, we don't go across until the following morning, and there's no accident. My life would have been so different. You, me, Kalden – we'd have been a family. I might have had more children.'

'I'm sorry it worked out for you like it did, but there's no point in speculating about what might have happened in different circumstances. It's in the past and long gone. The future's all that matters. And talking about the future,' Amy started to button up her jacket, 'I've got some shopping to do. We've finished our coffees so we might as well go our separate ways now, don't you think?'

'If that's what you want.'

'Well, we've met – I wondered if I'd be confronted by someone who looked like me, but I wasn't – and I now know where I came from and what happened to my birth father. I don't think there's anything more to be gained by talking for longer.'

'I'd very much like to see you again, Amy. But that must obviously be your decision,' Patricia said, and she stood up. 'You've got my address and you can always contact me. There's so much I want to know about you ... about your life ... everything ... I know I don't have the right; I'd just like to know, though. So I do hope you want to meet me again. You can say where and when. Anyway, I can see that you want to get off now, so I'll say goodbye.'

She smiled at Amy, and walked out into Chalk Farm Road, her vision blurring.

They met at the bottom of Pond Street the following Saturday afternoon, and made their way to the lower part of Hampstead Heath.

'We're lucky with the weather,' Patricia said as they strolled past the first of the ponds. 'Planning to go for a walk in England is always tricky – you never know if it'll rain. We used to walk for miles, Kalden and I. But rain's not a problem in Ladakh,' she added with a smile.

'I know,' Amy said shortly. 'I've been reading up about it.'

'I'm so glad you suggested meeting today. I was desperately hoping you would write again.'

'I wasn't going to. At least, I don't think I was. But as Andrew pointed out, I didn't ask you the big question, the one that deep down I must have wanted the answer to most of all.' She stopped and turned to Patricia. 'Why did you have me adopted? If you loved Kalden as much as you said you did, why didn't you keep me?'

'Believe me, I wanted to,' Patricia said quietly. 'I wanted to keep you very much. Every day for the last thirty-two years, I've regretted that I didn't fight harder to keep you, no matter how difficult it would have been. I've never stopped thinking about you, wondering what you were doing, hoping you were all right.'

'So why didn't you fight harder, as you put it?'

'I don't think I've ever really been able to answer that question satisfactorily to myself.'

'Have a try, why don't you?'

'I was eighteen – which was very young in those days. I was totally dependent upon my father, and I was still trying to cope with losing Kalden. It was a different world then. There was a real stigma if you were an unmarried mother, and my father was one of those people who always worried about what others thought. He was a strong, domineering person – an ex-army man, a major – and it wasn't easy to stand up to him. He made me choose between being cut off from my family and living on my own with a small baby to look after, or giving you up for adoption and staying at home. In the end, I agreed to give you up – I couldn't see how I could manage by myself without any help.'

'Other people in your position did.'

'I know they did, and I've always wished that I'd tried harder. I did try, though – I went to the benefits' office and to the housing people, but they were no help, and I looked at the bedsits I'd just about be able to afford. You can't imagine how squalid they were. You couldn't bring up a baby in such a place.'

'What about your mother? Was she in favour of you giving your child to goodness knows who?'

'No, she wasn't. If she could have helped me, she would have done. But she didn't have any money of her own, and she was far worse than I was at standing up to my father.' She glanced at Amy's face. 'It must be virtually impossible for you to understand what it was like thirty years ago. Unmarried mothers have it much easier today, what with benefits, crèches, the so-called sexual revolution, and less hostility in society generally. But back in 1963, when I was expecting you, I genuinely didn't feel that I had any real choice.'

'Your father sounds pretty horrible.'

'Horrible's too strong a word. He was a complex man, and a very unhappy one, but to give him his due, he thought he was doing what was best for me. But I'll tell you about my family another time – if there is to be another time, and I hope that there will be.' She paused. 'I don't know if I've made you understand why I gave you away. I hope I have. Above all, I hope you believe me when I say that it wasn't an easy thing to do, and that I regret it very much.'

'I do believe you regret what you did. You would do: you're on your own now, and you're getting older, with no family around you. Most people would regret doing the thing that caused that.'

'You must think what you want. I know it's more than that. And whatever you say to me, you can't stop me from being thrilled that you got in touch. Just to see you ...' Her voice caught.

Amy glanced at her quickly, and looked away. 'We'd better go back now. It's getting dark and I'm sure we've both got things to do.'

They turned round and started walking across the Heath in the direction of Pond Street.

'Can we meet again?' Patricia asked. 'I still don't know anything about you and what you've done over the years.'

'I'm not sure that there's any point. I don't need a mother now.'

'I know that. But I'd like to think that we could have some kind of relationship, nevertheless.'

Amy shrugged her shoulders, and they walked on in silence for a few minutes. 'What did Kalden look like?' she asked suddenly. 'I know you said he was good-looking, but apart from that. Have you got any photos of him?'

'Not a lot, but some. They're at home. Why don't you come for tea one afternoon and I'll show them to you?' She saw the indecision in Amy's eyes. 'I'm sure you'd like to see what he looks like, especially as you're so like him to look at. You wouldn't be committing yourself to anything.'

'My eyes are like his, I know.'

Patricia smiled. 'It's not just your eyes – your whole face is like his, and your mannerisms. You're very like him in lots of ways.'

'Maybe I will come and have a look at your photos, then. I could come next Saturday afternoon, if you like.'

Patricia's shoulders relaxed.

Chapter Twenty-One

Patricia stepped back from the front door. 'Come on in.'

Amy walked slowly into the downstairs room and looked around her. Her gaze ran along the shelves and the mantelpiece, across the wooden coffee table, along the top of the small television set in the corner of the room.

Patricia followed her eyes to the television. She gave a little laugh. 'It is tiny, isn't it? I'm not really one for the TV. I prefer reading.' She indicated the crowded bookshelves on either side of the fireplace.

'Me, too.'

'I'll get us some tea. Is it normal tea you like? I got in some camomile, just in case. Or you can have coffee. I know you like coffee. It's only instant, I'm afraid. I'm not a great coffee drinker, although I drink it when I'm out.'

'Whatever you're having is fine by me.'

'Normal tea, it is, then. I know you don't have sugar in your coffee. What about in tea?'

'No, thanks.'

'Sit down, do. I won't be a moment.' Patricia hurried into the kitchen, pressed the switch on the kettle and leaned against the worktop.

'I see you like nineteenth-century literature,' she heard Amy call from the front room.

'I do, very much,' she shouted back, pouring boiling water on to the tea bags in the pot. She placed the pot on a tray next to the things she'd put out earlier, picked up the tray and carried it into the front room.

'Jane Austen's my favourite,' she said, putting the tray on the coffee table. 'Do sit down.' She took the chair closest to her and Amy sat down opposite her. 'I read modern literature as well, though. I'm not totally locked in the past.' She laughed again, poured two cups of tea and handed one to Amy.

Amy gave her a polite smile.

'I've made a sponge sandwich, if you'd like a piece. I still use the recipe I got from school.'

Amy picked up her cup. 'I'm not hungry, thank you.'

'Well, I'm going to have a piece.' She leaned forward and cut two slices. 'There's a slice for you if you change your mind.'

'Thank you.' Amy looked around the room again. 'You certainly don't like to be surrounded by photographs, that's for sure. You've not got a single photo out.'

'They're in the upstairs room, where I usually sit. We'll go up and look at them when we've had our tea.'

'How long have you lived here?'

'It must be about twenty-seven or twenty-eight years now. I moved away from my parents as soon as I could support myself. Things had never been right from the day I told my father that I was expecting a baby. In fact, they'd actually gone wrong long before that, but I didn't see it. When I think back, the way I looked at my parents changed from the moment I met Kalden.'

'That's not altogether surprising, is it?'

'No, it isn't. And it's not surprising, either, that after you'd been adopted and we tried to put the past behind us, we couldn't. I couldn't get over losing you. How could I?'

'Did you have a job? After all, there was no baby to get in the way of you doing what you wanted.'

'I did teachers' training, as I'd planned to do, and then taught in a school not far from here. After about a year, I decided to leave home and I started renting this house. My father died two years later, and Mother died a year after him. I didn't want to move back to our house in Belsize Park Gardens – too many memories – so I sold it, and bought this place from my landlord. He'd been thinking of selling so it worked out quite well. I also stopped teaching full-time – I'd never really enjoyed it – and started working as a supply teacher.'

'You've lived here for a long time, then.'

'I suppose I have. Anyway, that's enough for now. The rest of the details about my family can wait for another day. I hope I get a chance to tell you them, though – they might stop you from being too critical of your grandparents – but all in good time.' She stood up. 'We seem to have finished our tea, so if you want, we can go upstairs. I'd like to introduce you to your father.'

She went across to the narrow staircase in the corner of the room, and Amy followed her.

'The room on the left is where I always sit,' she said as they reached the landing, and she stood back to let Amy go into the room ahead of her.

Amy took a couple of steps into the room, and stopped short. Her eyes widened and she stared around her. Then she walked very slowly round the room.

Posters and maps of Ladakh covered every inch of the walls; books of every shape and size, all of them about Ladakh, were piled up high on the bookshelves; photographs taken from books, from a computer, by a camera, stood on every shelf.

She stopped in the centre of the room and turned to face Patricia, questioningly.

'It's my Ladakh,' Patricia said quietly. 'I so wanted to be there with Kalden. And look, Amy.' She went over to the table next to the armchair by the window and picked up the silver-framed photograph that stood next to an album. 'This is your father. This is Kalden.'

Amy went to Patricia, took the photo from her and stared at it.

Then she raised her eyes and looked around the room again. 'This place is like a shrine.'

Patricia followed her gaze. 'Yes, I suppose it is in a way.'

Amy's forehead wrinkled. 'You've made a room in your house into a shrine for someone who died years ago.'

'I can see that it must seem somewhat strange to you, but when I'm in here, I feel as if Kalden knows that I love him. More than that – I feel as if he's still alive and with me.'

Amy put the photo back down on the table.

She straightened up, and looked into Patricia's face. 'But you already had a shrine to Kalden: you had me,' she said, her voice rising. 'What was I but a shrine – a real, living shrine with Kalden's blood in my veins? Not something you had to build out of photographs and books. A part of Kalden was still alive and could have been with you, but you gave that part away. Like it was nothing. If you'd kept me with you, brought me up and loved me, you would have really shown Kalden how much you loved him. Wouldn't you?'

'Not like it was nothing. You were never nothing. I loved you – I wanted to keep you. I ...'

'Gave me away, that's what you did. Abandoned me. What kind of love is that?'

'I told you I couldn't keep you. I really couldn't. On my own, unmarried with a baby, no job, next to no money, it would have been impossible. In those days ...'

'In those days, you say! Well, let me tell you about *those days*. In those days, mixed race children were looked down upon – in the classroom, in the playground, in the shops, in the street. Did you think it would be easy for me in those days, Patricia? Did you? Or were you too busy thinking about you, and how hard it would be for you?'

Patricia stared at her, her face grey.

'Everywhere we went, my parents and I, people took one look at me and knew I was adopted. Mum and Dad did their best to protect me from the names people called me, the looks I got, but it was *your* job to do that. I was *your* daughter.'

'Oh, Amy ...'

'If you'd stopped thinking about yourself for one moment and thought about me, you would have seen how difficult it was going to be for me. That I'd have a harder time than English kids who were adopted, even with the most wonderful parents in the world, which I had.' Tears streaming down her cheeks, she stepped back from Patricia. 'You selfishly turned your back on your baby. You should have kept me, no matter how hard it was going to be. That's how you would have shown Kalden that you truly loved him.'

'Amy,' Patricia whispered. 'Oh, Amy, I'm so sorry.'

'I won't have another cup of tea, thank you. I'm going home.'

Chapter Twenty-Two

Almost two weeks later, Patricia stood a little way down the leaf-strewn road in which Amy lived, a carrier bag in her hand, waiting for Andrew to leave the house. When he'd finally driven off, she took a deep breath, went up the drive to the front door and rang the bell.

The door opened. Amy stared at Patricia in surprise. 'I didn't expect to see you again.'

'I know that. But there are still some things to be said.'

'I rather thought we'd rather said it all.'

'Please, Amy. I promise I won't take up much of your time.'

Amy gave a slight shrug and stood back to let Patricia enter the hall. She closed the door behind her and led the way into the sitting room. 'You can have a coffee if you want.'

'No, thanks. I don't want anything.' She sat down and leaned her bag against her foot.

'I think you do,' Amy said, sitting opposite her. 'You obviously want to defend yourself.'

'Defend myself? Well, that's one way of looking at it, I suppose. Make a better job of explaining myself is how I'd prefer to describe it.'

'It doesn't really matter what words we use, does it? We each know how we see it, and that's what matters.'

'I deserve everything you said two weeks ago, Amy. I completely failed you and I failed Kalden. I accept that.'

'Well, that's something we can agree upon.'

'I've been thinking a lot about why I didn't fight hard enough to keep you, and I've decided that while my father deserves much of the blame, I'm not sure that it was his fault alone. Deep down, I've always felt responsible for Kalden falling, and I wonder if part of the reason why I agreed to the adoption was that I didn't think I deserved to be happy: I had to be punished for Kalden's death.'

'And what about me and my happiness? Again, it's about what you deserved, and not what I deserved. No matter how happy you are with the parents who've chosen you, there's always something that doesn't feel quite right. Especially when you look as different from your parents as I did.'

'I realise that now. I'm just trying to help us both understand why I gave you away, and I'm saying that I don't think it's down to one thing only. It's a combination of things: the nature of my father, the fact that I felt guilty about Kalden dying, my character. There's probably more of my mother in me than I realised. She never stood up for me against my father, but how much of that was due to James, and how much to flaws in her character, I don't know. I may have the same flaws.'

'Who on earth is James?'

Patricia bent down, opened her bag and took out several photographs. She spread them out on the table, and pointed to one. 'That's my brother, James. Your uncle, or he would have been. He died when he was seventeen. If he hadn't been injured in the war, there'd be no you. James would have gone to Ladakh with my father, not me. His illness dominated the lives of all three of us. Looking back as an adult, I'm sure that my mother always felt guilty about what happened to him, even though it wasn't her fault at all.'

Amy picked up one of the photographs. 'Is this your father?'

'Yes. I brought one of him in uniform as he was a military man through and through. And this is my mother, Enid.'

Amy glanced down at the photos, then looked curiously at Patricia.

'So what happened to James that made your mother feel so guilty?'

Patricia picked up the picture of her brother. Looking at his face, she began to tell Amy his story.

'You're sure the coffee's all right? I remember you saying you didn't really like coffee.'

'It's perfect. Thank you.'

Amy sat back in her chair. 'I'm not saying that what happened to James all those years ago makes what you did all right. It doesn't. You could have moved on. Lots of people suffered losses in the war and got over it. But I sort of understand you better.'

'I'm glad about that. I so want us to be friends. And apart from telling you about my family, there are things I can tell you about Kalden that you might find interesting. For example, he'd have been a monk if we hadn't met.'

'A monk!'

'That's right. He was going to join the monastery outside his village. But I think we'll leave his story for another day. If you're willing to meet up again, that is.'

'That's a cliffhanger, if ever I heard one. A monk, indeed. Just wait till I tell Andrew.'

'Anyway, so far all we've talked about is me. I want to learn about you.' Patricia paused. 'When we first met, you said that you'd lost your baby earlier this year.'

'That's right. I was three months pregnant when I lost him. Andrew and I miss him so much, even though we didn't get to meet him.'

'It must have been an awful time for you.'

'It was. I missed having Mum around – and Dad was ill at the time, which made it even harder.'

'You must have felt as if your life had turned upside down.'

'You're absolutely right, I did. And to be honest, I still do. But I don't want to talk about it – I get too upset when I do.'

Patricia glanced at her watch. 'Well, I think I'd better get off now – I wouldn't want to outstay my welcome.' She leaned slightly forward. 'I'm not going to ask you to forgive me for what I did – no one could forgive that – but I really would like to be your friend, if you'd let me.'

'I suppose we'll have to meet up again,' Amy said. 'I've got to hear about Kalden and the monk side of things, haven't I?'

Patricia's face broke into a smile. 'Indeed, you have. What about coffee next Saturday?'

'So that's Kalden's story,' Amy said, playing with her empty muffin wrapper. 'When you live somewhere like England, you never think about what it must be like to live where there's virtually no rain.'

'No one would.' Patricia leaned down and picked up the paper bag resting against the table leg. She put the bag on her lap and took out an album. 'Here, I've brought you the book my father compiled. It'll give you a better idea of how the Ladakhi live than I can give you. It's got lots of photos of villages just like Kalden's and it'll give you some idea of the surrounding area. Take it home with you – Andrew might be interested in it, too.'

'Thank you.' Amy took it and put it on the side of the table. She opened the cover and glanced inside. 'Are there any photos of Kalden?'

'I'm afraid not. Father destroyed them all. However ...' She pulled a slim package wrapped in brown paper from the bag and handed it to Amy. 'I was able to have a copy made because I still had the original negative.'

Amy tore the paper away and stared at the framed photograph of Kalden, a replica of the photo next to Patricia's armchair.

'Thank you,' she said. She ran her hand lightly over the glass that protected Kalden's face. 'Thank you. That was very nice of you, very thoughtful.' She placed the photograph carefully on top of the album. 'Have you been back to Ladakh since I was born? You obviously love the country.'

'No, I haven't. I couldn't bear to go there alone, without Kalden. He's so much a part of the place for me. So, no. I've contented myself with sitting in my room – in my shrine, as you put it – and imagining that I'm in Ladakh.'

Amy picked up Kalden's photograph and looked at it again. Still holding the photo, she flicked through the pages of the album. Patricia sat quietly, waiting.

'I wasn't sure until this minute that I was going to say this,' Amy said at last. 'But I'd like to go to Ladakh, and I'd like you to come with me.'

Patricia shook her head. 'I can't.' She clasped her hands together in her lap.

'It's Andrew's idea. He said that you and I should go there together, and that he'll give us the tickets as a reunion present. I told him I didn't want to go with you, but that I might go with him next year. But it's suddenly hit me that I *do* want to go with you. Who better to show me Kalden's village?' She leaned across the table, and looked directly into Patricia's face. 'So, let's go to Ladakh together, Patricia. Please.'

'I don't know what to say. I need to think about it. It's where Kalden died. I never expected to go there again. Sometimes it's better not to go back.'

'But you've never really left Ladakh, have you, so you wouldn't actually be going back, would you?'

'Well, that's true. But I'm not sure. No, I don't think I can.'

'It's been a really sad year for me – first I lost my baby, then I lost my dad, and in a way, I lost my birth father, too.

On the plus side, we've met and I've found out about my heritage. Now that I have, I want to see it first hand. I want to see the post house where you and your father stayed, and I want to see the mountains that Kalden loved. I want to visit the house where he lived – his family might still there be there, and his brothers are my uncles. That's what I want. And I don't want to go there alone, nor with Andrew – I want to go there with you.'

Patricia bit her lower lip. 'I need to think about it.'

'Well, don't think about it for too long,' Amy said, straightening up. 'Andrew's checked the flights, and we can go next week.'

'Next week! I couldn't. And it's too expensive, anyway.'

'As I said, it's Andrew's treat. He's an architect and a very good one at that. We don't have any children to spend our money on – at least, not yet, we don't. Andrew knows me better than I know myself, and he knows how much I need to go. Apparently, we can fly to Delhi at the end of next week and pick up a chartered flight to Leh. I thought we could stay in Ladakh for a couple of weeks.'

'Next week sounds very close. You don't think it's too soon?'

'We need to get there and back before snow closes the airport. And I want to go this year, not next. I might have a baby next year, and if I did, it wouldn't be so easy to take off just like that. The more I think about it, the more I want to see where half of me comes from. Silly as it sounds, I feel as if I'll be going home.' Her voice caught in her throat. 'So, are we going to get on that plane next week? Will you do the only thing for me I've ever asked of you?'

A strange sensation stirring within her, Patricia slowly nodded.

At the same moment, both glanced down at the photo that lay on top of the album.

Chapter Twenty-Three

Ladakh, September 1995

As they left Delhi further and further behind, their conversation died away. Amy moved closer to Patricia, who had a window seat on the crowded plane taking them from Dehli to Leh, and they both stared out of the window towards the ground.

'I can't wait to get my first glimpse of Ladakh,' Amy said. 'If we ever see it, that is – there are so many clouds you can't see the ground.'

'They must have heard you – they're breaking up. Look, you can see the mountains now.'

Amy leaned across Patricia and gazed down at the snow-clad peaks of the Himalayas. 'Wow, that's a view worth waiting for!'

Feeling the warmth of Amy's body against hers, Patricia's mind flew back to the first time she'd felt the heat of her baby in her arms. She sat very still, hardly daring to breathe, not wanting the moment to end.

'I'm glad we didn't leave it any later to come,' Amy said, sitting back against her seat. 'Some of the streams are already freezing over. They look like skinny little satin ribbons tied round the mountains.' She glanced towards the window. 'I wonder how you can tell when the bit of mountain under you is in Ladakh.'

'I've no idea.' Patricia smiled at her. 'Of course, you might suddenly feel that you're home. You did say that you felt as if you were going home.'

Amy gave her a half smile. 'I did, didn't I? Well, we'll see if that's what happens.'

Patricia turned back to the window.

A little later, she caught sight of a stretch of clear ground between the mountains. 'I'm afraid your inner signal wasn't working, after all – that looks very much like a landing strip. And the airport'll be the building next to it. We must have been flying over Ladakh for quite a while now.'

Amy leaned in front of her again. 'Isn't it tiny? There doesn't seem to be a lot of room to land. I'm glad I'm not the pilot. I'm not going to look out again until we've landed.' She settled back, checked her seat belt and stared ahead of her.

Patricia pressed her face against the window and gazed down at the concrete strip. The window misted up and she wiped it clear with her elbow. Thirty-two years earlier, while she and Kalden had been on the road to Manali, her father had been down there at the airport, walking on the same bit of concrete that she was about to walk upon.

Her heart gave a sudden lurch. It felt like yesterday.

Their plane rose, circled one of the mountains, swooped down into the valley and approached the runway. Patricia grabbed Amy's hand. The plane hit the ground and shuddered to a stop. Both let out an audible sigh of relief. Amy pulled her hand away. As soon as the seat belt light went off, she stood up to get down their overhead baggage.

When they'd collected the rest of their luggage from the airport's solitary baggage belt, they headed towards the exit to find a taxi to take them the few kilometres into the town. All of a sudden, Amy came to a halt in front of a large, hand-painted sign on the wall at the side of the exit.

'So that's why Andrew booked a couple of nights in Leh,' she exclaimed, 'although I'd wanted to get off to the village as soon as possible. It says here that you must wait at least thirty-six hours before going into the mountains.'

'That's because of altitude sickness. You have to get acclimatised before you go to the higher ground. It would be awful to spoil our trip by being ill. I've got some medicine for it, but it'd be better not to have to take it. When I came here with my father, we had the journey from Srinagar in which to get used to the altitude, but it's different when you come by plane. And anyway, we ought to have a rest after such a long journey before we start travelling around.'

'Whatever you say. From this point on, you're the boss.'

With the jagged peaks of the Himalayas dominating the horizon behind them, a stretch of stone-coloured desert on one side of them and farmland on the other, they trailed along the narrow streets and cobbled lanes of Leh, stopping every so often by the open stalls to look at the things for sale, and occasionally wandering into the shops selling curios and jewellery, where Amy darted among the silver, amber, coral and turquoise stones.

'The people must be very religious,' Amy remarked at one point as a group of red-robed monks passed them in the street. 'Look at all the monasteries, shrines and monks that they've got. Every time you go round a corner, you find an old monastery or a monk.'

'They are religious, but not in a way that's oppressive.'

Amy turned to stare after the monks. 'Kalden would have looked like that if you hadn't met him.'

'But he would have been alive.'

They glanced at each other, and for a few minutes, they walked along in silence, each lost in her thoughts.

'I'm sure this is very different from the way Leh used to be,' Patricia said, breaking into the silence. 'I've never been here before, but Father and I read up about it before our trip.'

'Trekking's very big now, and you can see that they're catering for the tourists who come for the mountains. I bet most of them come through Leh at some point, even if they don't fly into the airport. But tourism's good. It brings money into a country.'

'You're right.' She smiled at Amy. 'You only have to think of the toilets. The flush toilets we've got in our hotel were unheard of thirty years ago.'

'So what did people do?'

'Use a hole in the upper floor of the house. Everything went down to the straw and ash that was on the floor below. It was cleaned out once a year and put on the fields.'

Amy wrinkled her nose. 'Yuk!'

'It's a cold climate so there were no flies and no smell. The Ladakhi don't waste anything, or at least they used not to. I've no idea how they manage to have flush toilets today, though – they've no more water now than they used to have.'

'However they do it, I'm glad that they do.' She threw Patricia a half smile. 'And talking of things that are different, I like your new hairstyle. It suits you.'

Patrica blushed and put her hand up to her hair. 'I thought I ought to do something about the way I looked.'

'It's really nice. It's taken years off you.'

'Well, thank you.' She put her hands to her cheeks. 'You're embarrassing me and I can feel myself going bright red. Don't look at me, look at the vegetables on the stall. They don't sell just wheat and barley any longer, but all kinds of vegetables and rice. They must import the rice – I can't see how they could grow it here. And cabbages and potatoes. And look at the fruit. They never used to have apples and plums.'

'And not tight jeans, either, I'm sure! Have you seen what those men are wearing?' Amy said with a laugh as three young men, each wearing sunglasses and carrying a radio, came towards them. They grinned at Amy as they passed by and nodded their approval. 'I want any uncles I have to be wearing the homespun clothes that I saw in the photos, and not manmade fibres.'

'Me, too. I do hope the villages haven't changed as much as Leh,' Patricia said as they turned into the road that led to their hotel. 'I can't imagine what Father would have made of all the traffic today, and cement being used for buildings, instead of mud bricks. I think it's just as well that he never saw the changes. He was a man who liked tradition. Like me, he was somewhat locked in the past.'

'But we're unlocking your past by being here, aren't we? That's what you want, isn't it?'

'Of course it is.' Patricia threw Amy a quick smile. 'I don't want to destroy all my memories, though. To be honest, I'm quite nervous about what we'll find in Alchi tomorrow.'

'I can't wait to get there. Leh's nice, but I'm dying to see the places you went to with Kalden. I wish there was a bus earlier than four in the afternoon. With it taking three hours to get there, it'll be too dark to see anything by the time we reach the guest house.'

'We'll go straight to the guest house from the bus, drop off our bags and have a short wander around. I'm sure there'll be time to do that before it gets too dark.'

'I hope you're right.'

As they reached the hotel, Amy stopped abruptly. She turned to Patricia in sudden alarm. 'I've just thought – suppose Kalden's family isn't pleased to see you again! After all, if the two of you hadn't decided to run away, he'd probably still be alive today. Maybe they'll blame you for him dying.'

'That thought had occurred to me, too. On the whole, though, I'd be surprised if they thought like that. It happened so long ago. They'll still be desperately upset about him dying, of course, but I would have thought that their hostility towards me – if they had been hostile – would have almost certainly gone by now. Anyway, we'll find out soon enough.

And maybe it's just as well to be prepared for the fact that they might not welcome us with open arms.'

Biting her lower lip, Amy pushed open the entrance door and went into the hotel.

Her hand on the door, Patricia glanced back along the street. She'd never been to Leh with Kalden so the streets of Leh held no special memories for her. But in one day's time, she'd be walking on the same ground that she'd walked with him, and that was going to be very different.

Her heart beating fast, she followed Amy into the hotel.

They arranged for the taxi driver to return in three hours and wait for them outside the entrance to Kalden's village. Then they got out of the taxi, tucked their lunch packs into their rucksacks and stood in front of the opening in the village wall, watching the taxi drive off down the stony track.

'Well, the old Alchi was still very visible,' Patricia said, turning to look at Kalden's village, 'despite the number of guest houses and restaurants. I wonder what we'll find here? I do hope the character of the village hasn't changed too much.' She took a few steps back from the entrance. 'Let's not go in for a minute. We can give ourselves a moment or two, can't we? I don't feel quite ready.'

Amy smiled at her. 'Of course we can. We've got plenty of time. Come on, let's go and look at the view.' And she ran over to the edge of the ripe barley fields and stood gazing up at the shadowy peaks. 'I can see why you fell in love with the place,' she called back.

'It is lovely, isn't it?' Patricia said, coming over to Amy's side, and together they walked slowly towards the small stream that flowed at the end of the fields. Beyond the stream, the plateau shimmered as it stretched into the hazy distance, reaching out to the purple slopes of the mountains.

Patricia glanced to her right, stopped and pointed. 'Look

over there. That's the way to the missionary house. There's a *chorten* not far along the track – you can just about see it from here – at least, you can see the prayer flags. The *chorten* is hidden beneath them all. The missionary house is some distance beyond that.'

Amy glanced towards the *chorten*, then turned to look back at the village and at the monastery high up on the rock-face above it. 'That monastery looks as if it's going to fall on the village at any minute.'

Patricia smiled. 'It's been there for goodness knows how many years so I don't think that's very likely.' She took a few steps towards the village. 'It all looks just the same – it looks just like it did when Kalden was alive.' Her smile faded. 'Perhaps I should never have come back. Perhaps I should have let the past remain in the past.'

'We had to come back. I needed to come here. And in a way, so did you. I can't explain why I feel that, but I do feel it, with all my heart. This is something we both had to do, and we had to do it together. Now,' she said gently. 'What do you think? Shall we walk around for a bit longer or shall we go into the village?'

Patricia glanced at the entrance to the village. 'I think the village. But we must start at the beginning, and that's outside the village, at the post house. That's where I first saw Kalden. He came to see us the night we arrived. Oh, you should have seen him, Amy. There was something so wonderful about him. I used to think of him as my golden man. Yes, we'll start at the post house.' And she started to walk quickly towards the small stone house a little way down on the opposite side of the track.

When she reached the short path that led to the house, she stopped and waited for Amy to catch her up. 'The man who lived here was called Wangyal,' she told her. 'He and his wife moved to his sons' house for the time that we stayed here, but he used to come over every day and look after us. He seemed a nice man, although we couldn't really have a conversation with him. I'm afraid he'll have probably died by now.'

Side by side, they stood and stared at the house.

'Well, standing here isn't going to get us anywhere,' Amy said at last. 'It doesn't look as if there's anyone at home now, but we could knock and see.'

'Someone must live here – it's part of the mail delivery system. At least, it used to be. Maybe it's all been modernised by now. In fact, it must have been, when I think about it.'

Amy turned to Patricia, her face alive with nervous excitement. 'I'll go and knock, shall I? If there's anyone at home, I hope they speak English.'

'That's a point. It's ages since I said anything in Ladakhi. I do remember a few words, though. Obviously, there's *ju-le*, but you know that already – we've been using it in Leh. And, if I remember rightly, *Nga england-ne in-le* means I'm from England.'

Amy giggled. 'I think you can go and knock.'

'Come on. Let's go together.'

They knocked three or four times but there was no answer.

'They're out.' Amy's voice shook with disappointment. 'I was so looking forward to seeing inside.' She moved to the window and peered through it, shading her eyes to see more easily into the dark interior.

'Someone might come,' Patricia whispered. 'Come away from there. We can try again later.'

'I will, but come and have a quick look first. Was it as gloomy as this when you lived here?'

Throwing an anxious glance over her shoulder, Patricia hurried to Amy's side and bent down to look through the window. She caught her breath sharply and straightened up. 'It could be in a time warp. I think everything's in the same place, down to the pots for the butter and barley flour.'

'And the chair? Is that the one your father sat on when he hurt his foot?'

She went closer to the window and looked through it again. 'I think it might be,' she said slowly. 'It's amazing, nothing seems to have changed. Maybe there are a few more bits and pieces around the room, but not a lot. And thank goodness there's no television in the corner. But we'd better go now.' She moved away from the window. 'I'd hate to be caught looking into someone else's house.'

'Me, too,' Amy said, stepping back. 'If you're ready now, we could go into the village. It's a good time to explore as the villagers will be having their lunch. With fewer people around, it'd be easier to get the feel of the place.'

'I think I'm ready now, or as ready as I'll ever be. Shall we go through the little gap in the wall here or go along to the main entrance? The main entrance, don't you think? It's closer to Kalden's house. Well, it's closer to where his family live.'

They made their way back along the track to the large gap in the village wall and went though it. Pausing briefly just inside the wall, Patricia took a deep breath, and then she and Amy started to stroll along the dusty path that led through the heart of the village.

As they walked along, they looked from one side of the track to the other.

'I feel as if I'm being drawn further and further back into the past,' Patricia said, as she slowed to look down one of the narrow lanes that ran between the lime-washed houses. 'Nothing's changed. It's just as it was all those years ago, just as it's always been in my mind.'

They reached the centre of the village, and paused. Patricia looked all around her, her gaze settling on a side lane to the left of her. She took a few steps towards it. 'Come on,' she said. 'We'll go down there.' Amy followed her.

A little way down the lane, Patricia stopped in front of a large house with highly ornate carvings around the balcony, windows and doors. She went closer to the house, and stared at it. Her eyes filled with tears, and she covered her mouth with her hands and turned to Amy. 'My father loved those carvings. Being here is making me feel closer to him: he loved Ladakh. And I keep expecting Kalden to walk out of one of the lanes at any moment and come over to me. I can feel him here. Oh, how I wish you'd known your father!'

Amy put her arms around her and hugged her. 'I'm getting to know him through you. And just like you, I feel that he's here – you've made him come alive for me.'

'*Ju-le.*'

They jumped in surprise. A man of about seventy was standing in front of them, a smile of welcome on his face. He was wearing a long, homespun robe tied round the middle with a woollen cummerbund, out of which a wooden pot was sticking. Two cords of turquoise beads hung around his neck, and on his head he wore a close-fitting skin hat.

'*Ju-le*', the man repeated, his glance going from one to the other.

'*Ju-le,*' they said in unison, and smiled at him.

His brow wrinkled. He took a small step forward and peered more closely at Patricia, his smile slowly fading into a question. He glanced again at Amy, then back at Patricia. An expression of bewilderment spread across his face. He put his fingers to his lips and turned again to look at Amy. Slightly changing his position to stand squarely in front of her, he studied her face. Then he turned to Patricia.

'Patricia?' he asked hesitantly.

Unable to speak, she nodded.

He pointed to his chest. 'Tenzin,' he said.

She gasped. '*Ju-le*, Tenzin, *ju-le.*' She caught Amy's arm. 'It's one of Kalden's older brothers.'

'He remembered your name. He must have liked you a lot to have remembered you after so many years.' Amy smiled warmly at Tenzin. The smile he returned to her reached from one side of his face to the other.

'How are you, Tenzin?' Patricia asked. '*Kamzang*? I think that means are you well, or something like that.' She laughed and shook her head. 'I can't remember anything at the moment.' Then she started to cry. 'Kalden's brother. I can't believe it.'

'No English,' he said, shaking his head. 'Tashi English.' He beckoned to them to follow him. 'Tashi English,' he repeated, and he started walking quickly down one of the lanes, looking back to make sure that they were behind him.

'I think he's taking us to their house,' Patricia said, drying her eyes on her sleeve as they hurried after him. 'Tashi's the son of Deki and Tenzin. Or maybe Anil or Rinchen. I don't know. It doesn't matter.'

'Anil! Rinchen! Tashi!' Tenzin called loudly as he approached the large house they were heading towards.

'It *is* Kalden's house!' Patricia exclaimed. 'And it's just as I remember it.'

Tenzin reached the house, stood in the doorway and again shouted up the lane for Tashi. Indicating that Amy and Patricia should go with him into the house, he led them through the downstairs room to the staircase, up the stairs and between the wooden pillars that stood at the entrance to the kitchen, decorated with garlands of wheat, barley and peas.

They followed him into the large living area and hovered uncertainly in the centre of the room. He pointed towards a long bench next to the wall, and they went and sat on it. Then he sat down on a bench opposite them.

Minutes later, they heard the sound of footsteps running up the stairs, and a man of about forty appeared breathlessly at the top of the staircase. He stopped sharply at the sight of Patricia and Amy, and looked questioningly at Tenzin. Tenzin spoke to him and he came slowly into the room, closely followed by two more men, similar in age and appearance to Tenzin.

Tenzin said something to the three of them. They looked at Patricia, then their eyes moved to Amy and stayed on her. Tenzin made a further comment and they nodded, an expression of delight spreading over their faces.

'Tashi English,' Tenzin said.

Anil and Rinchen sat down next to Tenzin. Tashi pulled a small wooden stool close to Patricia and Amy and sat on it.

'Tenzin tries to tell you I speak English,' Tashi began. 'I learn in school in Leh. I not speak very good, but I understand and can say some things in English.'

Tenzin started speaking quickly to Tashi. Tashi held up his hand in a gesture that asked him to slow down. 'Tenzin say we are all very happy to see Patricia again,' he began. 'Very happy indeed.' He glanced back at Tenzin and grinned. Then he looked at Amy. 'And we also very happy to meet Kalden's daughter for first time,' he added, with a shy smile. 'This be Kalden's daughter, we think.'

'Yes,' Amy whispered.

'You have same face as Kalden, but more pretty.' He turned and told his fathers what he'd said, and the three men laughed and nodded.

Patricia leaned forward on the bench, her face suddenly serious. 'Will you translate something for me, Tashi?' she asked.

'I try.'

'I want you all to know that every single day for the past thirty-three years, I have thought of Kalden.'

Tashi nodded. He translated Patricia's words into Ladakhi. The older men looked at her with sympathetic understanding. Then Tenzin said something to Tashi, and Tashi turned back to Patricia and Amy and translated his words.

'And Tenzin want you to know that at every visit, Kalden talks about Patricia. For thirty-three years, he never forgets Patricia.'

Her world went black.

Chapter Twenty-Four

Patricia's eyes flickered open. She saw that she was lying on the bench, covered by a blanket. Amy was crouching beside her, holding her hand, her face anxious and unnaturally pale. Tashi, Anil and Rinchen hovered behind Amy, looking awkward and unsure of what to do.

Out of the corner of her eye, she saw Tenzin coming over to her with a pot of what she guessed would be butter tea. He handed it to Tashi, said something to him and went back to the stove.

'Tenzin say you must drink this,' Tashi said. 'You better when you drink it.'

Tenzin returned with a pot of tea for Amy. She stood up to take it from him. Their eyes met and they smiled shyly at each other.

'I'm able to sit up now,' Patricia said, and she swung her legs over the side of the bench. 'I feel much better.' She tried to smile. 'I don't know what came over me. Yes, I do. It was the shock of it.' She pushed the blanket to one side, smoothed down her hair and took the drink that Tashi was holding out to her. '*Ju-le*, Tashi,' she said, and she put the pot to her lips.

Tenzin poured some *chang* for each of his brothers and Tashi, and they all sat down again, watching Patricia with concern in their eyes.

'Are you really all right?' Amy asked, sitting back down next to her. 'You don't think you should lie down some more? I'm sure they wouldn't mind.'

'No, I'm fine, really I am.' She turned to Amy, her face white, her eyes questioning. 'What they said. I just want to know what they're talking about, what they mean. I saw him fall from the bridge near Chiling. I saw him die. No one could have survived that fall. And if he had survived the fall – which he couldn't have done – he could never have survived the cold night. I don't know what they mean.'

Amy looked across the room to Tenzin, and then back to Tashi.

'Patricia thought Kalden was dead, Tashi,' she began. 'She thought he'd been killed when he fell from the bridge near Chiling. I thought he was dead. I thought I'd never see him. But you're saying that he wasn't killed. That's what you are saying, aren't you, that Kalden is still alive?'

'Yes, Kalden still alive. He not killed.'

He turned to his father and translated what Amy had said to them. The three brothers looked at Amy and Patricia, and nodded. Tenzin started to speak, but Tashi stopped him. He spoke briefly to Tenzin and turned back to Patricia.

'I tell Tenzin I know what happened. I hear it many times. I able to tell you the story.' And Tashi began to tell them what had happened all those years ago.

Kalden had seen Patricia trip over the wooden plank and had jumped on to the bridge to get to her as quickly as possible. The bridge had swayed sharply sideways and he'd been thrown off his feet. He'd tried to grab the handrail, but hadn't been able to, and he'd been thrown off the bridge at an angle. With falling planks striking him, he'd slammed hard into the side of the mountain, felt an agonising pain in his leg, and passed out.

At some point later, he'd opened his eyes and found blackness all around him. He was in terrible pain, he'd told them. His leg and back hurt, and his body seemed to have been pierced by a thousand needles. He'd cautiously felt around him, and realised that the needles were thorns and that he was in the middle of a mass of rose-bushes. The thorns were digging into his flesh, and with every movement

303

he took, they dug further in. But they had broken his fall and were stopping him from plunging to the bottom of the ravine.

He realised, too, that they would be some protection against the cold of the night.

He didn't fear the cold. He was used to going into the mountains in winter and he understood the cold. But he knew that he must keep awake throughout the night, and every time that he started to close his eyes, he pushed the thorns deeper into his skin.

Morning came and, in the early light of day, he saw that he was covered in blood and that his leg was twisted. Carefully looking down the steep mountain slope, he saw the jagged rocks below, and he knew that it had been a miracle that he'd survived. And then there was another miracle: he heard the sound of voices on the bridge above him.

But no one would be able to see him, he realised, as the ridge hung over the slope and he was almost hidden by the rose-bushes. He called out to the men, but his voice was feeble. He called again, and again, his voice getting weaker and weaker. They'd never hear him, he thought in fear and desperation.

But the men had known that someone had fallen the night before, so perhaps a part of them had been listening for any sounds that there might be. However it came about, they heard his weak cries and one of the men called over the side of the bridge to him, telling him that they would get to him, giving him strength.

The men then went back to the hut, fetched rope and wood, and returned to the bridge. As soon as they'd made a cover for the hole in the base of the bridge, they crossed to his side of the ravine and prepared ropes to lower to him.

Fading in and out of consciousness, he could hear them working above him, and at last, after lowering a pony-man and a basket made of rope, they brought him safely to the top of the slope.

He'd been feverish and in a very bad state and had been taken to a house in Chiling. The family there had looked after him with the aid of the local *amchi*. Wooden splints had been put on his leg and herbal powder was put all over his torn skin to clean the wounds and keep infection away. Two days later, Tenzin had arrived.

The men who had found Kalden were the pony-men who'd met Lobsang and Patricia in the hut the night before, so they knew Kalden's name and the village he'd come from. One of them had gone there to tell his family what had happened, and Tenzin had come back with him to help with the care of his brother. When Kalden was finally strong enough to travel, Tenzin took him home, and his family cared for him until he was well again.

'And his leg?' Patricia asked.

'It was bad,' Tashi told her, 'but he can walk and this is what is important.'

Patricia and Amy looked at each other, and then at Tashi.

'I know what you wish to ask,' he said with a smile. 'You ask where is Kalden now?'

'Yes,' Patricia said. 'Where is he, please?' Amy took her hand and moved closer to her.

'He is in monastery outside village. When he well again, he could not look for you, Patricia – he not know where you are – so he go into monastery. But he comes to us many times. And every time he comes, he talks about you.'

'Can I see him, Tashi?' she asked. 'I want to see him again. And I want him to meet his daughter. Will that be all right? Can we see him?'

Tashi turned and put the question to Tenzin, who answered him.

'We begin to prepare for harvest now,' Tashi told them. 'Kalden will come with monks tomorrow.'

Tenzin spoke again, smiling warmly at Amy and Patricia.

'When Kalden come tomorrow,' Tashi said, 'we take him to house where you live when you in Ladakh. You go to post house, too, Patricia. His daughter comes here, to our house, so you and Kalden can talk. Is that good?'

'That's very good, Tashi. Thank you.'

'Where are you living now? We invite you to stay with us.'

'Thank you very much for your offer, but we've already got rooms in a guest house in Alchi. All of our things are there. In fact, the taxi driver will be here any minute now to take us back to Alchi. It isn't far away, though, and we'll come back early tomorrow morning.' She started to stand up. 'I keep thinking I'm dreaming and that I'll wake up any minute now. I hope I don't.'

'You not dream, Patricia,' Tashi said with a smile.

Tenzin said something as he stood up, and Tashi looked towards Amy. 'Tenzin ask the name of Kalden's daughter.'

Patricia opened her mouth to reply, but she felt a slight pressure on her arm from Amy, who stood up next to her.

'My name is Nima,' she said.

The post house stood in front of Patricia, the front door slightly open. She knew that Kalden was already in the house because Tashi had told her he was.

One of the children from the village had been waiting for their taxi to appear down the track and at the first sight of the taxi, he'd run off and come back with Tashi. Tashi had told her that Kalden knew that there was a visitor for him, and that the visitor would meet him in the post house, but he did not know who that visitor was. Then, wreathed in smiles, he had taken Amy off into the village, and Patricia had heard him tell her that he was going to introduce her to more of her family.

She'd watched Amy until she was out of sight, then she'd started to walk nervously towards the post house, her steps getting quicker the closer she came to the house. She'd reached the top of the path, and had stopped.

She stared at the house. He was in there. Her Kalden was in there. Unbelievably, she was going to see him again, touch him again.

Her heart thudding, she began to walk down the path. Reaching the door, she pushed it open wider, went into the downstairs room and closed the door quietly behind her.

The man in the chair where her father used to sit was reading a book, his back to her. He was dressed very simply in a light grey cotton shirt and casual trousers. The back of the head bent over the book was darkened by a haze of close-cut, greyish-brown hair.

'Kalden,' she said softly. His back stiffened. He straightened up and stared ahead of him at the wall. The knuckles on the hands that gripped his book went white. 'Kalden,' she repeated, moving closer to him. 'I thought you were dead.' Her voice caught in her throat. 'I thought I'd never see you again. I didn't know. I didn't know.' She broke off, unable to say more.

Slowly he stood up. Leaning slightly to the left, he turned to face her, and a look of disbelief spread across his face. He took a step towards her, moving awkwardly, his eyes questioning, bewildered. 'Patricia?' he asked. 'Is it Patricia?' He took another step, and another, each step bringing him closer to her. 'Patricia?' he repeated.

He stood before her, inches from her, her golden man.

'Oh, Kalden.' Her eyes filled with tears. 'It *is* Patricia. Your Patricia.'

He took her face gently in the palms of his hands, and

intently studied her features: her eyes, her nose, her mouth, the indentation in her chin. Then he raised his fingers to her forehead and lightly traced the thin lines than ran from one side to the other.

Her breath escaped in a small sigh. Closing her eyes, she let her head fall slightly back and stood there, trembling under the touch of the fingers that ran along each quivering eyelid. His breath was warm against her face as he wiped away her tears with his thumbs. She opened her eyes and looked into the depths of his dark brown eyes, and saw the turmoil of emotion in them.

Her tears trickled over his fingers. Neither of them spoke.

With a slight smile, he ran the palms of his hands down the sides of her cheeks. Her lips parted as she gazed up into his face, and she heard him draw in his breath.

'My Patricia,' he murmured, his voice full of wonder.

Slowly, he ran a finger along first her upper lip, then her lower lip. She caught hold of his hand, put his fingers to her lips and kissed them, one by one. Then she kissed the palm of his hand, and pressed it to her heart.

'I have loved you, Kalden,' she said quietly, 'from the moment I saw you, and I've never stopped loving you, not for so much as one second.'

'Me, too, Patricia. I always love you.' His voice broke. 'I think I never see you again, but I want to. Every time I go out of monastery, maybe to Alchi or Likir or Leh, and I see English-looking people in the streets, I look among them for you. And I talk to them. I ask them if they know Patricia, but no one knows my Patricia. Every time I come back to village, I come first to post house, and I dream I see you sitting outside house with a book. When I not in monk's robes, I wear English clothes so I feel close to you.'

'I thought you'd been killed when you fell off the bridge. But you weren't. Lobsang said we had to go on with our journey – he was worried about the snow. We left you and you were still alive. I can't bear to think of it. If only we'd waited for another day, for just one day. If only we'd given ourselves the time to look for you in the daylight, we could have been together for always. We could have been happy for all these years.'

She grasped his hand more tightly.

'We not look back, Patricia.' He lifted his other hand and ran his fingers through her hair, then he let his hand fall to his side. 'You were right to go on that day. Lobsang was right. Snow often come very early on road to Manali. But that is now long ago. Today you are here and that is most important thing – most wonderful thing.' He shifted his weight to his other foot.

'Your poor leg. I should have thought,' she said quickly, and she released his hand. 'We must sit down. You sit here again and I'll get the stool.' She pulled a stool over to the chair and sat down next to him.

'Not like that,' he said with a smile. 'You sit so I can see your face.'

Changing her position so that they could look at each other, she sat as close to him as she could get. He raised his hand to her face and lightly touched her cheek. Then he sighed deeply and put his hand back in his lap. 'You are even more beautiful today than day when I meet you, Patricia. But I must not talk like that now. I am a monk. Tell me about your life in England. Tell me if you have a husband.'

She stared into his eyes. 'In my heart, you have always been my husband, Kalden. There could never have been anyone else.' Then she took a deep breath. 'Before I tell you what I did when I got back to England, there is something I have to tell you first – I can't talk about my life in England without telling you.'

He looked puzzled. 'What must you tell me?'

309

'When I left Ladakh, I didn't know that I was carrying a baby, but I was. We have a child, Kalden. We have a daughter. I called her Nima. She's thirty-two years old and she's here with me now.'

He sat very still, staring at her. Then he turned his head to look at the wall in front of him. His hands went to his forehead, trying to make sense of her words.

'I have a child?' he asked, turning back to her. 'I have a daughter? This is what you are saying. I have daughter and she is here in Ladakh? In the village?'

'Yes, she is, and she's longing to meet you.'

He stood up and looked down at her. 'We have a daughter?' A slow smile spread across his face. 'A daughter. This morning, I get up and I am alone, like every morning. But now I am here with beautiful Patricia. I am not alone, and I have a daughter.' He held out his hand to her. 'We go now, Patricia. We go to our daughter.'

She stood up and took the hand he stretched out to her. In his eyes, she saw a reflection of the love and happiness that she felt. Self-conscious, they smiled at each other, then they let their hands fall to their sides.

Patricia took a step back. 'She's in your house, Kalden. She's with Tashi and Tenzin. If she's not there, they'll know where she is.'

Trembling, he led the way to the door, pulled it open and stood aside to let Patricia go out first. As she started to walk through the doorway, she saw the figure standing at the top of the path, and she stopped.

'You go first,' she said, smiling up at him. 'I think there's someone out there who's very impatient to meet you.'

Patricia sat with Amy in a restaurant in Leh, their suitcases at their side.

'You're very quiet today, Amy,' she said.

310

'Am I? I'm sorry.' Amy bit her lip. 'I suppose it's that I feel really sad to be leaving. I've only just met Kalden, and now we're leaving him. He'll be on his own again – I know he's got his family, but that's different. And you must feel the same. We will come back again soon, won't we? And Andrew must come with us next time.'

Patricia smiled at her daughter. 'Yes, we'll come back as soon as we can. But for now, we've got a bit of time left, so if there's anything you want to buy before we leave, I suggest you do it here. Leh Airport's not like Heathrow – there aren't any shops there.'

'Thanks for reminding me,' Amy said, getting up. 'I haven't bought anything for Andrew yet, and I want to get him something typically Ladakhi. I'll do that now. I won't be long.'

'I hope you find something,' Patricia called after her.

Smiling to herself, she opened her book and stared at the page with unseeing eyes. In her head, she was planning her return to Ladakh on the first flight after the winter snow had gone. She and Kalden had spent their eleven days together catching up on the missing years, but they'd only just scratched the surface, and there was still so much left to say.

As they'd strolled across the plateau, walking slowly because of his leg, he'd told her about his struggle to go on living after he'd lost her, and how his great sadness had made his family anxious about him. Finally, he'd realised that he had to put aside his misery and accept the destiny that he'd known was his from the moment that he'd reached the age of understanding.

Although he was sure that he'd lost her forever, he'd never been able to bring himself to make a lifetime commitment to the monastery – it would have been too final; it would have killed off the small ray of hope that flickered deep within him, that kept him alive. As a result, he'd gone into the monastery as a short-term monk. This meant that he had greater freedom over the clothes he wore when he wasn't in the monastery, and he was able to visit his family and help them out at times when extra help was needed.

She had wanted to be able to picture his life, and he'd described his room in the monastery: his low, narrow bed and hard mattress; his straight-backed chair and wooden table; the shelving on the wall for his books and texts. Most of his life as a monk was spent chanting the texts and performing the religious rituals for his village and the neighbouring villages, he'd told her. Every family paid him in food, or in cash, which was happening more frequently.

He gave the money to the monastery. He was grateful to the monastery for giving him a home and security, and he had made a life for himself as a monk, but it was not the life that he would have chosen for himself: that life would have been a life with Patricia.

And Patricia had told him about her life, about her father's unyielding attitude when he'd learnt that she was pregnant, and how she'd been forced to choose between parting with her baby or leaving home and managing without help or money. She'd cried as she'd told him how much she'd longed to keep their daughter, but had had no way of doing so. With horror in his eyes, he'd listened to her describe how Nima had been pulled from her arms and given to another family.

A part of her had died at that moment, she'd said. From then on, her life had closed in on itself, and the years that had followed had been lonely years. Her daily thoughts of Kalden had been the only things that had kept her going. And then Nima had come back into her life, and it had begun to be a life again.

On their last evening in Ladakh, while Amy had been saying a temporary goodbye to her family and to the people she'd met in the village, she had walked with Kalden into the fields and they'd stood quietly beneath the night sky, a canopy of black silk against which the stars shone out with a rare brilliance.

Their eyes had met, and Patricia knew that they each felt the same inner peace.

This visit to Ladakh had been about the past, she mused as she fingered the pages of her book, but it had opened the door to a future, a future that they hadn't yet had time to talk about. There would be time for that on the next visit.

A shadow fell across her book and she looked up to see her daughter.

'I think we ought to get a taxi now, Patricia,' Amy said with a reluctant sigh. 'I bought a butter jar made of apricot wood for Andrew, and I've got us a really good book that teaches you Ladakhi. I'm going to learn to speak the language. We can learn together, if you want.'

'I do want. That's a really good idea. And so's the butter jar – Andrew will love it.' She looked at her watch. 'You're right. It's time to leave.'

She put her book in her bag, stood up and went out into the street. Pausing, she turned to stare at the distant mountains.

'We'll come back again soon,' Amy said softly, moving to her side. She tucked her arm through Patricia's and turned to look at her, her eyes full of love. 'Let's go, Mother,' she said.

The driver lifted their suitcases out of the taxi. Patricia paid him and they made their way towards the entrance to the airport building. As they drew close, they saw a figure move out from the shadows and into their line of vision.

Amy caught hold of Patricia's arm. 'It's Kalden! He's come to say goodbye.' She started to run forward, then she

313

stopped and came back to Patricia. 'No, you go first,' she said. 'Here, leave your case with me.'

Her heart full, Patricia walked forward, her eyes fixed on Kalden.

Enveloped by the golden rays of the late morning sun, he stood still and watched her approach. She went right up to him, stopped and stared up into his face.

He smiled slowly. 'When I tell you about advantages of being short-term monk, Patricia,' he said softly, his eyes alive with love, 'there is one thing I forget to tell you. It is very important thing and you must know it. I forget to tell you that biggest advantage of being a short-term monk is that such a monk can leave the monastery forever, if he wishes.'

She caught her breath.

'And if she wishes,' he added.

He held out his hand to her, and she took it.

About the Author

Liz was born in London and now lives in South Oxfordshire with her husband. After graduating from university with a Law degree, she moved to California where she led a varied life, trying her hand at everything from cocktail waitressing on Sunset Strip to working as a secretary to the CEO of a large Japanese trading company, not to mention a stint as 'resident starlet' at MGM. On returning to England, Liz completed a degree in English and taught for a number of years before developing her writing career.

Liz has written several short stories, articles for local newspapers and a novella. She is a member of the Romantic Novelists' Association. *The Road Back* is Liz's debut novel.

For more information visit www.lizharrisauthor.com and you can follow Liz on twitter @lizharrisauthor

More Choc Lit

Why not try something else from the Choc Lit selection?
Here's a sample:

Highland Storms
Christina Courtenay

Winner of the 2012 Best Historical Romantic Novel of the year

Who can you trust?

Betrayed by his brother and his childhood love, Brice Kinross needs a fresh start. So he welcomes the opportunity to leave Sweden for the Scottish Highlands to take over the family estate.

But there's trouble afoot at Rosyth in 1754 and Brice finds himself unwelcome. The estate's in ruin and money is disappearing. He discovers an ally in Marsaili Buchanan, the beautiful redheaded housekeeper, but can he trust her?

Marsaili is determined to build a good life. She works hard at being a housekeeper and harder still at avoiding men who want to take advantage of her. But she's irresistibly drawn to the new clan chief, even though he's made it plain he doesn't want to be shackled to anyone.

And the young laird has more than romance on his mind. His investigations are stirring up an enemy. Someone who will stop at nothing to get what he wants – including Marsaili – even if that means destroying Brice's life forever …

Sequel to Trade Winds.

Visit www.choc-lit.com for more details including the first two chapters and reviews, or simply scan barcode using your mobile phone QR reader.

The Scarlet Kimono

Christina Courtenay

Winner of the 2011 Big Red Reads Best Historical Fiction Award

Abducted by a Samurai warlord in 17th-century Japan – what happens when fear turns to love?

England, 1611, and young Hannah Marston envies her brother's adventurous life. But when she stows away on his merchant ship, her powers of endurance are stretched to their limit. Then they reach Japan and all her suffering seems worthwhile – until she is abducted by Taro Kumashiro's warriors.

In the far north of the country, warlord Kumashiro is waiting to see the girl who he has been warned about by a seer. When at last they meet, it's a clash of cultures and wills, but they're also fighting an instant attraction to each other.

With her brother desperate to find her and the jealous Lady Reiko equally desperate to kill her, Hannah faces the greatest adventure of her life. And Kumashiro has to choose between love and honour …

Visit www.choc-lit.com for more details including the first two chapters and reviews, or simply scan barcode using your mobile phone QR reader.

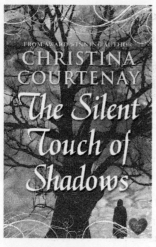

The Silent Touch of Shadows

Christina Courtenay

What will it take to put the past to rest?

Professional genealogist Melissa Grantham receives an invitation to visit her family's ancestral home, Ashleigh Manor. From the moment she arrives, life-like dreams and visions haunt her. The spiritual connection to a medieval young woman and her forbidden lover have her questioning her sanity, but Melissa is determined to solve the mystery.

Jake Precy, owner of a nearby cottage, has disturbing dreams too, but it's not until he meets Melissa that they begin to make sense. He hires her to research his family's history, unaware their lives are already entwined. Is the mutual attraction real or the result of ghostly interference?

A haunting love story set partly in the present and partly in fifteenth century Kent.

Visit www.choc-lit.com for more details including the first two chapters and reviews, or simply scan barcode using your mobile phone QR reader.

'A dramatic, moving and intensely romantic story.'
TRISHA ASHLEY

The Silver Locket
Margaret James

Winner of CataNetwork Reviewers' Choice Award for Single Titles 2010

If life is cheap, how much is love worth?

It's 1914 and young Rose Courtenay has a decision to make. Please her wealthy parents by marrying the man of their choice – or play her part in the war effort?

The chance to escape proves irresistible and Rose becomes a nurse. Working in France, she meets Lieutenant Alex Denham, a dark figure from her past. He's the last man in the world she'd get involved with – especially now he's married.

But in wartime nothing is as it seems. Alex's marriage is a sham and Rose is the only woman he's ever wanted. As he recovers from his wounds, he sets out to win her trust. His gift of a silver locket is a far cry from the luxuries she's left behind.

What value will she put on his love?

First novel in the trilogy.

Visit www.choc-lit.com for more details including the first two chapters and reviews, or simply scan barcode using your mobile phone QR reader.

The Golden Chain
Margaret James

Can first love last forever?

1931 is the year that changes everything for Daisy Denham. Her family has not long swapped life in India for Dorset, England when she uncovers an old secret.

At the same time, she meets Ewan Fraser – a handsome dreamer who wants nothing more than to entertain the world and for Daisy to play his leading lady.

Ewan offers love and a chance to escape with a touring theatre company. As they grow closer, he gives her a golden chain and Daisy gives him a promise – that she will always keep him in her heart.

But life on tour is not as they'd hoped. Ewan is tempted away by his career and Daisy is dazzled by the older, charismatic figure of Jesse Trent. She breaks Ewan's heart and sets off for a life in London with Jesse.

Only time will tell whether some promises are easier to make than keep …

Second novel in the trilogy.

Visit www.choc-lit.com for more details including the first two chapters and reviews, or simply scan barcode using your mobile phone QR reader.

To Turn Full Circle
Linda Mitchelmore

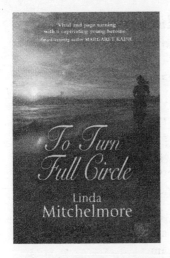

Life in Devon in 1909 is hard and unforgiving, especially for young Emma Le Goff, whose mother and brother die in curious circumstances, leaving her totally alone in the world. While she grieves, her callous landlord Reuben Jago claims her home and belongings.

His son Seth is deeply attracted to Emma and sympathises with her desperate need to find out what really happened, but all his attempts to help only incur his father's wrath.

When mysterious fisherman Matthew Caunter comes to Emma's rescue, Seth is jealous at what he sees and seeks solace in another woman. However, he finds that forgetting Emma is not as easy as he hoped.

Matthew is kind and charismatic, but handsome Seth is never far from Emma's mind. Whatever twists and turns her life takes, it seems there is always something – or someone – missing.

Set in Devon, the first novel in a trilogy.

Visit www.choc-lit.com for more details including the first two chapters and reviews, or simply scan barcode using your mobile phone QR reader.

Please don't stop the music

Jane Lovering

 Winner of the 2012 Best Romantic Comedy Novel of the year

 Winner of the 2012 Romantic Novel of the year

How much can you hide?

Jemima Hutton is determined to build a successful new life and keep her past a dark secret. Trouble is, her jewellery business looks set to fail – until enigmatic Ben Davies offers to stock her handmade belt buckles in his guitar shop and things start looking up, on all fronts.

But Ben has secrets too. When Jemima finds out he used to be the front man of hugely successful Indie rock band Willow Down, she wants to know more. Why did he desert the band on their US tour? Why is he now a semi-recluse?

And the curiosity is mutual – which means that her own secret is no longer safe …

Visit www.choc-lit.com for more details including the first two chapters and reviews, or simply scan barcode using your mobile phone QR reader.

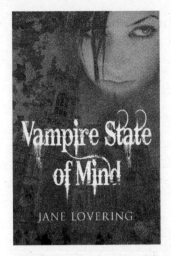

Vampire State of Mind
Jane Lovering

Jessica Grant knows vampires only too well. She runs the York Council tracker programme making sure that Otherworlders are all where they should be, keeps the filing in order and drinks far too much coffee.

To Jess, vampires are annoying and arrogant and far too sexy for their own good, particularly her ex-colleague, Sil, who's now in charge of Otherworld York. When a demon turns up and threatens not just Jess but the whole world order, she and Sil are forced to work together.

But then Jess turns out to be the key to saving the world, which puts a very different slant on their relationship.

The stakes are high. They are also very, very pointy and Jess isn't afraid to use them – even on the vampire she's rather afraid she's falling in love with ...

This is the first of a trilogy in Jane's paranormal series.

Visit www.choc-lit.com for more details including the first two chapters and reviews, or simply scan barcode using your mobile phone QR reader.

Love & Freedom
Sue Moorcroft

Winner of the Festival of Romance
Best Romantic Read Award 2011

New start, new love.

That's what Honor Sontag
needs after her life falls apart,
leaving her reputation in
tatters and her head all over
the place. So she flees her
native America and heads for
Brighton, England.

Honor's hoping for a much-deserved break and the chance
to find the mother who abandoned her as a baby. What she
gets is an entanglement with a mysterious male whose family
seems to have a finger in every pot in town.

Martyn Mayfair has sworn off women with strings attached,
but is irresistibly drawn to Honor, the American who keeps
popping up in his life. All he wants is an uncomplicated
relationship built on honesty, but Honor's past threatens to
undermine everything. Then secrets about her mother start
to spill out ...

Honor has to make an agonising choice. Will she live
up to her dutiful name and please others? Or will she
choose freedom?

Visit www.choc-lit.com for more details
including the first two chapters and
reviews, or simply scan barcode using
your mobile phone QR reader.

Never Coming Home

Evonne Wareham

Winner of the Joan Hessayon New Writers' Award

All she has left is hope.

When Kaz Elmore is told her five-year-old daughter Jamie has died in a car crash, she struggles to accept that she'll never see her little girl again. Then a stranger comes into her life offering the most dangerous substance in the world: hope.

Devlin, a security consultant and witness to the terrible accident scene, inadvertently reveals that Kaz's daughter might not have been the girl in the car after all.

What if Jamie is still alive? With no evidence, the police aren't interested, so Devlin and Kaz have little choice but to investigate themselves.

Devlin never gets involved with a client. Never. But the more time he spends with Kaz, the more he desires her – and the more his carefully constructed ice-man persona starts to unravel.

The desperate search for Jamie leads down dangerous paths – to a murderous acquaintance from Devlin's dark past, and all across Europe, to Italy, where deadly secrets await. But as long as Kaz has hope, she can't stop looking …

Visit www.choc-lit.com for more details including the first two chapters and reviews, or simply scan barcode using your mobile phone QR reader.

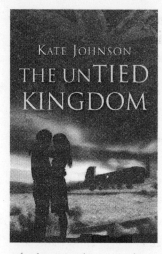

The UnTied Kingdom
Kate Johnson

Shortlisted for the 2012 RoNA Contemporary Romantic Novel Category Award

The portal to an alternate world was the start of all her troubles – or was it?

When Eve Carpenter lands with a splash in the Thames, it's not the London or England she's used to. No one has a telephone or knows what a computer is. England's a third-world country and Princess Di is still alive. But worst of all, everyone thinks Eve's a spy.

Including Major Harker who has his own problems. His sworn enemy is looking for a promotion. The General wants him to undertake some ridiculous mission to capture a computer, which Harker vaguely envisions running wild somewhere in Yorkshire. Turns out the best person to help him is Eve.

She claims to be a popstar. Harker doesn't know what a popstar is, although he suspects it's a fancy foreign word for 'spy'. Eve knows all about computers, and electricity. Eve is dangerous. There's every possibility she's mad.

And Harker is falling in love with her.

Visit www.choc-lit.com for more details including the first two chapters and reviews, or simply scan barcode using your mobile phone QR reader.